ALSO BY SUSAN CHOI

My Education

A Person of Interest

American Woman

The Foreign Student

TRUST
EXERCISE

TRUST EXERCISE

A Novel

SUSAN CHOI

HENRY HOLT AND COMPANY
NEW YORK

Henry Holt and Company
Publishers since 1866
175 Fifth Avenue
New York, New York 10010
www.henryholt.com

Henry Holt® and 🏛® are registered trademarks of
Macmillan Publishing Group, LLC.

Library of Congress Cataloging-in-Publication Data

Names: Choi, Susan, 1969– author.
Title: Trust exercise / a novel / Susan Choi.
Description: First Edition. | New York : Henry Holt and Company, 2019.
Identifiers: LCCN 2018032027 | ISBN 9781250309884 (hardcover)
ISBN 9781250222022 (international)
Subjects: | GSAFD: Love stories.
Classification: LCC PS3553.H584 T78 2019 | DDC 813/.54—dc23
LC record available at https://lccn.loc.gov/2018032027

Our books may be purchased in bulk for promotional, educational, or
business use. Please contact your local bookseller or the Macmillan
Corporate and Premium Sales Department at (800) 221-7945, extension
5442, or by e-mail at MacmillanSpecialMarkets@macmillan.com.

Designed by Meryl Sussman Levavi

Printed in the United States of America

3   5   7   9   10   8   6   4

TRUST
EXERCISE

Trust
Exercise

NEITHER CAN DRIVE. David turns sixteen the following March, Sarah the following April. It is early July, neither one within sight of sixteen and the keys to a car. Eight weeks remain of the summer, a span that seems endless, but with the intuitive parts of themselves they also sense it is not a long time and will go very quickly. The intuitive parts of themselves are always highly aggravated when they are together. Intuition only tells them what they want, not how to achieve it, and this is intolerable.

Their romance has started in earnest this summer, but the prologue took up the whole previous year. All fall and spring of the previous year they lived with exclusive reference to each other, and were viewed as an unspoken duo by everyone else. Little remarked, universally felt, this taut, even dangerous energy running between them. When that began, it was harder to say. They were both experienced—neither was a virgin—and this might have both sped and slowed what took place. That first year, in the fall, each had started at school with a boy- or girlfriend who was going to some other, more regular place. Their own school was special, intended to cream off the most talented at selected pursuits from the regular places all over the city and even beyond, to the outlying desolate towns. It had been a daring experiment ten years before and was now an elite institution, recently moved to an expensive new building full of "world class," "professional" facilities. The school was meant to set apart, to break bonds that were better off broken, confined to childhood. Sarah and David accepted this as the sort of poignant rite their exceptional lives would require. Lavished, perhaps, extra tenderness on the vestigial boyfriend and girlfriend in the process of casting them off. The school was named the City-wide Academy for the Performing Arts, but they and all the students and their teachers called it, rather pompously, CAPA.

At CAPA, the first-year Theatre Arts students studied Stage-craft, Shakespeare, the Sight-Reading of music, and, in their acting class, Trust Exercises, all terms they were taught should be capitalized as befitted their connection to Art. Of the Trust Exercises there were seemingly infinite variations. Some involved talking and resembled group therapy. Some required silence, blindfolds, falling backward off tables or ladders and into the latticework of classmates' arms. Almost daily they lay on their backs on the cold tile floor in what Sarah, much later in life, would be taught was called corpse pose in yoga. Mr. Kingsley, their teacher, would pad like a cat among them in his narrow-toed soft leather slippers, intoning a mantra of muscle awareness. *Let your awareness pour into your shins, filling them slowly, from ankle to knee. Allow them to grow liquid and heavy. Even as you can feel every cell, cradle it with your sharpened aware-*

ness, you are letting it go. Let it go. Let it go. Sarah had won admission to the school with a monologue from the Carson McCullers play *The Member of the Wedding*. David, who had attended a theatre camp, had done Willy Loman from *Death of a Salesman*. Their first day, Mr. Kingsley slid into the room like a knife—he had a noiseless and ambushing style of movement—and once they'd fallen silent, which was almost immediately, had cast a look on them that Sarah still saw in the back of her mind. It seemed to mix scorn with a challenge. *You look pretty nothing to me*, the look flashed onto them like a spray of ice water. And then, like a tease, it amended: . . . *or maybe I'm wrong?* THEATRE, Mr. Kingsley had written in tall slashing letters of chalk on the board. "That's the way it is spelled," he had said. "If you ever spell this with 'ER' at the end you will fail the assignment." These words were the actual first he had spoken to them, not the scornful "you look pretty nothing to me" Sarah had imagined.

Sarah wore a signature pair of blue jeans. Though she had bought them at a mall she would never see anyone else wearing them: they were specific to her, very snug, with elaborate stitching. The stitching went in whorls and patterns spreading over the ass, down the fronts and the backs of the thighs. No one else even had textured jeans; all the girls wore five-pocket Levi's or leggings, the boys the same five-pocket Levi's or, for a brief time, Michael-Jackson-style parachute pants. In Trust Exercises one day, perhaps late in the fall—David and Sarah were never quite sure; they would not speak of it until summer—Mr. Kingsley turned off all the lights in the windowless rehearsal room, plunged them into a locked lightless vault. At one end of the rectangular room was a raised platform stage, thirty inches or so off the floor. Once the lights were turned off, in the absolute silence, they heard Mr. Kingsley skim the length of the opposite wall and step onto the stage, the edge of which they faintly discerned from bits of luminescent tape that hovered in a broken line like a thin constellation. Long after their eyes had adjusted, they saw nothing but this: a darkness like that of the womb or the grave. From the stage came his stern, quiet voice, voiding them of all previous time. Stripping them of all knowledge. They were blind newborn babes and must venture themselves through the darkness and see what they found.

Crawling, then, which would help prevent injury, and also keep them well off the stage where he sat listening. They listened keenly also, as, both inhibited by the darkness and disinhibited by it, by the concealment it gave, they ventured to venture. A spreading aural disturbance of shifting and rustling. The room was not large; immediately, bodies encountered each other and startled away. He heard this, or presumed it. "Is that some other creature with me, in the darkness?" he whispered, ventriloquizing their apprehension. "What does it have—what do *I* have? Four limbs that carry me forward, and back. Skin that can sense cold and hot. Rough and smooth. What is *it*. What am *I*. What are *we*."

In addition to crawling, then: touching. Not tolerated but encouraged. Maybe even required.

David was surprised to find how much he could identify by smell, a sense to which he never gave thought; now he found it assailed him with information. Like a bloodhound or Indian scout, he assessed and avoided. The five guys apart from him, starting with William, superficially his most obvious rival but no rival at all. William gave off a deodorant scent, manly and industrial, like an excess of laundry detergent. William was handsome, blond, slender, graceful, could dance, possessed some sort of race memory of the conventions of courteousness like how to put a girl's coat on, hand her out of a car, hold a door open for her, that William's rigid crazy mother could never have taught him as she was absent from his house for twenty hours at a stretch working two full-time jobs and in the time she was home, locked herself in her bedroom and refused to help her children, William and his two sisters, with meals or housekeeping let alone finer things like their homework; these were such things as one learned about one's fellow fourteen-year-old classmates, within just a few weeks, if a Theatre student at CAPA. William was the heartthrob of Christian Julietta, fat Pammie, Taniqua who could dance, and her adjuncts Chantal and Angie, who screamed with pleasure when William swung and dipped Taniqua, when he spun her like a top across the room. For his part William exhibited no desire except to tango with Taniqua; his energy had no sexual heat like his sweat had no smell. David steered clear of William, not even brushing his heel. Next was Norbert: oily scent of his pimples. Colin: scalp scent of his ludicrous clownfro of hair. Ellery, in whom oil-scent and scalp-scent combined in a way that was palatable, almost appealing. Finally Manuel, as the forms said "Hispanic," of which there were almost no others at CAPA despite the apparent vast numbers of them in the city. Perhaps that explained Manuel's presence, perhaps he was some sort of token required for the school to get funding. Stiff, silent, with no discernible talent, a heavy accent about which he was clearly self-conscious. Friendless, even in this hothouse of oft-elicited, eagerly yielded intimacies. Manuel's scent, the dust-steeped unwashed scent of his artificial-sheep's-wool-lined corduroy jacket.

David was on the move now, crawling quickly, deftly, ignoring the shufflings and scufflings and intakes of breath. A knot of whispers and perfumey hair products: Chantal and Taniqua and Angie. As he passed, one of them grabbed his ass, but he didn't slow down.

Almost right away, Sarah had realized her jeans marked her, like a message in Braille. Only Chantal would be as distinctive. Chantal wore every day without fail a thigh-length cardigan in a very bright color like scarlet or fuchsia or teal, belted tightly at the waist with a double-loop belt with punk studs. Different cardigan, same belt, or possibly several identical belts. The moment the lights had gone out someone had scooted beside Sarah and scrabble-grabbed until finding her breasts, then squeezed hard as if hoping for juice. Norbert, she'd been sure. He'd been sitting nearby, staring at her, as he generally did, while the lights were still on. She'd leaned back on the heels of her hands and shoved hard with both feet, regretting she was wearing her white ballet flats, which were turning quite dingy and gray, and not her pointy-toe three-buckle boots with the metal-tipped heels she'd bought recently with her earnings from working both weekend opening shifts at the Esprit de Paris bakery, which job meant that she rose before six every day of the week, though she often did not go to sleep before two. The tit-grabber, whoever it was, had silently tumbled back into the dark, without even a sharp exhalation, and since then she had continued on the heels of her hands and her feet, crab-shuffling, keeping her ass down, her thighs folded up. Perhaps it had been Colin, or Manuel. Manuel who never stared at her, who met no one's eyes, whose voice she wasn't sure she'd yet heard. Perhaps he was pent up with violence and lust. ". . . all kinds of shapes in the dark. This one is cold, it has hard edges, when I place my hands on it, it doesn't respond. This one is warm with a strange bumpy shape: when I place my hands on it, it moves. . . ." Mr. Kingsley's voice, threading the darkness, was intended to open them up, everything was intended to open them up, but Sarah had closed and grown porcupine's bristles, she was a failure, her most recent recitation in Shakespeare had been awful, her whole body stiff, full of tics.

More than anything she feared running up against Julietta or Pammie, both so earnest and so unself-conscious, like children. They'd be joyfully stroking whatever their hands lit upon.

She'd been found. A hand grasped her left knee, ran its palm down the front of her thigh, the swirled ridges of stitching. She could feel its heat through her jeans. Just like that, in the pit of her stomach a hollowness came, a trapdoor swinging silently open, as if Mr. Kingsley's voice had been the nagging wind, ineffectively rattling the lock, which this hand had now sprung.

The one hand remained on her thigh while another found her right hand and raised it, laid it flush on a lightly shaved face. It took her thumb, limp and helpless, adjusted its position, and pressed it as if meaning to make a thumbprint. She felt beneath the pad a slight bump, like a mosquito-bite welt. David's birthmark, a flattened chocolate-colored mole, the same diameter as a pencil eraser, on his left cheek, just offshore of his mouth.

They had not, to this point in their scanty acquaintance, discussed David's mole. What fourteen-year-olds talked about, even took note of, moles? But Sarah had wordlessly noticed it. David wordlessly knew that she had. This was his mark, his Braille. Her hand no longer passively lay on his face but held it, as if balancing it on his neck. She slid her thumb over his lips, as distinct in their shape as his mole. His lips were full but not feminine, closer to simian. Slightly Mick Jagger. His eyes, though small, were set deep and resembled blue agates. Something intelligently feral about them as well. He was not at all normally handsome but did not need to be.

David took her thumb in his mouth, tongued it gently, did not slobber it, kissed it back so it lay once again on his lips. The thumb traced the cleft of his lips as if taking their measure.

Mr. Kingsley's voice must have continued, unraveling guidance, but they no longer heard him.

David had never in this way deferred a kiss. He felt skewered by lust and as if he could hang there, afloat on the pain. Up floated his hands, in tandem, and closed over her breasts. She shuddered and pressed against him and he lifted his hands just a fraction away, so his palms only grazed her nipples where they strained the thin weave of her cotton T-shirt. If she was wearing a bra it was a soft wisp of one, a silk rag encircling her ribs. Her nipples rained down in his mind in the form of hard glittering gems, diamonds and quartzes and those faceted clumps of rock crystal one grew in a jar on a string. Her breasts were ideally small, precisely the size of the cup of his hand. He weighed them and measured them, marveling, brushing them, with his palms or the tips of his fingers, the same way again and again. With his now-cast-off girlfriend from his previous school he'd evolved the Formula and had then become imprisoned by it: first Kissing with Tongue for the fixed interval, then Tits for the fixed interval, then Fingering Her for the fixed interval before, culminatingly, Fucking. Never a step neglected nor a change to the order. A sex recipe. Now with a shock he realized that it needn't be thus.

They knelt, knees to knees, his palms cradling her breasts, her hands clutching his skull either side of his face, her face pushed into his shoulder so that a patch of the cloth of his polo shirt grew hotly wet from her breath. He turned his face into the weight of her hair, basking in her aroma, exulting in it. How he'd found her. No word to describe it except recognition. Some chemical made her for him, him for her; they were not yet too fucked up by life that they wouldn't realize it.

"Make your way to a space on the wall and sit against it. Hands relaxed by your sides. Eyes closed, please. I'll be bringing the lights back in stages, to smooth the transition."

Well before Mr. Kingsley completed his speech Sarah broke away, crawled as if fleeing a fire until she hit a wall. Pulled her knees to her chest, crushed her face to her knees.

David was scorch-mouthed, felt strangled by his underpants. His hands, so exquisitely sensitive moments before, were as clumsy as if stuffed inside boxing gloves. He palmed and palmed his hair, which was short and unvarying, off his forehead.

As the lights came on each stared steadily forward into the room's empty center.

The crucial first year of their learning continued. In classes with tables, they sat at separate tables. In classes with chairs set in rows, they sat in separate rows. Hanging around in the halls, in the lunchroom, on the benches for smoking, they adhered to separate nodes of conversation, sometimes standing just inches apart, turned away from each other. But in moments of transition, of general movement, David's gaze burned a hole through the air, Sarah's glance darted out, then away, like a whip. Unbeknownst to themselves they were as noticeable as lighthouses. In repose, even when they both stared straight ahead, the wire ran between them, and their peers changed their paths to avoid tripping on it.

They needed distance to give them fresh darkness. At the end of the year, one knee restlessly bouncing, eyes sweeping the room's farthest corners, knuckles manically popping, David paused next to Sarah and asked, thickly, for her address. His family was going to England. He'd send her a postcard. She wrote the address briskly, handed it to him, he turned on his heel.

The postcards began a week later. On their fronts, nothing special: London Bridge, the humorless guardsmen at Buckingham Palace, a picturesque punk with a three-foot-high Mohawk. Unlike David, whose family regularly traveled to places like Australia, Mexico, Paris, Sarah had never been out of the country, but even she recognized the postcards as generic, pulled at random from the souvenir-shop carousel. The backs were something else, densely written edge to edge, her address and the stamp barely squeezed between lines. She felt grateful the mailman kept bringing them; he must be squinting at them, as she did, but with different emotions. At least one postcard a day, sometimes several, that she fished out as soon as the mailman had come, leaving the bills and coupons for her mother to find when she got home from work. David's handwriting was effusive, almost feminine, with tall loops and wide flourishes and yet great regularity, all the letters at just the same angle, all the t's and l's just the same height. The content was much like the form: exuberant with observation, and yet deftly measured. Each card made a little vignette. And in the lower right corners, squeezed next to her zip code, one or another of the tentative endearments that wrung the air from her lungs.

The vast southern city they lived in was rich in land, poor in everything else—no bodies of water, no drainage, no hills, no topographical variety of any sort, no public transportation or even the awareness of the lack of such a thing. The city, like vines with no trellis, sprawled out thinly and nonsensically, its lack of organization its sole unifying aspect. Gracious neighborhoods of live oak and chunky brick mansions, such as the neighborhood where David lived, lay cheek by jowl with wastes of gravel, or US Postal Service facilities resembling US Army bases, or Coca-Cola bottling plants resembling wastewater treatment facilities. And chintzy, labyrinthine apartment complexes of many hundreds of two-story brick boxes, strewn about scores of algae-stained in-ground swimming pools, such as the complex in which Sarah lived, might exhaust themselves at their easternmost edge on the wide boulevard, lined with tattered palm trees, which on its opposite side washed the gates of the city's most prestigious club for Jews. David's mother, on the family's return from London, was pleasantly surprised to find him interested in racquetball and swimming at the Jewish Community Center, for which, since enrolling at CAPA, he'd shown only contempt. "Have you even still got a racquet?" she asked.

He produced a racquet from the back of his closet. He even produced a towel. These dangled limply from his hands when he arrived at Sarah's door. The actual distance from the club, across the boulevard, to Sarah's door had been vastly greater than suggested by the many continuities. The walk—without the benefit of sidewalks or crossing signals, for their city wasn't built for pedestrians—from the JCC parking lot to the southern gate of Sarah's complex had taken close to twenty minutes, in the heat of the damned, along a median planted with scorched rhododendron but not any trees, during which several separate motorists had pulled over to ask if he needed assistance. In their city only the poorest of the poor, or fresh victims of crimes, ever walked. Once inside Sarah's sprawling and mazelike complex, David reeled—it was enormous, a city of its own, without signs. Sarah and her mother had moved there when Sarah was twelve, their fifth move in four years but the first Sarah's father had nothing to do with. Sarah and her mother only stopped getting lost in the maze of carports when they put a chalk X on the bleached wooden gate separating their assigned parking space from their back patio. July in their city: an average daytime temperature of ninety-seven degrees. From the sole clue David held, her apartment number, he could never have guessed that she lived on the far, western side from the club, near the opposite entrance. Sarah had given him directions from the western entrance which he'd disregarded, knowing he wouldn't be coming that way. He had been too ashamed to explain this to her, his plan involving a ride to the club, too ashamed of not having a car of his own, though neither of them had a car of their own, being only fifteen and not legal to drive for a year. It didn't cross his mind that she felt it as keenly, the utter dispossession of not being licensed to drive in that city of cars. It was part of the excruciating in-betweenness of no longer being children, yet lacking those powers enjoyed by adults. The "streets" within the complex weren't real streets at all but a tirelessly branching metastasis of walkway, or driveway, the former distinguished by borders of dying impatiens, the latter by bordering spaces to park. It took David over an hour to find Sarah's apartment. He might have walked two or three miles. David had imagined he would take her in his arms as he'd done on that day in the dark, but he only stood, glued to her threshold, with his sun-boiled blood spreading stains in his eyes. He thought he might vomit or faint. Then the shared air of their childhood touched him: that particular air of their city, mustily buried and cool, from its unending journey through air-conditioning ducts that the sun never reached. No matter if one lived in a mansion or a little brick box, that air smelled just the same. David stepped toward it blindly. "I need a shower," he managed to say.

For his ruse he'd been forced to wear shorts, knee-high socks, infantile white sneakers, a sporty T-shirt. The outfit embarrassed Sarah. He looked alien to her, unhandsome, though this quibble peeped faintly at her from beneath the hard weight of her lust. The lust in its turn was eclipsed by another and unprecedented emotion, an onrush of sad tenderness, as if the man he would be, full of unguessed-at darkness and weakness, had for a brief instant shown through the boy. The boy pushed his way past her and locked himself in her bathroom. Her mother worked long days somewhere; mother and daughter shared the small, dowdy bathroom, so different from each of the four bathrooms in David's own home. In this strange realm he showered with a smooth brick of Ivory soap, passing it between his legs, firmly lathering every square inch, meticulous and patient because truly frightened; he'd never had sex with a girl he loved. He'd had sex with two girls before this, both of whom now dissolved in his mind. His mind, slowly dilating as his blood temperature came off the dangerous boil. He'd made the shower water cool, almost cold. He stepped cautiously out of her bathroom, a towel circling his waist. She was waiting for him in her bed.

MR. KINGSLEY, THEIR teacher, lived with a man he called his husband; he twinkled at them provocatively when he said this. This was 1982, far from New York. None of them, except for Sarah, had ever known a man who might call another man his husband while twinkling provocatively. None of them had ever known a man who had lived many years in New York, who had been a member of the original Broadway cast of *Cabaret*, who referred to Joel Grey, when reminiscing on these times, as "Joel." None of them, again except Sarah, had ever known a man on whose office wall might hang, among other fascinating and risqué memorabilia, a photograph of an exuberant and barely clad woman, heavily made up, flinging her arms wide and high, who somehow despite zero resemblance was strangely reminiscent of Mr. Kingsley himself, and who was rumored to *be* Mr. Kingsley, though no one believed it. Sarah's first cousin, her mother's sister's son, was a "leather queen," Sarah said calmly to platter-eyed classmates; this cousin lived in San Francisco, often wore women's clothes to sing torch songs, and in general gave Sarah a key to Mr. Kingsley's esoterica that her peers wholly lacked. This was how David had first noticed Sarah: her aura of knowledge. He sometimes saw her laughing with Mr. Kingsley, and their laughter seemed shared, on the same remote plane. David envied this, as did everyone else, and he wanted to annex that plane for himself.

In 1982, none of them, except Sarah, had ever known a gay person. And equally, in 1982, none of them viewed Mr. Kingsley's gayness as anything but another aspect of his wholesale superiority to all other adults in their world. Mr. Kingsley was impossibly witty and sometimes impossibly cutting; the prospect of talking with him was terrifying and galvanizing; one longed to live up to his brilliance and equally feared that it couldn't be done. Of course Mr. Kingsley was gay. They lacked the word for it, but intuition supplied the frisson: Mr. Kingsley was not just gay but an iconoclast, the first such they'd ever encountered. This was what they longed to be themselves, little though they could put it in words. They were all children who had previously failed to fit in, or had failed, to the point of acute misery, to feel satisfied, and they had seized on creative impulse in the hope of salvation.

Strange, appropriate disruptions and traumas foretold summer's end. Hurricane Clem crawled toward them from the Caribbean, turning his wheel on the nightly newscast. Sarah's mother took her week's vacation, and sat home regarding Sarah with weary suspicion and making her put masking-tape X's on the windows and fill up the spare water jugs. Sarah only got away by claiming she needed to use the library, on the campus of the college very near David's house. She and David got themselves dropped off far apart from each other and both mistakenly far from the library, and even once they had found each other, felt somehow misused. They walked in the dizzying heat, end to end of the summer-struck campus, hopelessly looking for somewhere to be, too hot and upset to link hands. Periodically, a grounds worker in a golf cart piled with tarps and sandbags would drive past and throw them a look. There were no college students on campus. The whole campus including the library was closed. Crossing an ocean of parking-lot asphalt they came upon the football stadium, like a ruin of Rome standing silent and bleached in the heat. They squeezed through a bent scissor gate. Behind a snack bar, at the base of a popcorn machine, on a pair of flattened boxes that smelled of stale grease, Sarah let David fuck her, her mouth crushed in his ear, her legs looping his waist, her hands struggling to hold his sweat-slippery back. His rhythmically agonized exhalations scorched the side of her neck when he came. For the first time she didn't, and felt an aloneness. They hunched away from each other to get dressed again. David didn't brush off the bits of junk stuck to her legs, or make some comment that let Sarah feel it was all right to laugh. David, fighting with the laces of his sneakers, wished he hadn't come without her. He wished he hadn't felt her so rigid beneath him on a bed of cardboard. It had been very different from the times in her apartment when they'd had all her bed and her carpeted floor and the hallway and even the living room couch and armchair across which to spread their desire, when they sometimes would surface as if from a dream, and laugh to find themselves in a new room, and he'd touched every inch of her skin with his lips, and pushed his tongue in her cunt, and seized hold of her hands when she bucked and cried out, both of them startled and thrilled by her pleasure.

After dressing, they walked off the campus, having wound up so close to its edge, and found they were at the same plaza where Sarah's French bakery was. In a store Sarah liked, David watched her try on jewelry, weird handcrafted stuff made with unpolished rocks. When Sarah's mother's Toyota appeared outside the shop window, Sarah rushed away without letting him kiss her in front of the clerk. David stayed longer, and left with a ribbon-tied box.

*

REMEMBER THE IMPOSSIBLE eventfulness of time, transformation and emotion packed like gunpowder into the barrel. Remember the dilation and diffusion, the years within days. Theirs were endless; lives flowered and died between waking and noon. Hurricane Clem made landfall, and turned the boulevard David had crossed at midsummer into a raging brown river that sucked cars from the curbs and turned trees upside down. The first day of school was delayed for a week, confirming their suspicion that a lifetime, not a summer, had passed. They couldn't possibly still be fifteen. They took the natural ambition, at that age, to shock the peer group with a summer metamorphosis to greater extremes, being actors. Chantal returned to school with an Afro. Norbert tried, with uncertain success, to conceal himself under a beard. The most passionate female friendships had somehow expired. Sarah did not know why, as she came back through the doors to the Black Box, her whole body grew rigid when Joelle Cruz came shrieking her way. The previous spring she had practically lived with Joelle. Joelle had an older sister, Martine, at the school, and Sarah had spent fewer nights at home than with Joelle, in the back seat of Martine's grimy car, as they drove around in quest of liquor, or drugs, or a bouncer who'd fall for their cheap fake IDs. Joelle had introduced Sarah to coke, *Rocky Horror*, and wearing ballet flats with jeans; now her very flesh repulsed Sarah. It was too damp and pink. Sarah could smell Joelle's pits. Sarah felt that she did nothing different; she only *was* different. She didn't blow Joelle off. She didn't speak coldly to her. But no; she had changed. She was not Joelle's friend anymore. It felt so ordained, so engrained in the utterly new circumstances of sophomore year she was sure Joelle knew it as well, even willed it, perhaps, an overt act to which Sarah only responded.

But Joelle's irrelevance was irrelevant to Sarah, even as Joelle stood there talking to her. Everything was irrelevant to Sarah apart from David. She imagined his acknowledgment flashing toward her like a mirror. She and David had traveled so far ahead, just the two of them; they'd disappeared past a horizon, discarding their school selves behind. If they kept the shucked skins it was just for the sake of disguise. For Sarah it went without saying that their summer would be their secret, like a Mount Olympus (had she known what this was at the time) where they whispered together like gods. She had not even thought to explain this to David. She assumed that he already knew.

David burst into the Black Box not as a winking mirror but a spotlight, bearing down bright and hot, and swinging his arms in a slightly hitched way. He was hiding something he exposed by his very attempt to conceal it, flanked by a dozen of their classmates who clung to his charisma like lint. Sarah found herself holding a tiny gift box with a bow while they all stared at her.

Colin crowed, "David's gonna get down on one knee!"

"Look at you, *red* as a *beet*!" Angie laughed.

"Open it, Sarah," begged Pammie.

Sarah shoved the box back in his hand. "I can open it later."

"Open it now," David urged. Perhaps Colin and Angie and Norbert and Pammie and everyone else of whom Sarah was so grotesquely aware were invisible to him and he could not even hear what they said. That glimpse, of herself alone at the heart of his gaze, only lasted an instant. His indifference to their audience struck her as a dare or a test. She didn't see as a counterindication to this angry idea of hers his hot blush as deep as her own; if her face was as red as a beet, his was red as a burn, he'd come out in lurid blotches that overlapped with his boy's patchy stubble to make a mess of his face.

"I'll open it *later*," she said as Mr. Kingsley came in, waving his arms around his head to indicate that while it was glorious to be reunited, would they please shut their traps and get into their seats.

David wound up two rows behind Sarah; she didn't have to look to know exactly where he was. Facing forward she burned with her sense of a wrong. By her or to her? Her head would not turn, she would not look his way no matter how hard he willed her to do it. Adrenaline was roaring through them both, its warning urgent and obscure. Just minutes before, David had been striding through the big double doors, in fact bouncing, in fact *funny-walking from light-ness of heart* because he was finally stepping onstage in the role of her boyfriend. Sarah his girlfriend. David viewed these roles as sacred; they were the two roles he most cared about. Who gave a shit about Hamlet? He'd been afraid the little box was too small, that she'd be disappointed by a box that could fit in the palm of her hand. But when she opened it, the silver chain would unfurl, the blue stone would lie in the hollow he loved at the base of her neck. Something like his own radiance would pour from her—not the fright, or disgust, he had seen. Or the shame? Of him, obviously.

David struggled to jam the box back out of sight. He needed to get it to his locker, destroy it, the indigestible lump that it made in the front of his jeans was a joke. To David, love meant declaration. Wasn't that the whole point? To Sarah, love meant a shared secret. Wasn't that the whole point? Sarah felt David's eyes on her all through the class and kept perfectly still, held them there with her mind. Years later, in a future in which she enters theatres only as part of the audience, Sarah will see a play in which an actor asks, "Can't there be a silent language?" and be surprised when her eyes fill with tears. Two rows in front of David, aching with the effort of keeping perfectly still so his gaze, like a moth, won't take flight from the back of her neck, Sarah doesn't yet know the words for this language that doesn't have words. She won't understand what it means, when David stops speaking this language to her.

"Ego Reconstruction," said Mr. Kingsley, "requires a foundation. My darling Sophomores: one year older and wiser than when we first met. What might that foundation be?"

They wanted so badly to please him. But the question of how never had a clear answer. Say the right thing? (But what could that be?) Say a deliberately wrong but funny thing? Ask another question in response to his question, as he often did when responding to theirs?

Pammie raised her hand, eager and hopeful. "Modesty?"

He laughed at her in disbelief. "*Modesty!* Explain why you think so, and please don't be modest. Please flaunt your thought process, Pammie, so maybe I can fathom what it is."

Pammie's plump face, beneath gold barrettes, flushed to the roots of her hair. But she had an odd stubbornness, a capacity to dig in her heels and argue. She was a Christian, a disposition unremarkable outside the walls of their school but within it unsupported, even mocked, and in the previous year she'd grown used to defending herself. "People who have too much Ego are stuck-up," she said. "Being modest is the opposite of being conceited."

"Let me make one thing clear: we can never have 'too much' Ego—so long as we're in control of it."

Control of the Self: each of them feared they lacked this. Sarah, for example. Earlier that year she had asked her mother to file paperwork to get Sarah a hardship permit, a driver's license for people as young as fourteen who needed it to support their family financially, which Sarah had argued she did, offending her mother completely. In their subsequent fight, Sarah put a kitchen chair through the sliding glass door to their back patio, the repair of which cost her the whole summer's worth of her bakery wages. "And you think you could *drive*," Sarah's mother had said.

David, for example. That day Sarah gave back the box, he had crushed it using only one hand, in the process cutting open his palm. When she later tried to ask, "Can I open it now?" he'd replied, "I'm not sure what you're talking about." Whether these examples proved self-control or its lack remained unclear to him.

"The foundation we require for Ego Reconstruction is Ego

*De*construction," Mr. Kingsley concluded. They'd all heard about it last year, from the then-Sophomores and now-Juniors, who had constantly harped on this mystery while refusing to share even the slightest detail. "You'll get there when you get there." "You're still Freshmen! Don't try to climb a ladder in midair." "The last time I checked, you couldn't cross a bridge by starting in the middle." The then-Sophomores and now-Juniors were a strikingly effusive, tight-knit class who seemed to possess some special aura the now-Sophomores lacked that wasn't just the advantage of age. The then-Sophomores and now-Juniors were more photogenic, individually and together. In a school with no athletic program, they gave the impression of a cheerleading corps. Their clothing was coordinated, their teeth square and white. They had coupled early and lastingly, the exception of one couple, Brett and Kayley—whose saga of rupture, grief, and joyful reconciliation over the course of a few weeks the previous year had been consumed school-wide with the avidity usually reserved for soap operas—being the sort that proved the rule. The few then-Sophomores still single were exclusively affiliated, as Third Wheels or Best Friends. There were no loners, like Manuel, or irredeemable losers, like Norbert. There was no one like Sarah, whose fearful secret it was that during the Brett-Kayley hiatus, she had spent a night with Brett at his father's condo, during which he'd talked about Kayley, and cried, and at one point interrupted his kissing of Sarah to throw all his bedcovers out the window. After he and Kayley made up Brett had grabbed Sarah's wrist in the dusk of a Showcase rehearsal and warned her, "Don't tell *anyone*," and she'd been so afraid of the stain she might make on his image she hadn't even told David.

Though now David angled away when he saw her approaching. When unavoidably they met in classrooms David stared coldly and Sarah stared even more bitterly coldly and it was a contest, to pile up coldness, to shovel it furiously from their hearts.

"Let's form a circle," Mr. Kingsley said.

As so often before, they grew uneasily aware of their crotches as they sat down cross-legged, and felt the icy touch of the linoleum numbing their asses. Most of them had privately concluded that Ego Deconstruction/Reconstruction was some sort of fleshless orgy, and they were helplessly blushing, their skin crawling with arousal and dread. The wall of mirrors doubled their circle, around which Mr. Kingsley paced in orbit. His gaze was cast somewhere beyond them. His very way of gazing told them plainly how far they fell short—of last year's Sophomores? Of their own potential? Of the actors he'd known in New York? They felt their deficit all the more sharply because the unit of measure was wholly unknown. Sarah tried to see David, but he'd placed himself near enough to her left or her right that she couldn't see him, while far enough that she couldn't sense him. Would David be chosen? Would Sarah be chosen?

"Joelle," Mr. Kingsley murmured, in a tone of regretful admonishment. Sadness, almost, at her failure, but what had Joelle done? She was pink year-round, and a summer's worth of sunburn had her mottled and peeling all over her face and down into the cleavage broadly exposed by her tight V-neck top. The new raw pink skin turned bright red at the sound of her name; all the curls of dead, half-peeled skin seemed to rustle with fear. Her surface was disgusting, Sarah thought. "Joelle, please stand at the circle's exact center. You're the hub. Invisible lines radiate out from you to each one of your classmates. These lines are the spokes. Your classmates, and you, and these spokes, make the wheel. You're the hub of the wheel, Joelle."

"Okay," Joelle said, blushing fiercely, a fountain of blood pounding under her skin.

"I'd like you to choose one spoke now. Look down the length of that spoke. Someone's at the other end. Someone you're bound to, by that spoke passing through you, and passing through them. Who's the person you're looking at?"

The linoleum doesn't feel cold anymore. Please, no, Sarah realizes, staring straight ahead at Joelle's middle, at her soft belly concealed beneath the tight top.

"I'm looking at Sarah," Joelle says huskily, her voice almost a whisper.

"Tell her what you observe."

"You didn't call me all summer," Joelle barely chokes out.

"Go on," Mr. Kingsley says, gazing somewhere miles away; he's not even looking in Joelle's direction. Perhaps he's using the room's giant mirror to watch Joelle's burning skin, her glittering eyes, her too-tight top, out of the corner of one eye.

"And I would call you, and you wouldn't call back, and I mean, maybe it's me, but it's like, I feel like—"

"Stand up for your feelings, Joelle!" Mr. Kingsley barks out.

"We were best friends and you act like you don't even know me!" The strangled grief in her voice is far harder to bear than the words. Sarah is frozen, a statue, she's staring blindly at the opposite wall with its door to the hallway as if she could will herself out of this room, and then suddenly it's Joelle who bolts: Joelle stumbles headlong through the circle, practically stepping on Colin and Manuel, she wrenches open the door and, unleashing a wail, disappears down the hall. In her wake no one breathes, no one looks anywhere but the floor, no one even looks at Sarah. Life is suspended. Abruptly, Mr. Kingsley wheels on Sarah.

"What are you doing?" he demands, and Sarah flinches in alarm. "Go after her!"

Sarah lurches to her feet and out the door, unable to imagine the faces she's leaving behind, even David's. She isn't even able to find where he was in the circle.

The halls are deserted, the slippery black-and-white checkerboard rapping harshly against the hard soles of her boots. Her punk boots, cruel-toed with metal stilettos and three large silver square buckles each. Behind closed classroom doors on the west hall the

Freshmen and Juniors doze through the requirements, English and algebra, social studies and Spanish. Down the south and east halls, the real life of the school can be heard: the jazz band splashing through Ellington; the lone pianist's hands prancing over the keys in the dance studio and the thumping of bound, bloody feet. The smokers' courtyard is empty, its sun-bleached benches bearing only acorns from the massive live oak. The outdoor classroom, a walled-in rectangle of grass with a stage at one end, is also empty, its street-side gate padlocked. Sarah wills David, not Joelle, to appear in these secretive places, David to be sitting on the empty smokers' bench, David to be sitting underneath the oak tree. The rear entrance leads to the rear parking lot, where the students park and also eat lunch, on the hoods of their cars, when the weather is good. Joelle is outside the doors, doubled up, honking with sobs. Joelle clearly meant to escape in her car but was slowed by her grief; the keys to her Mazda poke out of one fist. This is the brand-new, rocketlike little Mazda Joelle bought with cash—more than ten thousand dollars in cash—she once showed Sarah, stuffed in a coffee can under her bed. Sarah didn't know where this money came from. Drug sales, she assumed; possibly something else. Each day Joelle drives the car to a friend's house a few blocks from home and then walks the rest of the way, so her parents won't see it. Joelle is not convoluted but simple, not sullen but sunny, yet she has the extensive clandestine life of a career criminal, and this used to enthrall Sarah. Now Joelle appears stripped bare, her essence exposed. She's just a party girl, overeager to be liked. The insight startles Sarah not because of its unkindness but because this, she suddenly knows, is the sort of insight Mr. Kingsley is constantly trying to extract. He paced with impatience last year when they told each other, during Observation, such things as, "You're a really nice girl," or, "I think you're handsome." Yet at this moment, Sarah equally knows, there's a story unfolding into which her true feelings don't fit. She is supposed to hug Joelle, make it up to her. She knows this as surely as if Mr. Kingsley stood there, supervising it all. She has the strong feeling he *is* there.

Joelle, precociously fleshy and pungent, so obliviously manifests the carnal that Sarah's own self-conscious carnality becomes disgusting to her, along with her own flesh, her own scent. Joelle's enormous breasts are heavily freckled, their trapped clefts and creases are constantly sweaty; Joelle's crotch, encased in her jeans, trails an olfactory banner like some sort of sticky night flower to inflame jungle bats. Joelle sleeps with much older men; at school, she disregards boys as if they're not even incipient men. She only has eyes for Sarah.

Half closing her eyes, almost grinding her teeth, Sarah takes Joelle into her arms. Joelle clings to her gratefully, soaks her shoulder with tears and slick snot. This is also self-control, Sarah thinks. This brute willing of the self to take action. Until now, Sarah thought self-control was only restraint: *not* putting the chair through the glass.

"I'm really sorry," she hears herself mumbling. "I'm so messed up right now, I didn't mean to seem distant. Things have just been so crazy. . . ."

"What's been going on? I could *tell* you had shit going on! I just *knew*—"

Soon the counterfeit is complete. Sarah intended to confide in no one, and if someone, Joelle least of all. Now, as if reading a script, she tells Joelle about the decoy tennis racquet, the empty snack bar. Confession made, she's in receipt of Joelle's whole devotion again. Joelle's sobs turn to mirth, her abject supplication to glee. She clings to Sarah no longer from the weakness of grief but to prevent herself rolling merrily on the sidewalk. Having bought back a friendship she no longer wanted by defiling the one thing she cared about most, Sarah knows it doesn't matter that she enjoins Joelle to a "secrecy" that puts Joelle into raptures. Joelle is practically wrapped like a vine around Sarah as they stumble back into the classroom and almost literally into David, because they've been gone for so long class has ended, and David's the first on his feet, to escape. At the sight of David, Joelle bursts out laughing and covers her face. David shoulders roughly past Sarah and Sarah feels bonfires ignite on her skin. Mr. Kingsley, also on his way out, says as if as an afterthought, "Sarah, come by and see me tomorrow at lunch."

Not even David in the course of escaping fails to hear the summons, or fails to understand what it means. Even Joelle, who has so misunderstood her entire transaction with Sarah, understands what Mr. Kingsley's summons means. Joelle tightens her hot grip on Sarah with sisterly envy. Sarah has become the kind of Problem they would all like to be.

"THAT WAS KIND of you yesterday," Mr. Kingsley began, after closing the door behind her with a resonant click. He'd indicated the chair she should sit in, and perhaps it was the novel sensation of sitting in a chair in his office that induced her to say, right away, "I didn't want to be kind." She was aware of a dangerous urge to spar with him.

"Why not?" asked Mr. Kingsley.

"I don't feel close to Joelle anymore. I thought, with everything you've taught us, that honoring my feelings about that was what I should do. But yesterday it seemed like the way that I felt didn't matter."

"How so?"

"You wanted me to go after her and make her feel better, and tell her we still were best friends. And I did, even though I was lying. And now I have to keep lying because she thinks that we're best friends again."

"What makes you think that's what I wanted?"

"Because you told me to go after her!"

"Yes, but that's all I told you to do. I didn't tell you to make her feel better. I didn't tell you to lie, and say the two of you were still friends."

"Then what was I supposed to do? She was crying. I felt guilty." Now Sarah was crying, which she had sworn she wouldn't do. All the anger she'd brought into the room was transformed into sobs. There was Kleenex on the end of Mr. Kingsley's desk nearest her chair, as if people often sat where she was sitting and cried, whether out of anger or some other emotion. She took a handful and blew her nose in it.

"You were supposed to stay with her in that moment, with tenacity and honesty. And that's what you did."

"I wasn't honest. I lied!"

"And you're aware of the lie, and aware of the reason you told it. You were there in that circumstance, Sarah. More there than Joelle."

That this disparagement, to her, of her classmate might be considered a dishonest behavior of Mr. Kingsley's wasn't among Sarah's thoughts at that moment. His comment seemed true in some way, and for a moment her crying subsided. "I still don't understand how telling a lie makes me true to my feelings, unless you're saying that making someone feel better is more important than telling the truth."

"I'm not saying any such thing. Honesty is a process. Standing up for your emotions is a process. It doesn't mean running roughshod over everyone else. If you weren't a person of integrity, I don't think you'd be sitting here challenging me about what happened yesterday." Sarah prickled with alertness to hear him describe her as "challenging" him. It was clearly the right thing to do. "I'll be counting on that integrity of yours when the English students are here in the spring," he went on. "They'll need the guidance of someone like you."

This futuristic leadership role seemed far less real to Sarah than her current crises. "I feel like, in telling her we're still friends, I've put myself in a trap."

"You'll find your way out."

"How?"

"I said *you'll* find your way out."

Sarah cried with renewed force, for such a long time that she eventually grew aware of an unfamiliar luxuriousness. Mostly she cried alone, on rare occasions in front of her mother, but either way the emotion alongside of grief was impatience. Her own impatience, her mother's impatience, with her tears. Mr. Kingsley seemed to grow more contented and patient the more that she cried. He sat smiling benignly. Under the narcotic of his patience she felt tempted to share the real reason she was crying, but thinking of it she cried too hard to speak, and then she'd been crying and thinking so long, she felt she'd actually talked about David, perhaps even been told what to do, and a strange peace overtook her that might have just been exhaustion. Mr. Kingsley still smiled benignly. He seemed more and more satisfied.

"Tell me about life outside school," he said when her guttering breaths had grown calm.

"Like what? Um. My mom and I live in the Windsor Apartments."

"Where are those?"

"You don't know? Oh my God, they're like the biggest apartment complex in the world. Every building and carport and tree looks the same. The first year we lived there, every time we went out we got lost coming back. We had to put a chalk X on our gate." This made him laugh, and she swelled with pleasure.

So MUCH OF what they do, with Mr. Kingsley, is restraint in the name of release. It seems they have to throttle their emotions to have complete access to them. Access to one's own emotions = presence in the moment. Acting = responding with authentic emotion under made-up circumstances. They fill their notebooks with such singular declarations, each of which, as they're writing it down, seems to offer the key, or perhaps the keystone, that will make the whole structure cohere, but later, when Sarah reads her notes over, she hears a repetitive melody that never climaxes or ends, like the maddening song that the ice cream truck plays in the summer. Sarah doesn't blame the information, or Mr. Kingsley, its source, any more than she would blame the book she is struggling to read, *Tropic of Cancer* by Henry Miller, for its impenetrability. Clearly she's too young to read *Tropic of Cancer*, but she can't accept this; if she knows what the words mean, the book's meaning ought to unfold. Stubbornly she keeps trying. Similarly, with acting, stubbornly she keeps trying. Similarly, with David, stubbornly she keeps up her half of the duet each blames the other for starting, this new flavor of longing embittered by outrage but no less exclusive to them. It's still a promise, Sarah stubbornly believes. Still a performance that each reserves just for the other. Sarah hides her fear that she's wrong—that she doesn't have talent, or David—beneath a youthful indifferent swagger, an insistence that she's willing to do anything.

By late September, the mainstage rehearsals have started. Their school day already ends late, at four p.m., unlike the day at normal schools, which ends at two thirty. But during times when there's rehearsal, which is more than half the year, rehearsal starts at four thirty and can go on for three or four hours. At dismissal the whole mass of Theatre students pours across the parking lot to U Totem for junk food: Funyuns and hot-pepper-spiced pork skins, individual servings of ice cream, rolls of SweeTarts and stacks of Kit Kats. Joelle shoplifts most of her items and never gets caught. Back in the parking lot they gorge on their feast, throw their wrappers in the outdoor trash cans, wash their hands before hitting the mainstage. For all their shoving, shouting immaturity, their indifference to nutritional standards, their unhygienic disorder as expressed in their lockers, their backpacks, and, for those who have licenses, cars, there are certain fastidious habits all the Theatre students observe as a group, by reflex. They would never dream of eating on the main-stage, in the wings, in the house with its red velvet seats. They may be teenagers, but there is nothing teenage about their dedication to this space, their cathedral. They'd as soon defecate in the aisle as eat candy bars here. They'll retain some of these habits the rest of their lives. Long after they've left the theatre, and their theatre dreaming, behind, they'll still spell it "theatre." The alternate spelling will always seem ignorant to them. The master's pride in a difficult tradecraft: they'll have Mr. Kingsley to thank for bestowing this on them, whatever else they conclude about him.

These long days, this life conducted almost wholly away from their parents, in a nearly unsupervised world of their peers, is the source of the ardor they feel for their school. Freedom, selfhood—those intangibles they might have once thought were reserved for adults—turn out to be already theirs. Even Sarah, still months from her license and perhaps an eternity away from a car after having to spend all her earnings on fixing the sliding glass door, tastes free-dom now that Joelle will drive her anywhere, anytime, in the Mazda, despite the fact that they live an hour's drive from each other, on opposite sides of the city. It's a swift balm to Sarah's resentment at having been forced to renew their friendship. Sarah and Joelle are both on costume crew, and have nothing to do until Mr. Freed-man, the costume designer, has finished the measurements, but they stay for rehearsal because they would not dream of leaving; they sit in the house with their tedious history homework. David is on props crew, which also has nothing to do because props crew is waiting for certain artistic conflicts to be resolved between Mr. Browne, the props master, and Mr. Kingsley, the director, but the props crew stays also; everyone stays, regardless of whether they have to, except for certain Freshmen who don't yet understand the ethos or whose parents object to a twelve-hour day.

From her seat in the house Sarah sees David, at a break in the blocking, cross from stage right to stage left very near the rear wall. He disappears in the direction of the shop. All the curtains are up in the fly space; the stage is a thrillingly vast, utilitarian maw in which the actors mill, waiting. Sarah rises quickly from her seat, tells Joelle she's going to the bathroom. Outside the theatre doors, she hooks left to follow the hallway that leads to the shop's outside door. As if on cue, the door opens and David steps out. It's past six; the hallway is empty. They're alone, for the first time since that late summer day on the college campus. The hall is empty but this emptiness is momentary; the shop door is just here, farther down is the loading-dock door that leads into stage left, the sets crew is not building yet, awaiting, as is the props crew, resolution of conflicts about the design, but any moment they'll wander through here, through their realm.

Sarah and David have torrents of accusations they have hoarded for weeks, to unleash on each other. Now their fury deserts them. "Hey," David says, a hot blush rising out of his polo shirt collar.

At the sight of that blush, Sarah's own chest seems to swell and implode. Heartbreak doesn't flow through the heart but along that frail shallow canal of the sternum.

"Hi," Sarah says, staring at his sternum where it hides from her under his shirt. She longs to lay her head there in repose from this agonized longing.

"Where are you going?" he asks.

"I don't know," she says honestly.

They reenter the shop together. Its workspace takes up the full height of the building. Circular saw, band saw, splintered scrap plywood, sawdust on the floor. At its far side, a steep ladderlike staircase leads up to a mezzanine level of storage; at the back of the storage area, a door opens onto the second-floor hallway, a realm of musicians' rehearsal rooms. Over the summer, someone has cleared out all the old flats and dismantled set pieces and other detritus and the storage mezzanine is quite empty. They pass out the door in the opposite wall and now stand in the second-floor hallway. Sarah crosses the hall to the double doors leading into the band room. These double doors are set back from the hallway a couple of feet so they form a wide, shallow alcove; she tries the double doors, which are locked. When she turns back, David catches her mouth with his, pressing her into the alcove's corner so she feels the protruding door hinges bite into her arm. Not protected or hidden at all; back pressed into the corner, she can see the whole length of the hallway. There is only the chance that none of their classmates will wander this way. These thoughts crawl along the bottom of her mind, clear but disregarded, as she devours David's mouth with her own. This is his power over her: not his cock or his hands but his mouth. Cock and hands are precocious enough. They belong to a fortunate, confident man, and have traveled in time for unguessable reasons to append themselves to a teenager. Unlike them his mouth is not a foreign power; it's her own missing part. Seeing him for the first time, last year, she had stared with recognition at his mouth, at its unhandsome, simian quality, his lips slightly too wide for his narrow boy's face. His mouth is nothing like hers because made for hers; her first time kissing him had been the first experience of her life that had exceeded expectation.

Gasping for breath, she takes his skull between her palms and fills the whorl of his ear with her tongue, because she's learned this disables him, even more than when she struggles to take his whole cock in her mouth. Then, some indelible scruple or shame interferes with his pleasure, while her tongue in his ear makes him swoon. They'd even made this a joke, in the course of their summer: they called it his kryptonite. Now he moans, unrestrained, and literally falls to his knees, pulling Sarah down with him. With his free hand he yanks open his jeans, fumbles his thick erection through the vent in his boxers. Her clothes have no such apertures, it's necessary to pull off her jeans entirely, at least from one leg, which means removing a boot, then her panties as well; heaving breath, they're both tugging and yanking her clothes in the middle of the black-and-white checkerboard floor of the hallway with all the unself-conscious diligence they might have brought to stretching canvas across the wood frame of a scenery flat. Then Sarah is naked, from the toes of one foot to her waist, and the hot, slippery fit is accomplished; despite their fierce mutuality to this point, they're both shocked to find themselves copulating in a public space of their high school, and now they bear down even more frantically, until with awful wrenchings of his face David comes, in his throes knocking Sarah's head unexpectedly hard against the door of the band room, which is now at her back. At almost the same time they hear another door open and quickly slam shut: the door to the shop mezzanine.

They're both trembling, their fingers useless as sausages, as they restore themselves into their clothes. They don't exchange another word; Sarah does not even know whether their eyes meet and part as they peel off in different directions, neither going back through the shop mezzanine door. David strides toward the rear stairs that will lead to the loading dock entrance, Sarah turns the corner to the main hallway and goes down the wide central stairs, across the piazza, back through the theatre's doors.

"Where've you been?" Joelle says, then starts laughing. "You bad girl." She hands Sarah her compact, and Sarah stares at her mouth in its dusty porthole. Her lipstick is rubbed off, her lips swollen and tender-appearing, strangely large for her face, like his mouth.

AT LAST, THE ends and the means seem to match.

They have a new Movement teacher, who will teach them to move. They will learn to move by moving; they will learn to free their movements by free movement. The Movement teacher's mission is so simple Sarah finds it idiotic. There is something else about the Movement teacher Sarah vaguely dislikes. She's not sure how to feel when she realizes her dislike stems from the fact that the new teacher is female. Mr. Kingsley, Mr. Browne, Mr. Freedman, Mr. Macy who does set design, dramaturgy, and theatre history: all men. Ms. Rozot will teach them Movement. From the moment they meet her, they all disrespect her, covertly. Something in Mr. Kingsley's gaze, as he introduces Ms. Rozot, warns them: they may mock her but they'd better keep it quiet.

She is a dancer and "multidisciplinary performer," and she trembles with joy at the prospect of being their teacher. "Teaching is a sacred trust," she gushes. "You are the future." Despite their secret disrespect they are secretly flattered. They'll give her a chance.

Since the tryst in the second-floor hallway, David has severed the wire. There is no longer even anger as a point of connection. His gaze backpedals from Sarah's like a magnet escaping its likeness. He has mastered the trick of existing elsewhere even when they are in the same room. An alien lives in his body; amnesia has sponged clean his brain. With each confirmation that David has vanished, Sarah feels more anguished and exposed, as if her moment of desperate abandon were still going on with the whole gaping class in attendance. Movement class will be held in the Black Box; they arrive as the Seniors are leaving, and Sarah sees David pausing with Erin O'Leary. Erin is a Senior, petite and blond, her flawless face grave with the consciousness of her preeminence. Erin has a film credit, a SAG card. She drives a pale blue Karmann Ghia convertible. The sheer quantity of her superiorities is laughable; she's like an implausible fictional character. Her tiny body, with its ideal, tiny hips and tiny breasts and compact little ass, drags generalized attention like a net. The boys, even the Senior boys, fear her: she is rumored to date real, established actors whom she meets on her "sets." The girls loathe her. She travels in a cylinder of rarefied air, untroubled by her social isolation: she's only here because it's trashy to drop out of high school. Next year, she'll attend Juilliard.

"Where are you headed?" David says to Erin.

"Restoration Comedy. You?"

"Movement."

"Ugh, I hated it. We ought to get showers."

"Oh, you're okay," David says, to which Erin laughs charmingly. She is so perfectly, adorably small that the crown of her glossy blond head barely grazes his chin. She gazes up at him, contentedly submissive. A girl who can do anything she wants. Can date a Sophomore if she wants. Anoint him.

Sarah plows into the Black Box, blind with revelation. Her cheeks, armpits, and crotch squirm with needles of heat, her familiar stigmata. Within the fist of her chest, her ribs snap like so many dry twigs. "Welcome!" Ms. Rozot is exulting. "Welcome to *Movement*." Right away Ms. Rozot has them leave their chairs, their books and jackets and purses, and come down to the great square platform of the stage. Sarah has difficulty relinquishing her pile of books, folders, spiral-bound notebooks, the tattered, fractionally digested paperback of *Tropic of Cancer* on the top of the heap like a cake decoration; she has been pressing the pile to her chest like a shield or a bandage, and giving it up she feels physical pain. Her chest groans at the fresh exposure. She can hardly stand straight. David is somewhere behind her, she can feel him there—looking at her? When she can't turn around and look back? Perhaps they're all looking at her. They all know her dilemma. Yesterday, trying to escape David's baffling absence, which she now understands, she'd climbed up to the fly rail and instead of solitude found Pammie, Pammie's face blotched and sticky with tears. Twenty-four feet in the air, they'd had no recourse but to speak to each other, two girls compelled by their classwork to a level of intimacy far beyond what they shared with the rest of the world, and yet also two girls who had never once traded a single superfluous word. "You love him, don't you," Pammie said.

The Black Box was just as it sounded, a black box of a room with a large platform stage at the center low enough to require no stairs, four sets of riser seating on each side, and aisles around the platform and around the sets of risers. During performances, black drapery made the aisles behind the risers backstage, four velvet hideaways also clandestinely useful at times, but today the drapery is furled, the box is open to its walls and its faraway ceiling, crisscrossed by the lighting catwalks. They are to walk, walk, walk—move, move, move!—all through this marvelous space; they must make themselves free to explore every inch. Not the catwalks or ladders, no. [Laughter.] "All right, you are all very clever! You will explore all *terrestrial* inches. In literature, there is an idea called automatic writing. You write without resting your pen. The pen must keep moving and moving; perhaps it is writing 'Why the fuck do I have to keep writing?'" [More laughter, shocked and charmed, at her profanity. Her profanity, tinged as it is with her accent, is more charming than shocking. Is it possible they could respect her?] "Well, this unbroken movement, of the pen, unlocks the secrets within. And if the pen can do this, then how much more the whole body? Let your body lead you. Your only order to it: *never stop moving*. Otherwise, it is in charge! I will help you with music."

Oh, no, they can't respect her. It's perfectly ridiculous. And the music she's playing! Cat Stevens. The Moody Blues. Satirically, then, they walk, walk, walk!—making faces at each other, swinging their arms, bouncing on the balls of their feet, speeding up comically so they're marching like robots. Whenever Norbert and Colin pass each other, they make absurd faces. Then, when they pass each other again, they both make absurd faces and leap in the air, still without breaking stride. This behavior spreads, evolves. Most of the boys adore Monty Python, and embarrass the girls at lunch with their flawlessly recalled and completely unfunny enactments of skits, by which they, the performers, are slain with hilarity. In the Black Box, the boys do "silly walks," and then pratfalls-in-motion to show they are slain with hilarity. By and large, the girls grow increasingly serious as the boys grow increasingly ludicrous. The girls no longer walk, they glide, they skim, they *slice*. The music changes to classical stuff without words. The girls begin taking on speed. An additional layer is added: high speed without hitting one another. They are weaving a mad tapestry with their movements; some unpredictably change direction in the hope of collisions. No matter what they do, no matter how subversively they do it, Ms. Rozot cries from the sidelines:

"Good!

"Move! *Move! MOVE!*

"Ah—you are *making something.*"

Indeed they are. Somehow, silliness dies. All the theatrical forms of movement—the "silly walks" and pratfalls, but also the arm-swinging ("I am carefree!") and the deliberate direction-changing ("I am a rogue!")—leach out of the room. Unexpected collectivity has slowly emerged in its place. Perhaps most important, embarrassment has been given up. Without their having noticed it, they're no longer embarrassed. Their speed has equalized until they're all traveling at about the same rate. Their winding paths, their cloverleafs and hairpins and loops, knit some underlying pattern as if they learned this maypole dance beside their parents as children, as if it binds them to something, and makes of them something.

Sarah's face is streaming tears. At the point where she ought to curve left or curve right she goes straight, and plunges out the Black Box doors and down the hall, running, her speed snatching the tears from her face.

There's a single toilet stall at the back of the girls' dressing room, off stage right, which no one ever uses except during performances. Sarah locks herself in and succumbs, her whole body folded and violently jerking as if she'll throw up in the bowl. Her mind startles her with the wish to be dead. To be dead, instead of in pain. Suicide, she realizes, isn't opting out of the future, it's opting out of the present, for who can see more of the future than that? Reference to the future, to its unbroken promise, is the reflex of those for whom the future's mirage still exists. Such people are lucky, deceived.

As if Sarah's thoughts had conjured her, Ms. Rozot comes into the dressing room and insists on discussing the future. Sarah cannot imagine how, apart from her own mind's self-defeating wizardry, this unwanted hippie Frenchwoman could have located her in this bathroom. Ms. Rozot is brand-new to the school. More than half the school's experienced students and teachers do not even realize this bathroom exists. Outside the stall door Ms. Rozot says, "Sa-rah? Sa-rah?" mispronouncing both *a*'s the same way, like the "o" sound in "odd." "Sarah, are you in there? Are you in pain?"

"Please leave me alone!" Sarah sobs angrily. Why is solitude so fucking hard to achieve? If only she had a car, she thinks for the billionth time. She would lock all the doors and just drive.

"Sarah, I want to share with you something. I think it will help you. Young people like you experience pain more *intensely* than those of us just a bit older. I speak of emotional pain. Your pain is greater, in duration and strength. It is harder to bear. This is not a metaphor. It is a fact, of physiology. Of psychology. Your emotional sensitivity—it is superior to that of your parents, your teachers. That is why these years of your life, when you are fifteen, sixteen, seventeen, are so difficult, but also so important. That is why developing your talent at this age is so crucial. This heightened emotional pain is a gift. A difficult gift."

Despite herself, she's listening. "Are you saying," she manages after a while, "that in the future, when I'm older, things won't hurt as much?"

"Yes, exactly. But Sarah, I am saying something else. Don't turn away from the pain. When you are older, yes, you will be harder. That is a blessing and a curse."

Ms. Rozot does not insist Sarah open the door, and this alone opens Sarah. They linger, she does not know how long, on their opposite sides of the door. "Thank you," she whispers at last.

"Please take your time," says Ms. Rozot, departing.

IT'S BEEN OBVIOUS from the beginning who are Broadway Babies and who aren't. Those who truly can sing, who can *give them the old razzle-dazzle*, who live for that *one singular sensation*, have for the most part drawn attention to themselves from the first day of school. They cluster around the Black Box piano during rainy-day lunchtimes and sing *The Fantasticks*. They wear the *Cats* sweatshirts to school that they got on their holiday trip to New York. Some of them, like the Junior named Chad, are enviably serious musicians who can not only sing but play Sondheim, for real, from sheet music. Some of them, like Erin O'Leary, don't just sing but dance like Ginger Rogers, having apparently put on tap shoes at the same time as they took their first steps.

Sarah's failure to be Erin O'Leary used to be a point of pride, if a wobbly one. Now Sarah is furious with her coarse heavy hair, the opposite of Erin's dandelion floss, with her wide hips the opposite of Erin's trim ones, with her big unskilled feet in their dirty misused ballet flats the opposite of Erin's miniature ones which make scissoring blurs through the air. Sarah is furious with the faltering squawk of her voice, the opposite of Erin's "songbird." Historically, Theatre students like Sarah (and David) who couldn't sing or dance solaced themselves with Uta Hagen, Beckett, and Shakespeare. They reminded themselves they were serious Theatre Artists, that Broadway was cheeseball one end to the other. Of course they kept this knowledge to themselves, out of respect for Mr. Kingsley and genuine awe for his musical talent. They were never troubled by their condescension, or at least Sarah wasn't. But now that it's mainstage auditions again, all of them are reminded, some of them more painfully than others, of how much they're exalted by big musicals. David loves *Jesus Christ Superstar*, knows all the words, sings along tunelessly with the album when he is alone. Sarah has the same secret relationship to *Evita*. They are serious; but how much better if they *also* could sing, if they could startle and move their classmates on those rainy days standing around the piano? If, implored by Mr. Kingsley, they could deign to play Christ, or Evita—for the good of the show, given that they were best for the role?

Such secret talent isn't theirs, however. They remind themselves— though not in conversation, for David and Sarah don't speak to each other, or have any idea where the other is sitting, so many rows distant as to be reduced to just a dark head tilted over a book, remote and indifferent and hateful and completely ignored (in fact, not even noticed)—of how corny *Guys and Dolls* is, how glad they both are to be taking a pass on auditions, how much more absorbing they're finding *Endgame* (David) or the first scene of *King Lear*, beyond which she has never yet managed to penetrate (Sarah). They do not share these similar feelings, the similarity having no meaning for them. They do, of course, actually watch the auditions, their hearts in their mouths, almost sick with vicarious hope.

It is, Sarah bitterly thinks, like an Erin O'Leary coronation. Erin will be Adelaide, of course. Acknowledging this, she sings "Adelaide's Lament," Mr. Bartoli, the dance department accompanist who also serves as musical director, practically bouncing off the bench as he plays, so acute is his pleasure in playing for her. Many, many of the boys, including many who, like David, can't sing, but who, unlike David, don't care, sing "I got the horse right here," making up for their laughable voices with a lot of mugging and humorous gestures. Some of them will get cast, as the gamblers do not have to be melodic and do have to be funny. David flushes with the consciousness of his own cowardice, the fraudulence of his appeal to Erin. Soon Erin, like Sarah, will find him repulsive unless he can make himself worthy. Sightlessly staring at *Endgame*, he vows to himself that he'll audition for the musical next year. In their department, auditions take place constantly—for the grade-level Showcase productions; for the Senior Directing Projects; for the Outdoor Shakespeare every May; for the Spring Mainstage (Drama) and, as now, Fall Mainstage (Musical)—and each round of auditions tends to confirm a corresponding, slightly different pecking order: the purely social pecking order of the sophomore class, in which both Sarah and David rank high; the pecking order of the Serious Actors, which David has started to climb; the pecking order of the Adults-in-Training, the perpetual Stage Managers, whose skills Mr. Browne ferrets out even when they are trying to hide them (Sarah fears this is her fate). But only fall auditions for the mainstage musical reveal a pecking order applicable to the whole school, for only in the fall musical does the whole school take part. The dancers happily subordinate themselves to chorus roles. The instrumental-music students hold their own auditions, for the mainstage orchestra. Among the Theatre students it is often repeated that the dramatic and musical mainstage productions are equal in status, but everyone knows this is bunk. Playing the lead in the dramatic mainstage doesn't even rate as highly as playing a secondary character in the musical. None of them, not even those who arrived at the school with an actual hatred of musicals, question this valuation. None of them wonder what things might be like if, say, someone other than Mr. Kingsley ran the Theatre program. Brilliant as he is, his hierarchies must be objective, and even last year, when it was still a point of pride to Sarah not to be Erin O'Leary, she had asked her mother for ballet, jazz, and tap lessons, so as to do better in the in-school lessons. Her mother had said, "Are you kidding? Isn't that what you're already doing all day, instead of preparing for college?"

As the auditions wear on, Sarah puts down *King Lear* and she, Pammie, Ellery, and Joelle, who will all work on costumes, compile a cast list. The female roles are a gimme; it's hardly possible to guess wrong. The male roles, more numerous, sometimes make for a dark horse or two, and the fun lies in guessing at these. Norbert is auditioning, and Ellery sinks in his seat and grabs Sarah and Joelle, on either side of him. "Girls," he whispers, "give me strength."

"Why aren't you auditioning?" Sarah asks him.

"Just because I'm beautiful and black doesn't mean I can sing."

Last year, as Freshmen, they had taken sight-reading, and been obliged to stand at the piano and warble the length of a page of sheet music chosen with indifference to their ranges, if they even had ranges. It hadn't been much of a showcase for vocal, or even sight-reading, skill, and a few of them, as often happened, had bombed, while a few others unexpectedly triumphed. Taniqua and Pammie, both church chorus veterans, had amazed with their sheet music literacy and their competent voices. At the opposite end of the spectrum, Manuel, when summoned to the piano, went rigid, his sheet music snapping in the breeze of his quivering hands. His skin, always dustily brown, turned mesmerically red like a coal in the fire. Just when they thought he would faint, his mouth slowly hinged open—and hung that way, mutely, as if he were an abandoned ventriloquist's dummy. A rustle of incipient laughter passed over the room. "Quiet," Mr. Kingsley had said, striking the first note of whatever it was he had given Manuel to sight-read. They were all forced to watch Manuel's pitiful trembling outlive the note's lengthy vibration. "One more time," Mr. Kingsley had said, striking the key and renewing the note in their ears. Was it possible for total petrifaction to grow yet more total, yet more petrified? It apparently was. Manuel was going to stand there enacting the meaning of "dumbstruck" until either Mr. Kingsley showed mercy or the bell rang to end class. "You're not off the hook," Mr. Kingsley had finally said, dismissing Manuel with surprising anger. In general Mr. Kingsley's anger was reserved for his pets, who wore it as a badge of distinction. Mr. Kingsley didn't bother being angry at people of whom nothing much was expected.

Now, as Mr. Kingsley called, "Next!" to the auditioners waiting concealed in the wings, Ellery clamped Sarah's elbow again. "Am I dreaming?" he squeaked.

Manuel had come onstage, an apparition. Perhaps it wasn't Manuel. He wasn't dressed like Manuel, in the slightly too-small and slightly too-youthful striped T-shirts you could tell, just from looking, had been bought from the sale rack at Sears, or maybe from the Purple Heart Thrift Store, by Manuel's unknown mother, after being discarded by whoever had bought them at Sears. The shirts Manuel wore every day had pills, and faint, ancient stains of the kind that defeated all efforts, and they squeezed his upper arms and his neck. For pants, Manuel wore corduroys that had almost no cord left. And regardless of weather conditions, Manuel never took off his jacket, the same fake-wool-lined corduroy jacket they'd first seen him in, and that seemed to them now as permanent as a turtle's scuffed shell. The onstage Manuel was missing this traditional garb, though not dressed any better. He wore a pair of black slacks that were shiny with age, and a grayish-white button-up shirt that, despite being short at the sleeves, was tightly buttoned at the cuffs, emphasizing the bony excess of his wrists. The feet were encased in hard black leather shoes that looked too small, and the usual bushy brown hair was combed back from the face exposing large, startled eyes, unfamiliar to all, beneath an equally novel, creased brow. A sheaf of paper was gripped in the hands. The Manuel-apparition looked like a waiter, an unhappy and poorly dressed waiter. Sarah realized with amazement he was dressing, as well as he could, for the part. *Guys and Dolls* would of course call for old-fashioned menswear: leather shoes, slacks, a button-up shirt. Not one other boy, for the sake of the audition, had made the slightest alteration to his everyday clothes. They'd all auditioned in their Levi's and polos and dumb slogan T-shirts.

It did seem possible this was a dream. As on the day of the sight-reading test, a titter passed over the house, instantly extinguished when Mr. Kingsley stood up from his place in the center of the third row. "Okay, Manuel. What do you have for us?"

Ellery squeezes Sarah's hand, and Sarah squeezes back. On his other side he has Joelle's hand. On Sarah's other side is Pammie. Joelle and Pammie are squeezing their eyes shut and clutching their cheeks; Pammie is so agonized she balls up in her seat like a hedge-hog. Both Joelle and Pammie, for their separate if equally feminine reasons, feel a motherly pity for Manuel, though neither has managed to befriend him. He doesn't afford the slightest opportunity, speaking to no one—not even Pammie, with her pious childlike fearlessness, can get him to answer her cheery "Hello!" Sarah hears Pammie fervently mumbling. It's possible, in fact likely, that she's praying.

"What do you have for us?" Mr. Kingsley repeats.

Manuel again turns that mesmerizing color of a live coal. At length he says, barely audibly, "I am going to sing the 'Ave Maria' of [a bunch of syllables Sarah can't hear]." Strings seem to be tied to his elbows, equally pulling on him from both sides, so that, in his tensile, motionless state, he might fly to pieces. Then the stage-left string breaks, and he lurches toward Mr. Bartoli, extending his music. Mr. Bartoli pages through it, nods. "Shall I begin?" he asks.

Manuel wrings his hands in a fretful grandmotherly way, abruptly drops them to his sides. Mr. Kingsley, still standing, his back to the rest of the house, says, "Manny, I know you can do it."

He speaks as though he and Manuel are entirely alone. Yet no one in the house fails to hear him, to the very last row.

It's possible for silence to change quality. The silence had been enforced, the silence of quashed merriment. Now it's the silence of genuine puzzlement. Mr. Kingsley never uses nicknames or pet names. To indicate an altered attitude he sometimes calls them, instead of their given names, Ms. or Mr. and then their last name. This denotes bemusement, disapproval, and much in between, but whatever the case there is always a distance implied. "Manny" observes no such distance. "Manny" doesn't even observe that there might be some forty-odd people elsewhere in the room.

Mr. Kingsley sits down again. The back of his head, with its limited features, its expensive haircut, and the ends of his spectacles' temples hooking over the backs of his ears, is nearly as expressive to them as his face—it radiates a peremptory certitude. "Come on. You know what I want. Give it to me." If the back of his head can say this, just imagine the front. (Ms. Rozot: "If the pen can do this, how much more the whole body!") Manuel—Manny?—seems to be in wordless communication with this hidden front of Mr. Kingsley's head. He gazes into it, receives something from it—he looked different when he first came onstage, and he somehow looks different again. With what might almost be called self-possession he nods to Mr. Bartoli. Mr. Bartoli raises his hands, brings them plunging back down. Manuel sucks air into his lungs.

To this point in her life, Sarah has associated opera with Bugs Bunny in braids, PBS, overweight men wearing tunics, shrieking women, and shattering glass. She's never understood, certainly because she's never seen a live opera but also because she's never heard a half-decent performance, not even in part, on TV, that opera, in fact, is the highest redemption of longing. That it's her own anguish, salvaged by music. The victorious army's fight song, in defense of her mute, savaged heart.

Now she understands why Ms. Rozot has warned her to not turn away from her pain.

Manuel sings. His Spanish accent, which he drags like a weight on his uncertain journeys amid English words, is a bona fide now. Who else among them could sing this, even if they were blessed with the voice? Who else among them is blessed with the voice? Manuel sings, it seems, to horizons beyond the light booth. His eyes are cast up, anxiously, as if he's aware he is barely retaining the fickle attention of God. So plaintively does he exhort this remote audience that Sarah glances back over her shoulder, expecting to see ranks of angels, their feet floating just off the ground. Instead she sees the faces of her classmates, rapt with unself-consciousness, the joyful respite from the problems of self. She too has passed out of herself, so thoroughly, so happily, that for a moment even David's face is strange to her, and not just because his eyes are full of tears.

Her body twists forward again as if slapped, as Manuel, like a fountain, upraises his arms and their glorious burden, his final note, into the air. As if they awaited this gesture, the house detonates: clapping, whistling, foot-stamping, Ellery leaping up to shout, "*Hombre!*" Onstage Manuel, streaming with sweat, grins while wringing his hands. We've all had this dream, Sarah thinks. The dream in which, to the world's surprise and our own, we turn out to be best.

Mr. Bartoli pushes the piano bench smartly behind him, crosses to Manuel, claps him on the shoulder, and pumps him warmly by the hand. They're only forty-odd kids but they make the noise of a full house. They keep going, on their feet, so that except to the rows nearest him, Mr. Kingsley goes almost unnoticed when, pushing his spectacles onto the top of his head, he roughly draws his sleeve across his forehead and eyes. Then, "Someone write down the date!" he shouts at them. "Manuel Avila's public debut!"

IN THE PARKING lot, at lunchtime, Sarah sits hunched on the hood of the Mazda with Joelle, Sarah scratching sometimes in her notebook, the two of them smoking clove cigarettes, Sarah ignoring the sandwich her mother has packed her. Her mother packs for Sarah, every morning, even when they're not speaking, as now, a sandwich of meat from the deli, sliced cheese, Grey Poupon, a slice of tomato, and lettuce on some kind of a bakery bun that will have either poppy or sesame seeds. "Your sandwich looks like a restaurant sandwich!" Joelle once exclaimed in wonder, and since then Sarah doesn't unwrap it, but when lunchtime is over drops it into the trash as they're going inside. She does so with her face turned away, as if not having seen herself do it might mean that she hasn't. On the far side of the lot the pale blue Karmann Ghia pulls in, perhaps some litter from the Del Taco drive-through carelessly tossed on the floor, perhaps David, ridiculous in a pair of Ray-Bans, enthroned on the passenger seat, but if Sarah has not in fact seen this, it might mean it isn't the case. No one can prove it's the case. Her eyes are night headlights; they only see what's just ahead. It's an unending labor, this policing of vision and thoughts.

"You look exhausted," Mr. Kingsley says, once he's shut his office door with a click that broadcasts the length of the hall. The ticket of admission. The door has shut on faces pretending absorption in the bulletin board, as if anyone need consult beyond his or her memory to obtain the full cast list, which was posted last week (Sky Masterson: Manuel Avila). Her fellow students are loitering in the hallway outside in the hopes of obtaining what she's just received: his particular summons. Pride and humiliation strangely mingle their tastes in her mouth, or perhaps it's the tart, rancid coffee to which she has lowered her face. He's handed it to her, in a Styrofoam cup, from his personal drip coffee maker. Pride she's been chosen, humiliation at what she presumes are the grounds for his choice. They all know the students with whom he is sometimes seen driving away, at lunchtime, in his olive Mercedes; whom he detains with no more than a look, as the rest of the class filters out of the room; behind whom he closes the door to his office at lunchtime. They're the Troubled students, the borderline ones, whose sufferings are eagerly whispered the lengths of the halls. Jennifer, who missed school for a month and now only wears sleeves that hang well past her wrists. Greg, the incandescently beautiful Senior, with whom Julietta and Pammie are madly in love, who despite his impeccable clothes, dazzling smile, and kindness, was thrown out of the house by his father, and now lives at the YMCA. Manuel, whose stark poverty is newly palatable because coupled with talent. And Sarah, about whom they say—what?

She's so in love with David she let him fuck her in the hall! And now he's dumped her.

"I don't get a lot of sleep," she concedes.

"Why not?"

"I have this job. At a French bakery. I have to be there at six in the morning on weekends. Both days."

"What time do you go to sleep on the nights you have work?"

"Maybe two."

"What time do you get up on weekdays?"

"The same. About six."

"And you're going to bed when? On weekdays."

"The same. One or two."

"You're going to kill yourself," he observes, and she thinks he's predicting an event in the future, her actual suicide, and then realizes he's speaking figuratively, or probably figuratively, about the long-term effects of not sleeping enough.

"I am really tired," she agrees, and just like that, she is crying again. Her shoulders hitch, and try as she might she can't stop bringing up chunks of wet, ragged noise. She knows it's expected yet knows equally that sometimes, some greater forbearance is also expected. Mr. Kingsley is not Ms. Rozot. Jennifer the failed suicide, Greg the orphan by force, impoverished Manuel, and her, Sarah—they've all been robbed of heedless childhood and that's why they've been chosen, their precocious adulthood acknowledged. All kids want such glamorous knowledge. The darkness of it. The hardness of it. The realness of it. The cold fact that life really is fucked. And Sarah, with her Morrissey T-shirts and her unfiltered

Camels and her sleep deprivation and her willful compliance with sexual hungers, she's been asking for this awful dispossession, with one mind she's been hot on its trail, and now that she's got it she longs to go back. If she could only go back, and eat the sandwich her mother packed her, with its thoughtful tomato.

She cries, as expected by him, and she eventually masters her tears, as also expected by him. She cleans her face and blows her nose with his Kleenex and disposes of it in his trash. She even takes out her Sportsac of makeup and unhurriedly fixes her face. When she snaps shut her compact she feels his approval as clearly as if he had spoken. "So," he says, pleased. "Why don't you tell me what's actually happening."

She tells him. Not all that same day; they're already out of time. But now she is a regular. Their meetings wholly evident, and wholly unacknowledged, as is any exclusive liaison, by those it makes complicit, yet excludes. David sees, and grinds his molars together by day and by night to the point that the dentist has threatened to make him a mold to wear while he's asleep. David, God help him, has no consciousness of discarding Sarah, but of being discarded. Here's a girl, unlike any other girl he's ever been with, who, once told of his love, doesn't grab hold of his hand, hang herself on his arm, drag him out to the mall or the movies with the chattering flock of her friends, but to the contrary, spooks like a horse when he walks in the room. Swathes herself in cold air and then dares him to try and reach her, and how can he? Is it possible their whole love affair was a misunderstanding? David had known she slept with guys who were older than he, in some cases much older. Seeing her embarrassment, their first day back at school, David had felt like a charity case. She'd *allowed* him, but he shouldn't let anyone *know*. And then the thing in the hallway, strange proof: she'll come to him when nobody's looking.

Or is it possible, Sarah says to Mr. Kingsley, that their whole breakup is a misunderstanding? Isn't it possible, Sarah begs Mr.

Kingsley, that David still loves her? How could he say that he did, and then not?

"Do you love him?"

"Yes." Then, unnerved by her certainty, "I mean, maybe. I think."

"Have you told him how you feel?"

"How could I?"

Acting is: fidelity to authentic emotion, under imagined circumstances. Fidelity to authentic emotion is: standing up for your feelings. Is this not the one thing, the *one* thing, he has tried to teach them? At first she thinks he's barked out of anger, then grasps that he's laughing. Perhaps he is laughing at her, but at least he's not angry. "God," he says, and even in the sanctum of his office his laugh is a stage laugh, artillery fire. "Thank you. I forget sometimes: it's a process. And, you know, it never ends. That's the beauty of it."

She doesn't know what he's talking about, but once she's cleaned herself up yet again with the box of Kleenex, she puts on her wise, weary face. "So it is," she agrees.

"What about your mother?"

"What about her?"

"How are you getting along?"

"I don't know. Not that bad. Not that well. Even when we're not fighting we don't really talk."

"She drives you to work on the weekend. You must talk in the car."

"Not really. It's so early in the morning. We just get in the car and drive there."

"I think the bakery job is too much. You should be sleeping on the weekend. Having fun."

"I need the job," she says tersely, because Mr. Kingsley is as unlikely as her mother to sympathize with her implacable pursuit of a car. She's unaware that her tone might suggest the brusque pride of the abjectly poor, particularly when paired with her tatty punk wardrobe. She does resent the absence in her life of a pale blue Karmann Ghia convertible, but she knows she's not poor. Not rich, certainly, in the little two-bedroom apartment behind the chalk X with her mother's long-serving Toyota. But not poor.

He is silent a moment, thoughtful. "You and David come from very different worlds."

"How do you mean?"

"David comes from a world of privilege."

She doesn't wonder how he knows this, or whether he's guessed. "I suppose more than me."

"He's not working."

"No. He doesn't have to. When he turns sixteen, his mother and Philip will buy him a car."

"Who's Philip?"

"His stepfather."

"Ah. Is that a recent thing?"

"It can't be that recent. His mom and Philip have a two-year-old baby."

"So David's the big brother," Mr. Kingsley says, smiling.

She smiles also, to designate David this way. "He already was. He's the oldest from his mother's first marriage. Then his mother left his father for Philip, David thinks because Philip had money. David's real dad never had any money. David says his parents, his mom and real dad, burned his childhood house down to collect the insurance. So in that sense, originally, he's not from such a privileged background," she concludes, overwhelmed by her flood of disclosures.

But Mr. Kingsley does not judge her craving to talk about David. He does not judge her breathless uncertainty, now that she's stopped. He reaches out, across the corner of his desk, and takes her hand. "You got to know each other," he observes. She nods mutely, all fluency diverted again from her tongue to her eyes.

That night when Joelle drops her off, after ten, her mother's at the kitchen table in her robe. Usually by this hour she's behind the closed door of her bedroom. Her mother's brown hair, streaked with kinky white strands, hangs down loose to her shoulders. She's wearing men's athletic socks on her feet. "Your teacher called," she says.

"Who?"

"Mr. Kingsley."

"Mr. Kingsley called here? Why?" Some terrified animal group—a quad of quail? a mess of mice?—explodes into flight inside Sarah's rib cage.

"I have no idea why. I know his stated reason. He called to ask about your bakery job. He asked if I could possibly let you stop doing it, for your health and well-being. He seemed to think that I force you to do it and keep all your earnings."

"I never said that to him!"

"I told him I don't have the slightest control over how you spend your time, at the bakery or anywhere else. I'd like to know what made him feel entitled to call me about it."

"I don't know, Mom."

"I'd be very happy if you quit that job, and I could quit driving you there at five thirty *both* weekend mornings, but you're so determined to buy your own car, you're so convinced that not owning a car at the age of fifteen is some sort of awful deprivation, you've somehow convinced me I'd be mistreating you by *not* giving you rides to your job. And now your *teacher*, who keeps you at your *school* for twelve hours a day painting pieces of canvas and gluing flowers on hats, this man calls to suggest I'm mistreating you by forcing you to work, as if I'm making you sing for your supper? How dare he! Who the sam hell does he think he is?"

"I don't know, Mom. I never said that to him."

"I happen to agree with him that you should quit that job, but that doesn't mean that I want his opinion. Your life outside school isn't any of his goddamn business. You *know* that, don't you?"

"Yes," she says, edging toward her bedroom. Already, his phone call's impact has changed shape. In the instant, she'd felt his betrayal, the violation of their special alliance. Now she grasps that he's mounted a challenge to her mother's authority. He has intruded for the sake of intruding. How proud she feels, to command his attention.

THE REHEARSAL ROOM, with its long mirrored wall and its frigid linoleum floors. So much has happened here, in this fluorescent-lit refrigerated box, where their twins stare at them from the room in the mirror. The room in the mirror is just as bright and cold as this room, just as provisional-seeming, with its plastic/chrome chairs, its foam/Naugahyde mats, its piano and bench, shoved aside, cleared away for their bodies. In this room they've crawled through the unrelieved darkness, encountering and groping each other. They've lain on their backs and been corpses. They've cradled each other, fallen into each other's linked arms, formed a wheel and by turn had the hub stare at them and deliver a verdict (Norbert to Pammie: "I think you're the nicest girl in our class, and if you were thinner, you'd be kind of pretty"; Chantal to David: "I don't fuck white guys, but if I had to fuck a white guy, I'd fuck you"). Now, coming into the room, they're told to set it up as a theatre. Three or so rows of chairs facing this way. At their front, a pair of chairs facing each other. As always, Mr. Kingsley will stand. "Side aisles, please," he says, and they hurry to compact the rows so there's clearance between the row ends and the walls. They take their seats, clustering in their usual ways: the black girls, the white boys, the rest filling in in accordance with vague, shifting rules of attraction/repulsion. The two chairs "onstage" remain empty. Sarah, coming in late from the bathroom, takes the empty chair at the back by Manuel, for no reason apart from its emptiness. Manuel is wearing a nice shirt; it seems lately he has better clothes, though this impression of hers isn't consciously made, it's landscape. Memory will reveal it.

"Sarah, please take one of the two chairs up front. Either one."

She's so startled to be singled out that for a moment she doesn't stand up, though her gaze whips to Mr. Kingsley, questioning. Nothing in his gaze answers. He is loftily perched on the battlement tower, conducting the movements of miniature troops. As she stands she's aware of Manuel quickly moving his backpack as if it might be in her way.

Last year, she'd had her wisdom teeth out. They'd come in unusually early, the dentist had said, and been unusually large in a way that would certainly cause crookedness that was harder to fix afterward; there was some sort of joke to be made here about oversize premature wisdom and irreparable crookedness, but she'd never worked it out to her satisfaction before the teeth were swapped for blood-soaked wads of gauze. They'd drugged her to do the procedure, her mother sitting in the waiting room, reading the paper, while Sarah lay prone and unconscious beneath the hot lights; and no sooner had the teeth been yanked out and the gauze wads stuffed in than Sarah had apparently swung her legs down from the chair, while the dentist and nurse washed their hands with backs turned, and before either of them, or the receptionist, or Sarah's mother, or other patients in the waiting room could quite process that Sarah was walking, she'd walked out of the office, and out the door of the building, and across much of the parking lot until, giving chase, the receptionist and nurse had at last detained her as she attacked the locked doors of her mother's Toyota. She retained not a shred of a dream's memory of this dental escape. In fact she'd thought her mother was joking, until she'd gone back for her follow-up visit and the dentist had said, "Should I tie you down first?"

This transit to the chair at the front of the room is equally unremembered. She finds herself facing herself in the full-length and full-width mirror. The other chair faces away from the mirror. An advantage she's failed to seize.

"David," Mr. Kingsley says. "Please take the other chair. Please move the chairs together so that your knees touch."

Their classmates do not make a sound, but almost as one they lean forward. The sitting knee-to-knee is unfamiliar, but that's not the piquant novelty. They who have stroked, rubbed, groped, and gripped in every possible configuration, at the behest of their teacher, in the name of their Art, can hardly be impressed with kneecap contact. What is impressive is the blunt singling out by Mr. Kingsley himself of what they've all, themselves, grown sick of tiptoeing around: David and Sarah and their all-important drama, of which they're so proud that they won't even share it. In Ego Reconstruction they skate over each other with ridiculous comments like "I appreciate the effort you made cleaning woodshop." They're haughty emotional hoarders; it's about time they were brought down a peg. At the edge of her vision, Sarah feels the hungry encroachment, made only worse by the pockets of sympathy—Joelle and perhaps Pammie wide-eyed with anxiety for her, while Norbert's lip curls at one corner. He's hardly the only one eager for blood.

David's knees, touching hers through their two pairs of jeans, do not feel like parts of a person. All four of their knees bump and flinch, blind bewildered convexities. It's necessary to sit strangely primly, squeezing her thighs together, to maintain the commanded contact. Unbidden, unbearable, she recalls David's face as he'd first entered her, in her twilit bedroom, on that hot afternoon. *I feel like*, he'd kept trying to tell her. *I feel like* . . . He'd felt like their bodies were *made for each other*, the tired cliché stripped of all but its startling truth.

She squeezes her eyes tightly closed, balls the memory up.

"Sarah, open your eyes," Mr. Kingsley commands. "Sarah and David, make eye contact, please."

She raises her eyes to his face. The blue agates grudgingly stare. The horizon dividing his lips. The button of his mole. His collarbone, partly disclosed by the V of his polo shirt, rising and falling a little too quickly. She seizes on this as a clue, and hope, which she'd thought she'd forsworn, explodes invisible and noiseless from her chest; but its force must be felt, because David recoils, the blue agates receding to points. "This is not a staring contest," Mr. Kingsley is saying. "I want you to find a soft gaze. I don't mean soft like weepy." (Does he say this because either of them appears weepy? Sarah will not weep. She will, she tells herself with absolute bloodless conviction, sooner stop breathing than let herself cry.) "I don't mean soft like tender." (Does he say this because either of them appears tender? She's already forgotten her vow of an instant before, her eyes well, they desperately rummage in David's for some tenderness, then catch sight of themselves in the mirror and boil themselves dry with the heat of their shame.) "I mean neutral. Receptive. A neutral gaze, without anxiety or accusation or expectation. Neutrality is the self that we offer the other, alert and open, unencumbered. No baggage. This is how we come to the stage."

Now that he's got them up there in the chairs, maintaining eye contact, disallowed from staring, accusing, expecting, or experiencing anxiety, allegedly neutral, alert, unencumbered—for some minutes he seems to forget about them. He wanders the edge of the room, unhurriedly talking. What it means to be present. Integrity of the moment. Acknowledgment of . . . Freedom from . . . Of course one feels and one knows what one feels and at the same time is master of feeling, not slave; feeling is the archive upon which we draw, but the archive has doors or perhaps it has drawers, it's got storage, an index, the metaphor for the archive of feelings has been lost on Sarah but she gets the idea. You're fucked if it isn't in order.

"David," Mr. Kingsley says abruptly, returning to stand over them. "Please take Sarah's hands. Sarah, please take David's hands."

David has advanced, receded, tilted, and swum in her paralyzed vision, his red polo shirt has grown blobby and almost subsumed him, but at the command David's back in the chair with a merciless thud, all sharp, unkind edges and nails for eyes.

They join hands.

David's hands are horribly inanimate, like meat, these hands of his that have been so alive to her.

Her own hands' surfaces crawl in protest, these hands of hers that have wrung the pillow clutched against her gut, and pleasurelessly slimed themselves between her legs, in failed service of her longing for him. Her hands have regained him, and he feels like a corpse.

"I want you to communicate through your hands," Mr. Kingsley instructs. "No words. Only touch."

David's hands remain inert. They do not squeeze, stroke, slap—but how are hands meant to communicate with hands? In fact, his have done so already. They don't even hold her hands. Sarah's hands are frozen to maintain the appearance that his hands hold hers. Her elbows are locked at her sides, her wrists and forearms tremble from the strain; if she gave up, her hands would clatter to her sides, David wouldn't catch them.

Mr. Kingsley is orbiting slowly. "Is that the best you can do?" he demands. "Those hands know each other, don't they. What do they remember? What could they tell us, if they knew how to talk? Or maybe they'd lie to us. Maybe they already are."

He can see, Sarah thinks. He can see the hands aren't really joined. They are linked but they somehow don't touch. How stupid they must seem to him, that they can't even follow his simplest direction. She is powerless to clasp David's hands, to seize them, to communicate with touch. Sweat drenches her scalp; she can feel it worming under her hair. The floor beneath her seems to rise and tilt, again and again, describing the same arc without ever completing it. She is slowly falling out of her chair, a black sunstroke stain marring her vision. Far away David's face hangs in the air, his cheeks tumescent with blood and his sightless eyes gleaming with rage. Sarah splits from herself; David might crush her fingers in his, snap the slender bones like so much dry spaghetti. If only he would. At length she grows dimly aware she is shaking with sobs. She hears the ugly noise long before she is able to pinpoint the source, and like the victim who is forced to inflict her own torture, unwilled she remembers the first time she came, and the wails she hadn't realized were hers until she felt David weeping with joy on her neck.

The tone of Mr. Kingsley's accusation has shifted and sharpened, for Sarah has brought the authentic emotion. She might not have done so with her hands, but poor thing: she is doing her best.

"Is that the best *you* can do?" Mr. Kingsley is shouting, red-faced. He's shoved his glasses on top of his head, snagging a chunk of his hair which now sticks up in unprecedented disorder. "This is the girl you walked *miles* for. In the *heat*. With a stupid *tennis racquet* so your mom would think you'd gone to the *club*. Because you *loved* her, David. *Don't lie to her now and don't lie to yourself!*"

Their classmates are slack-jawed. Is there any possibility this is a play? Among them, emotional exhibitionism is commonplace. Confession is commonplace. Shrill recrimination, and reconciliation, are commonplace. This is different, in what way they cannot in the moment define. Some feel the urge to call out, as if at a sporting event, with encouragement or admonishment or outright insult. "Don't give in to that cunt!" Colin wants to call out to David. Pammie wants to rush over to Sarah and conceal Sarah's bowed head with her arms. Pammie once sat behind David while he sat behind Sarah, and thought to herself, If a boy ever looks at me for half a second the way he's looking at the back of her head, I'll die and go to God a virgin, I will not even need to be kissed. Chantal wants to say, "C'mon, be a man, David, the fuck are you getting so red-faced about?" Norbert, who would gladly lick Sarah's ballet flats, wants to slap her across the face and say, "This is what you get for loving that dick when you could have had me." Some who find their view blocked are tentatively kneeling on their chairs or fully standing. Sarah finally snatches her hands away, covers her face with the sieve of her fingers through which mucus and tears leak in clear, gooey threads that become sticky stripes on her arms.

"Foul!" Colin shouts, and relieved, nasty laughter erupts.

"Take five!" snaps Mr. Kingsley, displeased by the class's irreverence. But he has one hand on Sarah's right shoulder, the other on David's left shoulder, and he leans in: they are not yet excused. Sarah cannot, will not, uncover her face, but she feels his lips brush the crown of her head.

"Well done," he says into her hair.

Then she hears him speak softly to David. "I won't rest until you cry."

Sarah peeks between her fingers. Mr. Kingsley is smiling, in cold enjoyment of his prophecy. It is only a matter of time. David's face is almost purple with effort. David lurches from his chair, knocks over several more as he less walks than falls out of the room.

"Take five, sweetie," Mr. Kingsley says so that everyone foot-dragging, shoe-tying, purse-digging, faking some reason to stay in the room—everyone except David, who's left—clearly hears. "You know where to find the Kleenex."

Take five, sweetie.

"WHAT ELSE DID you tell him?" shouts David, who hasn't spoken to her, even deigned to acknowledge her lowly existence, in months and who now strikes like a holy avenger as she and Joelle cross the parking lot toward Joelle's car.

JOELLE: *(interposing herself)* Shut up, David! Leave her alone.

DAVID: *(actually shoving* JOELLE *to one side with the palms of both hands, so* JOELLE *reels on her stiletto-heel boots, almost loses her balance)* Did you tell him you won't even talk to me, but you'll fuck me in the music room hallway?

SARAH: I won't *talk* to you?

DAVID: *(over her)* Or was he *watching us* fuck, did you set that up too?

JOELLE: *(regaining her balance, roaring with terrific volume)* You're an *asshole*—

SARAH: *(too stunned to speak—but* DAVID *has already turned his back on her,* ERIN O'LEARY'S *little car has pulled up; he gets in, slams the door, and his blond chauffeuse, expressionless behind sunglasses, drives him away)*

SARAH'S MOTHER: Your life outside school isn't any of his goddamn business. You *know* that, don't you?

MR. KINGSLEY: Please begin, Sarah.

Sarah and David sit at the front of the room in the two chairs again. Their knees no longer touch, they are permitted to sit very slightly apart. David looks at Sarah without looking at her. He sees her without seeing her. He sits in the chair without being there. She doesn't comprehend, not why he does this, but how; if she could do it, she would; she understands for the first time that David is the real thing, that David is going to make it in theatre, he may even make it so far, matter so much, that he can spell it "theater" if he goddamn feels like it, and she also understands that here at CAPA, with Mr. Kingsley, David is already finished. He will never play a lead. He will never be a star. He will leave the school with his weight of charisma untapped, unacknowledged, unpraised, obscured beneath a miasma of stale smoke and alcohol fumes, the "silly walks," the polo shirt, the tennis racquet not merely discarded but utterly invalidated and forgotten by all but a few stubborn memory-keepers.

SARAH to DAVID: You're angry.

MR. KINGSLEY to SARAH: No mind-reading. Again.

SARAH to DAVID: You're bored.

MR. KINGSLEY: *(Exasperated)* Live honestly, Sarah!

SARAH to DAVID: You're wearing a blue polo shirt.

DAVID to SARAH: I'm wearing a blue polo shirt.

MR. KINGSLEY: I don't *hear* listening.

SARAH to DAVID: You're wearing a blue polo shirt.

DAVID to SARAH: I'm wearing a blue polo shirt.

SARAH to DAVID: You're wearing a blue polo shirt.

MR. KINGSLEY: Who's in the moment here? *Any*one?

DAVID to SARAH: I'm wearing a blue polo shirt.

What is the moment? thinks Sarah. Where is the Now she's supposed to respond to? How does repetition not void all the moments, like a great spreading darkness behind which David hides, safe from all observation, and nursing his hatred of her? But such thinking, such hapless confusion, is exactly the reason they're failing at this, it's exactly the reason Mr. Kingsley, again, makes the gesture of rapid erasure: get-the-hell-off-the-stage.

COLIN to JULIETTA: Your hair is curly.

Indisputable. Julietta's emblem is her corkscrew-curl hair. Her hair stands up and sideways from her head and bounces when she walks and is an extension of her radiant smile. Julietta's cheeks are downy and pink at all times. Her eyes sparkle. Her mother is French, and has bequeathed to Julietta adorably unique pronunciations, like, for the common white spread, "MY-OH-*NEHZZZZ*." Julietta's mother has also bequeathed to Julietta an ecstatic Christian faith. Unlike Pammie, Julietta never seems to feel obliged to defend her religion. When her classmates inform her God doesn't exist, she beams at them without condescension. She loves them for sharing their thoughts! Just as Jesus loves them, and they don't even need to believe it.

Julietta dazzles Colin with her smile: what a perfectly right thing he's said! "My hair is curly." She chuckles.

"Your hair is *curly*." Damn, girl, when you look "curly" up, there's your hair!

"My hair *is* curly." Oh, is it ever, Colin. You cannot talk my hair out of curling. Isn't it funny?

"*Your* hair is curly," tries Colin. Come to think of it, Colin also has thick, wavy hair. Anywhere else Colin's hair would be "curly," but here it's competing with Julietta's storybook hair, her bouncy fairy-princess hair, her hair from an idealized painting of some nature-maiden with springtime's own blossomy vines for her hair! Does Colin's hair, his coarse tufty hair, even count?

"My hair is curly." Julietta shrugs. Big deal. Plenty of curly hair here.

"Your hair is curly," Colin says suddenly, his voice rough with impulse, as if the words got ahead of their sound. He stares a narrow bead at her, and just like that, Julietta flushes crimson as if he'd unbuttoned her jeans. A disbelieving titter streaks the room. Damn, how did he *do* that? He's good. Colin is usually so busy playing the rude Irish thug of his ancestral imagination they forget that he's actually good.

Silence! Mr. Kingsley snaps his fingers, then nods sharply to Colin. Next level. Colin still leads.

The next level is subjective observation. Subjective: an opinion, a feeling. A judgment. Very often a confession. As opposed to ostensibly simpler *obj*ective: a statement of fact. By and large they tend to think of the objective as describing the follower (here Julietta, who speaks second, responds) and the subjective as describing the leader (here Colin, who speaks first, makes the leading statement). But that's only because their dichotomous thinking is undeveloped.

Without a pause Colin says, "You're a virgin."

Whoa!

"Oh shit!" cries Angie, unable to "button it," as Mr. Kingsley will sometimes snap out, though he usually says it with no more than a look or a snap of his fingers. He does so now, angry *SNAP!* and they all wiggle, agonized, in their chairs, some straining forward with avidity and some cringing backward with dread. The composure of the audience member is a lesson they strangely have never been taught at this school of performance. They're only shushed and snapped at as if they were dogs.

Julietta had already been maximum crimson. As they watch her, her usual roses-and-snow very slowly fades back as the heat of her blushing fades out. She is taking her time, perhaps wondering, as many of them are, if Mr. Kingsley is going to call foul because "You're a virgin" is really objective—but *is* it? Isn't that up to her? Isn't it subjective—Colin's mockery of her—until she confirms it as fact? Yet she can't *not* confirm it as fact, the rules state that she has to repeat, only changing the pronoun and verb conjugation, which makes her assent meaningless—so does that, after all, make the statement *sub*jective? Their dichotomous thinking is undeveloped, this conundrum is pulping their brains. Pammie clutches her temples, then covers her eyes.

But Julietta, in her protracted silence—for she's entitled to silence as one of the actor's most versatile tools—has tilted the balance of power. Her complexion is fully restored. She is not smiling. Nor is she scowling or exhibiting uncertainty, embarrassment, or fear. Julietta regards Colin with unbroken composure which Colin tries to return, but they see him shifting his hams on the hard plastic chair, tilting his face slightly at her. He's mirroring her, but poorly.

"I'm a virgin," Julietta says, as if making this notification by her choice alone.

"You're a virgin," says Colin, strangely trapped by her into neutrality. Any scorn, any glee he exhibits will confirm his juvenility.

"I'm a virgin," Julietta repeats patiently. There's no kindness mixed into her patience. No unkindness either. Only acknowledgment that Colin might need to be told more than once.

"You're a virgin," says Colin increasingly sadly.

"I'm a virgin," Julietta says, pitying Colin's sadness. His thinking is still undeveloped.

The class loses count of the number of times Julietta and Colin exchange this statement. Sometimes Mr. Kingsley will stop repetitions for obvious reasons. Eruption and resolution. Power-trade. Clear successions of tone, giddiness to sadness to indifference, as random as changes of weather. Other times he allows repetitions to drone on and on. Then, even to those who aren't speaking, the words will become nonsense sounds that no fresh inflection will ever renew.

At last, interposing between Julietta and Colin, Mr. Kingsley says, "Thank you. Excellent." The class is sitting very still, all hilarity, amazement, discomfort forgotten. Their shared mental condition is akin to hypnosis.

Julietta and Colin remain in their chairs for a moment, regarding each other. Then Colin stands and with goofy sincerity holds out his hand. Julietta shakes it.

"YOUR EYES ARE blue," Sarah says, perhaps the least observant observation she could make. Almost hostile in its insipidity.

"My eyes are blue," says David, with such perfect neutrality he cannot be charged with indifference. He might have said, "One two three four," or hummed notes. No: humming, by the nature of song, would be far more expressive.

"Your eyes are blue." She's learned if she stares straight at him he goes foreign to her and she no longer sees him, yet Mr. Kingsley cannot accuse her of avoiding eye contact.

"My eyes are blue." Perhaps David's doing the same, staring at her so that, like the sun, she blinds him.

"Your eyes are blue."

"My eyes are blue."

"Your eyes are blue."

It's been weeks of the same. A punishment everyone shares, for neither of them will give up an inch, not a flush nor a flinch nor above all a tear. It exalts Sarah almost, this death of her heart, this drought of her tears. Perhaps she is actually getting somewhere: at least, she's learned something from David. An utterly passive, compliant resistance. In the beginning, their rigid impasse fascinated their classmates. Now, it's a purgatory. Their classmates hate watching them even more than they hate sitting there. They never fulfill the objective. They never win praise. They are never allowed to advance. Unlike everyone else, they're exclusively paired with each other.

"My eyes are blue."

"Your eyes are blue."

"My eyes are blue."

"Stop," Mr. Kingsley barks, flicking a hand in disgust. They are both now persona non grata. In unconscious tandem they stand up, turn away from each other.

"HABLAS ESPAÑOL," JOELLE says to Manuel with a twinkle of mischief. The room rustles with reinvigorated interest. They've never heard Joelle speak in Spanish, they've hardly heard Manuel speak at all, and repetitions in Spanish are unprecedented, they're not even sure they're allowed. How cool of Joelle! Their estimation of her rises sharply.

Manuel smiles, surprised. "Sí, hablo español."

"No additional words," Mr. Kingsley says. Manuel colors slightly.

"Hablo español," he amends.

"Habl*aaaaaaas* españ*OLLLLLL*," Joelle mugs, in the voice, perhaps, of a chain-smoking Chihuahua. They're all sitting up, wide awake now, delighted.

Manuel colors a little bit more, but he feels her warmth: it's conspiracy, not condescension. "Ahh-*BLOW*," he bleats with crazy nasality, and they all burst out laughing, "ehhhhhhhsPAÑOW-ELLE," so it rhymes with "Joelle"!

Joelle shimmies her shoulders and pushes her breasts toward him, raising one arm in the air. "AAAAAAAHHH, BLAAAAAAAAS!" she sings with power if not beauty, tinting pink from the effort, *middle C, up to G*, they-sing-with-her-in-their-minds, "EHHHS-PAHN-NYOLL!" she concludes, *A, B, ending up on that high C* . . .

"Woo, girl!" Angie calls out, and she isn't admonished, they're all breathlessly watching Manuel, will he, will he, will he?

Manuel is smiling back at Joelle with his lips slightly pursed, as if to say, "You naughty thing, someone ought to spank you, but not me, I'm too likely to laugh." They've never seen such animation, such knowledge, in Manuel's face before, and then, as if timing is another of his secrets he's kept hidden from them, without windup or warning he does it, unleashes his voice in the room, "*Ah, ah-ah-ah-ah-ah-AHHH-BLOHHH*," he unfurls bafflingly—how can such sound issue forth from a kid in a chair—"*eh, eh-eh, ehhhhh, eh-eh EHHSS . . . PAHNNNN . . . NYOLLLLL*," his concluding bass note rolling through like a velveteen landslide. Their howls of approval are equally meant for Joelle, she and Manuel are heaving with laughter, sliding out of their chairs, they are total subversives, and yet Mr. Kingsley is laughing and clapping the hardest of all.

*

IN THE FUTURE, Joelle will run away. She will simply disappear, halfway through senior year. Rumors will abound of her reasons, her means, her location. Her father beat her with a belt and a stick and tied her to a tree; she'd been sent to live with him by her mother, for being too wild. Her father has the FBI looking for her, he has doors broken down, Joelle's spotted all sorts of places: Tampa; Waikiki; New York; the background of the Aerosmith video for "Love in an Elevator," in which she is said to be one of the dancers. Confirmation of any of this awaits a farther future than the one in which she runs away.

In the future, Pammie will decide to be an astronaut. It's no frivolous decision, though she's remained, to her grief, overweight. She must go back to school and learn physics. After physics, a diet.

In the future, Taniqua will become one of the most recognizable television actresses on earth. She'll play a cop on a long-running show about rookie cops growing and changing in the course of becoming experienced cops. Taniqua will play the absolutely humorless female cop, whose awful past (of course), full of poverty and abuse and incarcerated fathers and drug-addicted mothers and shot-to-death brothers, accounts for her absolute humorlessness. Her old classmates, from her youth, will hardly believe it's bright, sassy Taniqua who's playing that humorless cop. They'll keep thinking that her hidden sense of humor, its belated revelation, will have to provide a plot point, but year after year it does not. Nor do her good singing voice or her dancing. None of these seemingly central aspects of Taniqua will ever appear in her signature role. She'll play that role for years, and be rich.

In the future, Norbert will be a manager at Whataburger. This will be so consistent with their cruelest expectations of him that they'll dislike him even more, for not proving them wrong. Norbert, so incurably himself. So stubbornly immune to all those means of metamorphosis.

In the future, Ms. Rozot's prediction in fact will come true. Things, at least the sorts of things implied in that discussion, like heartbreak, will hurt less, although the range of hurtful things will expand. Heartbreak will come to seem like a rather luxurious reason for pain. There will also be the failings of the body and the wallet. The extinctions of friendships. The crimes against children committed by grown-ups. And the inexplicable, small kindnesses, which somehow pierce Sarah most deeply of all, as when she left the house one summer day so distracted she forgot to zip her sleeveless summer dress, so a wide slit was open from armpit to hip, through which her bra and her panties could clearly be seen, and she walked this way, obliviously, all the way to the park, where a strange woman cried, "Sweetie! How have you been?" and embraced her.

And while Sarah stood bewildered in her arms, the woman said in her ear, "Your dress is open. I'll keep hugging until you've zipped it."

And Sarah zipped, and then they stepped apart and said goodbye as if actual friends, keeping up the charade until turning and walking their opposite ways. And Sarah recalled, for the first time in years, that acting was truthful emotions in false circumstances. She already missed that strange woman, her make-believe friend.

IN THE FUTURE, David will be so changed it will be hard to give credence to the David she first knew in these mid-teenage years. It will be hard not to see that young David as sort of a sham, a lightweight cocoon through which the future David, knobbly and heavy and hard, is already beginning to obtrude. Or perhaps this younger David really is an insubstantial shell. Perhaps they all are.

Mr. Kingsley no longer asks her to his office. There is no more of their confidential chatting, about her and David, or her and Joelle, or what a help he expects her to be when the people from England arrive. There is no talk between them at all. Sometimes, he winks at her in passing. Most times he looks straight through her. She's aware of having missed some opportunity, squandered some advantage, in the course of having tried to do exactly the opposite. One Friday afternoon instead of driving to the Empanada Outpost with Joelle and whoever else Joelle has in her car, Sarah returns to the deserted department hallway. On Fridays rehearsal doesn't start until five thirty, because of lesser pressure to finish by nine, it not being a school night. Instead of dining at U Totem on Fridays, they all walk in raucous packs or drive in dangerously overladen cars to one of the real restaurants they've adopted, where they are well known and in some cases greatly disliked. They are grimly tolerated at La Tapatia Taqueria, where they consume the free chips by the bushel. They are just short of banned at Empanada Outpost, where they will only be served if they all sit outside on the rickety deck. They are adored and spoiled at Mama's Big Boy, the once unremarkable Big Boy somehow entirely taken over by gay male waiters, who will give them free pie if they sing. Fridays can feel like a festival, the five thirty rehearsal start time often drifting toward six if Mr. Kingsley himself isn't back from wherever he's gone for his dinner—never any of the cheap nearby places that they go for theirs.

In the deserted hallway, Mr. Kingsley's door is closed. There was no reason to think he would be here, as he is other days when they just have the half-hour break and he spends it at his desk typing in gunfire bursts, his rimless spectacles precariously balanced at the end of his nose, his door half open but his severe absorption a deterrent to all but the most desperate, or confident, students.

She slides down the wall to the floor, hugs her knees to her chest. Perhaps Joelle will bring her a pineapple empanada, though she isn't hungry and can hardly recall the last time she was hungry. The cold ache, like a fist pressing onto her diaphragm, has long since replaced hunger. She's almost used to it, this pressure of sadness like a stone on her diaphragm's bellows. Or maybe she's not used to it, but it's actually lessened? She thinks of Ms. Rozot's promise to her as a prophecy. If she can just stick it out long enough, she will earn the bewitchment and stop feeling pain. Every morning she X's a calendar in her mind's eye: one day closer to feeling less pain. She tries a deep breath, even stretching her legs out along the cold floor so her diaphragm has ample space. She can't do it. She can't fill her lungs. She can't shift the stone and inhale all the way. And this was the first thing he'd taught them: how to breathe. The location of the diaphragm and its unequalled importance, perhaps even exceeding the brain's. As they mastered three-part breathing, he explained to them, two things would happen: they would come to understand the diaphragm's true dimensions, and they would come to understand the true scope of its powers. Until now, they had probably only used half (or a third!) of their diaphragm's total capacity. Even worse, they had probably thought that their brains were in charge of their bodies. Wrong. It is the diaphragm—opened to its full capacity, regulating influx and outflow, tuning us in to ourselves and the world, tuning out all the static, enabling clear thought—that's in charge of the body and mind, which of course are all one. And Sarah hasn't just lost control of her own diaphragm, she's perhaps lost possession of it. It's usurped by a stone.

She stretches out full length on the spine-chilling floor of the empty hallway. What if these floors had been carpet or wood? Could soft texture or warm temperature have changed memory's substance? The unrelieved hardness and coldness of the linoleum floors will always be to Sarah an inseparable part of the lessons learned here. For the first time all year she sincerely attempts it, flat on her back on the floor with the bulletin board above her. She has to scoot a little closer to the center of the hall, so her arms and legs lie properly without touching themselves or her sides. Palms up, eyes closed. The air-conditioning turns her torso to gooseflesh beneath her thin blouse, her nipples hardening with discomfort, but she forbids herself from crossing her arms over her breasts. Relaxation requires discipline. Strangely, she seems to hear better lying here on the floor. The air conditioner's resonant hum, which she's not sure she's ever heard before, seems to have different parts: a dull, buried knocking, a rising note over a rumbling low note, a scrape as of a chair across the floor. The foot of Mr. Kingsley's door is inches from her head. From behind the door, perhaps from the bowels of the building buried deep beneath the floor, Sarah hears a tuneless vocal noise and an abrupt creak.

Hard as she can, she pulls air through her mouth, as if hauling a rope. It's no use. There might as well be someone sitting on her chest. David sitting on her chest, as he did once. In the summer. When she'd reached around, grabbing his buttocks, forcing him to lean over her face.

She scrambles up to a seated position, back hitting the wall as with almost no warning Mr. Kingsley's door opens. Manuel steps out, sees her seeing him. He pulls the door shut behind him. She's against the wall next to the doorframe and so cannot see into the room and has no way of knowing for sure if Mr. Kingsley is in there.

Without a word to her Manuel turns and walks quickly away, disappears around the corner of the hall.

She rises also, before the door can open again, and goes the opposite way from Manuel.

Last year, she'd had Mr. Banks for geometry. Mr. Banks was rumored not just to have sex with some girls at the school but to have had a baby with one, who had dropped out a few years ago. No one knew the name of this girl or had ever seen her, or her baby. No one disliked Mr. Banks. He was tall, with muscle packed on his torso that shifted and bulged when he raised up one arm to write proofs on the board. He wore snug, short-sleeved polos that clearly displayed a dark upside-down U on his right upper arm with bent-back ends that it sat on like feet. All year Mr. Banks had made Sarah and William his pets, ostentatiously excusing them from proofs because, he told the rest of the class, they knew what they were doing while nobody else had a clue. Mr. Banks would say, "William, man, he's going to be sitting here doing the books for my outside business, and I'm going to be paying him, right under this table, while the rest of you fools still don't know how to measure circumference." Sarah, Mr. Banks would announce, was going to brush her hair like a shampoo commercial for his special enjoyment. Sarah would do so, bending forward so her hair hung like seaweed in front of her face, and then whipping her head so her hair fell back onto her neck. "You're supposed to do that in slow motion," Mr. Banks would complain. "C'mon, L'Oreal." At the end of the year, when Mr. Banks informed Sarah he was taking her off-campus for lunch, she hadn't been surprised or dismayed. She'd known he wouldn't touch her, whether through superior instinct or naïveté rewarded by luck, she couldn't have said. She'd followed him to the front parking lot and climbed into the cab of his huge pickup truck with the two bumper stickers. One said, "Easy Does It." The other said, "My Other Car Is Up My Nose."

"What does that mean, anyway?" she had asked.

"It means my life was ruled by an addiction to cocaine."

"So, what—you turned your other car into cocaine?"

"I had to turn it into money first. Here I thought you were so smart."

"What about that thing on your arm?"

"My brand?"

"It's a *brand*?"

"Like they do onto cattle. It's the letter omega, from Greek. You don't know that either? You've had me fooled, girl. I thought you were some kind of genius." He'd shown her his coin laundromats— his outside businesses—on their way to a hamburger stand in a part of town she'd never seen and could never have found her way back to, everyone black except her, standing outside their cars, their burgers in hand, in wax paper, the older woman at the open-air counter wagging her finger at Mr. Banks, meaning "How old is this girl?" and Mr. Banks telling her off with a gesture, and the two of them laughing.

In the truck, driving back, Sarah had said, "That's the best burger I've ever had. Thanks." This was back when she ate, and enjoyed it.

"You're welcome," Mr. Banks had said. "And thank you for your charming company."

That was all that had happened. It hadn't seemed unusual or wrong to have gone to lunch with him. Even her hunch that he wouldn't kiss her, implying the less likely odds that he might, hadn't made the lunch feel secretive. They hadn't skulked, walking out to his truck. They hadn't skulked, coming back, amid everyone else coming back from wherever they'd eaten.

Despite all the rules—the repetitions without extra words, the relaxation with arms never touching their sides, the breaths drawn in three parts—no rules exist to define their relations with teachers. They can have lunch with teachers, or not. They can shed tears and tell secrets, or not. Vague norms emerge and dissolve, are specific to people, don't apply generally or across time or across the whole group. They're arrived at by instinct, by naïveté rewarded with luck, or by naïveté not rewarded with luck. When Sarah's mother had said, "Your life outside school isn't any of his goddamn business," and asked Sarah whether she understood, although Sarah said yes, she didn't agree. Her disagreement perhaps was the same thing as not understanding.

MANUEL'S PARENTS APPEAR on opening night and seat themselves as best they can, near the back, until Colin, who is working as an usher, at Mr. Kingsley's direction persuades them to move to the second row center, the first and second rows having been taped off and marked "VIP." Colin's first attempt to move the parents doesn't

work, they are politely bewildered. He has to fetch Joelle from backstage, where she is covered with loops of duct tape and safety pins,
in readiness for wardrobe emergencies. Joelle comes out and with
much compensatory smiling and laughing explains to the parents
that seats have been saved just for them. They move with great reluctance, as if expecting to find they're the butt of a practical joke.
They're both short compared with Manuel, solemn as carvings,
exceptionally ill at ease. When the performance is over Sarah, having slipped upstairs into the light booth where Greg Veltin is
running the board, sees Mr. Kingsley, his arms piled with flowers
right up to his chin, press one of the bouquets on Manuel's startled
mother. Mr. Kingsley's husband, Tim, is helping him distribute the
flowers, and the two men, very alike with their clipped, glossy hair,
their expensive wool V-necks over brightly hued shirts, and their
knife-pleated trousers and glittering shoes, seem to diminish Manuel's parents even more just by talking to them, despite how clear it
is they're raining down compliments. Mr. Kingsley is wearing his
glasses, and Tim wears a mustache, and this is probably how Manuel's parents can tell them apart, Manuel's parents who are a paired
species also in their dowdy church clothes.

Sarah feels relieved when Mr. Kingsley and Tim have moved on
to the cast, who receive their flowers with regal entitlement.

The show is a thorough success. Erin O'Leary is adorable as
Adelaide; dorky Tom Dieckmann, who cannot really sing, is nevertheless the perfect wiseacre as Nathan; and Manuel's wooden acting is wiped from the spectators' minds when he raises his voice in
a song. Watching him act almost seems like a requisite penance, the
price of the voice. Slantwise Sarah looks at Greg Veltin, so adorably
handsome with his freckles and thick auburn hair and his tall, slender body. Last year, in *Anything Goes*, he had danced like Astaire.
That too was vicarious grace, of the sort that exalted them all. No
less can Greg sing, perhaps not like Manuel, but with his own irresistible brightness, as clean as a sailor's white suit. Pammie and

Julietta have made a cult of him, Pammie in particular barely able to breathe in his presence. She goes pink as a ham if he says hi to her. Not long ago Sarah used to see him ride off in Mr. Kingsley's Mercedes at lunchtime. Now he sits in the light booth. "Why didn't you audition this year?" Sarah wonders, she hopes not rudely. Everyone has wondered and been too shy to ask, assuming the reason is his personal crisis, about which he is so placidly unforthcoming.

"You know," Greg says, as if it's a question he hadn't considered, and finds genuinely interesting, "I think I just realized I had stuff to learn in the wings. I mean, there's such opportunities here that we shouldn't pass up. Like this light board? Mr. Browne says it cost twenty-four thousand dollars."

"But you're one of the best singers and dancers at school. Anybody can run the light board."

"Thank you," Greg says. "That's so sweet."

"I mean it," Sarah insists. "You would have been perfect as Sky Masterson."

"Manuel was amazing."

"You would have been better."

"You're the sweetest," Greg says kindly, shutting her down.

The party is at Mr. Kingsley's huge, beautiful house that he lives in with Tim. Only the current Seniors have been here before, in their sophomore year, the last time Mr. Kingsley was willing to host. "Does anyone want to tell me," he says before doing the toast, "why Tapatia Taqueria won't let us rent their backyard anymore?" Everyone laughs. There's Martinelli's Sparkling Cider and soda and all sorts of cookies and snacks laid out on fancy platters on a big buffet table inside, but outside, alcohol trickles into the yard from their cars. Here a bottle of Jack Daniel's, there a six-pack of Bartles & Jaymes. The yard is vast, landscaped, labyrinthine, with brick walks and large shrubs and places to sit out of view of the house. They know Mr. Kingsley will ignore pot and alcohol out in the yard so long as they're discreet. Out in the yard, their conversation mostly concerns where to go next, understanding as they do that for the hosts and for themselves, the party is a pleasant obligation. Mr. Kingsley and Tim are no more interested in hosting a wild party than the back-yard denizens are interested in being wild in this genteel locale. They'll stay an hour, go in and say thank you, get back in their cars, and be wild someplace else.

Inside, a very different party is proceeding on completely different lines. Here, no one wants to be anywhere else. They're taking turns at the piano and singing, they're hoping Mr. Kingsley will talk about Broadway, they would never imagine Mr. Kingsley might want them to leave. Yet they'll all leave, exalted and tired, long before overstaying their welcome.

The two parties share some guests, trade some guests, enjoy the presence of most guests exclusively. Julietta and Pammie, Taniqua and Angie, Erin O'Leary and Tom Dieckmann, among many others, are inside eating chips, drinking soda, and singing their throats sore. Tim has a few solemn Juniors and Seniors around him on the screened-in porch, talking music and art. Joelle rolls easily from indoors to outdoors and back. A tight crowd in the kitchen, earnest chitchatters clogging the stairs. David's so allied with shadow that Sarah's not even sure whether he's here, and, like Joelle, but for different reasons, she restlessly goes back and forth, in and out, from the sting of Colin's bottle of Jack Daniel's in the supple darkness to the caustic orange grit of Doritos in the house's harsh light. She's unable to feel at ease anywhere. She gets past the earnest chitchatters who are clogging the stairs and goes up, looking for a bathroom that doesn't have people sprawled outside its door. Down the second-floor hallway are posters for shows, real professional shows in New York. *Godspell. Follies.* The hallway is lined in beige carpet that swallows all sound, and Sarah ventures its length, as if her noiselessness means she is also unseen. Here at the end of the hall is a spreading mosaic of photos in colorful frames, Mr. Kingsley and Tim standing shoulder to shoulder and grinning in various rooms, or at various scenic vistas. Sometimes Tim has his arm around Mr. Kingsley's shoulders, and sometimes Mr. Kingsley has his arm around Tim's. They always look hale and collegial. Sarah wonders if it is a prejudice in her, deep-rooted, unconscious and unintended, that makes her unable to see that they're lovers in any one of these pictures. She wonders if, on the other hand, there's some persistent reticence on their part, posing for a third party, that makes every picture this way, independent of her. She wonders what a photo of her and David would look like, if it could capture some aura they both sought to hide.

There's a narrow little staircase at the end of the hall, uncarpeted and steep, as if it's recently grown up from being a ladder. She climbs it, directly into a room with sloped walls she realizes was made from an attic, now beautifully finished and furnished with a round braided rug and a bed and a sort of tall cabinet with a full-length mirror on the inside of one of its doors, before which Manuel stands, tucking in a blue shirt. "Do you *live* here?" she exclaims.

"No," he says, badly startled, one palm flat in his waistband, and then with surprising aggression, "Why are you here, always hanging around?"

"Hanging around? It's a party."

"There's no party up here."

"Then why are *you* here?"

"I'm changing my shirt, if you'd leave me alone," he says, closing the door to the cabinet, but not before she's seen several more expensive-looking bright-colored shirts, the same ones she's noticed him wearing at school.

"Did he give you those?" she asks.

"They're mine."

"Why are you keeping them here at his house?"

"Why don't you go somewhere else? Maybe the music room hallway? I hear you put on good shows there."

She almost falls back down the steep narrow stairs.

In the kitchen, trying to get out the back door, she runs into Pammie. She has to leave, her determination to leave is so total it leaves room for no other thought. She'll walk, never mind that her apartment is more than a half hour's drive. She'll walk all night, straight to the bakery for her six a.m. shift, seven hours has to be enough time to walk there. "Come with us!" Pammie cries eagerly. Julietta is with her; Sarah cannot even open her mouth to object before they've borne her off like happy thugs, each of them holding an elbow. The yard has emptied out substantially, the drinkers and smokers have said their goodbyes to their host before getting too drunk or too high. David is nowhere to be seen, perhaps never was here. Greg Veltin is waiting in the backyard gazebo, he's especially asked to speak with them. "We brought Sarah," Pammie says breathlessly. "Is that okay?"

"Of course," Greg effuses. It's perfect they've also brought Sarah. It's perfect she's here. He wants them to hold hands with him, is that too strange? Sarah looks across the murk of the gazebo, its ocean-floor light, at Pammie's rapt face. In Greg Veltin's presence, it shines like the moon. They are sitting in a circle on the gazebo's slightly splintery floor. Greg reaches out and takes Pammie's hand, and with his other hand takes Julietta's, and Julietta reaches her spare hand to Sarah, and Sarah reaches hers to Pammie, in a trance of surrender, not having the slightest idea what they're doing. Greg Veltin resembles Jesus—a clean-cut and freckled and auburn-haired Jesus—sitting cross-legged, holding the hands of these sophomore virgins who love him so much they would happily share him in marriage (they've discussed this at length, although with each other, not him). "I cherish your friendship," Greg tells them. "I feel so lucky to have friends like you, and I want you to know that I love you, and that, if things were different—God, I'd be so in love with you girls I wouldn't know how to choose! But luckily"—and he squeezes Pammie's hand and Julietta's hand with such a surfeit of feeling the two pairs of hands jump—"luckily," he repeats, "I'm gay, and so I don't have to choose, and I can cherish all of you forever."

"Oh my God!" Pammie cries, both her hands flying up to her mouth.

"You're the first friends from school I've told," Greg continues, incredibly—this adored, handsome Senior who can dance like Astaire and who is so clearly, inevitably, no-other-possibility gay that Sarah cannot believe she never realized—but that was fifteen in a nutshell, she'll think when she's twice, and then three times, that age. The obvious and the oblivious sharing the same mental space.

Julietta has burst into tears. "I'm so honored," she sobs. "I'm so honored you told us."

"I am too," Pammie says ardently, for in the instant, she also knows she has already known, and is also amazed by the gift of Greg's trust, a far greater intimacy than she'd dreamed of before.

The three of them have fallen into a joyous group hug. "Sarah, Sarah!" they laugh and cry helplessly, trying to extend their arms to her, too clumsy in their happiness to keep her from slipping away.

THEY KNOW SO much about each other, yet so little.

They know that William's mother makes William and his two younger sisters keep their toothbrushes and toothpaste and combs and whatever other personal items they use in zippered travel cases, which they must carry to the bathroom and back to their bedrooms every morning and night, and that if William's mother finds toiletry items left behind in the bathroom—the bathroom that only William and his sisters ever use, because his mother has her own bathroom off her bedroom—she will throw them away. She will throw away, as punishment for their failure to abide by her rule, a forgotten toothbrush or stray comb. They, William's classmates, know this, but they don't know William's mother's first name, or where William's father might be, or whether he's even alive.

They know that Julietta's parents store flour and rice in sealed plastic tubs against a coming apocalypse, but they don't know if Julietta herself believes in this apocalypse, or is worried about it. She certainly doesn't seem worried.

They know that Colin's father hits Colin, "punches his lights out," "knocks his block off," "smacks him clear to next week," but they don't know what Colin has done to deserve this, or whether he's angry or sad to be beaten. They don't even know if the words Colin uses to mean getting hit are his own words, or words he's been taught.

They know, at least some of them do, at least one of them does, that Sarah has let David have sex with her in the music room hallway, right out in the open, where anyone could have seen them.

They don't know that Sarah works weekend mornings at a French bakery, on the opening shift. Alone, Sarah carries the wide baking sheets of croissants, chaussons aux pommes, pains au chocolat, and brioches. She pulls the greasy pastries off the trays, to which they are lightly adhered, trying not to poke holes in them with her fingers. She fills up the display case. The baker, whoever it is, has finished the baking and left at some point before Sarah got here. She wonders who it is, why they never cross paths. The pastries are still warm. The curled, browned, brittle croissants make her think of the discarded shells of locusts she sometimes found hooked to the trees, when she was a little girl, and they lived on a street that had trees, before her father moved out. Sometimes in the very early mornings she would put on her sneakers and slip out of the house while her parents were asleep, and a blanket of white fog lay over the lawns, reaching just to her knees. Strange exhalation of the lawns at daybreak, magic child's-height fog she could pierce with her legs like a giant. In a certain season, she can't recall which, she could pull fragile locust husks off the trees and, if she wanted to, crush them in her fist, though she never did so. It would have seemed like such a waste of so much hollow intricacy, so many chambers and hinges and spikes, like an alien spaceship in miniature. She couldn't have been more than eight then. Half a lifetime ago. She had never been tired in the morning, couldn't imagine what being tired felt like. Running back through the fog as it melted away like a dream, to see her dad leaning out the front door of the house for the paper.

Now, she is always so tired she doesn't even realize she's tired. Words stall on her tongue. Tears gather prematurely in her eyes. Waking dreams drift and coil through her mind, similar to ideas, but perhaps not the same.

THEY KNOW SO much about each other, yet so little. Manuel knows, or thinks he knows, about her. A whore would have more dignity.

She knows, or thinks she knows, about Manuel. Furtive and smug. The closed doors, and new shirts.

And yet she doesn't know where Manuel lives, doesn't know his home number. Can't conceive where such information might be found. She's already forgotten the morning, freshman year, that a four-alarm fire broke out on the far side of the massive apartment complex she lives in with her mother, a complex so massive they couldn't even see smoke from their carport and only found out what the sirens were about from TV, where they'd seen the complex filmed from the air, and the flames six or eight blocks away. Distant though the fire had been, it had made for bad traffic, and her mother had dropped her off late, but when she went in the office to get her late pass the office ladies had cried, "Oh my gosh, honey, are you okay?" because in the office they knew her address—they'd actually looked through their records, when they'd seen the big fire on the news, to check if they had any students in danger.

So of course home addresses are known in the office, but she doesn't think of this. She isn't scheming. She lacks not just the skills for, but the very resolve for, premeditation.

Nevertheless, even in her tiredness, she's alert. Having noticed some things, she keeps noticing more things. Her work on costume crew is basically finished, she has not been assigned as a dresser, but she's still responsible for the general state of the costumes; the costume shop and dressing rooms are her wheelhouse, she patrols them, tidying and repairing. Particularly the hats were her thing for this show; she monitors their clusters of feathers or fruit or their bands of grosgrain, she gets out the glue gun if need be. In hushed hours before run-through starts, when nobody's around, she'll check the boys' dressing room, where they neglect their fedoras, leave them tossed on the floor. She'll re-form the crowns, dust them off, put them pointedly up on the shelves with the masking-tape labels where the boys should have put them themselves. The male cast members share two extremely overtaxed garment racks, cardboard dividers sticking up at dense intervals bearing their character names. "Gambler 1," "Gambler 2," "Sal Army guy," "Sky Masterson." They do a lousy job of hanging up their costumes. This Friday after school, before the show's second and last weekend begins, Sarah's going to be slaving away at the ironing board. She wiggles her fingers into, pries apart the crushed mass of male clothes between "Sal Army guy" and "Sky Masterson." Here's a pale green shirt, perhaps it's a color the store would call sea foam. The label: Armani. Duh, this isn't part of Sky Masterson's costume. She almost laughs at Manuel's lame deception. But of course, no one else is alert to his shirts. No one else has realized, as she has, that he wears these shirts only at school, changes back into cheap, crappy shirts, poor boy's shirts, before going home. Despite its crushed condition, the fabric of the shirt feels newly stiff and fresh. No gray ring in the collar, no yellow stains at the pits.

Sarah extracts it. She turns on the iron, waits patiently for it to heat, and then irons the shirt with great care, even using the sleeve form. When she's finished she folds it with buttons centered and sleeves underneath, the way she's seen men's shirts come from the dry cleaner's, and then she takes it into the costume shop and hides it on a high shelf, above the boxes of notions and buttons, stuff that currently isn't in use.

In the course of the week and weekend, two more shirts appear, of the same sort and in the same place, and she does the same thing with them both. She watches Manuel for signs of unease. He always looks slightly uneasy. He never makes eye contact if they happen to pass near each other. Their enmity is an agreed-upon fact and requires no further acknowledgment. Joelle is his dresser and he and Joelle are now buddies, they're constantly laughing and joking in Spanish. Joelle might even know Manuel's address but Sarah doesn't think of asking her, no longer cares where Manuel lives and doesn't recall why she did. She isn't aware of a plan for the shirts. She's just stealing them, because they make her angry, though whether at Manuel, or Mr. Kingsley, or both, she isn't sure. Her anger is intense but obscure.

The last performance, as always, is a two p.m. Sunday matinee, which, as always, feels anticlimactic, but there has to be time for the strike. After the show they'll all remain to strike the set for however many hours it takes.

Manuel's mother reappears for this final performance, without the father this time. Instead she's accompanied by a young woman, slender, serious, conservative slacks and blouse from, perhaps, T.J.Maxx or some other large store that sells cheap office wear. She has a black purse with a very thin strap. She resembles Manuel, like Manuel is a full head taller than the mother; she walks close to the mother, sometimes taking her arm. This time, the mother appears more at ease, the young woman unsmiling and watchful. It's the mother who leads the young woman, with visible pride, to the taped-off row of VIP seats. They settle themselves, tip their heads together, converse only with each other in the midst of the house's exceptional noise, all the greetings and huggings and jokings and families trying to find six or thirteen seats together, it's the final performance. Sarah leaves the light booth where she's been sitting with gay Greg Veltin, goes back to the costume shop, but it's too chaotic in there, all the cast members in costume and makeup fawning over Mr. Freedman, the costume designer, and giving him gifts. She waits until the first act is well under way, Mr. Freedman watching tonight from the house; then rooting through the costume shop's wealth of potentially useful garbage finds a plastic shopping bag with handles and slides the three ironed shirts in, in a stack. Settles them flat on the bottom to keep them unwrinkled. Tonight everybody is toting a sack of something, mostly gifts for Mr. Kingsley, teddy bears that say "Thank You!" or boxes of chocolate, despite Mr. Kingsley having recently said, "I'm on very strict orders from Tim: NO MORE CHOCOLATE. Let's say thank you without calories!"

Once, she would have filled a box with pain au chocolat at the bakery, because despite orders from Tim, Mr. Kingsley's great passion for chocolate is known. She would have tied the box closed with a ribbon, paid for it out of her wages, bought Mr. Kingsley a card at Confetti!: The Celebrate Store and toiled over just what to say.

This show, she's not giving a gift. She does not think he'll notice.

The show ends, the ovations end, cast members with their makeup very imperfectly removed bound out of the dressing rooms to be gushed over by their family members and to line up for pictures. Impromptu and fragmentary encores. "Sue me, sue me, go ahead, sue me, I LOVE YOOOO!" Then family members are reluctantly drifting away, cast is due back onstage in ten minutes for strike, they should get off the rest of that makeup. Manuel has a word with his mother and the woman who must be his sister, goes back in the boys' dressing room where his brand-new secret shirts constantly disappear. Sarah, standing in the piazza outside the main theatre doors with the bag, not sure which lot they've parked in, almost misses the mother and sister, catches sight of them just as they're stepping outside. She has to run to catch up. "Excuse me," she calls. If she had planned this, she might have worked out how to say it in Spanish. Joelle could have helped. But clearly, she hasn't planned this. "Excuse me. These are Manuel's, to take home."

The women turn toward her, surprised. She thrusts the bag at the mother, so she has to accept it. "Manuel's?" the mother says skeptically, glancing inside.

"They're a gift, from Mr. Kingsley, for Manuel," Sarah says, very clearly, although in English. But the sister can surely speak English. "Because Manuel is his boyfriend," Sarah adds, quickly turning away.

"*What* did you say?" says the young woman sharply. But Sarah has dashed down the hall, disappeared.

". . . AND YOU'LL KEEP these director's notebooks for the whole of spring term. Any questions?" asks Mr. Kingsley.

"Where's Manuel?" Colin asks. They have not seen Manuel since the *Guys and Dolls* strike. That was back before Christmas. A whole month ago.

Sarah watches Mr. Kingsley's face closely. Culpability is what she would like to discern. Disquiet is all she expects. She finds neither, nor anything else. "Manuel's having family issues," Mr. Kingsley says smoothly. "Hopefully he'll be back with us soon."

But he never is.

"BITCH," JOELLE SAYS in her ear. "Get your own fucking ride."

"AND IT STRIKES me as inappropriate, extremely inappropriate, for the children to be working at school for twelve, sometimes fourteen hours a day—"

"We're not children," Sarah breaks in.

"Certainly the rigors of our program don't suit everyone," says Mrs. Laytner, their remote principal, an irrelevant person in pearls. Mrs. Laytner attends opening nights with a fresh corsage pinned to her jacket, she cuts ribbons on new lighting boards, she is quoted in the local newspaper when their school is named a Top Ten. She's never in Sarah's recollection even walked down the Theatre hall. "Pre-professional training for children this age is a major commitment. But we believe that our students—"

"And his methods, this teacher's methods, also strike me as inappropriate."

"Unconventional, maybe. Mr. Kingsley is a brilliant man, an unconventional but brilliant teacher; we're incredibly lucky to have him. His methods are directly adapted from groundbreaking—"

"It's my understanding they're methods designed for adults."

"I think if you're concerned about his methods, it would make much more sense to sit down with Jim and have a discussion—"

"No!" Sarah exclaims.

"It's time we heard from Sarah," agrees Mrs. Laytner. "Sarah, do you feel, as your mother's concerned that you might, uncomfortable in our program? In any way overwhelmed?"

"No," Sarah says.

"Do you think Mr. Kingsley's way of teaching is inappropriate for students your age?"

"No," Sarah says.

"Of course she's going to say no," Sarah's mother objects.

"Isn't this why we're here? To ensure her well-being? Sarah, do you feel overworked here? Under too much pressure?"

"No," she says.

"Is anything concerning you at all about school right now?"

"No," says Sarah, who still cannot draw three-part breath, still can't eat, still can't sleep through the night. "Not at all."

*

"YOU'RE TALL," DAVID declares, startling her. Their repetitions, Sarah's and David's, have taken on the pointless, leaden feel of international diplomacy, of the greatest number of people, the highest level of tension, the longest list of conditions, the profoundest concealed boredom, brought to bear on the tersest and least meaningful utterances. It is the falsest emotion under the realest circumstances, except for now, when unexpectedly David's tone changes. Game over, it says. Ignore everyone else. Look at me. I am talking to you.

"You're tall," David repeats. This is supposed to be objective repetition. The two of them, unique among their classmates, have never been allowed to advance to the subjective repetition. Even Norbert can ace the subjective. But Sarah and David are too immature, too determined to pursue their private drama at the expense of the group. They won't process emotion, they hoard it. They are stuck in a rut. They are narcissists. Mr. Kingsley delivers these indictments as they sit knee-to-knee in the chairs, as if Sarah and David aren't present, as if their immaturity and narcissism and stuckness also mean they are deaf. In a way, Sarah is. Having fought for the right to remain in this school, in this class, in this hard plastic chair, she stares, unflinching, deaf, blind, into David's unavailable agates and he stares back, no one home, curtains drawn. Until today, when he sits forward slightly. "You're *tall*," he tells Sarah. Her heart lurches. Sarah's height is average. She is shorter than David. If he took her in his arms, her cheek would find rest on his sternum.

"I'm tall," she says carefully, as if afraid to misconstrue him.

"You're tall," he confirms.

No one else in the room with them now. The rest of them mere furniture. Mr. Kingsley has moved right in front of them, blocking the spectators' view, his arms crossed and his thin lips compressed with displeasure. Even he's furniture.

"I'm *tall*." Gentle skepticism: Don't you think that's a little bit silly? When we made love, my face smushed in your chest. Turning my head, I could feel your heart denting my cheek.

Telepathy received. Private smile: No argument here. But despite that, "You're tall," David says.

"I'm tall," Sarah says, trying it out.

"Take five," Mr. Kingsley says peevishly. Secret codes aren't authentic emotion. Sarah and David aren't behaving with integrity here. They just can't seem to stop being cryptic; this is not a game, people, it's *life*. The familiar condemnation rains down on their heads as without argument they return to their seats. They know everyone sees their disgrace but to them it is weightless, familiar, like the blossomy tree-trash that falls in their hair and sticks there as they're walking outside. Outside it is March, in their hot southern city late spring. Wildfires of azalea ringing the houses. All the sticky-fingered trees. David is sixteen at last, and his mother and stepfather, as promised, have bought him a car. David drives Sarah home, and though their companionship is stiff and wordless Sarah sits in his new-smelling passenger seat as if perched on the wing of some fabulous beast. It is David but carries him, too. They feel hopeless delight that they'll never admit. So this is what they might have had. Flying through their city unwatched, their arms warming the narrow abyss where the gearshift stands guard between them.

At the chalk-X-marked gate Sarah smiles her thanks, David smiles goodbye. Sarah turns so she won't see him driving away. David keeps his gaze out of his mirrors so as not to see her recede, growing small. Their sadness is a shared secret now and perhaps that's enough. To dare further they need scrutiny, hectoring, the built-in limitations they first obtained from Mr. Kingsley but that are broadly available elsewhere, the countless ways of being cryptic, of behaving with doubtful integrity, though never, they both know, without authentic emotion. Whatever they have, it's authentic. There Mr. Kingsley was wrong.

* * *

BY THE TIME the English People were finally due to arrive, even their hosts had forgotten about them. The English People had been announced by Mr. Kingsley the previous September, what now seemed a lifetime ago. The previous September, Manuel had still been a nonentity. The previous September, Greg Veltin had still been the untouchable idol of all virgin girls. The previous September, they had just been embarking on repetitions with the accumulated fervor of long anticipation, and had not yet so failed as to have heard Mr. Kingsley declare, as he'd declared this week, that they were the most disappointing Sophomores he had ever worked with. The previous September, they had not yet been disgraced—yet now, these ancient arrangements, in reminding them who they had been, also offered the prospect of starting anew. They would be their best selves, in the eyes of esteemed visitors who had never known them otherwise.

The English People were a performing troupe from a high school in Bournemouth, a city in England. They were only fifteen and sixteen themselves, which was why the Sophomores had been granted the particular honor of hosting them. The previous September, when Mr. Kingsley had gathered them in the rehearsal room, he'd reversed his chair and leaned at them confidingly. "They're touring with what's supposed to be an absolutely terrific adaptation of Voltaire's *Candide*," Mr. Kingsley had explained, "and as you'll learn in European Theatre History, Voltaire was France's most famous playwright. Now, who's been to England?" Involuntarily Sarah looked at David, and as quickly looked away. For her, until now, England only existed in David's postcards. Now those Big

Bens and Piccadilly Circuses and Carnaby Streets with their punks seemed like jokes played upon her alone.

David's hand, and only David's, raised up. The elbow remained bent, denoting his reluctance to answer this question. Sarah remembered the first time she caught sight of his house, freshman year, from the kid-crammed back seat of Senior Jeff Tillson's car. Jeff driving some five or six nondrivers home after one of the mainstage rehearsals, the lengthy and confused overlapping directions, debating who lived nearest to school and each other, David repeatedly telling Jeff Tillson to take the other kids home until it came out that David's house was the closest to school, in its historic neighborhood of enormous old live oaks hiding tall stately homes behind veils of discreet Spanish moss. David wound up being dropped off first, and the car had erupted with cries of "That's your *house?*" while David, his face crimson, uprooted himself from the overpacked car.

The chief feature of David's house was that it was two houses: the gracious two-story in front and a luxurious garage apartment, just built, in back. Apart from the bathroom, the garage apartment was a single enormous rec room, with David's bed at one end and his younger brother Chris's at the other, and a pinball machine and sofa and stereo and TV in between. David's mother, in preparation for the English People, added a set of bunk beds, a dorm-size mini-fridge, and a microwave oven, whether to encourage total exile from the house or apologize for it, no one bothered to wonder. Eight hosts had been originally asked for, but only six had been needed, because David's family would house two of the boys, and Joelle's family two of the girls. The other two boys would stay with William and Colin, and the other two girls with Karen Wurtzel and Pammie. Julietta had ardently wanted to host but for reasons that went unexplained Mr. Kingsley chose Karen Wurtzel instead and Julietta fervently smiled her approval. There were also two adults, both men, both of whom would be hosted by Mr. Kingsley and Tim in their beautiful home.

Long ago in September, Sarah was still enough part of her class to laugh with everyone else when Mr. Kingsley said the English People were arriving over spring break to get accustomed to their hosts and temporary homes "before tackling CAPA, which—how shall I say?—can be intimidating to the *uninitiated*." Sarah was still enough part of her class to relish the smugly held knowledge that for all its feuds and sectarian fissures, their school as a whole was a clique, unwelcoming to the outsider. Sarah was still enough part of her class to anticipate the pleasure of pitying these eager, inferior English, of surprising them with kindness, and receiving their gratitude. But now Sarah was so far outside of her class that she might have been English herself. She was so far outside of her class that when spring break ended, and school resumed, she was at first unaware that there had been a revolution, for she had missed all the contributing events: William's guest, Simon, deserting the unpredictable austerity of William's home for the dependable luxury of David's garage apartment; Colin's guest, Miles, in protest of the other three leaving him out following Simon, and being followed by Colin; David's original guests, Julian and Rafe, mocking Colin's Irish heritage in a manner that Colin mistook for a special distinction; David's brother, Chris, deserting the apartment for points undisclosed, leaving Simon and Miles to nightly fight over who got Chris's bed versus who got the sofa, while Colin uncomplainingly slept on the floor.

Meanwhile, among the girls, surprisingly it had not been Joelle's house but Karen Wurtzel's that became the headquarters. Karen's English guest, Lara, had in no time at all learned and broadcast what facts about Karen nearly two years of Trust Exercising had not excavated: that Karen's mother, Elli, unlike Karen, was pretty and fun and would stay up till all hours drinking Bartles & Jaymes and watching telly and talking and laughing while Karen stayed locked in her room and only came out to ask her own mother to please make less noise. Joelle and her two guests, Theodosia and

Lilly, having hit it off like the proverbial house afire and spending the late hours after rehearsal driving Joelle's Mazda everywhere but the forty-five minutes to Joelle's inconveniently located home, started sleeping at Karen's; after which, as had happened with the boys, the fourth English girl, Pammie's guest, Cora, protested at being left out and migrated to Karen's, Pammie trying to follow, but finding herself not invited.

After these domestic rearrangements, which took less than a week, the clique hardened its form.

Their first day at CAPA, the English People debuted as a leadership class. Though in many ways they looked physically younger than their American peers, the boys—Simon, Miles, Julian, and Rafe—being slender and smooth, their faces and chests still entirely hairless, and the girls—Lara and Cora, Theodosia and Lilly—being girlishly skinny, with no hips or breasts, the English People nevertheless separately, and even more so en masse, seemed older, their wits sharper, their knowledge more extensive and at the back of it somehow impenetrable. Perhaps cultural difference explained this. Perhaps it was all a mirage they induced with their accents, poor imitations of which became a widespread affliction of the sophomore class. The impression of power they gave seemed not wrought, but inevitable. That David or William or Joelle or Sarah or any of them had imagined impressing the English was now so unimaginable as to best be forgotten.

The two English grown-ups—Martin the teacher/director and Liam the star—first appeared after lunch, given that they were grown-ups, not visiting students, and so didn't take classes. When everyone had assembled in the Black Box, Martin and Liam sat onstage with Mr. Kingsley, like Mr. Kingsley backward on their chairs, while Theodosia and Lilly and Lara and Cora, Rafe and Julian and Simon and Miles, sat anonymously in the risers with the rest of the students. Bantering back and forth with Mr. Kingsley about the Touring Life, One Hotel Seeming Just Like Another, and the Pleasures of Home, Martin and Liam seemed cut of that same kingly cloth as the aptly named teacher. Martin and Liam were capable of the same ostentatious air of relaxation: that manner of behaving as if unobserved, to broadcast the serene consciousness of being closely observed. Martin and Liam and Mr. Kingsley, entirely ignoring their students, trading theatrical badinage between their improperly utilized chairs, formed not a clique, grown-ups being understood not to form cliques, but another sort of unit, perhaps best called a club. To Sarah, the existence of the club registered just below thought, as a sensation of hopeless exclusion. To David the existence of the club registered as an angering challenge he wished to reject—but in such a way that Mr. Kingsley and Martin and Liam would be abashed, and desirous of winning his favor. To Joelle it was merely three men, two of whom she'd not before assessed. Joelle quickly found Martin too old and dismissed him to the same inert heap where lay gay Mr. Kingsley. Liam, by contrast, was in range. As if her eyes were a stethoscope, Joelle measured his blood: high temperature, swift tempo. Energy zigzagged unpredictably through him like the charge through a poorly wired lamp. He had arrestingly unique, ice-blue eyes such as you read about in fairy tales, but they transmitted to Joelle some sort of muffled desperation. This was a good-looking guy who would never be sexy, due to what sort of deficit or obstacle it didn't interest Joelle to discover. Dismissing Liam as well, Joelle returned to passing notes with Theodosia and Lilly about the packet of cocaine in Joelle's makeup bag, and with whom they should share it at lunch.

Liam had been Martin's star student some handful of years before this, and Martin had staged *Candide* specifically for him, which Martin's current students seemed to accept with no trace of resentment. Liam was twenty-four, six years out of high school. Of Martin's age no one was sure. Sarah would not learn Liam's story, including his age, until Liam told her himself, later on in this Month of the English. Mrs. Laytner had been unusually visible since the

English arrival, intersecting as it did with ambitions she had for the school. Their multimillion-dollar theatre, with its two hundred feet of flyspace, its four hundred red velvet seats, its twenty-four-thousand-dollar lightboard, would host touring dance companies, orchestras, and whatever else one found in such beacons as Los Angeles and New York. While the Bournemouth *Candide* marked the American debut of its director and precocious young actors, its greater importance was as CAPA's debut as a venue on the stage of its city. A first performance of *Candide* during the regular school day was reserved for CAPA students and teachers, but this was only to keep them from taking up space at the two weekends of public performances, all of which had sold out in advance, after a photo-filled feature in the city newspaper, more evidence of Mrs. Laytner's exertions.

By the day of the first performance, the CAPA "sneak preview," the English People are almost halfway through their stay. They seem both familiar and foreign, as if they have always been here and as if they have just now arrived. Familiar are their faces and voices, their postures, their gaits—any one of the CAPA students can pick out any one of the English from the ocean of heads in the hall, across the width of the lot ducking into Joelle's Mazda or vaulting into David's convertible Mustang. Foreign is almost everything else. Well as the Sophomores know one another's private lives, which Mr. Kingsley has made them yield up like paying dues into a fund, they've learned so little about their English peers they do not even notice how little they know. They don't know if Rafe lives in a large house or in squalid government housing, if Cora is a knowing virgin or a discreet libertine. They can't crack the code of their clothes, if there is such a code, or of their accents, which to them all sound the same. They don't know what roles any of the English people, apart from Liam, are playing in *Candide*, nor what roles there are, nor even what the title role is, if "Candide" is a name or a thing. Busy as they are with this quarter's Costume History and Shakespearean Monologue and American Songbook, not one of them has read *Candide*. They may imagine that its title has an exclamation point. They have never seen a rehearsal because it goes without saying that the English People have no need to rehearse. They have never seen sets, props, or costumes because these don't exist. The English People travel light.

Sarah sits alone in the full house, hidden amid instrumental musicians. She is doubly exiled from Theatre now, persona non grata among the Juniors also. Somehow the year-old secret of her one night with Brett has become current news. They hadn't even had sex; in her memory Sarah sees Brett's narrow, hairless body and his abashed and drooping penis, pallid and cold to the touch. But these details do nothing to lessen her crime, just as her self-isolation, her cold-shouldering of loyal Julietta and Pammie, her funereal clothes, sullen curtain of hair, and dragon's tail of cigarette smoke have done nothing to prepare her for being an actual outcast. She's ablaze with fresh humiliation and can no more see beyond its nimbus of heat than could anyone being burnt at a stake.

The house lights go down. Greg Veltin has a list of lighting cues he's been given by Martin. A lightboard operator being the only technician *Candide* requires, Greg Veltin is the only person at CAPA, indeed in the entire United States, who's seen a rehearsal, as rehearsals in fact there have been. Greg Veltin is looking forward to the performance. Greg's own paradoxes, of personality and persona, of social status and historical experience, perhaps uniquely equip him to look forward to it.

Greg Veltin brings up the first cue and out saunters Liam, in generically olden-times baggy white blouse and knee breeches. The stage is otherwise perfectly bare. At CAPA, elaborate sets, props, and costumes are always required to keep busy the students who will never be cast—or who once were but are not any longer. For example, Greg Veltin, once the next Fred Astaire, now anonymous lighting cues guy. Greg Veltin appreciates the blunt lack of bullshit in this English production. Apart from the lighting cues list that

Greg holds, the production consists entirely of the actor who plays the hero, and eight other actors who play, variously, the other human roles, a couple of animals, and some items of furniture, roles that aren't really performed but denoted, with a startling carelessness Greg Veltin knows is not actually careless. He has seen it repeated with flawless precision, the tossed-off gesture again tossed, with just the same strength to just the same distance, again and again, the definite vagueness maintained so you're never quite sure if the gesture denotes an object or an action or even the set, as for example when actors get onto all fours, as they do frequently, to play at being tables, or sheep, or South American mountains, or something else altogether.

Once Liam sauntered onstage Greg's concentration on his cues became complete; regretfully he couldn't spare attention to the audience reaction for fear he'd mess up. Pools of light bloomed and faded to indicate scene changes that otherwise might go unnoticed— despite, or perhaps because of, the incessant and bellowed narration. "ONCE UPON A TIME THERE LIVED A BARON IN A GREAT FANCY HOUSE," bellowed Cora, as the rest of them, the girls dressed like Cora in knee-length ruffled skirts and snug blouses, the boys dressed like Liam in loose blouses and snug breeches, charged onstage like attacking commandos, enacting a house, a baron, fine furnishings, servants, and many abuses of servants, while Liam, as Candide, wandered this frenetic landscape of events in such a haze of charismatic idiocy Greg couldn't decide whether Liam was doing absolutely nothing onstage or whether he was a genius. Sarah, alone in her row of musicians, saw expressionless Miles standing arms akimbo, to indicate being a wall, over which Theodosia, on tiptoes, mimed peeking. Behind the "wall" were Lilly and Rafe, Lilly flat on her back with her legs scissored open, Rafe on all fours energetically thrusting. "OH!" shrieked Lilly with gusto. "OH! OH! OH!"

"ONE DAY," competingly bellowed Simon, taking over for

Cora as narrator, "WHILST SHE WALKED IN THE GARDEN, SHE SPIED MASTER PANGLOSS INSTRUCTING THE MAID IN SCIENCE. SHE THOUGHT SHE AND CANDIDE SHOULD LEARN SCIENCE TOO!" Theodosia determinedly yanked her skirts up to her waist and leaped onto Liam, whose expression of idiocy grew so much more idiotic that Greg Veltin concluded he must actually be performing, although with unique subtlety as compared with the rest of the cast. Sarah saw, without seeing, the thrusting of groins, heard without hearing the squeals and moans. No part of this pantomime struck her as sexual; she stared as if at animals or children, organisms beneath her interest. An indeterminate sound that was equally titter and murmur had spread through the house, like an erratic wind on water. Mrs. Laytner, who had been sitting in the front row with Mr. Kingsley, rose abruptly and stalked up the aisle. The doors at the rear of the theatre swung in her wake.

Was the performance cut short, or was it simply short at its full length? Even with such headlong swiftness—the English People raced through *Candide* as if in reasonable expectation that large hooks would yank them offstage—it was possible for audience members to grow more discerning. This was their first real experience of double entendre, and they were starting to get it, the joke of the mismatch between words and acts; they could catch it before it flashed past. There was another mismatch, between the actors' acts and their blithe, even dopey expressions. Stupidly grinning, the English People—Rafe and Julian and Simon and Miles, Lara and Cora and Theodosia and Lilly, and, of course, Liam—energetically pantomimed killing each other and being killed by each other, by means of guillotine, gun, bonfire, dagger, and noose; they pantomimed natural deaths via drowning and sexually transmitted disease; they pantomimed raping and being raped and consensual fucking; and above all, it seemed, instances of both forced and consensual ass-fucking. In the audience the uncertain titters and murmurs and utter confusion gave way to real, emboldened laughter flaring up here and there threatening to ignite the whole house, then turning inside out and resurfacing weirdly as shame. Things were very funny and without warning weren't funny at all, they were deeply embarrassing, and just as quickly *that* was funny, that ridiculous seriousness—or was it? Were you an asshole for thinking it was? And why had you thought the word "asshole"? How incredibly funny!—or not.

Greg Veltin performed his last cue and turned his attention to Mr. Kingsley, still in the front row showing the rest of the house the expressionless back of his head. To his disappointment, Greg couldn't derive any clues about the state of Jim's, or rather, Mr. Kingsley's, face, from the back of his head. Greg was no longer sure what he'd expected, or what he had hoped for. The show was over—had they taken their bows? Not having started with raising a curtain, they couldn't end with lowering one, so just walked off the stage. As throughout, the audience, once released from the spectacle, could not reach consensus on how to react. Some stampeded for the doors. Some remained as if roped to their seats. Even these motionless ones, like Pammie, appeared torn between opposing impulses, in Pammie's case the passive immobility of shock, and the active immobility of rage. Pammie's seatmate, Julietta, didn't stay to find out. For Julietta, the only thing worse than watching the show would be talking about it.

"Hi-ho!" called an English voice in a manner both sarcastic and sincere. Assume friendly intent? Assume mockery?

Sarah looked up from her boots. She was sitting on the hood of her mother's ancient Toyota Corolla, at the corner of the front parking lot. Sarah was parked here to avoid everyone, and so far she'd succeeded. She would have succeeded even in the back lot which was unusually empty, her classmates having left for the day.

The Sophomores had no rehearsals, indeed almost nothing to do, until the end of the month. Instead of being performers this month they were supposed to have been learning the role of presenters— drumming up publicity and printing up programs, ushering patrons to seats, counting the box-office take. But *Candide* had been canceled.

Neither Martin, who had called out "Hi-ho!," nor Liam, who sat in the passenger seat of the car Martin drove, seemed regretful. Martin was the author of the stage adaptation of *Candide* as well as its director. Liam was not merely the star, but the star for whom Martin had chosen *Candide*. They were far from home, in a city the April climate of which was already hotter than their native one ever approached on its worst days of August, and they had brought, as their ceaseless plaint went, too many "jumpers" and "trainers" and not enough of whatever nursery words they employed to mean T-shirts and sandals, and they were living as houseguests, in some cases decreasingly welcome. Were Martin and Liam angered, or embarrassed, or even pleased, to find themselves idle where they had expected to be presenting six performances in the space of ten days? It was impossible to say, as Sarah knew, because we cannot read minds but can only react honestly in the moment.

"Hi," Sarah says carefully. There is much to confuse her here. She has never spoken to or been spoken to by either Martin or Liam, for all the hours she's spent in their presence at school. She has never seen either of them in a car without Mr. Kingsley, their host, at the wheel. Having just, at long last, received her own license, a milestone the enormity of which is equaled only by its sense of anticlimax and its failure to grant her relief from her pain, Sarah is hyperaware of those occasions when a body and a steering wheel conjoin. She wonders whether Martin is licensed to drive in this country. Somehow she doubts that he is. The car Martin is driving isn't Mr. Kingsley's Mercedes. It's a teenager's car, a stylish beater of the exact make Sarah desperately covets, a convertible Bug, midway through extensive dermatological renovation. Its shell is heavily plastered with what Sarah assumes is a rust medication. In this year of their sixteenth birthdays, cars, or the absence of cars, are the only significant emblems. Sarah knows she knows this car but she can't place it, the car having only recently appeared in the lot, around the same time as Sarah's mother's impoverished Toyota, which Sarah hopes is not connected to herself in the minds of her peers despite how hard she has fought for the right to drive it. The crucial thing is not to be dropped off at school by her mother. Sarah is allowed to drive from her mother's workplace to school, and from school to her mother's workplace. This is why she's still in the CAPA lot, although there's no rehearsal. Her mother's workday doesn't end until six.

"Fancy taking a spin in our chariot?" Martin goes on, Liam grinning encouragingly. It's Karen Wurtzel's car, Sarah realizes. Karen's father has been helping her restore it. Somehow in her taciturn remoteness Karen has made the car's deficits into an asset, proof that she actually knows about cars.

"I have to pick up my mother from work," Sarah says, so surprised by the invitation she does not think to lie.

"Where's her job? Is it near?"

"She's a secretary at the university."

"Might have been there, we've seen every bloody attraction, is it the one down past those fountains? Why don't we follow you there, you can drop off the car with your mum and then come on with us and have dinner."

It's so simple the way he describes it—like driving itself, when one thing shape-shifts into another, for example her solitary vigil in the front parking lot smoothly eclipsed by Martin and Liam making ridiculous faces they know she can see in her narrow rearview, secondarily framed by the bug-spattered glass of Karen Wurtzel's windshield. Down Fountain Boulevard she leads them, underneath the linked arms of the live oaks, the afternoon sun her attentive spotlight, the Toyota Corolla suffused with an alien splendor.

Sarah knows her hopeful excitement is the result of reprieve from exile, from her status which isn't quite that of a slut but a soiled castoff even Norbert ignores. She'll no more show herself this hope, which is the same as abject gratitude to Martin and Liam for noticing her, than she would show it to Martin and Liam, let alone to her mother, from whom she conceals everything with such thoroughness that her mother doesn't know there are visiting English at school, available to magically pluck Sarah from her disgrace. Prior to the English People's own disgrace, which seems to so little concern them, the CAPA Sophomores were under constant pressure from Mr. Kingsley and Mrs. Laytner to sell *Candide* tickets to family members and friends. Sarah had not sold her mother a ticket. Sarah's continuation as a student at CAPA is largely a condition of her mother's being able to forget that the school exists.

"You're early," her mother says, not without pleasure. "Would you like to use Petra's typewriter? She's gone for the day."

In the barely recalled past of junior high school, Sarah spent most afternoons with her mother, in her mother's little office, also not without pleasure. Her mother would take her lunch hour late, at two thirty, using it to pick Sarah up from her school and bring her back to the campus. There Sarah had been allowed a freedom she had not yet possessed anywhere else. She had wandered the full breadth of the university with its enormous crabgrass lawns, its famous old live oaks, its broad pebbled walks, its oft-photographed Spanish-style buildings, its backpack-wearing students hurrying along among whom Sarah would pretend to belong. The campus bookstore was where she had bought the paperback copy of *Tropic of Cancer* she still hadn't managed to read; the campus commissary was where she had sat alone, with a Dr. Pepper, pretending to read it, cultivating an air that aloneness was the state she had chosen, and sometimes actually feeling a fierce pride in being alone. But most of the time, she would return through the towering heat of the late afternoon to loiter purposelessly with her mother, slouching in her mother's extra chair, receiving unembarrassed the attentions of her mother's co-workers, rearranging her mother's collection of witty coffee mugs, all of which had been gifts from Sarah on Mother's Days past. She'd spent those afternoons with her mother so effortlessly that she's never given them a thought until now that they're as intimately strange as the object landscape of her mother's desktop.

"That's okay," Sarah says, picking up the photo of herself she most likes, the one from seventh grade. She looks far older than her years, is wearing just enough makeup, is smiling with unrecognizable confidence. There's neither the slutty excess of eyeliner nor the desperate excess of eye contact that marred her last three school pictures despite deliberate precautions to the contrary. She does not recognize the very pretty, very happy thirteen-year-old in the picture, perhaps because the picture has become for her an icon. She wishes she had some pretext for showing it to Martin and Liam. "I ran into Karen Wurtzel after school and she invited me to sleep over": the lie as always successful in direct proportion to her lack of preparation. Duplicity, or she'd rather call it storytelling, is her sole realm of inspiration, the entire basis for her mistaken belief she can act.

"Who's Karen Wurtzel?"

"You know, she lives in Southwoods."

"I don't know."

"She's in my class. She followed me here so I could drop off the car." No need to talk about the building's lack of visitor parking, the reason Karen isn't standing here also; Sarah had thought of saying this on the way up, which means it's too much detail and so she does not. Sarah's mother has long since chosen her battles, and theirs is now an almost marital understanding of tacit permission in exchange for unblemished appearance. Sarah's grades will never slip, she will never be addicted or arrested or pregnant.

"She's taking you to school in the morning?" confirms her mother by way of farewell, turning back to her work. Sarah feels a pang; her mother had been happy to see her. If they were a different mother and daughter she would go around the desk and kiss her mother's drooping cheek, but even in the past, when theirs was a shared world, they rarely touched each other.

Sarah goes back down in the elevator and finds Martin and Liam horsing around in the lobby despite the building's lack of visitor parking; through the glass doors Karen Wurtzel's car is visible parked in the fire lane. "We were just about to send out the search parties," says Martin, and when Sarah says it's good that they didn't she must show alarm, because both men laugh.

"Did we give you a scare?" Liam hopes.

The rear seat of Karen Wurtzel's car is almost not a seat at all and Sarah has to twist sideways to fit. "Now off to fetch Karen," says Martin. "Those Calamitous Bournemouth Yokels."

"The Captain Boffed You."

"Three Corpulent Britons Yodel."

"Troubled Cooks Bludgeon Yams."

"You have a future on Fleet Street, Liam. This Can't Beat Yours but There Comes Bonny Yanni."

"Who's Yonny?"

"Y-a-n-n-i. Greek fellow with long flowing hair, plays the keyboards and sings."

"Do you fancy him, then?"

"Oh yessss, he reminds me of you, you pretty thing, needs a shave like you do. Hasn't old Lillian taught you to shave, you inveterate son of a smothering mother?"

"I'll thank you not to mention my sainted mother."

"I'm humoring you as the way to her heart."

"Will you be my daddy then?" Liam grotesquely curls in the

narrow front seat and paws Martin's sleeve in the manner of an uncoordinated kitten. "Will you change my nappies? Waaahh! Waaahh!"

"Don't I already?"

"Now, Martin," admonishes Liam, leaving off his kitten act and sitting up. "I'm trying to impress this girl, aren't I?"

All this witty repartee is shouted back and forth across the stick shift as if for the peanut gallery, as Martin drills the little car down the street like a man fully licensed, or perhaps never licensed. Sarah need not acknowledge what Liam has said. Had he not made the comment she would have felt sure they'd forgotten her. As it is she can't be sure she's the girl that he wants to impress; perhaps "this girl" is Karen. The force of the wind as Karen's car speeds along isolates Sarah in the back seat, her tornado of hair intermittently blinding and gagging her. Concealed within these onslaughts she is able to contemplate Liam. He has the chiseled features of an idol, eyes so unlikely in their blueness and brightness as to suggest something doubtful, an improvised or artificial arrangement, hidden under his skin. Rejected as Sarah has been by Joelle—by Joelle, whom *Sarah* tried to reject—Sarah is unaware of Joelle's verdict on Liam, and had she known it she would have surely contradicted it. Yet Sarah comes to much the same conclusion. Liam is within range, although she doesn't frame it to herself the same way. But the impression of inexplicable deficit, of a queer gap between outward gifts—tall, handsome, lanky, flashing eyes, dazzling smile, the fringes of his hair tangling just the right amount with his eyelashes, one could go on and on—and inward integrity, this Sarah notices also. She envisions a cringing creature, some naked frightened non-human thing, having put on Liam's body like a suit. Now it has to be vigilant, it has to keep watch on the humans around it, to see how to act, so it isn't found out. And who was Liam keeping watch on? Martin.

The vision of the creature in the Liam bodysuit had to be forcibly struck from her mind. Liam was exceptionally handsome. Sarah repeated this idea to herself as if it were a lesson.

Martin wrenched the steering wheel and Karen Wurtzel's car dove roughly over a curb cut and into a small parking lot. Brief strip mall, a handful of storefronts, the retail totem pole at the parking lot entrance indicating Chinese takeout, shipping center, and TCBY, which stood either for The Country's Best Yogurt or This Can't Be Yogurt, Sarah wasn't sure which. Karen Wurtzel was standing in front of TCBY wearing jeans and a kelly-green polo with TCBY stitched above the left breast. She held a white plastic tub about the size of a medium popcorn. Martin braked just short of running her over and flourished grandly with one arm. "Thine Chariot Beckons You."

"Too Clever By Yards," complained Liam.

"Testy Can Be Youth," replied Martin.

Sarah watched a series of storms break across Karen's face and disappear before the men had looked up from their wordplay. "Hi," Karen said brusquely to Sarah without looking at her, as Martin and Liam got out of the car, Martin handing Karen her keys with a bow. Karen handed Martin the white plastic tub and Martin peeled off the lid and peered in. "This *Can't* Be Yogurt," he said.

With Karen driving, Martin took Liam's place in the passenger seat, and Liam climbed in with Sarah. "How's the water?" he asked. Their knees clashed in the inadequate space and Liam bent to study their conjunction. "They're talking about us," he reported to Sarah, who bent her head near his to hear him.

"What are they saying?"

"I don't know. I don't speak any Knee."

"How do you know they're not just making noises to fool you?"

"The way dogs do? 'Woof woof woof,' as if they're saying something? Dogs must think we're quite daft."

"I don't actually hear our knees talking."

"It's on a higher frequency, like a dog whistle. Perhaps dogs talk to knees. But they don't *have* knees, do they? Do they? Look, Martin! Who am I?" Liam sprang onto his knees in the tiny back seat and let his tongue idiotically loll from his mouth as the wind beat his hair from his face. "Arf arf!" he shouted into the wind. The toes of his upturned shoes were digging into Sarah's thigh; they were battered black lace-ups made of cheap or fake leather, sad-sack shoes yet he wore them as obliviously as would a little boy whose mother still bought all his clothes. He had fully committed to playing the pleasure-maddened dog and was barking and slobbering and nosing Martin's shoulder as best he could around the impediment of Martin's seat behind which Martin, twisting so as to face back, sheltered whilst whacking Liam's "dog" nose with a rolled magazine he'd produced from his satchel.

"Bad dog! Bad dog!" Martin cried as Karen wordlessly drove and Sarah, seated behind Karen, rode while trying to catch a glimpse of Karen in the rearview, spotting only herself. Her grim expression repelled her and she forced herself to laugh with crazy energy at Martin's and Liam's antics.

Karen parked in the lot at Mama's Big Boy and they filed inside, first Karen, looking at no one and speaking to no one, then Martin and Liam shoving and goosing each other, then Sarah, at whom Martin and Liam grimaced and clowned and for whom she felt herself performing as a mirror, laughing a laughter not her own, although it would become hers, she told herself. She would not mimic Karen's wounded hauteur, the flattened line of her mouth.

"Table for four," Karen told the host as the host pirouetted in welcome.

"Right this way!" the host cried. "Are you going to need high chairs, honey? Not even boosters?"

"I dooo want a boothstah, I dooo!" Liam said.

At the booth Karen slid in first. As if scoring a run Martin slid in beside her, slamming her against the booth's inside wall. "So terribly sorry!" he cried. "Are you injured? We must take a pulse—I'll be gentle. *Cold as ice.* Is there a doctor in the house? Perhaps a licensed dietician? Liam, crumple up these napkins for a fire, I believe Karen's heart has stopped beating—"

"Let *go*," Karen said, laughing, for even she could not withstand Martin's earnest assault—but it was different with Karen than it had been when Sarah mirrored Martin's and Liam's hilarity. Sarah knew she had been copying, while Karen had somehow reclaimed her own place. It no longer mattered to Karen that Sarah was here.

Sarah wound up seated opposite Karen. Liam, beside Sarah, sat opposite Martin, consumed by his role as Martin's foil, co-conspirator, and jester. "D'you know Liam used to have fatal stage fright?" Martin was telling Karen. "D'you know I used to have to tell him to bring extra pants on the nights he performed?"

"He liked to see me play dress-up," said Liam.

"In case of *accidents.*"

"D'you mean like that time you zipped your willy, Martin? Don't worry, Karen, it caused only minor deformity."

"I'll cause *you* a minor deformity!"

Neither Sarah nor Karen could compete with this, nor were they invited. But Karen needed only to train her attention on Martin. He'd cast her in the role of watching him, as he'd cast Liam in his multiple roles, and Sarah in her part as a sort of wordless prop by which Martin could give Liam occasional scoldings. "Poor Sarah's bored stiff!" Martin said. "She's going to be wondering why she came out with us instead of having all the great wicked fun she had planned."

"I was just going to pick up my mom," Sarah began.

"Devoted to her mum, just like you, Liam, and yet it's *me* discovering these points in common. Why aren't you getting to know each other? Do I have to do everything?"

Wit, or what passed for it; a nimbleness of insults and baffling allusions; the quick pivot, the cavalier non sequitur, the comically extreme reaction. Sarah had always imagined herself possessed of such talents. Hadn't she been a lunch-hour intimate of Mr. Kingsley's? But Martin's conversational virtuosity—or perhaps his unremitting energy for dominating social situations—overmatched her completely. She became quiet and even stupid in its presence. She tried to lay hold of Karen's passive spectatorship, which seemed, at least in the moment, to possess more dignity than her own tentativeness, but Karen's refusal to meet her eyes, to acknowledge her presence, to in any way admit her into comradeship, seemed to deny her Karen's manner toward Martin and Liam as well. Since becoming a student at CAPA, Sarah often had the classic nightmare of finding herself about to go onstage without knowing her lines, or even her role, or even the play, and though this situation lacked the abject terror of those dreams it was similarly paralyzing.

Although Sarah also spoke, laughed, ate half a club sandwich, even flirted with Liam—at least, had she been watching herself from a neighboring table it would have appeared that she did all these things. They had arrived at the Big Boy around five and now it was almost seven. "Crikey, we have shopping to do," Martin said. "Come along, come along. What did you tell people, Liam? Seven thirty or eight?"

"I don't know," Liam said. "I think I just said after seven."

"You're such a complete imbecile, or perhaps you're a dreamer, a beautiful dreamer, and we're all your beautiful dream."

"Why d'you look so much like my worst nightmare, then?"

"D'you ever have that nightmare," Sarah tried, "where you're in a play, but you never rehearsed, and you don't even know what play it is?" She'd done the thing she most despised, of attempting to parrot their accent. Mustering the strength to speak words, she couldn't even use her own voice.

"Yes!" Liam was shouting, as if she'd guessed the answer to a lucrative riddle. "All the bloody time! That's my *worst* nightmare!"

"Another remarkable point in common. There you go, Sarah,

you're drawing him out. I think you two ought to do the drinks shopping and Karen and I will do snacks, but don't take all night. We're already late and we don't even know if we're late for seven thirty or eight due to Liam's remarkable idiocy."

"Where are we going?" Sarah asked Liam once they were alone, cleaving the arctic glare of the supermarket with the rattling cart preceding them as if they were a young couple pushing a "pram." Separated from Martin, Liam had grown quiet, and intently attentive to her, and correspondingly handsome; he watched her push the cart as if enthralled. For a moment, after she spoke, he seemed to study her words on the plate of his mind, as if unsure how to consume them.

"To our place," he said.

"You mean—Mr. Kingsley's?"

"Yes. Jim's place. *And* Tim's. Mustn't forget Tim. Tim and Jim, Jim and Tim. D'you think they fancied each other because their names rhyme? *And* they wear the same size trousers." Liam giggled, exposing his compromised teeth—if only he would keep his mouth shut.

"I didn't know they were having a party."

"Is this a lager you like? We should get one of these big—boxes—Martin loves big American things—"

She understood for the first time that they were buying alcohol. "Do you have an ID? That proves that you're over eighteen?"

"You think they'll ask me to prove that I'm over eighteen?" Liam giggled again, perhaps at the thought of being mistaken for a minor—yet he had come here, with Martin's troupe, as a sort of honorary high school student. Didn't he think he resembled one? But he didn't, Sarah realized. Beneath the unforgiving grocery store lights, his skin was slightly worn, the corners of his eyes slightly creased. Or perhaps it was not the store's fluorescence, but the absence of Martin as a point of comparison, that made Liam's age abruptly visible. Either way, Liam said, as if he knew her thoughts,

"It doesn't matter. Martin will pay, and there's no mistaking him for a kid."

"How old is he?" Of course she knew he was older—the teacher's imprecisely superior age—but how much older she'd never been able to guess. She could not match him, agewise, to the other adults in her life.

"How old is Martin? He's bloody forty, isn't he? Old wanker." This was said with fondness. To cover her surprise Sarah wheeled the cart into a reckless U-turn now that it was heavy with Miller High Life and Bartles & Jaymes. Forty was much older than she'd thought, though she wasn't sure what she had thought, nor how this contradiction of what she had thought made her feel.

At the register Martin paid for the beer, wine, potato chips, and pretzels while Sarah, Karen, and Liam slunk out of the store as if they didn't know him. Barks of laughter—Martin's—and an unintelligible volubility—the cashier's—followed them through the automatic doors, which slid shut and then jerked open again for Martin, pushing the juddering cart. "Is everyone in this country a ponce?" he asked as he plowed the cart across the lot toward Karen's car. "I've never met so many poofters in my life. Teaching at your school, waiting tables at that burger restaurant, ringing me up at the grocer's—"

"It's the neighborhood." Sarah cut him off. Something in Martin's comment provoked a warning sharpness in her own reply, but as soon as she heard it, she faltered. "This is the gay neighborhood," she clarified, and now she sounded apologetic. "I mean, not just gay—it's the arts neighborhood, but it's where lots of gay people live. It's the fourth-largest gay neighborhood in the country," she unaccountably added, "after New York, San Francisco, and—I'm not sure of the third."

"Buggering Batman, Liam. Sarah here seems to specialize in Sodomitica. How did you know, Sarah, that sort of thing's *right up his alley?*"

"My cousin's gay. He used to live in this neighborhood," Sarah said, uncomprehending and unheard, as Liam, having leaped on Martin's back and snatched off his glasses, howled and waved the glasses in the air while Martin spun himself and Liam like a top, hugely waving his arms to emphasize his vision impairment. Unassisted, Karen unloaded the grocery cart into the VW's under-hood trunk.

"Did your mummies know your school's in America's fourth-largest gayborhood? Mind my specs, Liam, you're going to break them."

"Did *you* know, Martin? I'll bet you did. And you told me I wouldn't need my arse helmet."

All the way to Mr. Kingsley's they kept it up, though neither could entirely out-shout the VW's plosively stuttering engine. It brought a din as of German invasion to the crepuscular, secretive streets of Mr. Kingsley's neighborhood, the strangely underwater world into which one passed instantly upon turning off the garishly lit boulevard. It was a noiseless foreign world of boundless lawns upholstered in shadow on which globes of live oak and azalea floated like ships. Karen's unmufflered vehicle tore through it contemptuously, and Sarah could already see Mr. Kingsley standing at the hem of his own velvet lawn, eyeing their approach with his fists on his hips and that expression Sarah most feared, of unsurprised distaste, on his face. But as they came around the bend that revealed his house there was no Mr. Kingsley, only several familiar cars at the curb. One was Joelle's. One was David's. Karen parked her car in front of David's.

As she stood out of the driver's seat, Karen looked directly at Sarah for the first time all night. Not in friendship, but in cold inquiry. Sarah knew Karen wanted to see David's car inflicting on Sarah whatever soft violence an unmoving car can inflict. "Aren't you coming in?" Karen said. Martin and Liam hastily routed the booze and snacks from the under-hood trunk and disappeared around the side of the house toward the enchanted forest of Mr. Kingsley's backyard, with its deck and pergola and fairy lights. Sarah gazed forward yet she could see David's car through the back of her head, could see the ghosts of David and herself entwined like snakes in its dusky interior.

"Are you dating him or something?" Sarah asked about Martin, as much to banish her own thoughts as to deflect Karen's question.

Karen stepped away from the car and slammed the door, which left Sarah having to lever the driver's seat forward and reopen the door for herself, or climb out the open top. Either option would make her look like a clumsy fool and so she stayed in the car and returned Karen's unfriendly gaze.

"'*Dating*'?" Karen smirked. "We're just hanging out."

"Your mom must love you *hanging out* with some forty-year-old guy from England," Sarah said, hoping to shock Karen with Martin's shocking age, as Liam had shocked her.

But Karen only said, "She does. That's why we're not hanging out at my house anymore." With that Karen turned her back and crossed the lawn.

As soon as Karen had passed out of sight Sarah clambered out of the car on the curb side, averting her gaze from David's car as if it would blind her to actually see it. She stood so near the hood of David's car she could have laid her palm on it. She was seized with the wild conviction that David was sitting in his car, just an arm's length away, watching her, and that this had been the reason for Karen's cold gaze. Then Sarah understood that it wasn't just David sitting in David's car, watching her, but David and the new girl who rode in the passenger seat. English Lilly, ambient gossip reported. David and Lilly sat quietly watching Sarah smote by the thought of David's car, unable to even look at it—Sarah wheeled on them, her lips compressed in scorn. The car was empty. As if she'd meant to all along, Sarah pulled the door to David's car open and slipped inside. He never locked it; locking it would suggest that he might care about it. The car, once so clean and new-smelling, was now a squalid vessel for abuse. The passenger seat and footwell were heaped with books and refuse, empty bottles, empty cigarette packs, the twisted wraiths of soiled cotton T-shirts. The pull-out ashtray overflowed and propagated smears of gray, foul ash in every direction. The car phone lay strangled in its cord, its light-up buttons extinguished. Until recently, Sarah knew, that phone had worked. David had boasted so much about it, handing out the number to so many people, even Sarah had learned what it was. It had been a schoolwide pastime to call David's car. The phone appeared to have been beaten to death perhaps against the cracked dashboard. The one time Sarah rode in the car, its interior hadn't even been marked by a boy's carelessness. Now it overflowed with a grown man's despair. Sarah reached for the seat lever and lowered the seat all the way, and herself. The hushed night disappeared from view and she saw only the interior skin of this filthy armor of the boy she had loved.

Her face pressed into one of the leather seat's stitched crevices, she crushed her fist in the vise of her thighs, the car so vibrating with her lust, or her grief, its movement should have been visible from the outside. But, "Sarah?" called Liam's slightly too high-pitched voice, trailing off forlornly. He would be somewhere near the front of the house, seeing Karen's gaping convertible, top down and obviously empty, and David's car, also apparently empty. Surely he would not cross the lawn to make sure Sarah wasn't crushing her clitoris over a white-knuckled fist in the passenger seat of her ex-boyfriend's car, in the hope of the sort of orgasm that feels like one's pleasure torn out by the root: a punishment for the pleasure as well as a final end of it.

Still Sarah froze, heart racing in her chest, skull, and crotch. The scent of her lonely exertion wound into the car like an unwilled and shameful secretion, fear's trickle of urine or mystery's trickle of blood from the nose.

He didn't call her name again. A muffled sound, perhaps the door closing again, and then silence. David's car's clock said 7:42. When it said 7:48 Sarah raised the seat back to its previous position and left the car as if leaving the scene of a crime.

Mr. Kingsley's front door was unlocked. No Liam or anyone else stood in Mr. Kingsley's foyer, with its terra-cotta tiles and its bizarre human-size doll that was supposed to be called a "soft sculpture" and its rusty Mobil sign, with a winged horse, ostentatiously hung underneath its own spotlight. Quickly Sarah took the front stairs to the second-floor hall, the plushly carpeted one lined with posters and photos; she locked herself into the bathroom, washed her hands and her face, and redid her eyeliner and lipstick. When she came out again, there was Liam at the end of the hall, standing in an attitude of indecision. He seemed to be slightly tipped forward, hands dangling at his sides, wrists too long for the sleeves. This impression of infirmity passed when he saw her, and once again he looked handsome and young and his striking eyes flashed with charisma.

"You're mysterious, aren't you!"

"I went to buy smokes," she lied.

The smile remained on Liam's face but now it had been there too long. He was acting, she realized, and wanting direction but not getting it. This was the strange quality that hung around his handsomeness, a blur or a warp where he seemed to be lagging behind his own actions and wondering how they had gone.

"Isn't this house crazy?" she offered.

His gratitude seemed to cohere him. "It's a bloody fucking castle, isn't it! Let's hide—I hear the others." Grabbing her hand he hauled her up the steep attic stairs—half serious, as if their lives depended on it, half ridiculous, as if "let's hide" were an improv they'd just been assigned. The gleamingly beautiful attic room Sarah remembered from the night she'd discovered Manuel was now as squalid as—what? It took her a moment to understand the familiarity of the squalor. The room was as squalid as David's car which she had just left. The stately expanse of the varnished floor, the expensive charm of the low-angled ceiling and dormers, were made unrecognizable by trailing heaps of pungent laundry, scudding piles of takeout garbage, countless fallen soldiers of the armies of Miller and Coors. Retaining her hand Liam pulled her through the cluttered filth with no more compunction than a goat would show crossing its native terrain. Then they were standing at the window on the far side of the room next to one of the beds. Letting go her hand, Liam opened the window with exaggerated care, making almost no sound, and cupped a hand by his ear to indicate that they were eavesdropping. A murmur of voices entered with the damp evening air: composite talk and laughter, muffled by distance and leaves. A party concealed in the manicured jungle of Mr. Kingsley's backyard. From the height of the attic the party's constituent parts, its outlines, its individual words were as impossible to parse as were the individual leaves of all the shrubs and trees that loosely filled the air outside the window like a mound of black feathers. Peering out Sarah could see, here and there, bright glints from the small outdoor lights. They disappeared, then flashed again, whether from the movement of the breeze through the leaves, or from the movements of people, she didn't know. And then David's voice reached her, as clearly as if he and not Liam were standing beside her. David's low, sardonic voice made some sort of wisecrack, was answered by jagged laughter. In the instant of hearing his voice Sarah's chest seemed to fill with the same feathered darkness into which she was gazing: a mass crushing and weightless of pain and desire. Across that distance she hadn't deciphered the words he had spoken, yet it took her an instant to realize she hadn't; his voice by itself seemed so sharp she had almost flinched from it.

"Everybody's outside," Liam said. "All our lot, and David." After a moment he added, "He used to be your boyfriend—or was he just having us on?"

Her mouth was too dry to speak comfortably. "He wasn't ever my boyfriend."

"But he fancied you?"

"I don't know."

"'Course he did."

Stupidly she blurted, before thinking, "*Why.*" Now he would think she wanted compliments from him, when what she'd literally meant was *why* did David love me—which was the cowardly way to ask David, *Why do you no longer love me?* Of course Liam, in speaking to her, assumed she was speaking to him.

"Because you're lovely, that's why." He delivered the line beautifully, and a thrill rippled over her surface, in the depths of which David continued to lurk, the unanswered question.

"Stop," she said, wincing.

"You are. So. Lovely. D'you know who you remind me of?" he exclaimed, as if finally solving a conundrum. "*Sade.* D'you know who that is?"

"I don't look like her."

"You do," Liam said, feasting his eyes on her face until he seemed to embarrass himself. He broke off, and reaching outside the open window, brought in a saucer of cigarette butts. After patting himself all over, he produced a packet of Drum and papers, and sat down on the bed. "Fancy a ciggie?"

"Don't you want to go down in the yard?"

"With the rest of them? No. No." He dropped the packet of Drum and pulled her by the wrist to sit beside him. "No," he whispered hotly. "I want to stay here with you." When he jammed his tongue into her ear she gasped with repulsion as much as surprise, and twisted her head to take his tongue in her mouth, a less embarrassing arrangement that was even less pleasurable. She tasted the bitterness of her own earwax and bore down harder against him, in the hopes of erasing the flavor. It was a baffling struggle to accommodate his wildly poking, flicking tongue; no matter what they did, her tongue and his seemed to be at violent cross-purposes, each trying to poke the other out of the way. With an agonized groan Liam twisted their intertwined torsos until he'd crushed her to the mattress's uneven surface, and then her air went out of her all at once as Liam, wildly struggling to take off his jacket, let his full weight drop onto her chest. He finally wrenched the jacket off with the vehemence of a madman escaping his straitjacket, and at the same time she gasped in such a desperate effort to refill her lungs she made a noise like a squeak or a shriek—hearing her, Liam raised himself above her on the balls of his hands and grinned frankly into her face, for he'd taken her gasp as a sign of excitement.

And she was, in a strange way, excited. All the physical signs of Liam's ardor abashed and shocked her. He flailed; his dead white hairy limbs appeared impaled on the stem of his unaccountably wrinkly erection which he took in his fist and seemed to squirt redly at her, for he'd yanked back the covering skin. Sarah had never seen or even imagined an uncircumcised penis; she must have gaped at it, delighting him further. But along with these dismaying physical extrusions came verbal ones which made her shudder with astonishment. He talked constantly, mostly incomprehensibly, but what of his babble she grasped was unstintingly filthy. His voice rose and fell as he jabbered at her, like the voice of a gleefully mischievous boy who's found a pornographic novel and is reading it aloud. And the words he used! So much filthier for being nursery words a mincing mother might use as she wiped a fat baby. He called it his *willy*—"Oh my willy's going in!—it's going in!—so squashy wet my willy's in your *squashy wet tight squashy hot*—" Nothing could have been less suave—he didn't touch her so much as he yanked, poked, jabbed, squeezed as if her body were some sort of toy—and yet she heard herself, a rising note of protest or a siren of warning, "*Noooo, noooo, noooo.*" And the horrible pleasure, pushing outward from her like a flower of flesh with great muscular petals like tongues, in its enormous agonizing opening so overpowered her she could not even feel his "willy" or any other part of him anywhere in or near her, as if he'd shrunk to a speck and been swept out to sea on the flood of her unwanted pleasure.

Returning from this she found herself suffocated beneath a weight of damp flesh. Her bra, T-shirt, and jean jacket were shoved to her armpits, exposing her breasts; her jeans and panties were shoved to her ankles; her knees were splayed open; she was still wearing her black pointy boots. Her bottom, coldly soaking wet, felt glued to a puddle of slime. Over Liam's shoulder she saw the door of the room which was not even closed, and shoved him away with such force he fell off the end of the bed into foothills of trash.

"Didn't you like it?" he exclaimed.

"The door's *open!*"

Ah, she wasn't displeased, only charmingly shy! Agreeably he sprang across the room to close the door despite it hardly mattering now—and so was the window still open, through which, only minutes before, she had heard David's voice. What had the night heard of *her*, she wondered as she frantically tugged her clothes back into place, dodging his spidery efforts to re-entwine her, his slobbering kisses and praise. "God you're *so* lovely," he marveled again and again, like an actual idiot. She wished he would put on his clothes, cover his pale washboard chest and its brightly pink nipples. But he seemed perfectly at ease, sitting cross-legged on the heap of fouled sheets, his spent penis flopped between his legs like a stricken worm.

"Don't you think we should go downstairs?" she begged him.

"If you'd fancy a drinkie I can pop down and get us some beers."

"It's just—what if someone comes up?" That the door had been open—the unthinkable humiliation of exposure grew more narrowly evaded in retrospect, as if, with enough dawdling, the past might be rewritten and the awful thing take place after all. How often was she going to do this, fuck someone in public? If he'd only get dressed!

"But Jim isn't *here*. Did you think he was *here*? He's at the opera, he and Tim. They'll be gone hours."

"He and Tim aren't home?"

"No!" Liam laughed.

"But do they know we're here?"

"We're their guests! We're allowed to be here." At last he was pulling his clothes on, growing handsome again as his flesh disappeared. Halfway into his shirt, he pulled her against him and again pushed his pointy avid tongue down her throat. "D'you know I've been mad for you?" he asked huskily. "Wanking day and night, thinking about you. Almost drove poor Martin out of his mind."

"Oh my God." She laughed hollowly, twisting away. He tried to pull her hand into his just-buttoned pants but playing the coquette she escaped him, and rushed out the door and down the flight of stairs into the second-floor hall. A murmur of voices and music reached her from the opposite end of the house. As she pursued it Liam caught up, wearing the gaze of devoted assurance she longed for from David.

"I adore you," Liam whispered as they emerged, pungent and nest-haired and obvious, into the kitchen.

There stood Joelle and Theodosia and Lilly and Rafe and a handful of the popular Juniors, whom Sarah had never known Joelle to spend time with, sharing a joint. Joelle gazed at Sarah as if from the deck of a ship that was moving away from the dock toward a glorious distant horizon; and Sarah saw herself, in Joelle's steady gaze, marooned on the dock, shrinking down to a pinprick, vanishing.

"My my my," Rafe said to Liam, "where've you been, Master Candide? Learning your lessons?"

"I've been alphabetizing the porno. There's ever so much of it."

"Oh my God," Rafe said, blurting out smoke. "D'you all know about the porno? No end of it. Martin told us he'd thought he was putting on *8½* by Fellini and what came on was gents shoving their fists in each other's a-holes."

"Noooooo!" shrieked the popular Juniors, covering their faces, their mouths, or their ears.

"Martin's such a bloody liar, he knew exactly what tape he was playing," Lilly said to laughter.

"Do I hear my own revered name?" Martin said, appearing in the doorway that led from the yard with his dingy hair even more scrumbled than Liam's. "Did you miss me, my darlings?"

"We're just talking about what a pervert you are."

"Be good now, be good. For fuck's sake take the joint back outside."

Karen wasn't with Martin, or anywhere Sarah could see. Unobtrusively Sarah tried to peer through the darkness seeking Karen or David as she passed outside into the yard. Her palm was wet and cold from the bottle of beer she was clutching. The small of her back squirmed beneath Liam's palm where he kept it attached as if with adhesive. She craved escape from his touch at the same time as feeling wild gratitude for the obstacle he made, like a shield, between her and Joelle, between her and the prospect of David. No sooner did this occur to her than she became afraid he'd change his mind and in her fear grabbed his hand, and felt him gratefully squeeze in return. Then they were smoking in the gazebo with Simon and Erin O'Leary, who clung to each other with the stunned despair of lovers so overcome by their lust they cannot take the first step toward solving it; they could have walked indoors and fucked in any of several unoccupied rooms as Sarah had just done without meaning to, but the simplicity of this solution escaped them. Their mutual grip was white-knuckled. Also in the gazebo were Colin and Cora, Cora who had been housed with Pammie and had thrown her over and moved in with Karen. Sarah wanted to ask Cora where Karen was, but Colin and Cora, unlike Simon and Erin, were noisily necking, grinding and groping, indifferent to their audience. And Rafe was there, bantering filthily with Liam, his arm slung around Katrina from Dance. Every one of the visiting English had paired off soon after arriving, none of these couplings was news, there had even been time for breakups and betrayals—only the grown-ups, Liam and Martin, had remained outside the dance, bemused by it, exempt; "horny little fuckers," Martin had said. But now Liam had chosen Sarah—she could feel this information emanating through the darkness, altering her status, though in what way she couldn't yet gauge. And Martin? "We're just hanging out," Karen had sneered. Sarah remembered sitting in this gazebo with Julietta and Pammie and Greg Veltin, those three linked in a circle of joy to which Sarah could not stay attached though they'd reached out their hands to keep her. Theirs was a love she had rejected by reflex because of its very simplicity, its undiverted, untranslated eruption from the heart or the guts or wherever such feelings came from. Sarah didn't have such feelings anymore. Here she sat in the octopus arms of a man whose attractiveness she had to keep scolding herself to perceive and for whom she felt nothing but, now, an uneasy responsibility, as he slobbered and groaned his undiminished longing into her ear.

Rafe and Katrina and Simon and Erin and Cora and Colin no longer bothered to banter or smoke but only strove with mouths and tongues to swallow each other, and ground their crotches together, and collided their limbs with the gazebo's unyielding walls. When Sarah flinched from Liam's kiss he fell agreeably onto her neck and fed there like a starved, toothless dog. Apart from feeling wet, and as a consequence cold, Sarah's body was devoid of sensation. Staring into the darkness beyond the gazebo as Liam whimpered and gummed the tendons of her neck she saw David's profile float past, moving away, as if though mere feet of air stood between them they were no longer of the same world. Ever since arriving she'd been straining her powers of intuition to make some kind of contact with David and now he was passing so near she might have reached out and seized him. Her jaws opened but no sound came out. Yet David turned, and his gaze fell on her where she sat on the floor of the gazebo with Liam's mouth latched onto her neck and Liam's hand twiddling her unfeeling breast. David's gaze swept her mercilessly and then he'd passed out of sight, toward the house. Sarah wrenched herself upright. "I have to go to the bathroom," she said, and escaped.

Inside the house the kitchen counters were covered in bottles and bags, the sound system had been left spattering between radio stations, shelves of smoke hung in the air performing slow disintegrations where they had been deposited by unknown persons passing through. Every room Sarah saw was empty. Yet she was certain the house wasn't empty. Her body had come back to life, emotion pumping from her like a tide that touched all surfaces and lifted even the slightest piece of evidence, floating it into the light. Passing down the first-floor hallway to its very end Sarah flattened her hand on a door that was slightly ajar, pushed it open, and there were Martin and David, hunched in noiseless contortions of mirth. Their puckered faces were red. At her entrance they unbent, with effort and gasping.

"Oh my God," said David, "get that thing away from me."

The room in which she'd found them was a bedroom, vast and dim, holding a great bed lavishly made up in purple satin so dark as to look almost black. The bed stuck out from its wall like a tongue, was tumbled with pillows of all different sizes but all made of the same black-purple satin, like a crop of eggplants. The glow from two enormous lamps under zebra-striped shades would have barely outshone a candle. The far side of the room disappeared into drapery.

"Look who's here! Catch," Martin said and as she reached toward him in dumb obedience an object landed in her hands. David smacked it away.

"Jesus! Don't make her touch it."

"I'm sure it's perfectly clean. I'm sure they boil them after each use." Shaking with laughter, Martin dropped onto the bed and started rifling through a drawer in the near bedside table. "Maybe Sarah would prefer a different color? A tad longer or fatter? More pointy?"

"What *is* it?" she asked David as Martin pelted David with another of the objects.

"You're fucking sick!" David was trying to talk down to Martin, but his very desire to talk down to Martin guaranteed he could not. David wouldn't look at her, wouldn't touch the thing, whatever it was, but dodged it like a squeamish little boy, so that Sarah, inflamed, snatched it up from the carpet.

"You *really* want to put that down!" cried David.

"Oh, shame," Liam said, peering around the doorframe. "Martin's got in the toy chest again."

"Do you want to know what it is?" Martin asked her, with sudden seriousness. "My, David, you needn't man the battle stations, you're quite safe with me. Did you really fancy him?" This was to Sarah, for David had sprung from the room, he'd escaped her again. "I'd like to know his secret. He must emit some chemical. Lilly's mad for him, she says she's not going to come back to England, she's staying here to shag David the rest of her life. But you, sweetest Sarah, you're far too mature for Liam, let alone a wet-eared wanker like David. Come sit beside me. You too, Liam. Gather round, children," and in a trance Sarah sat down beside him on the eggplant-colored bed, seeing nothing but David and Lilly, David's blunt-fingered hands and Lilly's sallow, pointy face and her grim, willing mouth. Liam bounced onto the bed and pulled her onto his lap so that her legs dangled just short of the floor. "I feel like Prospero blessing Miranda and Ferdinand," Martin said, digging into the drawer. "Trade me the one you've got, Sarah. Give it here."

"Tell me what it is first," Sarah said, twisting out of Martin's reach.

"Naughty minx!" Martin said.

How well she could suddenly do it—act a complete part, while concealing, completely, a true self that did her no good. Saucy and sharp, she baited Martin, tossed and caught the rubber thing just beyond Martin's reach, felt Liam's insistent erection questing into her ass as he gripped her ever tighter to his lap. And all the while she was really with David, with his fumbled efforts over Lilly which he made to evade her, Sarah, and which wouldn't succeed. Indifferent to the stupid men for whom she played the role, indifferent to the prick pressing into her ass, indifferent to the thing dropping into her hand, indifferent to the room, she homed in on David. It won't work, she told him calmly.

"Sarah," came Mr. Kingsley's voice into the newly quiet room. "Please give that to me and go home." Beneath her Liam stood up and she slid off his lap onto her feet. Mr. Kingsley was standing before her, his hand extended, and she put the thing into it, staring into his face and at the same time past his shoulder into his husband Tim's face, which hung in the doorframe like Mr. Kingsley's pale shadow.

"Lucky you! That must be the shortest *Das Rheingold* in history," Martin brayed, as if by sheer volume he could transport them all out of the room.

"Tim was feeling unwell," said Mr. Kingsley, while pointing at Sarah a look that spoke words as if straight to her mind. You of all people should have known better.

"We had a bit of a misunderstanding," Martin blared on. This wasn't obliviousness, Sarah saw, but a hostile rejection of circumstance. Apart from Martin's voice the house was perfectly silent. Even the faint static from the untuned radio in the living room at some recent moment had ceased. "My lot came around looking for me," Martin shouted, "then their pals turned up looking for them. Inseparable they've all become."

"Sarah," Mr. Kingsley repeated, "please go home." As she rushed from the room Tim seized hold of her hand.

"Do you have a ride, sweetie?" he whispered.

"Yes," she said, or perhaps she nodded, or perhaps she said nothing; she wrenched her hand from his and ran down the hall out the door. Every car was gone from the curb. Every trace of the party was gone like a zipper drawn closed, leaving only her sharp breaths and the clicking of her boots as she ran down the street. She feared nothing more than Mr. Kingsley's Mercedes pulling up to display his disgusted but unsurprised gaze, but she must have longed for it, also, so vividly did the vision pursue her. No one, not Mr. Kingsley nor Martin and Liam nor Karen nor David nor anyone else whose body was, as it seemed bodies always should be, encased in a car appeared out of the darkness to enfold Sarah's seemingly naked, certainly lost, unprecedentedly vulnerable body into the proper housing and accustomed rate of progress of a car. Sarah ran, as she had never previously run, down streets unaccommodating of pedestrian activity, streets without sidewalks and where the signs were far apart or entirely absent. Mr. Kingsley's neighborhood was a sinuous maze and she was lost almost as soon as she'd gotten his house out of view. Soon she was too winded, and too self-conscious of the noise her boots made, to keep running but her walk was swift and frightened. In this city only the very poor and criminals who had made some sort of mistake while committing a crime ever walked. Sarah thought of her mother's shabby little car, so intimately familiar, with longing and rage. She would do anything to obtain her own car. She would prostitute herself or rob or kill if it meant she could have her own car. Since starting all over with saving her bakery wages she hadn't bought a single thing and if she could just get to twelve hundred dollars she was sure she'd have her pick of good cars; she read the *Auto Trader* every week with obsessive attention. She had long since ranked her dreams in order: Bug, MG, Alfa Romeo, in every case convertible. There were always beautiful little foreign convertibles for sale for around twelve hundred dollars in the *Auto Trader* "because those little cars are a big pain to keep running, they're worthless," said Sarah's broken and cynical mother, who for all her superior experience of life knew nothing about how to live.

And then suddenly Sarah had returned to the wide, loud, brightly lit boulevard and could see the sign for Mama's Big Boy glowing in the distance. It was a distance a car would travel in the blink of an eye but it took Sarah, walking quickly, what felt like ten minutes. She walked at the edges of the parking lots, not on the curbside bands of crabgrass, so as to look like someone walking to her car, not someone walking down the street, but even so, a few cars sounded their horns as they passed as if striping her with a paintbrush of noise. Were they warning or mocking? She didn't know, but she tried to walk even more quickly, as fast as she could without seeming to run. In the entrance vestibule of Mama's Big Boy she spilled her coin purse all over the floor trying to get her fingers around change for the phone. Her useless fingers, like so many hot dogs stuck onto her hands. Once she had finally managed to call David's car phone she was afraid that the ringing would stop. David was certainly parked somewhere with English Lilly grinding away on his lap, the curtain of Lilly's blond hair slapping them both in the face, Lilly's left knee like an ungreased piston squeaking against the edge of David's seat and with each squeak nearly knocking the phone from its cradle. At any moment David and Lilly's labored fucking in the front of his car would inadvertently answer the phone and then Sarah would hear what she already saw and heard all too clearly—but instead she heard a default outgoing message that David had apparently never bothered to personalize. She hung up. It wasn't even eleven. Mama's Big Boy was approaching its busiest hours, when people who had already been somewhere and people who were still going somewhere converged. There wasn't a single booth open so she sat at the counter, staring down at the enormous laminated sheets of the menu. "You again?" said her waiter of three hours before as he sailed past with pots of coffee aloft in both hands. Thankfully he wasn't working the counter, he wouldn't speak to her again, wouldn't say, "Where are those boys with the accents?" She had only enough for an order of fries and a coffee and when they came their two contrasting tastes, dull-grease-potato and acrid, equally filled her mouth with the warning saliva that comes just before vomiting. She couldn't sit on the stool at the counter for more than an hour, they had a rule against loitering, but she might not even make it that long. Some time later she went to the bathroom to rinse and stare at her unrecognizable face and when she returned the untouched fries and coffee were gone and someone new was on the stool, poring over the menu, and when she caught the counterman's eye he waved a hand dismissively and turned away.

Close to midnight, she definitely wanted David to answer, she didn't care if he had Lilly on his lap, but again he did not. Perhaps now he was asleep. Perhaps now everyone was asleep. Her mother in her lonely bed; her mother's car, which Sarah still felt might appear—willed to join her like a loyal animal—in its carport. Mr. Kingsley's Tim, who had not been feeling well at the opera, was asleep, and Liam whose incursion she still felt as a damp dull soreness between her legs was asleep. Mr. Kingsley and Martin—where were they? Had they placed silence and contempt between themselves, retreated to opposite ends of the house? And where was Karen? Never until this moment had Sarah considered that she might after all have to spend the night with Karen. She had expected Martin and Liam, whose idea it had been to spirit her away, to bear responsibility for the impulse as if it weren't an impulse at all but a rational plan—as if, like CAPA hosting the troupe, Martin and Liam would host *her*, safeguard her welfare and put her up—in a hotel?—and buy her breakfast and drop her off on time at school in the morning. She had expected this because they were adults. Yet she'd gone off with them because they didn't behave like adults, so that she couldn't understand, now, whether they'd deserted her or whether she'd been stupid to expect otherwise.

There were five Wurtzels in the phone book but only one in a familiar zip code. Sarah dialed the number and despite the late hour a smoky drawling voice answered, sounding not unpleasantly surprised.

"Karen?"

"This is Elli. I think Karen's already asleep. Can I give her a message?"

This Sarah had not been prepared for. She demurred, apologized, managed not to cry, and yet failed to hang up on the unsurprised voice. "Sarah," Elli Wurtzel's voice said after Sarah had choked out her location and situation, "I want you to stay standing there at the phone until a taxi pulls up. It's going to be an orange-and-blue taxi that says Metro Cab. It might take a while but it'll definitely come. It'll bring you to my house and I'll be waiting up for you. Don't disappear on me or I'll have to call your mom, and the cops. Okay? Do you understand?"

"Yes," Sarah said.

"Are you drunk, honey?"

"No."

"High?"

"No."

"It's okay if you are; I just want to be sure you don't leave there before the cab comes."

"I won't."

"I want you to wait inside, honey. Don't stand outside in the lot by yourself."

On this one point she disobeyed. She waited outside in the lot, out of sight of the waiters she felt must be watching and talking about her. Close to one in the morning an orange-and-blue car that said Metro Cab entered the lot, driven by a man with a brown beard and longish brown hair who asked, "Sarah?" then gestured her in. He found her gaze in the rearview mirror. "Hi, I'm Richard. I'm not running the meter 'cause Elli'll settle up with me direct. She's a friend."

"Okay," Sarah said. She'd never ridden in a taxi in her life. She hadn't even realized her city had taxis. In her childhood she'd watched a television show about New York cab drivers. The meter had something to do with the way that you paid.

They drove back down the boulevard, all the dead grass, crushed glass, strewn litter, cracked pavement, inexhaustibly vivid granular variety on which Sarah had trod exhausted in an instant. The cab climbed onto the freeway and whistled through the night, dismounting two exits west of Sarah's neighborhood among slightly dilapidated single-story brick ranch-style houses like those the city over except in neighborhoods of the wealthy, like David's and Mr. Kingsley's, or in poor neighborhoods, like Sarah and her mother's, or in the neighborhoods of people even poorer than Sarah and her mother; everyone else, in Sarah's experience, lived in houses like these. Even Sarah and her mother had once lived in a house just like these, when Sarah's parents were still together. Richard pulled into the driveway of a darkened house on the front step of which a petite woman with long brown hair was sitting in a frilly bathrobe, smoking a cigarette. As the car turned in, the woman stood quickly and came to meet it. "Thanks," she said to Richard, leaning one elbow on the sill of the open driver's-side window, as if it were the middle of the day. "I owe you one."

"You'll get my bill," Sarah heard Richard say, and Elli and Richard both laughed. Sarah got out of the car on the opposite side from where Elli was standing, and the car drove away.

Inside the house the air seemed made of sleep. All was warm, stale, damp. Sarah could hear the heavy inhalations and exhalations of sleepers; following Elli through a shag-carpeted living room dimly lit by the glow of a VCR's digital clock Sarah saw that a sleeper facedown on a couch, one long leg and one arm dangling onto the floor, was Liam.

"In here," Elli whispered, coming back to where Sarah stood rooted to the floor and taking her hand as if Sarah had perhaps lost her way in the dark. They left the twilight of the living room, passed through the near-complete darkness of a hallway with many closed doors, and entered the last door, from under which glowed a thread of gold light. "It's a full house tonight," Elli said when the door had been closed behind them. Her drawl was husky and bemused, as if no circumstance could distress it. They stood together in her densely cluttered bedroom, clothes and teddy bears and pillows heaped in such quantity that the underlying furniture could barely be seen. A lamp with a tasseled shawl pinned to the shade cast dim light on framed pictures of a much younger, rounder-cheeked Karen and a chubby little boy with the same face as Karen. Dolls and knickknacks and books were crammed into the overtaxed shelves: *Star Signs; The Complete Tarot; Recipes for Nutritional Health.* "This should fit you," Elli said, with effort tugging a pajama set loose from a drawer that was too full to be properly opened. When the set was uprooted Sarah could see that it was ruffled and trimmed with little marble-size pom-poms. "I got it for Karen but she won't be caught dead wearing it, and it's too big for me. I'm a two. Oh, honey. What is it? Is it a guy? You are *so* pretty. Karen never talks about you; I can guess why. You're gonna get in the shower—use the body wash."

Clutching the pom-pom pajamas, Sarah locked herself into the tiny bathroom, like a forest of candles and powders and creams in which toilet, sink, and tub had accidentally grown, funguslike, through the floral perfumed understory. Sitting on the toilet she turned on the shower and sobbed into its noise. Love was some kind of chemical error. In the shower she turned the water by increments from very warm to very hot until she thought her skin would burn, and felt the microscopic Liam—where he had floundered his chest against hers leaving streaks of hot sweat, where he had tongued his spittle through the grooves of her ear and down the cords of her neck, where he had greased her with his fingers and stuffed her with what she'd hoped to forget he referred to as "spunk," another nursery word connoting sickly stench, unlaundered linen, hidden stains, and shame—scoured and rinsed away like so many hairy little organisms from a cleanser commercial, protestingly sucked down the drain. No part of her body did not crave the annihilation of hot water and soap. She found the body wash, but didn't want to use the crinkly pouf that went with it and was obviously often used by Elli and seemed too personal, so in the end she poured the body wash into the cup of her hand and tried to get it over as much of herself as she could. She washed her hair twice, clawing hard at her scalp. Then it seemed she might have been in the shower too long. When she crept out of the bathroom Elli sat curled on the bed with a tray resting beside her on which was clustered an array of little jars. Elli smiled a bright and pretty smile Sarah found herself return-ing. Elli had a small mole on her cheek. She seemed to be fully made-up despite how late it was. "*There*," Elli said happily. "You look so much better." Elli patted the mattress and shifted the tray to make room. That Elli was a mother, Sarah couldn't keep lodged in her mind, let alone that Elli was the mother of Karen. Carefully Sarah climbed onto the bed, wishing the pajamas were longer. At home she slept in a 97 Rock T-shirt that came down to her knees.

"I can tell you have a broken heart," Elli said.

Sarah started to laugh and found herself crying instead. She cov-ered her eyes with one hand and felt a tissue box being pressed on the other.

"Don't be embarrassed, honey. You're lucky, having your heart broken. That means you were really in love. I'm dying to do your Tarot but I think you should sleep, just as soon as you swallow your supplements. Do you take supplements?"

"Um, no. I don't think so."

"You should. Our bodies need this stuff. And your body needs even more, because of the stress and the pain. You have to help the body renew. A lot of the sadness you feel is *physical*. That's really important to know. We're gonna make up your supplement mix and tomorrow once they've had a chance to work we'll talk about how you feel and if I need to I'll make some adjustments. Then I'll do up a week's worth and write you a list and you can get them yourself." As she spoke Elli uncapped one jar after another, shaking out capsules and tablets of all sizes and colors from which rose an unsettling odor of dead and dried things. The odor made Sarah think of those dirt caves beneath a dome of tree roots in which things often seemed to happen, whether magical or sinister, in the stories she read as a child. Elli had created a kaleidoscope of dingy color on the tray which looked as easy to ingest as a pile of gravel. "Sit up straight," she instructed, handing Sarah a tumbler of water. "Relax the back of your throat completely. It'll help them go down."

It was a long, queasy process, swallowing everything down. Some of the capsules contained gold, beige, or olive-green powder, some of the tablets tasted moldy or salty and sucked the moisture from her mouth like eating chalk. Herbs, minerals, essential spores, and elements of earth. Mechanically, Sarah wet her mouth, placed a pill from the tray at the back of her tongue, relaxed the muscles of her throat, washed it down, Elli talking all the while in her tireless, musical voice. "What I always tell Karen is how boys and girls, and women and men, mature at such a different rate—it's a medical fact that if you take a girl of sixteen like you, and a boy of sixteen, physically you might look the same age but *chemically*— and remember chemicals make our emotions and thoughts—that girl of sixteen and that boy of sixteen are at totally different levels. Emotionally, intellectually, the girl's years ahead of the boy. That jelly-looking one is fish oil, I know it's smelly but it lubricates your brain. *So* important. Even if you just took that alone, right away you'd feel calmer. And the truth is, the boys never catch up. Not entirely. Take my father, Karen's grandpa. That man is fifty-eight years old and he's barely more mature than Karen's little brother, Kevin. Kevin actually has much more of the feminine in him, because we're all a mix. When I talk about men and women or girls and boys I'm simplifying, because we're all a masculine/feminine mix though most women are more feminine and most men are more masculine, but it's not black and white, not at all. My father is a very masculine man and he's like an animal crossed with a child. Kevin's gonna be ahead of him by the time he's fifteen, I really believe that. But your guy, the boy who hurt you—I'm guessing that the masculine is dominant in him. Do I know who he is? Is he one of your classmates? Oh, honey—no, don't talk about it. Sometimes it helps to talk it out and sometimes it's just worse. Go to sleep." For Sarah woke up at six every morning, seven days in a row in a row in a row. Her head juddered downward, perhaps her chin actually struck her chest, the drained tumbler of water dropped out of her hand, she felt Elli's small, soft hands rolling her over, tugging the bedspread and sheets from beneath her, the bed continued restless a few moments more, the lamp continued to glow, but Sarah barely felt, barely saw, not even when the lamp's click brought absolute dark nor when the bed's jouncy movement subsided and was replaced by encircling pressure. "Can I cuddle you, honey?" came Elli's imperturbable whisper. "You poor thing, so tired. . . ." Sarah indeed was too tired to answer or move or to flinch from her bedmate's enveloping touch.

Trust
Exercise

"KAREN" STOOD OUTSIDE the Skylight bookstore in Los Angeles, waiting for her old friend, the author. Her old high school classmate, the author. Was it assuming too much, to say "friend"? Was it accepting too much, to say "Karen"? "Karen" is not "Karen's" name, but "Karen" knew, when she read the name "Karen," that it was she who was meant. Does it matter to anyone, apart from "Karen," what "Karen's" real name is? Not only does it not matter to anyone else, but the fact that it matters to "Karen" will probably reflect badly on "Karen" in the same way that so much about "Karen" reflects badly on "Karen." So "Karen" won't insist on providing her real name or anyone else's, although she'd like to say, for the record, that she can see right through the choice of "Karen" for her designation. With apologies to actual Karens, "Karen" is an unsexy name. It's too recent to have retro chic and not recent enough to feel fresh. It's a name without snap. It gives you a plain feeling but not plain enough, like "Jane," which is such a plain name that the phrase "Plain Jane," in contradiction of its meaning, has snap, it rhymes and suggests a romantic plainness, the phrase "Plain Jane" makes people smile. "Karen" has no such associations. "Karen" isn't pretty, or smart, or deceptively plain until she takes off her glasses. "Karen" is a yearbook name, filler, a girl with a hairstyle like everyone else's and a face you've forgotten. My name isn't and never was Karen, but I'll be Karen. I'm not petty. See: I've taken off the quote marks.

Karen stood outside the Skylight bookstore in Los Angeles, waiting for her old friend, the author.

She wasn't petty, she has never been petty, has never had enough self-possession, or possessed enough self, to afford pettiness, because petty is a way people are who have something to spare. Still: she'd like to say for the record that the choice of her name, this name Karen to which she's resigned, is not the only thing she can see through. She can see through a lot of the rest of it too, as easily as drawing a line from a column of things on the left to a column of things on the right, making crisscrosses like suture marks stitching the columns together. Remember, from when you were a kid? The column on the left might be pictures and the column on the right might be words but the matching pairs aren't side by side, they're mixed up, and you have to match them. It's not hard. If you knew me—if you knew Karen—or any of them, you could do it. In fact, the scheme is almost too simple—out of respect for the "truth"? From a failure of imagination? Is it better or worse that the code is so easy to crack? Sarah and David are the people they must obviously be, only their names have been altered, and not even altered that much—the new names are in the right spirit, they're true to their objects, in fact they're so apt they're unnecessary, their divergence from the truth is so inconsequential that they might as well be the same truth they've replaced. Mr. Kingsley, too, is the person Mr. Kingsley must obviously be; his new name, too, is in the right spirit. If certain colorful revisions of his character have been undertaken, they don't serve to disguise the historical person, though they do disguise something. That something, however, isn't Karen's to unmask; she's not here to expose without warning. Pammie, unlike Mr. Kingsley, is not a historical person but the way in which Karen's Christianity was found laughable. Julietta is the way in which Karen's Christianity was admired. Joelle is the intimacy between Karen and Sarah, disavowed and relocated onto a historical person very much like Joelle with whom Sarah did not have an actual friendship. Why give the pain of broken friendship to Joelle, why take it away from Karen? The reasons might be psychological. Why make Karen non-Christian, while making her laughable Christianity Pammie, and her admirable Christianity Julietta? The reasons might be artistic. All this is just speculation; Karen isn't the type to pretend to have superior insight into people she knew as a child and then turned her back on and then used as she wished for her personal gain. Not to finger-point. That would be petty.

Karen stands outside the Skylight bookstore in Los Angeles, waiting for her old friend, the author. Karen is thirty years old, the same age as her old friend the author. She hasn't seen her old friend the author since both were eighteen. In the dozen years since, much has happened to Karen. Much of what has happened has been therapy, and the rest of what has happened tends to be described in terms drawn from therapy. This is a tendency of which Karen is aware and about which she isn't apologetic. At least she knows where her language comes from. If, however, Sarah—for example—were to ask what she's been up to the past dozen years, Karen would avoid therapy-speak in her answer as carefully as she used to avoid Jesus-speak. She would do this to be taken seriously by a person devoid of belief. Despite Karen's not just disliking but disrespecting this person devoid of belief, that ancient shame would creep over her belief, her need for belief—her *belief* in belief—like a stain and Karen would, now as in the past, pass herself off as a person who didn't believe. That much hasn't changed. Oh, this and that, she would say. I've mostly worked as an office manager, personal assistant, personal organizer, stuff like that—you probably never knew it in high school but I'm highly organized [laughter]. It's kind of a curse, I can't see something without making it more efficient. I think it's a reaction to my mother [laughter]. But it's nice, in terms of making a living. People hire me to organize their stuff, I can pick and choose my clients, I can set my own hours. It pays well. It leaves me lots of time to travel. My brother and I—I don't know if you remember, I have a brother—just took a trip to Vietnam and Laos. Yeah, it was amazing. Beautiful.

Saying these things, if she says them, Karen will be aware of the deceptively offhand way she puts the most enviable aspects of her life in the foreground. She will be so aware of this effort to cultivate envy, and the effort to conceal the effort, that it's going to be hard to believe Sarah isn't equally aware, despite the ample evidence of Sarah's inability to grasp her, Karen's, feelings. Synonyms for "ample" include "bounteous," "copious," and "plenteous" but not, according to this particular thesaurus, "voluminous," which in *its* entry lists synonyms including "big," "huge," "roomy," "capacious," and . . . "ample." Sometimes synonymousness only travels one way. The dictionary tells us that "voluminous" travels out of the past from the Latin word *voluminosus*, meaning "having many coils," which travels from the Latin word *volumen*, a roll, which, reversing direction again, travels to the Middle Ages to become a word in English, "volume," which means a roll of parchment that's been written on. Anybody can look these things up. A given person's facility with words is not in fact their knack, gift, or talent; it only means they own a thesaurus and a dictionary. The way we were raised—by "we" I mean me and Sarah; by "raised" I mean given the ideas that most mattered to us, and it wasn't our parents who did this but our teachers and friends—talent was the only religion, the only basis for belief that wasn't mocked. Talent was a divine thing embodied in humans and you either had it or you didn't, you were blessed or you weren't. Either way, you worshipped it. If you were blessed with talent, you worshipped it by using it, and no sin was worse than letting talent go to waste. If you weren't blessed with it, you worshipped it by serving the people who had it. You had better be joyful, not jealous. Karen and Sarah, you girls *know* without you we could never do mainstage, you girls are a pair of wardrobe wizards, lucky us that you'll run costume crew! Did Sarah audition for mainstage every year despite having the range of a toad when she sang? Yes, she did. Did Karen audition for mainstage every year, she who soloed with her church choir? Yes, she did. Was either of them ever cast, even in a bit part, even once in four years? No, never. They were permanent members of that mysterious majority, the talented enough to get into the school but not talented enough to serve as its stars. They must serve as the background against which the stars shined. They must feel joyful to do this and never resent it, although admission to the school had seemed like a promise that each passing year was remade and then broken again. Every year one of the seemingly permanent losers was unexpectedly cast in a lead, which both kept hope alive and increased the humiliation. Senior year it was the guy we'll call Norbert. *Norbert.* By then, Karen had returned to her childhood world of dance with a vengeance, though instead of ballet she took modern and pretended to look down her nose at acting. She'd chosen acting as a fourteen-year-old: a mere child, she had chosen an art meant for children. Senior year she was gracious about it, happy to lend a hand with the costumes so that all the Theatre children could have a good time. Of course they should know she'd be studying modern in college. Sarah struck much the same pose, but with writing. Scribble, scribble, scribble went Sad Sarah in her Solemn Notebook. The only difference being that Sarah succeeded, having aimed lower and chosen a talent anybody could fake with the right kind of tools. Try and fake dance: you can't do it. True arts require discipline, they require that you sculpt muscle and bind it to bone. I haven't danced since college because I'm a realist and I understood early enough that I wasn't going to be a professional dancer any more than I was going to be a professional actor, because although I'm really lean I'm too short and too wide. I maybe should have been a swimmer but anyway. Anyway, Karen hasn't danced in a decade, but strangers still see at a glance that she used to dance seriously, they see it in her posture, that's how ingrained she made it, how much work she put in.

The hard work of herself, on the hard muscle and bone of herself. Nobody else's stuff dragged in to make something seem *ample*, *bounteous*, *copious*, *plenteous*, or *voluminous*.

I'd come to the bookstore fully intending to sit down in the audience. I imagined Sarah seeing me, maybe as soon as she stepped to the mic or maybe after she'd already started to read. Either way, I imagined her recognition of me would have the same sort of effect on her voice that bumping into the turntable had when we used to play records. Her needle would jump and then fall back again and she'd pretend to keep going, but there would have been that little break, that flaw in the smoothness. Maybe only she and I would notice, but I didn't need other people to notice, in fact I didn't want other people to notice. I wasn't after some public moment, with the crowd as my tool. When we were children, or students, or whatever we were at the place we'll refer to as CAPA, we were taught that a moment of intimacy had no meaning unless it was part of a show. The ways we liked and hated and envied and bullied and punished each other never seemed satisfyingly real unless Mr. Kingsley put them onstage during Trust Exercises, and he chose very few of our moments. Sarah and David, it should be obvious to anyone, were envied by all of us for the attention they got. In fact, that was their stardom, a different kind of stardom than being cast in a lead but in the long run more potent. Being a legit star at CAPA was a Pollyanna enterprise requiring that you have straight white teeth and be able to sing and to fit a whole set of ideas about life that we were too young at that point to recognize as ideas or as you might say a belief system. Unlike most of us I'd been raised in a religious belief system but even I didn't recognize at that age that CAPA stardom was also a belief system, and not just the way that life was. David and Sarah's different stardom gave the clue to some alternate universe where everything was reversed, and instead of discovery and love and success were distortion, disconnection, and failure. That was the show they starred in. The exercises Mr. Kingsley made them do, it occurred to me many years later, were a kind of pornography. I only meant to say that I decided to not surprise Sarah in front of an audience. I didn't decide this out of kindness to her. I just didn't want to give her the moral high ground.

One more thing, before Karen and Sarah's reunion. In her story, Sarah takes the actual friendship between Sarah and Karen, and turns it into a friendship between Sarah and Joelle. She also takes the actual end of that friendship, and turns it into a show that was watched by their classmates, a Trust Exercise. But it wasn't. The death of our friendship was private. The dying took place at a distance, but at the instant of death we were face-to-face without anyone else. It was my first day back at school after a break. I'd spent the fall and winter of my junior year at a Bible school and I hadn't seen Sarah since early that summer. Sarah had spent the summer in England with her much older lover. She had gotten to do this by driving her mother's car, without her mother's permission, away from a fight with her mother over her mother's refusal to give her permission to travel to England, through a red light and into an oncoming truck, totaling the car and receiving nonfatal but impressive-enough injuries. As soon as she was discharged from the hospital and her passport was ready, she left for England and didn't come back until the day before school started. I knew these details because my mother had given rides to Sarah's mother all summer, to the grocery store and the doctor, because Sarah had totaled the car and Sarah's mother couldn't afford to replace it. Sarah's mother was disabled, which for some reason Sarah's story doesn't mention.

I had gotten to school early my first day back so I could park in the front lot, where there weren't many spaces, because I wanted to avoid everyone I knew and they parked in the back. It was January and the air was actually cold, its dampness was cold, and the cold damp made a haze that in my memory softened the light so that I felt hidden and somehow alone, as if I was actually going to succeed, and get through the first day of school without having to see anybody I knew although it was a small school and all the same people every year and there was no way I'd even get through an hour without seeing them all. But even a few minutes without seeing them all would have made a difference. There were teachers' cars in the front lot but it wasn't half full. My plan was to sit in the smokers' courtyard, which opened off the cafeteria through a set of glass doors, so it wasn't a good place to hide but at least you could see people coming. I knew there was nowhere to hide and the best I could do was to see people coming, but then I pulled open the heavy front door of our school and there was Sarah. She seemed to be coming out. It was seven forty-five in the morning, forty-five minutes before the first bell. There was no one else, no other sound; all the adults were in the main office or locked in their classrooms.

Sarah was wearing some kind of punk outfit that was supposed to look uncaring—punk—but instead shouted effort. The effort of all those months working her bakery job to earn money, the effort of totaling her mother's car to make her mother too frightened to try and control what she did, the effort of crossing the ocean to spend the summer with a much older man, the effort of navigating Carnaby Street and choosing just the right clothes without knowing what any choice meant. The outfit was Doc Martens boots and shredded black fishnets and bleached cutoff jeans and a white, black, and red T-shirt with a spiky-haired guy sneering "Oi!" Her hair was short and she'd drawn thick lines around her eyes. Inside the lines her eyes didn't look larger, as she probably hoped, but sunk in from the rest of her face, like she'd put on a mask. From under her eye-liner mask she saw me, the person she'd most hoped to avoid, just as she was the person I'd most hoped to avoid, so that, thinking and acting the same way, our efforts canceled each other. And right away her gaze went hard with the anger we always feel at the person who spoils our idea of ourself.

I don't know what she saw in my gaze. Her story doesn't show my gaze, or depict it through somebody else, or maybe it does and I'm so self-deluded I don't recognize it. That's possible. What she should have seen was pure accusation, which doesn't take long to transmit. We looked at each other for just long enough. I don't think we stopped walking, me in, and her out, the same door. Everything we'd felt for each other, which had been dying down throughout the summer almost naturally, how a candle's flame slowly dies out when you cut off its air, flared and changed all at once into something else, instead of expiring. But our friendship was over.

KAREN STOOD OUTSIDE the Skylight bookstore in Los Angeles, waiting for her old friend, the author. Her old friend the author had arrived at the bookstore by car about fifteen minutes before, and had stood outside the store in the same spot where Karen was now standing. Her old friend the author had glanced into the store and then glanced at her watch, as if waiting for someone or some-thing, or as if concealing a hesitation by pretending to be waiting for someone or something. Then, as if the someone or something had arrived or the hesitation ended, she went into the store. During this time, Karen watched from a café across the street. At the café, Karen

had also been waiting for someone and something, and also hesitating. She had been waiting for her old friend the author, and for
whatever sensation it would give her to see her old friend the author
again. The sensation had been precise and satisfying. It had been a
sudden pressure on the sternum, a pressure that meant excitement,
and dread, and anticipation, and reluctance, all rolled together, but
with an emphasis on excitement and anticipation. Karen was very
good at parsing and naming her feelings. She'd been practicing this
skill for many years. The sternum-pressure sensation had also been
like hunger, a demand for action, unlike other similar sensations
which despite being similar were completely different, not demands
for action but warnings against it. Karen's hesitation had been waiting for this signal and once she had it her hesitation was over and
she got up and paid for her coffee and crossed the street to go into
the bookstore but before she had done this a new hesitation came
up, the hesitation about sitting in the audience. As already discussed,
Karen had intended to sit in the audience if she went to the reading
at all, but standing in front of the bookstore, looking through the
big windows at the other early arrivals milling around browsing the
shelves, Karen had all those thoughts mentioned above about audiences and power trips and moral high grounds and decided not to
sit in the audience but to stay outside on the sidewalk where she
wouldn't seem out of place because it was lively for an LA sidewalk
as this was one of those rare "walkable" neighborhoods LA is so
proud of. Karen had lived in Los Angeles for a period of several years
which had ended several years ago, but her brother still lived here,
she still wound up here a couple times a year, she still felt at home
here. She was still on her own turf, you might say. Karen had
browsed in this bookstore before but she hadn't bought anything.
She leaned casually against the plate-glass window, cupping her
palms around her eyes to make the inside of the store visible. The
sun was setting, its fiery light pouring from the café side of the
street, painting the solid parts of Skylight Books's storefront gold

while turning the window into a blinding mirror and throwing huge golden rectangles into the store, across the concrete floor and up the bookshelves standing all over the place at artsy angles to each other to form a sort of maze. Karen knew that because of the light behind her she could press her face to the window and be just a dark shape to a person inside. That was an advantage she hadn't expected. She could see, through the maze of bookshelves, to the part of the store where the readings were held. A lectern faced several rows of folding chairs. Some people were starting to sit in the chairs, while others continued to wander. Some of the wanderers pensively held stacks of books they'd already discovered, while others pensively gazed at the slender signs hung on the walls, describing the books that were shelved underneath. Art. Humor. Essays. Reference. Fiction. The words on the signs formed a system implying that people who shopped in the store all agreed what the different words meant. The day before, the day she'd arrived in LA, Karen had gone to a drugstore and among the signs on the aisles describing what each aisle contained—"Hair Care"; "Cough and Cold"; "Cosmetics"—was a sign that read "Personal Intimacy." "Personal Intimacy" was the way certain items were categorized in that drugstore. "Art," "Humor," "Essays," "Reference," and "Fiction" were the ways certain books had been categorized in the bookstore. "An author of fiction" is the way Karen's old friend the author categorizes herself. A category is a way to define, while a definition, according to the dictionary, is a statement of the exact meaning of a word. The dictionary tells us that fiction is literature in the form of prose that describes imaginary events and people, is invention or fabrication, as opposed to fact. The dictionary tells us that the imaginary exists only in the imagination. Logic tells us that what exists only in the imagination does not exist in reality, or actuality, which the thesaurus tells us are the same thing.

After the sun had dipped under the opposite buildings, the inside of the store looked brighter, and Karen could see all the way to the lectern and chairs without standing too close to the glass. Now she stood leaning on the streetlight, again knowing that this way she couldn't be seen from inside, where, finally, a pale thin man with a curtain of hair in his face came to the lectern, spoke briefly, and slumped out of view. Then Sarah came to the lectern. A curtain of hair fell in her face also; her hair was smooth and dark like an expensive piece of furniture. In high school, Karen and Sarah had done everything to their hair they could think of except take care of it. They had bleached it, shaved it, permed it, dyed it, as girls do when vandalizing themselves seems the best way of proving their bodies are theirs. Sarah seemed to have learned that expensive self-care also proved that her body was hers. Every inch of her surface was polished. It couldn't be an accident that her side-parted hair was just slightly too short to remain anchored out of her face every time her right hand, in a demure little movement, tucked it behind her right ear. She tucked; and it fell out, eclipsing her face. She tucked; it fell out. Karen wondered if this tic was as conspicuous to the people inside, who could hear Sarah reading, or if the sound of her voice made the gesture less noticeable.

In time the sound of applause was faintly audible through the glass. Then apparently there were questions. Sarah stopped tilting her head toward the lectern and looked straight at her audience so that the curtain of hair kept itself to one side and didn't need to be tucked anymore. Sarah listened intently, nodded, spoke, and smiled a few times. She looked less self-conscious and pretentious, more relaxed and intelligent. Her smile, which had always been one of her best features, also seemed somehow improved, like her hair. Sarah had one of those faces that, when she wasn't making a particular expression, tended to look preoccupied, worried, or mad. You couldn't know what, if any, thoughts were storming across her brain at any given moment, but a lot of the time it seemed as if you could see them, and that they were hostile. Back in high school certain teachers, the ones with thin skins and quick tempers, had always been telling Sarah to wipe that look off her face, which seemed to startle Sarah or injure her feelings—her eyes would widen and sparkle as if they were wet—so that you wondered if "that look" possibly stood for nothing, not hostile thoughts but no thoughts. When Sarah smiled, all this uncertainty about her thoughts disappeared. But she didn't smile often or at least didn't used to.

After a second burst of applause people started leaving their chairs and milling around again. The pale thin man led Sarah to a table that was covered with a white cloth and tidy stacks of books and Sarah sat down behind the table with a self-conscious attitude of being very closely watched doing this ordinary thing of sitting down and so trying to do it as if she wasn't in fact being watched, which only made her seem more as if she was performing—performing modesty, just as when she kept tucking her hair. Someone handed Sarah a Sharpie and a line formed in front of the table of people who wanted their book to be signed, and Sarah vanished from view behind the line of people awaiting their moment with her. At this point it might make you impatient to hear me change my mind again, but the truth is that after deciding not to sit in the audience I had never decided quite how to approach. I guess I'd thought of her leaving the store the same way she'd gone in, and the two of us there on the sidewalk. The sun had finally gone down, it was night and the sickly orange glow from the streetlight made the sidewalk feel private and maybe too private. I hadn't planted myself in her audience. I hadn't broken the fourth wall for my own satisfaction, but the line was a different arrangement. It promised each person a private encounter, but under the rules of encounters in public. Such as, everyone smiles and nobody runs. All these thoughts made up a lengthy hesitation during which everyone in the bookstore who was also hesitating about getting in line, or who was buying a book before getting in line, had now gotten in line so that when Karen entered the bookstore and got in the line, she was last. For a moment the store's brightness, blinding after the sidewalk's dim glow, made the decision to come inside seem like an error. Often the experience of our simplest perceptions, for example the feeling of blindness that comes from walking into a very bright space after standing for an hour in the dark, leads to an inaccurate thought—I've made a mistake—which leads to a feeling—anxiety—which reinforces the thought. One of Karen's favorite authors, because although Karen doesn't really read fiction, or much of anything that a store like Skylight Books stocks, Karen reads all the time and possesses some real expertise in a handful of favorite subjects, wrote a book that, once Karen had read it, enabled her to analyze her feeling-states as clearly as if they were passing through prisms, that didn't just make them visible but broke them down into all their components. Once you can do that, it's a challenge to not view other people as blind. Previous experience with the condescension of religious belief helps somewhat in correcting overestimations of yourself. Categorizing in ways that make sense from the gut, putting like things with like, helps somewhat, and being able to do that is why Karen's good at her job. While waiting in the line, which was completely made up of people pointed intently at Sarah, people who refused to even glance at each other because they didn't want to believe there might be someone else who had the same special connection with Sarah they'd formed just by reading her book, Karen had plenty of time to get out her own copy of Sarah's book. It still had Karen's bookmark stuck in it at page 131, commemorating the point at which the end had come, in Karen's opinion. If Karen, as the reader will learn, had no problem closing the door on her mother when her mother attempted to visit, Karen certainly had no problem closing the covers on a book that featured her mother but purged Karen in most ways that mattered.

As the line inched forward, a young female employee of the bookstore worked her way back. She handed each person a single Post-it Note, and if needed, a pen. "If you'd like Sarah to sign your book to you, please write your NAME on the Post-it exactly the way that you'd like her to write it, and then please use the Post-it to MARK THE PAGE that you'd like her to sign on. The title page is what most people choose. If you want her to sign just your first name, PLEASE ONLY WRITE YOUR FIRST NAME. If you want her to sign it to somebody else, PLEASE WRITE THEIR NAME. If this is for a birthday or some other occasion, please write BIRTHDAY or whatever the occasion on the Post-it. Thank you! Does anybody need a pen? No, you keep the Post-it. Use it to mark where you want her to sign. That way she can open right to it. It's your choice, but the title page is what most people choose. Does anybody need a pen? Oh, look at you—so organized!" While the time-saving system was being explained over and over again to every single member of the line, Karen had removed a block of Post-its and a pen from her briefcase, written "Karen" on a Post-it, and posted the flag on the edge of the title page. And yes, I used quotes on the Post-it. I wanted Sarah to use them when signing.

"I had my own Post-its," Karen told the employee, who wore a name tag that read "Emily." Emily's strenuous effort to save Sarah perhaps half a minute per signing demonstrated that Emily's own time was worthless to her.

"Ooh, you have the hardcover," Emily said. Karen being the last person in line, there was nobody left who required a Post-it or who needed the system explained. Emily loitered with Karen as by tiny degrees they approached the white table. Karen didn't do anything to encourage this loitering. "I *love* the hardcover design," Emily went on, as if it had been Karen who designed it. "Well," Emily wanted to clarify, "the paperback's really nice too. It's just a gorgeous book inside and out. Have you already read it?"

"I have," Karen said, interpreting the question broadly, without guilt. But there didn't seem to be an easy way to leave it at that. Emily seemed to be hanging on Karen's every word. Emily seemed to intuit some kind of special relationship between Karen and the book, or maybe this was just Karen having another inaccurate thought. "Very closely," Karen added, to make up for a meaning-less half-truth of which Emily would never be aware. This made Karen think about the historical problem she had of tending to try to please other people, even strangers, for less than no reason. She'd always hoped that making this problem historical—acknowledged and documented—would leave it behind in the past, but so far that hadn't worked out.

"Oh, wow!" Emily said, gratified. "A real fan!"

"Oh my God." Sarah's voice, up to now mellifluous and artifi-cial and vague as white noise, abruptly fell into a lower register, as if in the middle of singing inanely, she'd burped. For the second-to-last person in line had turned away, like a curtain pulled aside, reveal-ing Karen. It was the moment Karen had been waiting for, and, distracted by Emily the bookstore employee, she'd missed it. Or rather, she'd missed seeing it. She had heard it. But she'd wanted to see it. She had wanted to see Sarah exposed in a moment of panic. Instead she saw her quickly rising from behind the white table, unleashing the rarely seen dazzling smile. By "dazzling" we mean extremely impressive, beautiful, or skillful, and we also mean so bright as to cause temporary blindness. It's a frequentative of the verb "daze," by which we mean to make someone unable to think or react properly. In high school, the man we're calling Mr. Kings-ley assigned us, as fifteen-year-olds, the song called "Razzle Daz-zle" as the audition piece for our production of *Chicago* (music by John Kander, lyrics by Fred Ebb). Sarah, who never could sing, embarrassed herself at auditions. Karen, who could sing, nailed the song but apparently lacked some other quality required to be cast in the show. "Razzle Dazzle" is a cynical song about getting away with murder. Sarah rose up from behind the white table, dazzling with her rarely seen megawatt smile, and before Karen could step back, Sarah hooked her arm around Karen's shoulders and pulled her in for a hug, with the table between them, while the person named Emily squealed, "I should have known you were an old friend of hers!" Despite being a former dancer with excellent balance, Karen almost lost her footing while this awkward hug, which you'd almost think had been done for that purpose, was happening. Almost losing her footing, Karen was almost unable to think or react properly. She almost felt herself at a disadvantage. But that was an inaccurate thought.

I ALWAYS KNEW I was one of the ones who would leave. Whether it was talent or just willpower, something would get me far from my hometown. How likely you were to leave town after graduation was another way CAPA ranked people. Everyone assumed the stars would leave. Everyone assumed the people in the background would stay. Sarah was the exception to the rule, actually. Sarah was a bad actress, a worse singer, and a nonexistent dancer, but we could tell she would leave, rejected and depressed as she pretended to feel, with her self-destructive habits that were her best stab at acting, and her shredded punk clothes. Our senior year, when she went shrieking down the Theatre hall waving her Brown acceptance letter, no one was surprised. It was when I got my acceptance to Carnegie Mellon that everybody was shocked. But I'd known I was getting out somehow, while so many of the stars who were supposed to, Melanie who'd stood smiling in her own private dream while I crawled around on the floor buttoning her *My Fair Lady* shoes with a hook, or Lukas who'd thrown his *Music Man* shirt on the dressing room floor every night because he knew I'd pick it up and iron it, ended up boomerangs. The farther they hurled themselves out, the more quickly they landed back where they'd begun.

I wasn't a star dancer at Carnegie Mellon, but when I gave up dance I didn't run home, I did the opposite. I went to New York anyway, just when all our classmates who'd gone to NYU and even Juilliard were leaving. New York was "too hard, too expensive, too lonely," but I'd never expected New York would be easy or cheap or a place I'd have friends. I'd never been a star and I didn't expect to be treated like one. I did well in New York. I had a job, I had a place to live on my own. And then one night I opened the door of my apartment and there was my mother, in a brand-new ankle-length faux-fur coat that some man had bought her to keep her southern self warm in the cold New York weather. She'd gotten some man to get her to New York and she was grinning like a naughty little girl at how clever she was, actually hopping up and down on my doormat. I left immediately and moved to LA, where my brother was finishing school. It took our mother three years to unhook from the man from New York and rehook to a man from LA; by the time she caught up, an unexpected change had come over me. I wanted to go home. I loved it and missed it. I'd only wanted to leave in the first place because my mother lived there, and she no longer did. So I told her in no uncertain terms what would happen if she followed me again, and told my brother to do the same thing, but he couldn't. My mother had always forgotten about him, raising him with the sort of benign neglect that left him wanting more of her instead of realizing she was a toxin. My mother and brother still live in LA, while I live in the city all three of us think of as home. When I visit my brother, he doesn't tell our mother I'm coming. When he visits me, he doesn't tell her he's going. He pretends that he's traveling on business. And though I'm sad that this saddens my brother, what would happen if my mother had contact with me would be worse than his sadness, and both of them know this.

After I moved home, I often ran into the person we've been calling David. His boomerang flight had been longer than Melanie's, shorter than mine. He'd been back in our town for two years. He'd started a theatre company which put on the darkest, most disturbing plays David could think of in the same sorts of places where we'd gone to hear music in high school, the rusty ice houses or the abandoned warehouses or the seedy dance clubs. David had failed at acting at Northwestern and he'd switched to playwriting and failed at that because he never finished the plays he started and he'd switched to directing and turned out to be very good at it. People came to see the plays he put on, despite their being dark and disturbing and staged in weird inconvenient locations. The person whom we're calling Mr. Kingsley became a regular audience member, and then a regular donor, and then, as David's company started getting its shit together and applying for nonprofit status and grants, even a member of the advisory board. When you saw Mr. Kingsley and David standing around at one of David's fund-raisers, Mr. Kingsley drinking whatever red wine was on hand from a clear plastic cup, David drinking whatever showily cheap "blue-collar" beer was on hand from a can, the two of them talking intently as if they were completely alone in the loud, crowded room about whatever dark and disturbing play David was currently staging, you saw two members of the same Elite Brotherhood of the Arts.

Mr. Kingsley, when we were his students, never explained this Elite Brotherhood in the way that he was constantly explaining the idea of stardom, through everything he tried to teach us, and all the ways we didn't measure up. The idea of stardom, of honing your talent and unleashing it on the world, organized everything that we did—but what he never told us was that the Elite Brotherhood of the Arts organized the stardom. Mr. Kingsley was clearly a member. And now David was clearly a member. That was strange and even funny only if you stood apart and noticed that it *was* a brotherhood, with membership and rules, and not a God-given Order of Things. During the period when David's company got its shit together to apply for nonprofit status and grants, Karen lent them her organizational skill set, in case this hasn't already been guessed. She was the getter-together of the company's shit, though she never sought credit or even a paycheck. She was happy to make that contribution to David's success. So few of their peers had succeeded, so few had found stardom—but of all people, cynical David had made a place, right there in their hometown, for surviving ambition. Now the Theatre kids went straight from CAPA graduation to David's auditions, and Mr. Kingsley employed David as a "visiting artist" to teach the "master class" in directing. Karen donated her evenings and weekends to the company's "office" and "books" and its near fatal, before she intervened, unpaid-tax fiasco. David, in gratitude to her, insisted she come to a fund-raising gala, at which he dragged her over to Mr. Kingsley, who beamed and nodded and chitchatted with her while gracefully if not successfully trying to hide the fact that he had no idea who she was.

Karen was content, she told David, with having given up performing. She was just as content as he was. But David, perhaps because over the years he'd developed a sort of ardent artistic flattery as the only currency with which he could pay all the people he owed money to, refused to believe this. "Come on," he said. "You got into Carnegie Mellon. Unlike me you can actually sing. You can fucking tap-dance."

"I'm an awful tap dancer." This was true. The limitations of body type, mentioned above, made tap dancing an imperfect fit. In tap as in ballet you want lanky; only modern can accommodate the dancer who's built like a swimmer.

"For fuck's sake, only a tap dancer says, 'I'm an awful tap dancer.' You were good. Remember when we all had to sing 'Razzle Dazzle'? You killed."

"He didn't cast me."

"He never cast me either."

"And now you're a director and I'm your accountant. All is as it should be. You don't have to tell me I'm an undiscovered star just because you can't pay me."

"You had a dark energy onstage—don't roll your eyes! I remember. You didn't have a stupid Mentos smile."

"Stop."

"From the point of view of directing I can't fucking believe the deficit of talent in our class. Of course our estimation of our talent was completely overblown, but even if you adjust for that, we had a deficit. If you look at the school over time, there's only one person in its entire history who's ever become a global celebrity, and she went to the school for less than three weeks so we can't really claim her. But there's the handful of people who have been on a billboard over Sunset Boulevard once or twice in their careers, and we've produced one of those let's say twice every decade. Then there are the people who've managed to pay the bills as working actors— sometimes you see them on TV although they never break out. There's one of those maybe every two years. Then there's the people who should have made it at least as far as getting regular work, but they had shitty luck. There's a few of that type every year and I cast them in my stuff, all the better for me. But our class had *no one* even in that final category—except you."

"You're putting me in the shitty-luck category? I'd rather be in the talentless category."

"Come to auditions next week. Come on. Why the fuck not?"

I might have given a dry bark of laughter, or made a wry face, by which I would have meant, You're ridiculous, or I'm ridiculous, and either way I'm not taking this seriously. I would have shoved off the barstool unhurriedly, paid my tab, said good night. In high school, despite being members of the same graduating theatre class, David and I had never been friendly. Our shared connection to Sarah was more like a wedge than a bridge. But now that we both lived in our hometown again, conversations like this happened often between us. David was obsessed with the past, and not just certain parts of it. All of us, I think it's fair to say, fixate on things from our past, maybe wanting them back the way they were, maybe wanting to go back and change them. Either way, this fixation on parts of the past seems pretty common. David took the tendency to an extreme. The *whole* of his past obsessed him. The past was like the country he was exiled from, and any vestige of it, even me, was fascinating to him. David seemed to have decided, very early in life, that the best of his life was already behind him, and all his present achievements with his theatre company interested him only because they gave him a connection to his past. I interested him only because I gave him a connection to his past. I gave him the opportunity to talk about his past, even parts of his past that hadn't interested him at the time but that interested him now. And so he would remind himself of this or that thing I'd done, or talk about my unacknowledged talent, because it gave him the thing he most craved: a doorway, however indirect, to his past. He would have done it with anyone out of his past. In fact, he did. I often heard him engaged in the same sorts of conversations with other relics of those years who had rotated back into town.

These conversations about the past always happened at a bar we called The Bar—everyone called it The Bar—although it had a proper name. Our town had plenty of bars, so there wasn't an obvious reason this comfortable but ordinary bar would be known as The Bar. It wasn't a place we had gone to in high school, although it had existed then, giving off the same vibe of friendly, predictable after-work watering hole it gave off now, the difference being that then this vibe seemed inappropriately dull and now it seemed appropriately dull. In this one way, at least, David had broken with the past. It was The Bar, not one of the bars he'd drunk at in the past, where he liked to sit around and talk about the past.

Unlike David, I spent very little time at The Bar. To be clear, I spent very little time with David. The volunteer grant-writing, the tax-fiasco fixing, the dropping in once in a while to a gala to not be recognized by Mr. Kingsley, the conversations about my unacknowledged talent at the bar of The Bar, were things that happened maybe every couple months and made up a tiny fraction of my life. Most of my time I spent working for clients who paid me, or working on the house I'd bought. I also went to therapy, and started training as a therapist. I didn't drink. I'd never drunk much and then there was a time in my life when I eliminated things, some because I couldn't tolerate them, and some because I didn't require them, and drinking was a thing that I didn't require. I called my brother most nights to check in, and often ate my dinner while I listened to him talk. I sometimes watched a movie. I read a lot: History and Self-help are my categories. I've always liked being alone.

Some nights, though, I liked the thought of being with people, and then I'd drive to The Bar, usually with a book, although I rarely got to read it, because David was usually there. We almost always had some actual business, some organizational task I was helping him with, that would cause him to turn from whoever he'd been drinking with. David always had someone to drink with, often a small crowd. There was usually a woman riveting her attention to David like she thought there would be a quiz later, there were usually members of the theatre crowd and members of the broader arts crowd and members of the even broader drinking crowd, orbiting David, placing him at the center of things. Even when David was alone at the bar of The Bar, as he sometimes was because he'd gone into a State that held people off just as effectively as if he were swinging a spiked club around, he was still at the center of things. By which I mean that even when he pushed people away they kept their eyes on him, from the far side of the room, anxious to find a way back to his side, to regain his attention. When we were young, David had clumsy charisma; he knew he was attractive, but he didn't know in what way or why. More than a decade of dedicated self-abuse had ruined his looks and when he was tired or drunk, his face looked like a ball of molding clay that had been thrown against a wall. Yet his charisma, which you could no longer confuse with his looks, was more noticeable. It almost seemed independent of him. The physical David would sit slumped at the bar staring into his glass while his charisma stalked the room, pushing some people away, pulling some people close. Karen was always pulled close, on account of her usefulness to him as a loyal unpaid employee and her status as Link to the Past.

Tonight, then—a night in late January, many months before Karen's reunion with Sarah at the Skylight bookstore—David is seated alone at the bar, in a funk, when Karen enters wearing her jean jacket buttoned all the way up, a tasselled scarf wound several times around her neck, a pair of gloves, and a hat pulled low over her ears. It's as cold as it gets in their town, which is plenty cold for Karen, who hates to admit that she never got used to the cold in New York, but whimpered beneath its onslaught just like her mother, except without her mother's ankle-length faux-fur coat. From outside, as she hauls on the frigid door handle, Karen can't see The Bar's interior, only the glow of its lights, through the big windows which usually put the people at the bar of The Bar on display to the sidewalk outside, but which this night are frosted with condensation. But Karen isn't surprised, on entering, to find David immediately inside the door, on the right-most barstool, his usual place. When David isn't in rehearsal, he sometimes occupies this stool from three or four in the afternoon until two or three in the morning. It's David who takes an extra beat to notice Karen, maybe because of the hat and the scarf. As she pulls these off and steps up to the bar to order a Coke, David sees her. "The fuck," he says. "I was just thinking of you. Remember Martin?"

Karen finds this an interesting, excellent question. Like all her favorite questions it seems so simple and obvious that for David to have asked her seems idiotic at first. Does she *remember* Martin? But now the different layers of the question start to peel apart. Remember in what exact way? The dictionary tells us that "remember" means "to call something to mind, recall something forgotten." Well, Karen has never forgotten Martin, so in this sense she doesn't remember him. The dictionary also tells us that to remember is to keep something in memory. Without going down the rabbit hole and looking up "memory," let's give this one a check mark: yes, she does keep this something in memory. We also have, in this particular definition, "keep somebody in mind"—yes—"give somebody a gift"—you might say so, depending on "gift"—"send somebody greetings"—not lately—"commemorate somebody or something." Commemorate: remember something *ceremonially.* This meaning is suddenly very appealing. It sticks in Karen's mind, the way a lot of things do. David, who has his own share of problems, one of which is being too smart for every situation he puts himself in—he is too smart for his work life, his sex life, and definitely his life as a drunk, which takes up the biggest part of his time—would probably enjoy this little lecture on the meanings of "remember," but Karen wouldn't enjoy giving it, so she only says, "Sure, I remember Martin."

"Check this out," David says, and lays a news clipping flat on the bar. *Bourne Courier-Telegraph*, October 4, 1997: "Top Teacher Dismissed Amid Allegations." Beneath the headline are two short columns of print and one short column of a black-and-white photograph of a man with a narrow ferrety face, light hair fringing over his eyes and his ears, a narrow gap between his teeth, oversize glasses that weren't fashionable even ten years ago, a jacket and tie that he probably borrowed and that don't really fit. Even without the benefit of color you can tell that his skin is too white and his teeth are too yellow. The photo looks more out-of-date than it is, the way official photographs—Karen supposes this is the yearbook photo, the "Our Faculty" wall-of-the-main-office photo—never look like the day they were taken but like the day when their dingy backdrop first began to be coated with decades of dust. The man, of course, is the man we're here calling Martin. He looks just like and not at all like the Martin that Karen remembers. Karen can't even tell, staring at the dated photograph, whether the Martin it shows is older or younger than the Martin she knew. The Martin of the photo and the Martin Karen "keeps in memory" look exactly the same, and at the same time they look totally different. Now

Karen can no longer tell them apart. She wonders whether she does remember Martin at all, or whether she just made him up, looking down sightlessly at the utterly weird, unrecognizable photo that looks exactly like Martin. She's been staring so long at the photo that when David asks, "Are you done?" she doesn't realize he means finished reading the words. The words she has not even started.

"I'm done," she says, meaning something different than what David's asking. He picks up the clipping and puts it away. His fingers seem to be trembling. He seems to be having difficulty, now that the clipping is safely away, lighting a fresh cigarette. David is completely freaked out, which is the flip side of being a jaded unshockable guy; it's the soft inner lining his jaded unshockable costume is meant to conceal. Undetected by him, Karen puts on David's jaded unshockable costume. She's going to have to get the article at the library: she's careful to remember, to "keep in memory," the name *Bourne Courier-Telegraph*. She's going to have to pore over the article later, however much she would like to pore over it now. But she doesn't need to pore over it now to have the basic idea. She has that already.

"Where did you get that?" she asks.

"From Jim," David says, by which he means Mr. Kingsley. So freaked out is David he doesn't even remember that this business of calling the person we're calling Mr. Kingsley a chummy first name, for our purposes "Jim," is only for the Elite Brotherhood. "But first I got this letter from Martin," David says. David's urgently waving the bartender over, he's so desperate for fortification to get this explained, to the point of not even realizing what's happened to Karen. He doesn't notice his jaded unshockable costume slip off Karen, at this mention of getting a letter from Martin. He doesn't see Karen yank the thing back into place, and so misses the chance to tempt her to confess that when she moved back to town, although she swore to herself not to do it, she finally drove to the house of her childhood and knocked on the door, because some crazy part of herself imagined, a long time after it was expected, a letter from England arriving there for her, but—thankfully no one was home at her childhood home, and she never went back.

Unlike Karen, David had never expected to hear from Martin again. David hadn't spent much time with Martin for those two months, fourteen years ago. They'd never been in touch after Martin and the others had left. But Martin, in his letter, seemed to know all about David's success. Maybe Martin had actually heard about David somehow, and been reminded he knew him. Or maybe he'd remembered David, and for whatever reason decided to look him up and see if he'd made something of himself. You couldn't tell from the letter, which he'd sent to the company's post office box.

"Do you have the letter with you?" Karen asks, interrupting David's lengthy dissertation on the letter from Martin, in a possibly over-sharp tone. Karen would much rather see this letter herself, hold the thing in her hands, than hear David describe it. But of course David has misplaced the letter already. It doesn't matter, he reminds Karen in response to her outright annoyance. He remembers its words perfectly. When David and Karen were in high school, David tortured his classmates with recitations of the skits of Monty Python and the songs of Bob Dylan. He's always had a flawless memory for words that coexists in some way with a totally fragmented grasp of his life. This is a psychological or neurological phenomenon that perhaps has a name Karen might someday know if she goes into clinical practice.

"He congratulated me on everything with the company," David says. "He was really nice about it. It seems like he'd looked up reviews. And then he said, 'It's about bloody time someone shook things up in that starchy little burg you call home. I was sorry that it couldn't be *Candide* but I'm delighted it's you! Give the righteous moralizers a smack—you might knock their eyes open.' And then he said, 'Perhaps you've heard I have some troubles of my own with the morality crowd. It's the usual thing—if they can't find immorality to scold they make it up and it works just as well.' Then he talked about how he'd finally found the time to finish writing a play, and made arrangements to stage it, both directing and playing a principal role, but then 'here came this witch hunt in which, most regrettably, I am the witch.' And then he pretty much asked me if I'd stage his play. The one he's had to cancel."

Not understanding what "morality troubles" and "witch hunt" might mean, David had, first, forgotten about the letter for a few days while he dealt with his own theatre projects and created and recovered from hangovers. Then he saw Mr. Kingsley at a meeting or somewhere and asked him what he knew these days about Martin. Mr. Kingsley made a face—the sort of face a nun makes when the doings of the wicked are too regrettable to even discuss. Sitting at The Bar with Karen, his palm lying on top of the envelope in which he's put the article that Karen wants to keep looking at but will not admit wanting to look at, David makes his version of the face, which reminds Karen that David didn't fail at acting because he didn't know how. At least he can put on a face. Drunk as he is—or maybe because he's so drunk—he does a very good nun. A face hung on a hook and dragged low by a weight—the weight of wickedness that's too regrettable to even discuss. Mr. Kingsley had declined to discuss it. He'd made the face, and a couple days later—today—he'd dropped the news clipping by David's office. But who are the wicked Mr. Kingsley declined to discuss? Are they Martin, or Martin's accusers?

Although she's not known for promiscuity or a sense of humor—in fact, people probably think she's both celibate and unfunny—Karen often points out in certain public situations that she has never slept with David. Let's say Karen happens to be at The Bar the same night as some person from David's broadest circle, aka his drinking circle, whom she has never met and doesn't want to meet because she and this person have nothing in common. In such situations David without fail will insist upon introducing Karen to this random drunkard of his vaguest acquaintance. David without fail will describe Karen using such hyperbolic phrases as "one of my oldest friends in the world" or "goes back further than anyone" or "knows where all my skeletons are buried." Karen without fail will quip, "I'm the only woman in this bar who hasn't slept with him," or, "I'm the only woman he's ever known for more than a week who hasn't slept with him," or, most impactfully, "I'm the only woman in this town/county/greater metropolitan region who hasn't slept with him." David without fail winces visibly when she says this. It's as if his reputation as a guy who's irresistible to women—except Karen—is somehow undeserved, or unpleasant to him. Karen has never understood David's relationship to his sexuality, which like his charisma seems to stalk the world independent of David's intentions, doing whatever it wants. And Karen herself, whenever she makes the comment, without fail also winces, but on the inside, because the comment is compulsive and she never means to make it and wishes she didn't. It possibly suggests sour grapes, as if she wants to sleep with David, when she doesn't. Or it possibly seems mean-spirited or superior toward other women. And however it seems, it is unnecessary. Yet she always says it, always wincing; and David always gives her the opportunity to say it, always wincing. Why? What compels them?

Until the night David showed her the clipping, Karen would have said that David always introduced her because of his obsession with his past. And she would have said that she always made the comment because she was annoyed by his obsession with his past. But on the night of the newspaper clipping, Karen wondered whether the whole thing had to do not with the past, the thing David always brought up, but with sex, the thing Karen always brought up. Maybe Karen's insistence that she had nothing to do with David's sex life meant that Karen, in fact, had some ax to grind about David's sex life, its epic quality discussed by everyone, as if David were the star of some hit TV show that

Karen had been watching for decades with no option of turning it off.

That night at The Bar, as they began to talk about the "witch hunt" against Martin, it didn't take long for Karen to suspect that David wasn't shaken by the thought of Martin being a predator. Rather David seemed shaken by the thought of women lying about Martin, a person whom David, all these years later, viewed as a role model and sort of spiritual colleague, an example of how David thought a working theatre artist should be. In the fourteen years since David and Karen had seen him, Martin had remained teaching at the same school. He'd remained that irreverent, exemplary teacher, always winning the awards and always almost getting fired. He'd remained the guy students called "the biggest influence on my life" or "the only person at that school who *connected* with kids" or other such hyperbole. He'd taken his students not just to CAPA that long-ago time, but all over the world, offered them opportunities they'd never imagined, broadened their horizons, taught them to believe in themselves, and so on. All this information came out of the article, which David seemed to view not as one possible version of a possibly unknowable reality but as a simple window onto the life of someone David barely knew, whose past magically touched upon his—in other words, a sacred person. Karen knew David had always viewed the cancellation of *Candide* as proof of the hypocrisy—or, to use Martin's word, "starchiness"—of this "little burg" David and Karen call home. Karen further guessed the cancellation of *Candide* had played its role, alongside Beckett and Northwestern, in the way David viewed himself now: theatre rebel, proud discomfiter of paying audiences. Martin having paved the way, the article must seem to David like evidence of a world gone mad, in which the vengefully lying were rewarded and the truth-telling teacher and artist destroyed.

"Do you not believe he slept with his students?" Karen finally asked. Karen had realized there was nothing she could say, at this moment, that wouldn't shred the jaded unshockable costume she was still somehow wearing, that wouldn't shred it into rubbery strips. At moments like these, a most useful technique is to ask the other person a question. It shouldn't be a leading question, but Karen's question, we admit, had some slant. All we can say is, the room had some slant. I was trying to stay on my barstool. I was trying to remain an old, dear friend of David's.

"I'm sure he slept with his students. I'm sure *they* slept with *him*. They knew what they were doing! *We* knew what we were doing. Remember what we were like?"

"We were children," Karen said carefully, as if it were David who ought to be handled with care, David who might be injured by the conversation. But apparently, despite taking precautions, Karen still caused offense. David gave a scornful laugh.

"We were never *children*," he said.

THE ATTENTIVE READER might wonder, What ever happened to Manuel? Will Karen reveal his fate to us? I wondered this myself. After reading what I read of Sarah's book, before seeing her at the Skylight bookstore, I went to my bookshelf and pulled down my high school yearbooks. Yes, reader, I kept them. They were quality items, those yearbooks. Their title was *Spotlight!* With the exclamation. It is not without care that I turned the stiff, glossy pages. Few inscriptions marred the endpapers. What effusions the few did contain didn't reveal anything unexpected. No writer had claimed space with a colored Flair pen who did not find the yearbook's owner "a sweet girl," "so nice!" destined to other than an "awesome future." Turn the page, then; pass the frontispiece of none other than David glancing over his shoulder, wearing the last of his hair and a Mao jacket. Pass through Administration with a pang; those office ladies took more care of you than your own mother did. Pass through Dance and Music (Instrumental and Vocal), through the Winter Ballet and The Jazz Ensemble Takes Manhattan! Theatre is the headliner here. It not only comes last but has the most pages. Study them all: four classes of Theatre students each year for four years, and there's still the strong chance that "Manuel's" DNA includes chromosomes from another department. We're seeking the fate of Manuel in his various origins, for though I won't claim there was no Manuel, I guarantee there was no *one* Manuel. Of clear sources I count at least three.

The first Manuel was a Theatre student, "Hispanic" as the forms say, who lacked all discernible talent. No more could C. act than dance, no more sing than drive nails into wood. He could not even glue feathers onto a hat. What was he doing there? It isn't my puzzle to solve, but whatever the reason, it didn't expire. C. was our classmate all four years. He departed as he came, unremarkably. He neither achieved prominence nor prematurely disappeared. Although he never had a girlfriend or boyfriend while we were in school, last I heard he'd gotten married, gone into business, had a couple of kids, and was doing just fine.

The second Manuel was a Vocal Music student, also "Hispanic" as the forms say, whose name you may know if you listen to opera. He is one of the school's biggest success stories, and his voice, like Manuel's in the surprising audition, truly conjures the ranks of the angels. He never came out as gay while at our school but he certainly is. However, P.'s talent wasn't discovered at our school but years earlier in his childhood. Nor was he a protégé—or more—of Mr. Kingsley's. P. was the pride of the Vocal department, so consistently booked in professional opera from the age of thirteen that he never even deigned to audition for the school mainstage. He continued from our school to Eastman, and a stellar career. I saw him perform once, as Sharpless in *Madama Butterfly*, when I lived in New York. Afterward I briefly considered waiting for him at the stage door with the handful of starry-eyed others all cradling bouquets. But I had no claim on him. I'd known of him but he'd never known me. I decided against and went home.

The third Manuel is not a person but an observation. Is not a salient aspect of this character his special relationship with Mr. Kingsley? Does not this relationship so anger Sarah that she inflicts an unspeakable wound, a strange sort of revenge?

The attentive reader might also wonder, What did Karen know about Sarah's strange act of revenge? Again, I wondered this myself. Had I seen things I'd not understood? Had I known things I'd somehow forgotten? To the first question, Doubtful. To the second, No way. I never forget anything. But Sarah's reconstruction in her book of the lighting and set and backdrop were so true to my memories, I kept blaming myself that the action seemed unfamiliar. How completely Sarah transported me back to that costume shop, with its overtaxed garment racks poorly divided by signs made of wilting shirt cardboards. The iron, the ironing board, the hats left on the floor. Yes, exactly. All that, just like that. Enough to make me think the unfamiliar action must be equally true and I just hadn't noticed. But no: no one inexplicably disappeared from our theatre class—except me. And no one had a very special, perhaps too special, perhaps so special as to unleash in Sarah a thirst for revenge, relationship with the man we've agreed to call Mr. Kingsley—except Sarah.

But you've heard all about that very special relationship already. Or have you?

Two terms my therapist used that I liked, among many, were "projection" and "restraining force." I liked those terms because they were so concrete in the therapy context and so broad in the context of life. Projection: even if you don't do therapy yourself, you'll agree that for all its bad rap, projection is creative. It puts something, or rather someone, out there, that person supposedly having those feelings that are actually yours. While restraining force is creation's true opposite, not destruction but creation's cancellation. Not-thinking, not-feeling, not-doing. Projection or Restraining Force: Something or Nothing. The bald lie, or the stark truth that never gets told. There is no Manuel, or there are several. Sarah did nothing like that, or she did everything, even things she attributes to others. Karen knew nothing, or she knew everything but the form that the story now takes. Sarah tells this story to reveal a hidden truth—or to hide the truth under a plausible falsehood, scrambling history unrecognizable with the logic of dream.

Does Sarah think the story makes her out as a good or bad person? Looked at one way, she's a selfish, hurtful bitch. Looked at another, she might imagine she's rescuing someone.

But the truth or falsehood of Sarah's story, the purity or taint of her motives for being truthful or false—these aren't ours to determine or speculate on. We apologize for the digression.

NOT LONG AFTER that night at The Bar with David, Karen went to the main branch of the public library and obtained her own copy of the article in the *Bourne Courier-Telegraph*. After reading it she found her belief in Martin's guilt completely vindicated. Strangely, she could also grasp how David's belief in Martin's innocence might be completely vindicated. The article was one of those that used a local controversy to investigate the broader "culture wars." At the well-regarded high school in Bourne, Martin had won teaching awards year after year for his theatre program while also fending off rumors that he engaged in "behavior unbefitting an instructor." None of the rumors had ever been proved. Receptivity to them seemed to vary according to one's view of the utility of arts education. Conservative parents who viewed the theatre program as so much time-wasting twaddle called for investigation and accused the school's principal, an arts champion, of shielding a sex criminal. Progressive parents who viewed arts funding as being under siege called for the defense of Martin and the denunciation of a witch hunt in which, most regrettably, he was the witch. The difficulty of knowing which side had it right was made worse by the students, who almost always declined to speak out and the rare times they did, disagreed with each other. Finally, the previous year, a sixteen-year-old Theatre student at the school had told her parents that she and Martin shared a loving and consensual sexual relationship and that she was expecting his child. Martin denied being other than the girl's instructor. The girl's parents hired lawyers and demanded that Martin submit to paternity tests. Martin refused and was fired—but not charged with a crime, as the student retracted her claim. While the age of consent in the UK has been sixteen since the late nineteenth century, the article said, it is an offense for any person aged eighteen or older and who holds a position of trust (for example, a teacher) to engage in sexual activity with a person aged eighteen or under, as such activity abuses the position of trust. The school, perhaps in penance for its prior inaction, put out the word through alumni networks that it was seeking other victims of Martin's alleged abuse. Lest this sound too judgmental, the article concluded with a quote from a theatre colleague of Martin's: "Here's a person of incredible talent who's devoted his life to the teaching profession, and this is what he gets: fired from his job, his reputation destroyed, all on the basis of hearsay. And you wonder why talented people won't teach."

Not long after reading the article, Karen obtained a copy of Martin's play, which he had been hoping to produce, star in, and direct, until his witch hunt interfered, and she read it with the same interest she'd brought to the newspaper story. She got the copy of the play from David. David, after being shaken and shocked by the news about Martin, and then affronted and outraged, had turned finally sardonic and crusading. The sardonic crusading took the opposite form of the shocked shakenness, which played out at The Bar, an ideal location for sitting, drinking, and scolding the world for being "fucking insane." The sardonic crusading played out on the stage of David's theatre. This progression, from being shocked on a barstool to crusading onstage, was in fact David's cycle, the way his wheel always turned. First, David would passively suffer his shock. Then after a certain point, as if the suffering charged him with power, David would unleash a crusade to shock others, and make them suffer in turn. Then, exhausted or remorseful or both—because he always, in his crusading phase, attacked people and made them upset—David would feel shocked again and passively suffer. Rinse, wring, repeat. If I ever actually become a therapist, and David ever has money, I'd like to treat him. He interests me. He interests everyone, which is more than you can say about most people. I once heard an intoxicated commentator at The Bar opine that David did well with women because he was so unpredictable, but this was a drunk person's observation. David is completely predictable. Half the time he's in a funk and half the time he's ferociously active. Half the time he suffers and half the time he causes suffering. I'll leave it to a mental health professional as to whether this is textbook bipolar disorder or something more nuanced but for our purposes you only need to know that David's sardonicism—a real word, look it up—about the treatment of Martin led to his crusade to put on Martin's play. David recovered the letter Martin had sent him, mashed onto the floor mats of his car or in his bedsheets or underneath his coffee maker. He wrote to Martin fulminating against the idiocy and insanity of the world and asking for a copy of the play. You can easily believe that when Martin got this letter, he was gratified. So began a transatlantic correspondence between these long-separated members of the Elite Brotherhood of the Arts.

Karen was in David's office on the day the play arrived in the mail. You could say that she'd been staking out that play, stalking it, the same way she'd been keeping herself abreast of all the David/Martin developments: David's shock evolving into his crusade, David's recovery of the letter, etc. Karen had kept herself abreast by making herself indispensable to David, which was always very easy to do. David always needed some administrative favor and was always quick to accept someone's help, without asking why that person would offer. David, I believe, suffered from low self-esteem yet never had any difficulty believing in the singular importance of his work. This is a distinguishing trait of members of the Elite Brotherhood of the Arts. David also had no difficulty believing that this belief—in the singular importance of his work—was shared by others. When proposing to dedicate hours of your life to some project of David's, you were never in danger of David asking why you wanted to do that. David had recently relocated his office due to an unfortunate misunderstanding of the fire code, and Karen offered to unpack and overhaul his filing system, which she herself had created several years earlier, but which no one had ever maintained. In this way Karen was able to keep herself abreast of the David/Martin correspondence, and to read Martin's play, at her leisure. There were no surprises in the correspondence but there were some surprises, at least to Karen, in the play.

The first surprise was that the play was good. At least, to Karen the play seemed to be good. She's never claimed to be an expert on plays. But she read through it quickly. That seemed like a sign of a good play. Also, how much she thought about it afterward seemed like a sign of a good play. The play had startled her, yet seemed strangely familiar. That was the second surprise, that the events of the play seemed so familiar, as if they had happened to Karen—but in a different life, a life she hadn't known she'd lived, so that the play was a sort of dream-version, all jumbled but retaining some reminder, like a smell or a stain.

The play was set in a pub, and though it was full of English people drinking English drinks and saying English-sounding things, the setting might have been The Bar. It was the same sort of every-night place. The owner and bartender, "Doc"—the character Martin intended to play—is a taciturn figure. In the opening scene, the patrons argue about an acquaintance who's drunk himself to death, and whether this should count as suicide. The patrons try to get Doc to weigh in but he won't. Then a girl enters, seeming to want a handout. She's dirty and sexless—the audience should even think that she might be a boy—and also small and frail-looking. In spite of that, her arrival gets Doc riled up. For the first time, he says more than a couple of words. He yells at the girl, and kicks her out. Everybody else is uncomfortable but gradually things get back to normal, and the argument resumes. The scene ends.

Then come a lot of scenes about Doc and his patrons illustrating social ills and moral conundrums. They are well done if in no way original. Karen read these with absorption but felt no need to reach for the Post-its. Hence I'll skip to the almost-last scene.

The bar is dark and deserted, closed for the night. A clock shows that it's four in the morning. But then we hear a key turn, and Doc enters. And, surprise, with him is the Girl. Before, it seemed as though they were no more than enemy acquaintances, business owner and street hustler. Now it's clear they're something more. In the dramatis personae, neither character is given an age. Doc is described as "past his prime; a different life might have left him less stooped, less scowling." The Girl is described as someone who, "however long she lives, will never cease to look the waif." She is supposed to be indistinguishable from a boy in her dirty jeans and T-shirt, which means she's breastless and hipless, but does that make her ten, twelve, or twenty? The Girl sits at the bar while Doc moves around behind the bar and in and out a door through which we now see a pathetic back room, all peeling linoleum, bare lightbulb, and cot. This is apparently where Doc lives. Doc puts a plate of food in front of the Girl, and she eats. They seem to pick up a conversation from where they left off. Doc is angry at the Girl for how she lives. The audience should realize that concern, not accusation, was the subtext of his yelling at her earlier. The Girl says Doc might as well be angry with himself. Doc says, "We all make our own choices." The Girl says, "Do we?" Doc says, "We do when we can but you know that I can't." The Girl says she can't make Doc's choices either; no one can make another person's choices. Here Doc "collapses; whether physically, morally, or both" (to quote stage directions). It's a moment of reckoning—but for what? "Don't you see?" Doc says to the Girl. "Don't you see that I'm trying to repay you?" "Selfishly, as always," says the Girl. "Please, baby," Doc says. "Please do this for me." No blocking is provided, but the Girl apparently finishes her food and stands up. Doc apparently comes around from the back of the bar, or the Girl goes around from the front, because Doc "seizes the Girl in a violent embrace" (to quote stage directions). Is Doc the Girl's father, or lover, or both? The play doesn't answer these questions of Karen's.

Doc and the Girl exit to the back room, the door shutting behind them.

A shot rings out, offstage.

The Girl comes out from the back room and exits.

But the play isn't over. The lights come up one last time. It's a memorial. The bar is draped in black bunting, and there's a framed picture of Doc, and a vase of wilting flowers. All the same patrons, all wearing cheap-looking jackets and ties, are sitting around drinking and talking, just as in scene one, but now the suicide they're debating is Doc's. They all have different theories about why he did it, and make different pompous statements about the meaning of life. Suddenly, silence. The Girl has entered. She's better dressed, in clothes appropriate for church, although they look secondhand and don't fit. Despite her changed appearance, her evident intention of paying respects, all the patrons attack her. "Get outta here, you little whore!" and "Fuck off, you sticky-fingered bitch," they variously say. The Girl has no lines in response, but nor does she seem to exit. The play seems to end with her standing there. She enters; she's assailed by insults; and the word

end

is all that remains.

But Karen, reading that word, could see the end clearly, as Martin, writing that word, must have seen it clearly. Martin was a director as well as a playwright. What might seem missing, from a reading point of view, was actually something bestowed, on director and actors. Karen was once an aspiring actor. She remembers how to fill in those blanks.

In the trance that overtook her while reading, Karen was not sure how much time had passed. She remembered Mr. Kingsley once telling them that if they simply read Shakespeare at the same rate that actors performed it, they'd be able to read entire plays in a couple of hours. This was the sort of putatively encouraging but actually critical and discouraging advice Mr. Kingsley had constantly given them despite his never having, Karen would bet, read an entire Shakespeare play in two hours or even an entire Shakespeare play in his life, yet it was a piece of advice that had stuck in her head ever since. It had given her the obviously flawed idea that reading time and staging time must be similar when most times and certainly this time that wasn't the case. It seemed to have taken her minutes to read through the play, and yet the play took up one hundred plus pages and was stuffed full of invisible silence, and not just the kind that takes up time onstage. There was copious onstage silence, that might take minutes or hours to enact, but there was also a silence of meaning, a refusal to spell out the facts. This refusal Karen felt as a challenge, although it took her some time, of having feelings and trying to name them, before she hit on the name for the feeling. Challenge. Very personal challenge. This isn't to say that Karen felt the play was a personal challenge to her in the sense of a message from Martin, that letter he'd promised, belatedly sent. Karen isn't crazy. She doesn't hear the lampshade talking, or read messages in her eggs. This is to say that she felt, from herself, to herself, a strong *challenge* to enter the play's silences and to utter their meaning.

*

MANY WORDS ARE both nouns and verbs. Present/present. Insult/insult. Object/object. Permit/permit. A list of such words, compiled for the business traveler not fluent in English, is pinned to my bulletin board. It's meant to illustrate not just the words' versatility but the fact that in each word the emphasis shifts the same way, from the first syllable to the second, with the sense shift from object to action. "I have a PREsent to preSENT to you." "The stapler is an OBject to which I hope you won't obJECT." "This PERmit perMITS me to fire you." These example sentences are of my composition. I like the list of words because it's like a monotonous poem and also because the "rule" it represents applies only to those words and is otherwise useless. "Audition" is also a word that is both noun and verb, but it always sounds the same. It's a word that means, literally, "the power of hearing," or "a hearing," as well as "to perform an audition," a circular definition that is actually the first under "verb" in my dictionary. In the verb form most true to its source (*audire*: to hear), the action belongs to the listener: *David* is auditioning actors for roles in the play—he is "hearing them out." But actors, poorly educated egomaniacs though they may be, understand about power. They're the reason the circular verb definition—audition: to perform an audition—has become the most popular one: I'm auditioning this weekend, I auditioned for that, I auditioned for him, etc. "Audition" dramatizes the struggle between subject and object, between doing and being done to.

My hatred of actors and my resistance to including myself among them complicated the resolve I had made, after reading the play, that no one else but me would play the Girl. I wanted to act without being an actor, and definitely without having to act like an actor. But no less than I hated actors I also hated people who thought they were so good they just asked to be given a role. And so in the days leading up to auditions I never told David I was coming nor simply asked him to give me the part, never chose a piece, never rehearsed it, never reconciled myself to *being auditioned*—and never reconciled myself to not auditioning.

The morning of the auditions I printed out a monologue but I didn't learn it. I didn't even look at it. I drove to the club David used as a theatre, and sat outside in my car until I knew they were just about done—because I'd helped with the schedule, as usual making myself indispensable about these auditions that David had never suggested I come to, having almost certainly forgotten our long-ago conversation about my great talent because he'd been drunk at the time. Sitting in the car I was surprised to have no idea what I would do. I tried to audition myself. I listened hard and heard nothing. Then as if she'd been given a cue, around the time Karen sensed they were finished she got out of the car and walked quickly inside where a very young, petite, pretty actress was in conversation with David who'd clearly just auditioned her or perhaps relinquished subjectivity and allowed her to do the auditioning, from the looks of his slightly flushed face. Karen knew auditions made David anxious as if he were the one who had something to prove. Maybe that knowledge emboldened her. Grabbing a chair she sat down just across from him, shoehorning in on his conversation with the actress, who faltered and smiled and finally went for her bag while David's assistant director picked up his clipboard and flipped pompously through sign-up sheets that Karen had printed herself. "David's just about done if you'd give us a second," said the assistant director but Karen disregarded him and only focused on David. "You don't think I can do this," she said.

"Do what?" David said.

"You don't think I can do this," she said again, just the same way. David clicked.

"I don't think you can do this," said David.

"You don't think I can do this," said Karen.

"I don't think you can do this," said David.

"You don't think I can do this," said Karen.

"I don't think you can do this," said David.

"You don't think I can do this."

"I don't think you can do this?"

"You don't think I can do this," she confirmed, because you don't fucking listen, you have no audition, you have no sense of hearing at all.

"I don't think you can do this?" David said angrily.

"You don't think I can do this!"

"*I* don't think you can do this?"

"You don't think I can do *this*!"

"What the fuck is going on?" cried David's assistant director.

"Shut the fuck up, Justin! I *don't* think you can do this!"

"You don't think *I* can do this?"

"The purpose of repetition," Mr. Kingsley once said, "is control of context. People cry, scream, grab each other's crotches, rip their clothes off . . . repeating the same set of words . . ."

Karen and David didn't grab each other's crotches, or rip off their clothes. They did scream, with increasing gusto. Karen did cry, a bit, but only once she had gotten back home. REpeat/rePEAT weren't on Karen's noun-to-verb list, but they ought to have been, since they work the same way: an action, event, or other thing that's done over again/to say something again one has already said. "You don't think I can do this," repeated, also means, "There are things I would like to do over."

I'VE SAID THAT David interested me. Not Sarah. Sarah obsessed me. I don't use the word lightly. Remember that the two words don't represent differences of degree. The dictionary tells us that to be interested by someone is to feel "attentive, concerned, or curious." Curiosity is a friendly emotion and even a moral position. Those whom we make the objects of our curiosity we don't prejudge or condemn. We don't fear and loathe them. My therapist, in our time together, often urged me to "stay curious" and it was a nice thing for him to try and make me do, unsuccessful as he was, because curious is a nice way to feel.

Being curious toward, interested in, David made me feel like I'd bought into him, made a choice. By contrast, being obsessed by Sarah was a form of enslavement. "Obsess" comes from the Latin *obsessus*, past participle of *obsidere*, from *ob-* (against or in front of) + *sedere* (to sit) = "sit opposite to" (literal) = "to occupy, frequent, besiege" (figurative). When we say we are obsessed, we say we're possessed, controlled, haunted by something or somebody else. We are beset, under siege. We can't choose. I was obsessed with Sarah, meaning obsessed *by* her, deprived by her very existence of some quality I needed to feel complete and in charge of myself. If you'd asked Sarah, however, she would have said she'd done nothing to me. That's how it is with the people by whom we're obsessed. They've *obsessed* us, they've *transitive-verbed* us, but no one could be more surprised than they are.

So who makes it happen—obsession? Unlike the things that I did blame her for, I didn't blame Sarah for this. I didn't blame either of us. Obsession is an accidental haunting, by a person not aware she's a ghost. I knew Sarah was my ghost, but she'd forgotten I even existed.

Karen and Sarah, her old friend the author, went from Skylight Books to an expensive and stylish Mexican restaurant made out of huge white sheets of linen like the caravan of some sultan, if sultans ate Mexican food. The fact that it never rains in Los Angeles is most impressed on visitors by those business establishments that don't bother having a roof. Potted palms, white banquettes, service kiosks for the staff glittering with stemware and steak knives, all sat out under the orangish night sky with its one or two faint fuzzy stars. Aircraft cable crisscrossed overhead to form a grid from which hung fairy lights and bloated paper lanterns and the vast white linen sheets which were supposed to divide the night air into "private" dining regions so that the feeling, for a person who was sober, was of being surrounded by some giant's drying laundry. Karen could see Sarah was nervous. Even Karen's most attentive, private-practice-ready "listening face" couldn't downshift Sarah into some lower gear. Sarah was almost at the bottom of her daiquiri and Karen, as Sarah talked, gestured to the waiter to bring another daiquiri and another of what Karen was drinking, a fancy nonalcoholic limeade full of what looked like lawnmower mulch. Because the perspective of a nondrinking person seems to be unique, especially among people who read, allow me to break in again and observe that in my experience people who drink never don't when they find themselves with a nondrinker. In fact, they drink more. Nondrinkers make drinkers uncomfortable. The situation they're afraid of—getting drunk in the presence of someone who's sober—is exactly the one they create.

"But enough about me, what about you?" Sarah cried, at the end of a long recitation of unexpected things that had happened to her on her book tour, none of which could have been more unexpected than one of her characters turning up, in the flesh, to invalidate all Sarah's memories of her. "What have you been up to the past dozen years?"

"Oh, this and that," Karen said, smiling to show that she didn't feel that this question came too late to be polite and that it might not even be sincere. "I've mostly worked as an office manager, personal assistant, personal organizer, stuff like that—you probably never knew it in high school but I'm highly organized." Their shared laughter came right on cue. Just as she'd imagined, Karen told Sarah about her recent trip to Vietnam with her brother, in this way illustrating her carefree and well-funded life.

"Oh my God, your brother!" Sarah said, exulting in the fact that she remembered this person's existence. "How is he? What is he doing?"

Karen answered Sarah's questions in the same way she'd speak of her brother to any random stranger, citing all the most expected, least remarkable facts, that might belong to anyone. Single, lived here in LA, worked in corporate law. Karen's brother, with whom she shared a face, and many other less visible things. Karen knew that Sarah couldn't even pretend to find these unrevealing facts about Karen's brother to be exactly what she'd expected, or the last things she'd expected. Karen's brother had been so far beneath Sarah's notice, back in the past, that Sarah struggled now to fit him in the picture, and even seemed to think Karen would marvel at the sound of his name. "Kevin, Kevin, Kevin, oh my *God*," Sarah harped, as if Karen's brother's name were a piece of obscure trivia. "I remember . . . oh my God! He had this razor-blade necklace he thought was *so cool*, do you remember that thing?" Did Karen remember it? Did Karen remember every granule of the childhood landscape she shared with her brother, in which the razor-blade necklace, believe it or not, was not such a major landmark? Still, Karen nodded and smiled as if she and Sarah were keeping pace down Kevin Memory Lane, as if the razor-blade necklace turned and gleamed enormously above them like the sun.

How many rooms house the past? In their hometown, space came cheap. Even poor people's houses were flabby with space; they were just cheaply made. The apartment Sarah shared with her mother, Karen and Kevin's house that they shared with their mother, were crappy structures full of water bugs and mold, faucet handles and doorknobs that fell off, windows and doors that wouldn't open or wouldn't stay shut, but they were never cramped, there was always space, dank space, more than you could decently fill. Karen and Kevin, before and after their parents' divorce, always had their own rooms: enormous rooms with low, stained ceilings, dirty matted shag carpet, accordion-style closet doors that had come off their tracks, sliding windows in aluminum frames that stuck and shrieked and developed a weird, whitish rust, like salt deposits, that came off on your hands. One room like that was bad enough, but two was killing. All through their childhood Karen and Kevin had continually migrated into one room or the other, they resisted each having a room of their own, they understood in their bodies, if not in their minds, that two bodies in one room defeats the room, but one body in one room is defeated. And so each kept sneaking into the other one's room—sneaking, because throughout their childhood there was always someone holding the opinion that they shouldn't share a room, whether stating it directly or not. Before the divorce, it was their father and grandmother who held this opinion. After the divorce, their mother for a while had a boyfriend who held this opinion. In high school, it was Sarah who held this opinion—not consciously, because Sarah did not even know that Karen frequently shared the same room with her brother. It was just that Sarah would have found it bizarre that Karen, in a house with four bedrooms and three inhabitants, might share a room with her brother. And so Karen and Kevin, for the sake of not seeming bizarre to Sarah, withdrew to their two separate rooms. Kevin, Karen understood, had shared Karen's grim determination not to spook such a friend-prize as Sarah. It was possible that Kevin— twelve the year Karen met Sarah, still requiring "husky" jeans, soft and pale and pudgy and awkward and unappealingly bashful—felt that grim determination even more. Kevin gawped at Sarah from behind the doorframes. It was possible that Kevin had purchased the laughable razor blade on a chain, with saved allowance, from the head shop in the mall, in the hopes of winning Sarah's approval.

So, yes, in Sarah's version of Karen's childhood, Kevin barely existed, while in Karen's and Kevin's versions of their childhood, Sarah loomed. Sarah had impressed herself by remembering Kevin, while Karen knew it was too much to hope Kevin might forget Sarah. When Karen booked her current trip to LA, she deliberately failed to tell her brother that she was coming this particular day to intersect Sarah on Sarah's book tour. She didn't trust him not to want to come along. She didn't trust him not to challenge her vision of Sarah, which was the product of so much analytical labor, with his own vision which was sealed in the amber of a childhood crush. But at least Kevin had a vision of Sarah, unlike Sarah's nonvision of him, in which her drunken recollection of his name was another of the unexpected things that had happened to her. "Kevin! Oh my God. So did you guys move to LA together? That's so sweet. I remember you guys were so close." Yes, they were, but no, she didn't. She remembered no such thing. Karen, ordering Sarah a third daiquiri, smiled again.

"We were both living here for a while, and I really enjoyed it. But now I'm back home."

It took Sarah a moment. "You mean our hometown?"

"Home sweet home."

"You're *living* there?" Sarah's high-gear voice dropped an octave. She'd finally forgotten herself, and that sardonic quality of knowing—not necessarily caring, but knowing—that Karen remembered so clearly, returned. Sarah had always seemed to *know*. Not you, but something you wanted to know. Now she seemed to see their town, dumped over a neighboring table like so many dirty guacamole bowls. "I never imagined you'd live there. I'd sooner imagine I'd live there, and I never imagined I'd live there. How is it?"

"It's great. It's not the same place we lived when we were kids. I mean, that place is still there, but I don't spend much time there."

"I hated living there so much. I always felt so powerless."

"We were kids. We weren't supposed to have power."

"You had power. You had that car."

How Karen's crappy high-school car loomed for Sarah! It was one of the things that fascinated Karen about Sarah's book, this grievance about Karen's car. It was one of the things that kept Karen curious about Sarah, and not just enraged. If Karen wandered off in Freudian directions, a guilty pleasure, she might conclude there was, in addition to the obvious penis envy (phallus-envy? Karen's Freud is pretty rusty, please remember she majored in dance), also some obvious father envy going on, Karen's car representing Karen's father's role in her life, which while minuscule was larger than Sarah's father's role in Sarah's life, since Sarah never saw her father and didn't even know where he lived. Here we might understand "father" as meaning any form of masculine care. See, for example, Sarah's special friendship with the man we call Mr. Kingsley, and that friendship's mysterious end. See, for another example, Sarah's thing for David's car. That phone he failed to answer, that mess in his passenger seat. That orgasm Sarah gives herself, masturbating, because David's not there. Everything about the car represented David's broken promise to take care of Sarah, as if David was more— or *should* have been more—than just another fucked-up teenage kid. Why was *David* responsible for her? What about the adults in their lives? As if on cue, Sarah said, "Do you see anyone?"

And by "anyone" Karen knew Sarah meant David, and felt the satisfaction of the night arriving just where she'd intended, like a train pulling in right on time.

"I see David a lot. In fact, we're working on something together."

Another of Karen's observations about people who drink is that their drunkenness doesn't steadily accumulate like snow building up. It has valleys and peaks, of confusion and relative clearness. Although the confusion gets steadily worse, and the relative clearness gets steadily cloudy, there keep being these moments of reaching a peak, where the drunk person thinks she can see. She feels certain she isn't that drunk. That's where Sarah was, as the subject of David came up. Sarah was no longer high-pitched and hyper, she was no longer churning out fake excitement, she was tenderized down to her bones. She must have felt steady and safe in her own fortress walls. If it's possible to see a person's self-absorption clash against her curiosity, to see her inwardness and outwardness collide, then I saw it in Sarah. I saw her craving to talk about David meet her craving to learn a new David, from me. Before, she'd forgotten herself. Now, for him, she set herself aside.

"Tell me about him," she said.

ONE OF THE challenges I've faced in therapy is my total recall. All my life I've had a flawless memory. All my life people have noticed, no one more than my mother. When I was very young, my mother paraded my memory. There was the lighthearted way she'd use me grocery shopping instead of a list. Imagine me at four or five years old, Kevin a fat toddler stuck in the shopping-cart seat. Aisle by aisle I'd rattle off our kitchen shortages down to the teaspoon. We were out of milk and bread, we had three eggs, we had a frozen chicken breast in the freezer, the baking soda box was empty, there was only one sleeve of saltines. She'd ask me questions about the sugar bowl's level or the state of the lettuce when other people were in earshot, always hoping they'd make some comment, and when they did she was off to the races. "Believe me—she also knows how long it's been since I vacuumed the carpet." [Appreciative laughter.] "Believe me— it's no fun when your kid won't forget that you promised her ice cream—last summer!" [More appreciative laughter.] There was the less lighthearted way she deployed me in wars with my father or, later, her boyfriends. "Are you *sure* you want to say that to me? *Karen's* listening." "Karen, please *remind* Paul what he promised to do." As I got older, though, my mother stopped parading my memory. She stopped bragging about it or hitting her enemies with it. Instead, she started running it down. My memory had been the ultimate proof of any points that she wanted to make, but it strangely disproved any points of my own. I might remember some incident, sure, but *I did not understand it.* Anybody whose brain was so cluttered with dull trivia like the approximate number of ounces of toothpaste left in the tube didn't actually know what things *meant.* My mother first exploited my memory, and then insulted it, but the conclusion I reached didn't change. My memory was my innermost self and I had to protect it.

Therapy can seem like revision of memory. It can seem like you're saving your life by destroying your story and writing a new one. It can seem like therapy won't get its goddamn grubby mitts off you. At best therapy demands uncomfortable humility from the person with total recall, and at worst it can remind me of my mother—the difference being that therapy wants the emotional truth, while my mother runs screaming from any emotion or truth that's not hers. Was Sarah the same, as I'd always assumed? One thing I'd known about Sarah since high school was that her memory was well below average. She forgot things all the time, in every category. She forgot where she'd placed her bag, her jacket, or her lipstick the instant whatever it was left her hand. She forgot what assignments there were, or whether she'd done them. She forgot why she'd fought with somebody, and what had been said. The result of her forgetfulness—or the reason for it?—might be her "imaginative gift" for rewriting the past, but did this mean she was more, or less, likely to perceive someone else's emotional truth? If she forgot my emotional truth—assuming she'd ever known it in the first place—was she now all the more on the lookout for it? Or would she just lend me hers, like my mother would do, and ignore a bad fit?

Karen would have thought the latter—or she would have thought that she thought the latter. But as Sarah embarked on her fourth daiquiri, Karen realized that something had changed. It wasn't just Sarah's blood alcohol level. Sarah, who had been so obviously shocked and terrified in the bookstore when Karen appeared—who had been, at that moment, and whether accidentally or not, perfectly in touch with the emotional truth of the situation, which was that Karen despised her—had now nestled into a new, fraudulent understanding, of Karen's creation, with all the unquestioning trust of a baby. That new, fraudulent understanding was that Karen and Sarah had never ruptured. They had always been friends. They had never stopped loving each other, simply drifted apart. And Karen realized that she, Karen, had known all along that Sarah, for all her charisma and beauty and knowing*ness*, which is different from knowing, was fundamentally forgetful, insecure, untrusting of her instincts, and anxious for praise and acceptance. And Karen realized that she had known all along that Sarah, if given the chance, would ignore Karen's emotional truth if she was offered an emotional falsehood that made her feel better. And Karen realized that this weakness of Sarah's was something she, Karen, had been counting on. For all her self-deprecating misgivings about having come to Skylight Books without a plan, Karen let herself admit she'd had a plan all along.

"I'd have loved to see his face when you showed up at auditions," Sarah said eagerly. By now she had heard about Martin's new play—minus Martin's witch hunt—and David's production of it—minus David's crusading—and Karen's saucy, fun-loving decision to take David up on his bogus invitation to audition for him, if not the form the audition had taken. Karen had made Sarah laugh about David's shrewd use of his charm as a method of payment. Oh, yes, Sarah remembered this well. David's gift for making you feel only *he* saw your gifts. Despite the cool night Sarah was flushed, with alcohol but more substantially this memory of David, and the pleasure of talking about it. Although, in her new happy trust in her friendship with Karen, she didn't neglect to insist Karen *was* talented. "I mean, David's right, you *are* good," she said, "but I think you're right also—that he told you to audition because he loves pretending he's this great, supportive guy. That's why I love that you went. So what happened?"

Karen did a look of comical surprise—she hadn't mentioned already? "I got it." Sarah shrieked and threw her arms in the air.

"After all that BS about my unacknowledged talent I guess he had to cast me," Karen said. This was false modesty. Remember that the part—the only female part in the play—was written for a woman who "however long she lives, will never cease to look the waif." Remember that the character is slight enough to be mistaken for a boy. Karen is petite and in excellent shape but she's never since she turned ten years old "looked the waif" or been mistaken for a boy. That pretty young actress whose audition Karen wiped from David's memory—*she'd* been a waif. But David wound up casting Karen, to his own great surprise, and no more from pity than guilt. Her un-ideal physique was the proof that she had something better. "Didn't you and Martin have a thing?" David had asked Karen at The Bar, after telling her he'd given her the part to his own great surprise. Karen had lowered her lids at him, as if she hadn't expected the question—she had—and also found it in very poor taste. "Fine," David said, "but just do me a favor. Don't get in touch with him before the first rehearsal. I want to see the look on his face. I bet we'll be able to use that, for when the Girl first comes into Doc's bar."

"So he's Doc?" Karen confirmed casually.

"Fuck yeah. I told him that I wasn't going to do it if he didn't play Doc. I can't wait to see his face when he sees you."

"Me too," Karen said.

At the open-air Mexican restaurant, Karen didn't go into these details with Sarah, not even the detail of Martin's casting. But when Sarah asked, "Do you think there's any chance Martin might come see it?" Karen said, "David seems sure that he will," and watched Sarah first withstanding, then submitting to temptation.

"If he can come from England, I can make it from New York. I *have* to. I've never seen a single one of David's shows."

"Would you really?" Karen marveled. "We open in less than three weeks."

"Really," Sarah said. She glowed like a lantern, as if already absorbing David's stunned adoration at her unexpectedly attending the play. "Write down the dates on this napkin. I'll book a flight when I get back to my hotel."

"But are you serious?" Karen persisted.

"Of course I'm serious! I can't not. David's show? That you're in?"

"Because—if you're serious—"

"What?"

"No, it's crazy."

"Just tell me!"

"I just had this crazy idea—don't be offended. Just, remember all those times on costume crew? So my character has just one change. It's not even a quick one."

Sarah clapped one hand over her mouth, barely muffling a squeal. She had to take the hand away to speak again. "I'll be your dresser! I'll dress you!"

Do mothers iron anymore? Or should we say, Do people iron anymore? But admit, it was mothers, not people, who ironed. Even Karen's mother, trailing around in her ruffle-necked robe and her wedge bedroom slippers, had ironed. The ironing board permanently set up on its X-leg, wearing its silvery cover drawn tight by elastic. Lying on the floor under the board, Karen had been reminded by that elastic gathering of her own diapers, which in this memory were in the recent past. Karen must be two or three, lying under the ironing board, gazing up at the puckered elastic that holds the smooth, silvery fabric in place. Kevin must be an infant, kicking in a playpen or napping in his crib. Karen's father still lives in the house and Karen's mother is ironing his shirts. She sprays on the shirts from a can, the same way she sprays in a pan right before she cooks dinner, but the smell of the spray starch cooked hot by the iron makes Karen more hungry than does the smell of any actual cooking. The iron, coming down on the patch of damp starch, seems to be eating it, with a crackle and gratified hiss. And her mother, dreaming her way through the menial task as if nothing could be more romantic, is the mother whom Karen expects, the mother she'll always be trying to find. In the costume shop at CAPA, when Karen rediscovered hot spray starch, the sound and the smell of it kept her content all those shows that she did the costumes, that she dressed someone else for the stage. Hot spray starch sedated her. It recalled the ancient safety of her lost childhood. And it bound her and Sarah together, into a harmony, ironing costumes. Now those afternoons they spent in costume shop that at the time had given Karen nostalgia for being a child are themselves an ancient childhood memory. Nostalgia is a "sentimental longing or wistful affection for the past." It comes from the Greek *nostos*: to return home, and the Greek *algos*: pain.

ALL THOSE YEARS after he first arrived, Martin returned. He was picked up at the airport by David, who was hosting Martin in his terrible apartment. Karen knew such arrangements were *de rigueur* in the Elite Brotherhood of the Arts but she still wondered how much Martin would enjoy David's sofa bed after Mr. Kingsley's guest suite. Karen herself, indispensably helpful, hired a cleaning service to fumigate and sanitize David's apartment before Martin's arrival, as usual earning David's abject gratitude. Karen also booked Martin's travel, filed the paperwork for a visiting-artist grant from the state, drafted the press release announcing the production, and updated the theatre's website. In connection with none of these tasks did Karen publicize the fact that the Visiting Artist arrived trailing scandal. Among no one in David's theatre company was the scandal discussed. So far as Karen could tell, apart from David and herself and Mr. Kingsley, no one knew. Martin's alleged crimes didn't follow him to this American city where he'd spent time more than ten years before. But they didn't need to, Karen thought—the author would like to indulge in an adverb and write—serenely. Yes,

Karen felt serene thinking of Martin, preparing for his arrival. "Serene" means "calm, untroubled, tranquil" and often refers to conditions at sea. Martin crossed the sea, whether in serene condition or not we have no way of knowing. When met by David at the airport Martin might have been shocked by David's physical transformation. David at thirty could have been mistaken for a man nearing fifty. David was bald, his brow and jowls and shoulders drooped as if they were subjected to enhanced gravity, he couldn't clear his face of stubble fast enough, he'd gotten thicker all over and had the pallor of a chain-smoking drinker whose only time outdoors is the time he spends getting into and out of his car. Martin might have felt, seeing David, that the past was further past than he'd thought. Would he feel this way seeing Karen? Would he recognize Karen?

The play was being staged in a former warehouse building which now held a bar in the front half and a "performance space" in the rear half, indicated by poorly built risers and pipes hanging on chains from the faraway ceiling to which were clamped an assortment of secondhand stage lights with frayed wiring and wrinkly gels. Black moth-eaten stage curtains salvaged from some ancient extinct theatre had made the enormous dusty warehouse into a sort of maze of spaces that had to be connected at their edges but you couldn't tell where. People were always getting lost trying to find the bathroom or trying to find their way back outdoors. People got so tangled up in the black stage curtains that seemed to mark an exit or an entrance but didn't that sometimes they had to be rescued after crying for help. The bar was a huge plywood horseshoe with almost no seating. For some reason there were only a handful of barstools, each with some hunchbacked uncommunicative drinker permanently attached. Otherwise there were armchairs and sofas, obviously rescued from the garbage, strewn around the concrete floor. The night of the first read-through, the night of Martin's first full day in town, Karen arrived early and made a circular arrangement of furniture, rounded up some ashtrays, even got the bartender to give her a pitcher of water and glasses. Okay, she was nervous. No longer serene. But it was an expected and manageable nervousness. Its source was clear and its duration would be short. We never know, when life reunites us with someone, how closely our stories will match. By contrast with the first time they'd met, when she had felt herself so old but in fact had been so young, Karen now actually was old enough to understand that for Martin, there might have been no story at all. There might have been—for this person who'd not merely touched but deformed her—no sensation of contact at all. He might not recognize her. If he did, he might not recall a single detail of their past relationship. If he did, he might not recall the same details. If he did, he might not recall them in just the same way. But Karen required very little to gauge the disjuncture and make her adjustment.

The four other actors arrived first and chatted awkwardly with Karen. All were under twenty-five and nervous of Karen, whose position in the acting pecking order they did not understand. Karen could not have cared less to explain. Karen could have chatted with them in her sleep. To her as to this story and the play they were completely peripheral. They intrude on this paragraph only because David was late; David had asked them to come at seven thirty while he and Martin, David had told Karen, were coming at seven, because David was eager for an unimpeded observation of Martin and Karen's reunion. But David was late without realizing, as always. He came into the vast black dusty space with his self-conscious saunter which always advertised, even through a twilight murk, his awareness of his role as impresario, his keen pleasure and anxiety in making things happen—in this case, the reunion between Martin and Karen. The result might be discomfort or delight but either way he'd made it happen and he'd plow it into the play and make more happen. This was David's typically self-centered and not totally wrong point of view, that the moment was all about him. His point of view suited Karen. It kept her invisible.

"Hey hey hey, look who's back in the U S of A," David said as Martin, strangely small, hands crammed in pockets, shoulders overly shrugged, kept pace, a triangular smirk on his face in the corner of which drooped a cigarette. David saw the actors. "What the fuck are you guys doing here?"

"You told them seven thirty. It's a quarter to eight," Karen said.

"Is that *Karen*?" Martin exclaimed with the extreme emphasis of delight. He snatched the cigarette out of his mouth. He stopped dead in his tracks but the rest of him seemed to lean toward her, his grin most of all. However, his eyes contradicted. There had been flash and flutter in there. Panicked survey of options, swift choice of Enthusiasm. David, his glance bouncing back from the actors, entirely missed it.

"It is," Karen smiled.

"Aren't you looking fucking fantastic!" Martin said.

"Thank you." Karen accepted this tribute with the extremely dignified truncated condescension she'd once observed in an actress playing a member of the British royal family in some *Masterpiece Theatre* thing. Karen's mother had adored *Masterpiece Theatre* with the slavish adoration of somebody who thinks she's cultured but in reality is turned on by the clothes. For years Karen had scorned her mother's slavish adoration and yet kept on watching the shows, her mother in her gut like a worm. Then one night she saw an episode with an actress playing a member of the British royal family who looked down her nose at some man and said her stingy "Thank you" in response to whatever his compliment was. She said it as if she were holding her nose and also as if she were giving the man a great gift and was going to be embarrassed if he showed gratitude. There was such a complicated tender hatefulness in the way that she said it, and Karen, who was probably in college at the time, had thought of Martin, yes indeed she had. She'd thought of his British Difference and wondered whether there had been codes she had not understood. And now here she was actually saying the prim little "Thank you" to him and watching for a response. What did she see? His gaze was flying around like a game of Ping-Pong. He seemed to know that the exits weren't easy to find. Karen's nervousness changed from something boiling and popping its bubbles to something cool, stiff, and glossy. You might call the new thing confidence, from the Latin *confidere,* "have full trust," and who among us hasn't noticed that people with confidence tend to inspire it. Martin's gaze was ping-ponging; he had every reason to be on his guard—after all, he had come Trailing Scandal. But he also had every reason to crush his own instincts and to seize grounds for confidence where he could find them. Of course Martin wanted to normalize. What criminal doesn't. And Karen's dazzling little "Thank you" was so full of knowing contempt it seemed somehow flirtatious, and you could see she was smiling. Karen watched Martin get it together and give her his weasel/rake smirk in response. Even David, tuning in a beat late, thought there was a *frisson* between them and was happy. *Frisson* is a French word meaning "shiver or thrill," and it wasn't much used in this country until the late 1960s. Then, once the sexual revolution came, people needed it or wanted to need it. Karen's mother, of the negligee as daywear, adored the word *frisson.*

Karen, still smiling, let Martin peck both her cheeks, which he did while keeping up a nervous scolding of David. "You didn't bloody tell me we'd be seeing Karen!"

"Did he tell you I'm playing the part?"

Hearing this, Martin had to act so much more Enthusiastic he practically shot through the ceiling—but that was his nervous confidence convincing him that actually, Karen was flirting with him, that actually, it was All Right. This was how Karen was able to see that in fact, despite all her worry and doubt, Martin's story, and hers, were the same.

Equally pretending this wasn't the case they sat down and told each other piles of pointless lies about the past dozen years of their lives while the young actors deferentially supplemented the pitcher of water with several pitchers of beer.

Then, everybody sat down and they did the read-through.

"Doc hardly talks in Act One," David observed afterward, "yet the audience has to form an opinion about him—that gets exploded."

"Given it's my own bloody part I could gladly give myself more bloody lines," Martin said, provoking laughter from the young actors.

David talked more about the subversiveness of Doc, and Martin interrupted him with comments like, "Isn't he just a pathetic sod?" shrewdly disguising from the admiring young actors and David his neurotic need for limitless compliments on the complexity of his character as false modesty dressed up as jokey self-deprecation. It was a virtuoso feeling-state lasagna and everybody ate it up and gave Martin back just what he wanted: more laughter, along with protests that his character wasn't a "sod" at all but an Everyman and maybe even a Jesus.

In addition to dissecting Martin's high-level bullshit, which had the welcome effect of making her feel less ashamed of her youthful past self that had found him so brilliant, Karen entertained herself by trying to guess how long it would take any of the men to notice her sitting there, not contributing a word to the conversation. But they were all drinking beer, and she wasn't, so they weren't even on the same clock. "I think we ought to see the gun in Act One," she interrupted. "Like Chekhov says. If we're going to hear a gun in Act Two we've got to see it in Act One."

"Actually, he says that if we see it in Act One, it's gotta go off by Act Two. But, same difference. That's a cool point, Karen."

"I can imagine Doc, like, digging around for something under the bar at some point and just slapping the gun on the bar to get it out of the way," one of the actors remarked.

"All bar owners keep a handgun," said another.

"Is that true?" Martin said. "So bloody American. It's not true in England."

"Welcome to Bloody America."

"Maybe he takes it out when the Girl first appears, sorta slaps it on the bar like, Scram, or else?"

"I like that," said David. "We'll need a prop gun, but we needed one anyway. Recorded gun noises are lame."

"I'll take care of it," said Karen.

The four young actors planned to linger to see a band that was coming on later so David and Martin and Karen walked out as a trio onto the ruined street of cracked concrete slabs sprouting weeds and other former warehouses that hadn't yet turned into bar/performance spaces. A few blocks away were railroad tracks on the literal wrong side of which the whole area sat; on the right side, a few miles away across total wasteland, you could see the tidy shape of downtown sticking up, where the traffic lights worked. David might have parked anywhere, there was nothing but parking, but he'd parked directly behind Karen on the desolate street so that, going back to their cars, they were walking together. David's sports car, with the phone, was long gone. The driver's-side window of his current vehicle was a black plastic trash bag. Karen's much envied convertible was also long gone. She drove a practical unblemished car that David recognized only because he'd seen it so often. The shattered sidewalk and desolate street stretched away to an unseen horizon. Black infinity stretched overhead. Out here, on the literal wrong side of the tracks, there wasn't enough light pollution to lower the salmon-orange haze that was their city's night sky over them like a comforting blanket. David parking behind Karen was a companionable gesture, in the way of herd animals sidling up to each other at dusk, to less feel the darkness and cold. It made Karen wonder, as they unlocked their cars, whether he was less confident of his judgment than he'd pretended. "Even if he was fooling around with his students," David had said just a few nights ago, "it's not a fucking crime. Our standards have gotten so overreaching. We can't drive without wearing a seat belt and can't fuck unless the government says it's okay? We know they all consented."

"How do we know?" Karen asked in her I'm-not-arguing-just-curious tone.

"He says they did—and sue me, but so far no one's shown me one good reason not to believe him. Now they say that they didn't consent, years or a whole decade later. Why's that?"

"I don't know. It doesn't prove that they're lying."

"Well what about *you*? Whatever your thing was with him, you weren't some helpless victim. You gave him the keys to your car. He moved into your *house*."

"All true," Karen said.

"You weren't some helpless victim," David persisted. There was a strange fervor in his voice when they talked about Martin. "You could have walked away—you could have kicked him out! Mr. Kingsley kicked him out—and you took him in. If anyone was helpless, it was Martin."

"I'm not arguing with you," said Karen. No, she was not some helpless victim. It wasn't David's business to decide this, but it happened to be true. Still, that evening he had wanted to prove something, and this evening, as they unlocked their cars, Martin standing there dragging on his cigarette for dear life and pretending to admire the hideous view, Karen sensed David feeling unsure that he'd succeeded in proving it. And when David was feeling unsure, he wouldn't rest until extracting reassurance.

"Coming to The Bar?" David said with poorly hidden insistence.

"The cost of soda's too high. Heading home," Karen said.

"Do come, Karen, we haven't had a proper chat," Martin said with poorly faked insistence, so obviously wanting her to leave that she almost stayed just to spite him. But no.

*

MY FATHER WAS a carpenter. "Like Jesus," to quote him. Also like Jesus, my father had a lot of other skills. Electricity, plumbing. Anything you need to know to build a house, my father knew how to do. After he split from my mother he'd still come back to our house on the weekends, to do big things and small, reshingle the roof, clear the gutters, rewire the ceiling fan, unclog the toilet. Even that, my mother couldn't do herself. Once my mother had Ron, the first in a series of boyfriends, my father stopped coming, not that Ron knew how to fix anything. But my mother didn't want Ron to feel shown up by my father's grim competence. The things that got fixed were the things that I'd learned how to fix, by watching, but I couldn't keep up with the house's deterioration. By the time I was in high school, the house was returning to a state of nature. The grass was waist deep in the yard and there were oak trees taking root in the gutters. At the same time as our yard was taking over our house, my father's house was taking over his yard. He'd added a deck and a kitchen extension, turned his two-car garage into a television room, and built a giant carport to shade his driveway. On our weekends, I'd drive my beater over there and work on it with him. There was nothing he didn't know how to do: engine work, body work, he'd even salvaged leather seats for the interior. We didn't talk much, share feelings or thoughts. My father and I—this is the story I tell myself; who knows how his story would go—are too much alike to be close. We're both extremely competent, we both like to be left alone, we both had a weak spot for my mother and hate ourselves for it. Again, it's possible that if you asked my father about him and me he'd say something completely different, though it's more possible he'd say nothing.

When I was little my father supported us by doing carpentry and handy work, but at some point early on he started building sets and doing lighting for the opera, and got himself into the stagehands' union. That's what kept Kevin and me fed and clothed, my father's union job and his decency toward us even though my mother, then as now, barely worked and spent her alimony on her boyfriends. My father worked rock concerts and film shoots, pretty much anything that used lighting, but his most steady paycheck remained the opera, the downtown theatre, and summer stage in the park—all the middle-of-the-road, status quo stages that David despised. David, who'd grown up with more money than anyone else in our school, burned with contempt for those places, which he would say offered cultural diversion for the self-regarding rich. On the other hand my father, who grew up poor and never went to college, would have scorned David's rabble-rousing plays if he could have been bothered to know about them, which he couldn't. When I told my father, who knows every union prop master in town, that I needed a gun that shot blanks for a show of David's, my father made the huffing sound that lets you know he's laughing. "What's the show, *The Marxist Revolution*? Every time I see that kid interviewed in the Arts section he's insulting rich people, but I notice he's fine about taking their money. He's got his angels like everyone else." Although my father is Christian, by "angel" he didn't mean a messenger of God. He meant a rich person who donated money to keep David's theatre going.

"Yeah, it's a conundrum. Anyway, I was thinking that Richie could help me." Richie was a prop master friend of my father's.

"A prop gun or a blank gun?"

"A blank gun. It gets fired."

"So use the prop gun and a good sound effect."

"Dad, I'm not the director."

"I wouldn't trust this person with a blank gun. Who's his prop master? How do you know that they know what they're doing?"

"*I'm* his prop master. And I know what I'm doing."

"Just because there's no bullet, it's still dangerous. There's still the cartridge and gun powder. No screwing around. That's how Bruce Lee's kid died."

"That gun had a squib load in it."

"Because the prop crew were morons. You've got to know what you're doing."

"I do, Dad."

"Sure you do. It's the morons I'm worried about."

"Well, I won't let them touch it," I said.

I decided to take both a prop and a blank gun from Richie—for safety, we agreed. I even got two different models, so you couldn't mistake them. The prop gun was a Colt replica with a wooden hand grip. Like any prop gun, it was a real-looking toy that did nothing. The blank-firing gun was an all-black Beretta. I didn't even bring it to the warehouse until the full dress. It was the prop gun we used in rehearsal, the prop gun I held when, offstage, Martin and I acted out what the audience would hear but not see. Martin sat in a chair and I stood beside him, the prop gun in my hand, pointed down and angled away. I'd suggested blocking our movements backstage for safety and it was just the kind of detail David loved and believed in for the authenticity it would somehow convey. Doc sinking into his chair, the Girl taking position beside him, stepping her feet apart, bracing herself.

From that vantage, standing beside seated Martin, her gaze always fell on the same thing, Martin's skull where it sprouted his ear. The connection between skull and ear seemed a little too loose. She'd lost the original Martin, who'd previously been preserved by her total recall down to the yellowish grooves of his nails. The night of the read-through, when he'd come slouching in next to David, for an instant the two Martins shimmered on top of each other, more alike than different but still marking the time from the past until now. It was the slightness of the difference between Martin Now and Past Martin that made it so strange. It was the thorough difference of Karen Now from Past Karen, the shocking difference of David Now from Past David, and the only slight difference, a connoisseur's difference, between the two Martins, that made it so strange. Strange enough to make you think that you hadn't known Martin at all in the past. The original Martin, already so hard to attest to, was absorbed by the Martin of Now, and even Karen with her total recall couldn't get him back out.

And everything, and everyone, cooperated to help Martin supersede Martin. Everyone smiled and agreed, without being so crass as to put it in words, that the scandal reported in the *Bourne Courier-Telegraph* must not have occurred. Mr. Kingsley, who'd once thrown Martin out of his house, came to rehearsal all smiles and pumped Martin's hand. Martin was normal, delightful, as most people are if you give them a chance, and it felt good, I'll fully admit, to take part in his normalization, to drift with prevailing currents, to not be the sore loser or lone crazy history buff. It felt good and I let it feel good. I enjoyed rehearsal—I enjoyed the permission it gave me to not think about Martin. Running lines with Martin, being "seized" by Martin "in a violent embrace," joining Martin and the others at The Bar afterward, I finally stopped thinking about Martin for the first time in years. He finally got out of my head and went to sit across the room with his ferrety smirk and his yellow fingertips and his knobbly knees and his shaggy hair, and although I saw him sitting there, his reality didn't disturb me.

WHEN SARAH'S BOOK had first been published, the previous year, David got manic-crusader about it, as if he'd written it himself or perhaps more accurately as if he'd had a child, who had turned out to be incredibly precocious and possessed of all the qualities of David's own that David loved and none of the ones that he hated, and this child, this sort of genius-distillation of David, had written the book. David's first campaign was to get CAPA to feature the book on their marquee, where the mainstage productions were usually announced; in the big glass display case just inside the front doors; and on the brand-new still-under-construction website. You'd think this was a fool's errand, given Sarah's depiction of CAPA, which some would have called negative and yet others a whitewash, a difference we will not pursue, but as it turned out the administration at CAPA was apparently too dazzled by its association with a Published Author to even read the author's book and make up their own minds and so David succeeded. Next David went on a campaign to get the *Trib* and the *Examiner* to not just review Sarah's book but do big splashy front-of-the-section feature articles about it. David might have been a guy who drove a car with a black plastic trash bag for its driver's-side window but he was also a shrewd self-promoter who'd developed, over the years, very useful relationships with the arts editors at both papers and in this campaign he also succeeded. You might have thought Sarah had hired David to do freelance publicity but in fact David and Sarah had not seen each other since high school, any more than Sarah and Karen had seen each other since high school, or Karen and David had seen each other since high school, until Karen moved back to their hometown and found David there. It was from David that Karen first learned about Sarah's book. He'd yanked it out of his backpack and thrust it at her with that smirk on his face—lips tightly compressed, face twisted in an unsuccessful effort to conceal wicked glee—he always wore when vindicated. About what did Sarah's book vindicate David? Her writing "talent," which perhaps he thought he'd discovered, or encouraged? His importance to her, as measured by the number of pages devoted to his fictional self, and the far fewer number of pages devoted to fictional others whose real analogues might have been thought to rate more coverage? Karen assumed that it must be the latter, but later to her great surprise David told her, one night after rehearsal, that he'd never even read Sarah's book. This was a full year after the book had been published, and just a few days before Karen surprised Sarah on Sarah's paperback tour.

David seemed surprised that Karen was surprised. "I'm not a reader," he reminded her, as if she should know better. "I read plays and I read the newspaper."

"But you were so proud and excited about it. You, like, harassed people to give it publicity."

"Of course I did. It's Sarah's *book*. I'll do the same for you, whenever you fulfill whatever your huge ambition is."

"I have no huge ambition."

"Bullshit. I got you out to auditions!" As usual David steered the conversation back to his accomplishments, his self-satisfaction coexisting with his insecurity and self-hatred. It had to be the insecurity and self-hatred, Karen felt at first, that accounted for his not reading the book. Only the dread of a humiliating discovery could be powerful enough to counteract the burning narcissistic curiosity David must feel knowing Sarah had written about their CAPA years and so presumably about him. Yet it turned out he did not even know that the humiliating disclosure he might have feared, had he had any real self-awareness, had been spared him by Sarah for reasons which Karen will not try to guess. Even had the disclosure been there, Karen still could more easily see David devouring his portrayal than just taking a pass.

"Don't you want to know how you come off in it? Don't you want to see how she depicts you?" Karen asked.

"It's not *me*. It's fiction."

"My turn to call bullshit. That whole thing about fiction not being the truth is a lie."

"So I'm guessing you read it."

It made no difference to this conversation that Karen had read only half. The point was that disciplined Karen had failed to resist, while impulsive David had succeeded. "Of course I did," she snapped. "I'm still shocked that you didn't."

"And how did *you* come off in it? How are *you* depicted?"

You'll be surprised that she had no immediate answer. She

herself was surprised. All those years of work naming her feelings, climbing down the dictionary definition's ladder into the dark dusty tomb of a word's origin, yet she couldn't lay hold of one word to give David. "Incompletely," she said after so long a pause David must have forgotten the question. He laughed with too much amusement, as if she'd been witty.

That night in the Mexican restaurant-caravansary Karen told Sarah about David's manic campaigns on behalf of her book, which she hadn't intended to do. As already stated Karen hadn't known, arriving that night at Skylight Books, what exactly she would do, apart from stimulate herself with the reunion and respond accordingly. Still, much as she hadn't known what she would do, there were things she'd felt sure she would not do. She certainly wouldn't stoke Sarah's belief in the superior dramatic arc of her life by describing David's manic devotion to publicizing her book. Yet no sooner had they agreed that Sarah would be Karen's dresser than Karen said, "I think it'll mean a lot to David that you're involved in one of his shows. He was so excited when your book came out, he acted like it was his child. He got it put on the CAPA marquee."

"He *did*?" Sarah said, looking queasy. Another item on her list of crazy things that had happened to her on her book tour: unwanted proof that this place that she'd written about actually existed.

"'*READ the critically acclaimed novel by a CAPA alum, available at bookstores everywhere!*' Yeah, he went all out. He didn't tell you? I would have thought he'd have written to you."

"I had no idea. No, I never heard from him. I was hoping I would." This did not sound convincing.

"You could have written to him."

Sarah grimaced like a child. She was certainly drunk, her anxiety and illogical pleasure burning brightly in her cheeks. She dreaded to hear about David but longed to hear more about David's devotion. "Scared," she said, in a little-girl voice, of the prospect of writing to David.

Karen gave her a don't-be-silly look. "Why?"

"That maybe the book pissed him off."

What could have? The book's revisions and excisions seemed designed to spare David's feelings. But Karen didn't say this, let alone reveal that David had not even read it. "Are you kidding? He's so proud to be a fictional character."

"So he liked it?"

"He loved it. If there was anything he didn't like about it, it's that you didn't write about him even more."

Sarah's laughter trailed off; there was no more evading the subject. "And what about you?"

"Me?"

"I worried that it might have felt weird to you, reading that book. Too familiar."

"You worried about that?" said Karen, in tones of amazement. "Did you really?"

"I did. I mean, I do. I mean, I'm worried right now." Nervous laughter erupted from Sarah again.

"Well, it didn't feel at all familiar. I mean, you changed a *lot*. Wouldn't you say? If you were worried that I'd recognize myself in your book, I didn't." Did Karen here lie, by omitting some facts? She merely spoke literally. I've said I recognized myself in Sarah's story easily: recognized as in "identified" myself. I didn't recognize to "acknowledge validity of." I didn't recognize to "accept."

Sarah failed to recognize the kind of recognition I meant, as I knew that she would. Sarah's face bloomed with relief. "I can't tell you how relieved I am," she said.

MEANWHILE, AMONG *the girls, surprisingly it had not been Joelle's house but Karen Wurtzel's that became the headquarters.* Notice how, unique among all the CAPA kids, all the English kids, and even in contrast to Martin and Liam, Karen gets a last name. An ugly one, that sounds like German food. It has the effect in the story of making her seem unfamiliar and distant, not invited to the party. Aside from "Wurtzel," though, the sentence mostly is true, with some lies of omission, like the bulk of what Sarah has written. Likely it matters to no one but Karen that it was her own mother who turned their house into a crash pad, not just with permissiveness but a hard-fought campaign. She'd started with Karen's official guest, whose designation, like the others, we won't bother to change back from Lara, prying her away from Karen with confidences and cigarettes and staying up all night watching TV. Once the other English girls began coming around, the mother we're fine to call Elli—it captures her well—kept it going by keeping the fridge stocked with wine coolers and cookie dough. Elli doled out advice on love and sex, loaned her makeup, hair accessories, and clothes. Astrological signs were explained. The Tarot was consulted. Soon Karen's bedroom was hosting a nightly slumber party at which her mother was the guest of honor and Karen the least welcome. Karen went to sleep in Kevin's room, which earned her the girls' mockery and contempt. And so Karen took extra shifts at her job after school, set her alarm for extra early in the mornings, was simply gone, disappeared, every time the English girls needed a ride.

Elli tried to smooth it over by driving the girls to school in the morning on her way to her job, but she couldn't take off work to pick them up when the school day was done. A hodgepodge of people—David, miscellaneous Juniors and Seniors the English girls started going out with, even a creep of a cabdriver Elli strung along who did her countless favors in the hope of getting laid—got the girls from school to wherever they went after school, and from there to Karen's home at the end of the night. It was a pain in everyone's collective ass, it pissed everyone off, because Karen with her adequate car could have always driven the girls where they needed to go if she hadn't been such a sulky hypersensitive bitch.

This was where things stood when Karen, one day toward the

end of her shift, came out from the storeroom and saw Martin standing there on the far side of the fluorescent-lit case. She was thoroughly surprised and embarrassed. She had seen plenty of Martin at CAPA but she had never yet spoken to him, marginal as she was, socially unnoticed as she was. She was mortified that Martin should know she spent afternoons here, pumping excrement-resembling fro-yo into stale waffle cones. The previous year, when she'd just turned fifteen, Karen had gone to a "lock-in" at church and made out with a boy who ground his crotch against her bare thigh so hard he abraded her skin, and afterward a girl ridiculed her for having "carpet burn" in the wrong place. That was Karen's sexual experience to date. Coming out of the storeroom and seeing Martin, Karen assumed he was there by coincidence. She assumed he must like frozen yogurt. When he said he was there to see her, she might have literally let her mouth hang open from shock. But then, all was made clear. "The girls put me up to speaking to you, about how you won't give them rides," he said. Karen hadn't even finished flushing with confused pleasure that he was there to see her when all her blood had to change gears and instead flush with angry humiliation.

But then he yanked the lever in the other direction. "I told them to sod off. You're not their bloody chauffeur. I told them, 'If you can't even stay in the houses where you were assigned, you can't throw a fit about not getting rides.'"

"You said that?" exclaimed Karen.

"I very nearly didn't bring them on this trip. Should've known they'd be terrible guests. So this is your country's best yogurt, is it? Should I try some?"

Just like that he brushed off the girls and put himself on her side. Karen served him a cone of the fro-yo, which she had subsisted on her first weeks on the job and which now made her gag even when she just smelled it. She waved him off when he tried to pay for it. By now her co-worker had come from the back, tying his apron in place. Her shift was over. "How did you get here?" she asked when they walked out together. He'd already finished the cone. The crumbly little strip mall parking lot was empty apart from her own and her co-worker's cars.

"I walked." Martin shrugged.

"You *walked*? Nobody walks."

"I did. It took a long time, too. I hope I don't have to walk back."

"So now I'm *your* chauffeur."

Martin grinned, roguish. "Gives me a clever idea. I'll tell the girls you can't drive them because you've got to drive me. That way they can't be angry at you."

"I don't care if they're angry at me," Karen lied.

"But I care."

Skip ahead. Imagine Karen made witty, by the attention of this witty man who assumes that she somehow is witty, like him. And she is! Or at least, with him, believes herself to be. Imagine the driving around. Day after day there are hours and hours of driving around. Avoiding the vengeful girls, her outmaneuvered mother, is a game they automatically win, just by forming a team. Karen shows Martin all the places in her town she thinks are special. Martin does not make her feel naïve at her failure to notice that every one of these places is located in a corporate park. It's that kind of town, possessed of only artificial beauty, manmade "ponds" spanned by poured-concrete bridges underneath which the water glows a blinding ghastly green from spotlights magically submerged but somehow not electrocuting the resident ducks. Topiaries cut into the shapes of the letters which spell out the name of the multinational conglomerate whose headquarters are surrounded by these hedges and ponds cast impenetrable shadows on the closely clipped, comfortable grass. Overhead, at the top of the corporate tower, a beacon swings in circles, all night long, as if there were a coast somewhere within a thousand miles, and ships to warn. Beneath Martin's body, Karen's body comes alive the way it never has before, not at the "lock-in" when the boy scraped the skin off her thigh with his denim-clad hard-on, not under the covers while reading the dirty parts in *The Thorn Birds* and poking herself. Possibly it would have made no difference if it had been Martin or if it had been her yogurt-place co-worker whose name history fails to preserve. Possibly first love, despite all the fuss, is only mating with ideas attached. Martin, retrospection shows us, was scrawny, smelled and tasted like an ashtray, and had yellow nails, yellow teeth, and yellowish whites-of-the-eyes. Inside his underpants, where Karen's hand was urged, a single clammy mushroom thrived. Even in the nearly total darkness of the topiary shadows, Martin's penis seemed unwholesomely pale and wet. But this was love, a crazy clamor to receive recognition. Did it matter that the person who unleashed Karen's floodgates was much older—even older than she knew? Did it matter that he was a liar? Did it matter that he had practice, and she had none? Did it matter that after he opened Karen's floodgates Karen's "lake, river, reservoir, etc." never refilled, to stick with the floodgates metaphor? Karen has thought about this, believe her. She knows she's not a special kind of victim, for having gotten shown the ropes by a much older man who, it turned out, did not care about her. She knows this is perfectly common; just look at all the stories/plays/movies about it. She wanted him. In her ignorance and inexperience she thought he was handsome, worldly, earnest, and reliable, and now, with her knowledge and experience, she can see that he was ugly, provincial, duplicitous, and untrustworthy; even cruel. The fact remains that she wanted him. Her wanting him means that she chose. She doesn't have a case here, she's fully aware; this would be why she's kept her mouth shut and kept her problem to herself. Martin's "witch hunt" is made up of women who insist they have a case, but what's different about them, exactly? Karen's attitude toward them is violently mixed. She might defend them to David, but in her bowels she scorns them, these young women who made a bad judgment and now want to blame someone else.

In Sarah's story, Karen and Sarah barely know each other. Sarah winds up in Karen's car, Karen's home, and even Karen's mother's bed essentially by accident. In the ethics of friendship this means that she owes Karen nothing, because they're not friends; but in reality, as already revealed, this wasn't the case. They were friends. Sarah was the best friend Karen ever had, while Karen was, at the time, the only friend Sarah had with a car, not to suggest this was Sarah's reason for maintaining the friendship. In Sarah's story Karen resents Sarah's involvement with Liam, regarding it as an intrusion. There is likely some psychological truth to this. Girls are complicated. They rarely love each other without also hating each other. They often react to differences of situation with envy even if the difference, the thing their girlfriend has that they don't, is a thing they never wanted in the first place. When Sarah began dating Liam—the way it really happened being so much simpler and more inevitable than the way it unfolds in Sarah's story, because Sarah and Karen were always together, and Martin and Liam were always together, so that Sarah was almost obligated to get together with Liam once Karen was together with Martin—Karen did suffer a pang. Liam was, at a glance, better looking than Martin. And Sarah always had some intrigue or several, while Karen never had any. But the pang was fleeting. First of all, Liam was not so good-looking as Sarah's story suggests. It's true he had nice eyes and interesting bone structure. But his teeth were bad, as all their teeth were bad, and his Adam's apple stuck out too much. As depicted in fiction he had a very weird vibe. In the matter of Liam's weird vibe please refer back to Sarah. On this point she's flawless, unsparing, she practically admits that Liam was a rebound/placeholder because her more prestigious/precocious intrigues had collapsed. So Karen suffered a pang, because she'd enjoyed, briefly, being the one with intrigue, but the pang didn't just pass, it was wiped out, erased, by the greater pleasure of this best-girlfriends-double-dating situation. Not just willingly but happily did Karen drive herself and Martin, Sarah and Liam, around in her car. Not just willingly but happily did Karen, with Martin, watch Sarah, with Liam, saunter off into the topiary shadows of the corporate park.

As they drive home their last night from the corporate park Karen's outfit is ruined by grass stains and her vision is blinded by tears. In the morning, without the originally planned school assembly featuring the principal you've met as Mrs. Laytner thanking them for "sharing their art across oceans," the English People will finally leave. Mr. Kingsley will put them into three taxicabs and send them off to the airport without so much as a wave, though he might produce his tight-lipped, white-lipped smile. Parked outside Mr. Kingsley's house on this departure eve, Martin hugs Karen's head in his arms and strokes her hair with his nicotine-stained fingertips and says, "Oh, my sweet girl." This romantic comment remains a landmark of Karen's sexual life. The next day Karen and Sarah, conscious of their tragedy, skip school. Instead they go to a US passport office downtown. Because they are sixteen years old, "parental awareness" of their passport applications is "required" but incredibly easy to fake, far easier than faking the credentials for buying a beer. What a strange, neither-here-nor-there position for the government to take. Karen's mother isn't just aware of Karen's plans, she's ecstatic. She almost ruins it for Karen with her excitement. Sarah's mother is the opposite of ecstatic but we've mentioned this already. Sarah pays for her own ticket, Karen's mother helps Karen with hers, warning her to keep this escapade a secret from her father. Departure is six weeks away, as soon as the school year ends. In that time Sarah receives letters from Liam almost every other day. The letters are enthusiastic and stupid, like the letters of a dog. They sprawl across pages and pages, detailing such events as a car driving into a hedge and the driver having to climb out the back door because the front door was stuck on a branch. When not detailing such incidents the letters natter on about how pretty Sarah is and how much Liam is dying for their reunion. With each new letter Karen can see Sarah's interest in Liam declining further. Even Karen, who initially scoured the letters for mentions of Martin, can't bear to skim them anymore. Meanwhile Karen receives very occasional, jocular postcards from Martin that don't seem to track with her letters to him although it's clear he's received them. "Hi there, Karen! Thanks for the tape. Super mix. How's everybody in the US of A?"

In the days leading up to their flight, Sarah lives with Karen. She says her mother's kicked her out, although Karen doubts it. Given Sarah's mother's disability it's easier for Karen to believe that Sarah simply walked away. Sarah's mother calls the house constantly, Elli pulls the phone into her bedroom and closes the door but Karen doesn't need to hear to know what's being said. Elli is playing the fellow adult, commiserating with Sarah's mother about how stubborn girls are, promising Sarah's mother she'll bring Sarah around. As soon as Elli hangs up the phone she forgets all about Sarah's mother until the next time the phone rings. All Elli cares about is helping them pack. She calls in sick to her receptionist job at a realtor's office to take them shopping for the things they still need. One good scarf: they should both have *one really pretty silk scarf* to tie their hair back or to tie around their necks. Karen has never in her life worn a pretty silk scarf. And one cute light jacket, because it gets cold there, it's not like here, remember when the English People brought all the wrong clothes? By one cute light jacket Elli doesn't mean Karen's ratty jean jacket, she means something like Sarah's man's blazer with the maroon silk lining that shows when you roll up the sleeves. Sarah has a vintage style that Elli adores; for hours Sarah and Elli try on Sarah's clothes, put together different outfits, weigh the advantages of one item over another, the blazer, the old-man cardigan, the plaid kilt, the funky

khakis from the Army Navy store. Just one suitcase, girls: sophisti-
cated travelers travel light. Elli has never been out of the country.
It's possible she's never traveled on a plane. Karen doesn't know
where Elli's gotten these rules about silk scarves and traveling light.
Karen herself has never been on a plane. Right after her parents first
got divorced, Sarah flew to see her father a few times before he disappeared for good. "All by yourself?" Elli cries.

"They just put you with a stewardess. I don't even remember
the flights."

"Lucky you to be traveling with someone experienced," Elli tells
Karen.

At the airport Sarah shows she's taken this idea of being the
experienced traveler to heart. She's insufferable, explaining things
like how Karen shouldn't lose her boarding pass and how she has
to make sure she has her makeup in her carry-on bag because she
won't be able to get to her luggage before they've landed in London. Looking back, Karen's willing to acknowledge it's possible
Sarah was nervous, just as nervous as Karen. It's possible Sarah's nervousness took the form of bossy condescension toward her friend,
telling her friend the sorts of things even non–English speakers
could have figured out for themselves at the airport, and then, once
the plane was airborne, telling her friend things about London
which she herself only knew on the basis of postcards. "Carnaby
Street is where all the punks hang out. There's a Hard Rock Café
and then there's Piccadilly Circus which is totally cool. I don't care
about Big Ben—it's just a clock." The plan was for Liam and Martin to meet them at Heathrow—"Heathrow" was the name of the
airport but you never said "Heathrow Airport" only "Heathrow,"
experienced Sarah informed inexperienced Karen—and for all of
them to stay at a youth hostel, whatever this was, perhaps not even
Sarah was sure, and once they were done seeing London they'd take
a train down to Bournemouth, the city where Martin and Liam
both actually lived. What would happen after that remained obscure.

Karen, seated next to the window, presses her face to the glass. The glass is icy cold, its touch makes her eyes water. She sees a total blackness of night she's never even imagined, back home where the night sky is always hazed out. The plane vibrates and roars as it flies, which alarms Karen because it seems like it's working too hard. She will not seek reassurance from Sarah. She won't give Sarah the satisfaction. Sarah is smoking, listening to her Walkman, pretending to read. Gazing down on them from the future, on Sarah self-consciously holding her book in one hand, cigarette in the other, like a woman three times her age; on Karen chewing off the corner of her thumb while unaware of the red circular mark on her forehead from where she keeps compulsively pressing her forehead against the cold window, my heart goes out to them. Like a ghostly flight attendant floating in the aisle I gaze down at the two teenage girls, at Sarah who doesn't love Liam, and at Karen who is not loved by Martin, and I'm filled with melancholy that's almost compassion. It's sad the same way. But in the moment, staring into the darkness which she can't keep her eyes off in spite of how frightening it is, Karen feels only resentment of Sarah. Because in the days leading up to their departure, Karen hasn't heard from Martin at all, not even a jocular postcard. There's no way he doesn't realize she's coming, she's sent him the details more than once, and Liam knows she's coming, and Martin knows whatever Liam knows, and Sarah treats her plans with Liam as also being Karen's plans with Martin, and aren't they? Karen believes it, because Sarah does. Sarah believes it, because Karen does. Karen has given Sarah no reason not to believe it, she hasn't mentioned the silence from Martin. Karen has let Sarah have this mistaken impression, and now she hates and even blames Sarah for it, which of course isn't fair, but Karen is afraid and embarrassed and also their friendship, at this moment of greatest shared risk, has gone wrong. It's sick, out of whack. In fact it's been like this for weeks but Karen wanted to think it was Elli who made things feel wrong but now Elli is gone and the wrongness remains. An hour into the flight Karen clambers over Sarah without explanation, crashes into the phone booth–size bathroom and vomits all over the ashtray-size sink. Karen stares at her greenish-gray face in the mirror. It takes her all the paper towels in the holder to clean up the vomit. She stuffs the vomit-covered towels in the toilet, presses the handle, then jumps back with fright as a sucking roar tells her she's opened a hole in the airplane and her vomit has fallen into the sea. Retrospection streamlines the nine-hour trip and also inflates all the portents of doom. Did sixteen-year-old Karen really know, on the flight, what would happen? Did she and Sarah really sit side by side in cold silence, aware that their friendship had come to an end? Probably not. There were ideas that gave rise to feelings, and feelings that gave rise to ideas, but there was also lots of giggling, smoking, scribbling in journals, and sharing of the Walkman. We almost never know what we know until after we know it. The night rushed past the little round window and when the line of fire showed in the east Sarah pressed close to Karen, her coarsely permed hair tickling Karen's cheek, and they watched the sun rise until the light was so bright they could no longer look. The last hour of the flight was spent solemnly doing their makeup.

At "Heathrow," once they'd stood in all the lines and had their passports stamped—that's a thrill nothing has ever undone, Karen can feel it again to this day, the knowing she'd just made her life forever larger than her mother's; if she could just avoid falling behind, if she could just keep on moving, she'd always be that much ahead—an alarming crowd shouted and waved signs from behind a long railing. And there was Liam, the telegenic handsomeness he sometimes had under stage lights, or in photos, totally erased by his fish-belly paleness, his pimples, his flailing limbs like a spider's, and his over-pointy Adam's apple like a hard-on in his throat. And he was looking left to right frantically and waving a square of cardboard that said SARAH and when he caught sight of the person who went with that name his body froze and his mouth fell open with amazement as if he'd never believed she would come. He looked like a little child who'd just been offered candy. His joy was that unembarrassed and pure. And although the technology for reading minds has not yet been discovered, to quote a witty therapist Karen once knew, Karen was willing to bet, at that moment, that Sarah's thoughts were so preoccupied with what an unhandsome dork Liam was despite his eyes and bone structure, and with how far he fell short of the romantic ideal she'd tried to believe that he was, and with how little she wanted to let his tongue into her mouth, that she couldn't even see that pure joy on his face which she'd caused. Which is too bad, because a lot of us never get looked at that way.

In the first confusing moments, going out through the gate in the railing and struggling to get to Liam through the crowd, it wasn't obvious that Martin wasn't there. It still seemed possible that he was parking the car, or getting a coffee, or returning from a trip to the men's room. Liam grabbed Sarah around the waist while jumping up and down so that they banged clumsily into each other, and then Liam got his tongue in Sarah's mouth until Sarah pushed him off to arm's length. "Wait, wait! Let me look at you!" she said, as if she wanted to gaze in his face and not get his tongue out of her mouth. That was when Liam caught sight of Karen, it seemed for the first time.

"Oh wow, Karen! You came!" Liam said. "I thought Martin wrote you, about his big part? He got a summer stock part—"

"You mean he's not here?" Sarah said. "What the hell are you talking about?"

"He told me," Karen said before planning to say it. "I mean, he said he was up for a part. Probably his letter saying he got the part is still on its way to my house." Karen felt Liam looking at her in confusion. Clearly Martin had gotten the part, if there really was a part, a while ago. But Liam was too stupid to know she was lying. He was even more stupid than Karen.

"It's so cool you came anyway!" Liam said earnestly. "We'll all have a great time—"

"But *where's* Martin," Sarah demanded. "Can't Karen go where he is?"

"He's *touring*, Sarah. I can't just go along on his tour!"

"He really told you he might be on tour? How come you never told *me*? You came all the way here and he's not even *here*?"

"I'm sure my mum won't mind if Karen stays too," Liam tried interrupting.

"Your *mum*?" Sarah said.

It was interesting, actually, how everyone's primary feeling-state at that moment was disguised as a different emotion. Sarah's repulsion at being reunited with Liam took the form of outrage at Martin. Liam's passion for Sarah took the form of concern for Karen. And Karen's unbearable humiliation, which she had always expected and never expected, took the form of emotionlessness and not caring. "I still want to see England," she said to Sarah angrily. "Stop making such a big deal about it. I have to go to the bathroom."

In the bathroom Karen threw up again, but since she'd felt too sick to eat on the plane, all she threw up was smelly clear slime. She hadn't made it into a stall and she could feel the eyes and hear the feet of Heathrow travelers as they steered clear of her while she heaved and gagged over the sink and splashed cold water on her face. Did Martin somehow know? She's always wondered. Despite his obvious defects of character he's persisted in her psyche as a weird joker-god, malicious and omniscient. Karen finally left the bathroom. Her eyes felt scrubbed with salt. An endless punch was landing in her gut.

Karen, Sarah, and Liam went to the youth hostel where in a room like a prison cell Karen lay in a bottom bunk facing the wall with her suitcase on her feet so she could feel if someone tried to steal it and slept a feverlike sleep while Sarah and Liam did whatever they did, had whatever adventure they had, made whatever postcard pictures in Sarah's mind part of her life. Later Sarah would be someone who referred to Trafalgar Square and U2 in Cardiff and bangers and mash. Later Sarah would go home with Liam to Bournemouth and meet his mum who watched the BBC and spread Marmite on toast and waited hand and foot on Liam as if he were a king and on Sarah as if she were his new wife the Queen and who seemed to have no idea that Sarah was still in high school, and later Sarah would learn that Liam had been "on the dole" for his entire adult life and was perfectly happy about it, and later Sarah would break up with Liam and go back to London alone and live in the hostel again and somehow get a job at a nightclub as a cocktail waitress, and later Sarah would meet a guy at the nightclub who took her with him on a train to see U2 in Cardiff and whom she lost in a stampede for floor seating in the arena, and later Sarah would stop sending Karen these updates, each one so flashily stamped with different-color silhouettes of the Queen, because Karen never wrote back. Karen never even read the letters until many years later and still isn't sure why she read them at all. In London Karen lay in the bunk in the prison-cell room in the hostel, and knelt behind the door down the hall labeled "Water Closet" gagging over the toilet, and sat in the grimy vinyl chair in the hostel office while a robotic guy from Germany figured out how to place an international collect call for her. Bunk bed, toilet, telephone. That was London.

Karen and Elli had succeeded in keeping the escapade a secret from her father yet when he answered the phone he wasn't as surprised or confused as you might think to learn his daughter was in London and that she was sick, broke, and alone. The sound of his voice, unemotional but not exactly cold, drawling a little in a way she'd somehow never noticed before, coming out of the phone into her ear as she sat in the chair in the hostel in London, marks the beginning of Karen's true adult life, if these things can be marked. Karen hopes they can. She finds that sort of historical clarity helpful. At the time Karen couldn't have explained her decision to call her father and not her mother but it was part of that beginning of true adult life, paradoxically since it was a decision to make no more decisions, to seek out superior judgment, to acknowledge there was such a thing. Karen's true adult life began when she recognized she was a child, and remembered that, unlike her mother, her father viewed her as a child as well. Calling her father meant doing things his way, but at least he had a way. At least he had a way, and the will to stick to it. Karen put herself into his hands. All the way back to America, Karen remembered nothing, she kept nothing in mind and called nothing to mind. Now she was an expert traveler: she did it all with a mind that was totally empty. Her father was waiting in the airport for her with his belly buttoned into his work shirt and his big hairy hands gripping each other in front of his crotch. Elli sometimes called Karen's father "a fucking hick" with great scorn but Karen's father had command of the resources. That first night he said nothing to her, just let her sleep in the small, sad room that was always reserved for her and Kevin's rare visits and that wasn't decorated with anything but their school portraits, every single year but one (Kevin first grade/Karen third grade—Elli had forgotten to order the packets), framed and lined up on the wall. Paneling on the walls and shag on the floor Karen's father had nailed up and tacked down himself. Military-style bedsheets Karen almost couldn't wedge herself into, they were tucked on the mattress so tight. Then their strong detergent smell gave her a headache and kept her awake. This kind of thing had never bothered her before. The next day, the trip to the doctor. Back home again Karen's father tanned her bare butt with his belt the way he'd done when she and Kevin were very little, before the divorce. All of this had been expected and hoped for. Karen's father let her get back in bed afterward, brought a folding chair in and sat on it, watching his knuckles until Karen stopped crying. Eventually he said, "Who's the guy."

"Just some guy who was visiting from England."

"Does he know?"

"No."

"And you couldn't find him when you went over there?"

"No."

"Any other ideas where to look?"

"No."

All this was just a formality. Karen's father didn't want to deal with the guy any more than Karen did. "The place is an hour drive from here. They have classes to keep you at grade level. And church, obviously. It's a God-centered organization. They'll handle everything. And the adoption."

"Okay," Karen said.

"It isn't fancy but it's safe and it's clean. You don't need a hotel."

"I know," Karen said.

"It's not cheap but it shouldn't be cheap. For the sake of the babies. It's not a vacation."

"I understand. I'm sorry," Karen said, which she was.

In a strange way it was the perfect place to say goodbye to God. At some point, without noticing, Karen had stopped believing in God. So there was something sweet and sentimental for her about living someplace where no one could shut up about him. "Thank you so much, Karen, for the unconditional love you've shown in seeking God's will for the future of your child" was the kind of thing everyone from the math tutor to the caseworker to the janitor said every chance they got. And though she understood this was people euphemistically kissing her ass for not getting an abortion, it was still pleasant to be thanked and praised all the time, as if you were really "God's gift," another popular phrase. As her father said it wasn't "fancy" but in fact it was a lot more like a hotel than anywhere else that Karen ever lived. There were vases of real flowers, and soothing Jesus music, and more vegetables and fruits than Karen had known existed. She had her first kiwi fruit here, for example. Years later—in fact, recently—Karen came to understand that she'd been pampered so much at the home because the home was a farm for growing White Christian Babies Without Health Defects of the type that's so rare and in such high demand on the adoption market now. Even if she'd realized this then, she wouldn't have enjoyed the time less.

Exactly a month after Christmas, as everybody from the OB to her caseworker noted, as if Karen had been extra clever this way, Karen had her baby. The baby was female. The feeling-state of labor can't be kept in mind or called back to mind, although the final slippery escape, like a fish coming out, does turn out to be memorable. When her baby was clean, warm, and dry and all wrapped in a blanket Karen held it and smelled it and thought to herself, *I will never remember this smell*, and she was right, she has never remembered it. It's always just out of reach, like a dream. Later on there was a prayerful ceremony in which Karen was praised some more, for her selfless Christianity in having chosen life. Then her baby was taken away to be united with her Forever Family, whoever they were.

Two weeks later Karen transferred back to CAPA. She drove her old car to school, arriving early so she could park in the front lot, where there weren't many spaces. She wanted to avoid everyone that she knew and they parked in the back. It was cold and damp and the dampness made a sort of light haze that in her memory softened the light so that she felt hidden and somehow alone, as if she was actually going to succeed, and get through her first day back at school without having to see anyone. But it was a small school with all the same people every year and there was no way she'd even get through an hour without seeing them all. But even a few minutes without seeing them would have made a difference. There were teachers' cars in the front lot but it wasn't half full. Karen's plan was to sit in the smokers' courtyard, which opened off the cafeteria through a set of glass doors, so it wasn't a good place to hide but at least you could see people coming. She knew there was nowhere to hide and the best she could do was to see people coming, but then she pulled open the heavy front door of the school and there was Sarah. Karen and Sarah looked at each other for just long enough. Neither stopped walking, Karen in, and Sarah out, the same door.

THE WAY MARTIN had written his play, the Girl doesn't have a quick-change. If you'll remember, in the penultimate scene the Girl and Doc go offstage, into the back room which we've previously seen through the propped-open door, and know to be Doc's squalid home. Doc and the Girl close the door behind them, there's a pause, the shot rings out, the lights go out; then the lights come up again on all Doc's regulars sitting in the bar memorializing him, and only after they've said a few lines does the Girl appear, in her funeral clothes. It's a quick-change for the set: in the blackout the actors playing the regulars get to their marks, the stagehands put the portrait of Doc and some wilted flowers and black bunting on the bar, etc. The Girl has more than enough time, between going through the backroom door with Doc, and reappearing, to do her own costume change. So Karen's invitation to Sarah to be her dresser, in addition to being an inspiration of the moment, was also an idiotic gaffe. Karen did not need a dresser and Sarah would not need help realizing this. But in the weeks after Karen saw Sarah at Skylight Books, and before Sarah arrived to take up the sentimental task/have the funny old-times'-sake experience which Karen had offered despite it not existing to give, the staging of the play went through a series of evolutions that would almost make you think Karen had supernatural powers. First, David's set designer created a window in the bar's backroom door with a roller blind pulled over it, so that when Doc and the Girl went in the back room and closed the door, a spotlight threw their shadows on the blind, and the shooting could be seen in silhouette. Second, David decided that when the lights came back up he wanted the Girl already onstage, dimly visible to the audience if not to the regulars, so that when she stepped forward into the light, the regulars would realize she'd overheard them. This meant Karen couldn't start her costume change until the lights went out, and had to complete it before they came up again. It would be a quick-change. "You'll need someone to dress you," said David. Karen waited for the nightly post-rehearsal at The Bar to tell David that Sarah would do it. "*Sarah's* coming?" cried David.

"I saw her last month in LA. We thought it would be fun if she helped with the show," Karen lied, clumsily. David was sitting up slightly too straight, staring down the length of his nose and holding his cigarette out to one side. When David was affronted, you were reminded of how dangerously handsome he'd been at the age of eighteen. His eyes flashed out as if to remind you that you shouldn't have forgotten about it.

"Sarah's never seen a single show I've done."

"That's why. She felt like she had to see this one and even help in some way," Karen continued to deceitfully improvise, really disliking this situation of her own creation in which she had to prop up a pretense of Sarah, to mollify David. Once again Karen was reminded of the suffocating self-regard of Sarah and David, who never failed to see themselves as performing some extraordinary drama even when they'd been completely out of touch for almost thirteen years.

"Why this one? Because you're in it?"

"*No*, just because she realized it was about time she saw one of your shows. It's just an extra point of interest that I'm in it."

"When did you get back in touch with her? The way I remember, toward the end of high school you weren't even speaking."

"We were in high school," Karen said dismissively.

Maybe it was unfair of Karen to see Sarah and David as twin narcissists, each fixated on the other's ancient image and seeing in that hapless teenage lover some lost part of themselves that they still wanted back. Maybe it was unkind of Karen to see Sarah and David this way because the feeling-state attendant was one of impatience, resentment, and scorn. Karen had no room for other people's unresolved emotions because she had no room for her own lack of generousness. Karen suffers, herself, because she wants to be empathic and she can't. The best she can do is maintain healthy separation, and oftentimes she can't even do that. Karen's failures in the empathy department are so acute she finds that she can't look at David and Sarah, when David, getting out of his piece-of-shit car, and Sarah, getting out of Karen's car, confront each other on the broken stretch of sidewalk outside the bar/performance space where the first dress rehearsal will finally happen tonight. Picking Sarah up from the airport, Karen had let Sarah do all the work—grin strenuously with excitement, unhesitatingly hug, chatter and marvel nonstop—while in the privacy of nonparticipation Karen coldly dissected every pop and pulse of Sarah's tireless efforts. But as Sarah faced David across the expanse of smashed pavement, Karen found herself looking away. What passed between them in an instant smote Karen. She felt ashamed, witnessing it.

Then the instant passed and David, his old lope still visible beneath his new weight, crossed the space between them and grabbed Sarah into his arms in an overly hearty, hail-fellow-well-met way and Sarah gave a strangulated laugh, exaggerating the strangulation for humor, and said, "Careful! Don't squeeze too hard. I'm pregnant," and David stepped away as if he'd been burned.

"I found out right after I saw you in LA," Sarah said to Karen. "My hangover the next day was—well, it lasted a lot longer than usual."

"I guess that answers the question of what I can get you," said David. "I mean, there's a bar in the space."

"Oh! Water or juice would be great."

"Great! Okay," David said, and turning on his heel he strode across the street and into the building as if Sarah had ordered the drink to be brought to her there on the sidewalk.

"Congratulations," Karen said as they walked in.

"I'm only eight weeks. I didn't mean to say anything but I just sort of blurted it out. I was afraid I might blurt something worse."

"I'm sure David would have forgiven you. He's been thrown up on a lot in his life," Karen said.

Inside David was nowhere to be seen. Karen left radiant Sarah to be fawned on by Martin and made her way through the maze of black curtains, across big dark hidden reaches of the warehouse, and out the back door onto the old loading dock. David was there, sitting on the dock with his back to the wall, smoking and staring at the toes of his boots.

"Are you okay?" Karen said.

"I'm not," David said. "In fact I'm not okay."

Karen sat down on the dock next to David, which she hadn't intended to do. She'd intended to go inside and leave David alone. Telling herself to not think about it too much she put her arms around David and at her touch he slumped heavily and then jerked back to life with a terrible sound like an animal caught in a trap. His whole body heaving and jerking made him hard to hang on to. Karen guiltily wanted to stop, but only had to admonish herself a few times before he shrugged her off of his own accord, without anger, to get at his cigarette pack in his pocket. Before lighting up he scrubbed the loose-stretched hem of his ancient T-shirt roughly over his face.

"We'd better do this fucking rehearsal," he said, standing up.

Sarah watched Act One sitting alone in the fourth row while David went about the business of running rehearsal. But it was still there, Karen observed: that tension, like a wire strung between them that if you weren't careful you'd trip over it. Karen wondered how it could still bother her. Because it excluded her? Because it made such a claim for itself, to be a more important human condition than anyone else's? David was constantly on the move, stamping up the risers to the lightboard or climbing onstage or sitting in the

outermost seats to check sight lines, the whole time trailing cigarette smoke and slopping suds from his beer on the floor, but no
matter where he moved he kept his eyes away from Sarah so that
you knew he'd grown eyes in the back of his head, or on the out-
sides of his shoulders, wherever they needed to be to keep that wire
running the most direct path. It cut the room to pieces and the
rehearsal was a disaster of missed cues and misspoken lines and tech
glitches and no one, except possibly Karen and Sarah and David,
knew why. Once the second act started and Sarah was out of sight
backstage with Karen's costume the last shreds of David's focus
disintegrated and he shambled around with his fourth or sixth
beer like a sleepwalker. "David, David?" the lighting designer was
saying. "Is that the cue you wanted?" "David, David?" the sound
designer was saying. "Which song did you mean?" "David, David?"
the set designer was saying. "Should Doc yank down the blind?"
Karen had brought the loaded blank gun in for the first time and
she realized the blocking of the silhouetted shooting was going to
have to change again; holding the Beretta nose down with her fingers well away from the trigger she went out onstage and squinted
into the lights. "David!" she said and felt the whole chaotic room
of milling-around people who'd lost their leadership suddenly snap
to attention. "Whoa, don't shoot," someone said, and a shiver of
laughter broke out.

"There needs to be more space between Martin's head and the
gun. Once I'm standing on my mark, take a look from far left and
far right to make sure the shadows line up the right way."

"I thought it was a blank gun."

"It is, but it still has a cartridge with gunpowder in it. That's
what makes the shot noise, and it makes a shock wave. So no one fool
around and put this against your head or even point it at someone.
I'll point away from Martin's head at an angle for safety, but the
shadows should look like I'm aiming at him. Tell us if they line up."

"If you don't mind my asking," Martin said, "am I in any danger?" Martin had come out onstage to play this question for humor.

"Just don't piss Karen off!" someone said.

As the humorlessly responsible firearms person, Karen ignored this. "Even though there's no projectile in this weapon, the safest way to handle a blank gun is to pretend that it's real. I'm firing toward stage left, so I want no one stage left during the scene. There's no need for anybody to be there. Costumes are stage right, props are stage right, all the actors make their final entrances from stage right. Okay? Nobody hangs around stage left."

"Listen *up*!" David said.

Because so much of the bar's back room would be visible through the open door, and also because David insisted, the set designer had furnished the room with a little shelf of yellowed paperbacks, a full ashtray, a filthy manila folder with the neglected paperwork of an ailing small business sticking out the sides, a hot plate with a tattered cord, a few cans of soup, a pair of gray socks with large holes in the toes hanging over the end of the cot. Inside the drawer of the rickety table, which not even the front row could see, half-empty matchbooks, chewed pencils, hoarded change, a tattered old *Playboy*, and a pocket sewing kit. It was the sewing kit that pierced Karen when she opened the drawer to look in. It seemed like her own lonely, unloved competence hidden in that scratched plastic box.

Martin sat in Doc's chair at Doc's table; Karen stood to his side; the lighting instrument clamped to a pipe poured its hot light on them and threw their shadows on the closed window blind. Holding the Beretta with her trigger finger lightly balanced on the trigger guard, Karen pointed the gun. She stood to Martin's right. Martin sat facing front; at the sound of the shot he would tumble sideways, to the left. David shouted to Karen to step inches this way or that way, angle her arm up or down. Karen's arm was quivering and burning from being extended so long. She shouted to David that her arm would fall off and at last David said that it worked. One of the stagehands came out from the wings and taped around the chair's legs, Martin's feet, and Karen's feet, and taped an X on the inside hidden wall of the set while Karen sighted down the barrel. If she and Martin and the chair all stayed inside their marks and she sighted at the X, the shadows ought to line up from every seat in the house. "Let's do it!" called David, and Karen, setting the Beretta back on the table and rubbing her shoulder, went back out onstage, passing Sarah, who grabbed onto her hand.

"You're so good," Sarah whispered when Karen looked at her questioningly.

"Shoot it this time for real," David said.

"Somebody should tell them up front in the bar that we're shooting a blank gun," said Karen.

A good idea, all agreed. Someone went.

In the brief pause someone said, "It's a good thing we're out in the sticks where nobody can hear."

Someone else said, "In the sticks . . . no one can hear your blank gun."

Someone else said, "In space . . . no one can hear your bad jokes."

Then they were ready and began. For the first time, doing the scene, Karen felt a panic-pressure building inside, as if her rib cage was about to blow apart. Far away in the depths of a pit her mouth was speaking her lines but she couldn't hear what she was saying, she didn't know which line was next. She'd had bad dreams like this. She must have said them all; Martin/Doc "seized her in a violent embrace" and for the first time although they'd done this countless times she felt his body, scrawny and aged and hot with effort and forceful, and her own body bristled and rippled all over.

Then they'd gone through the door, Karen pausing as the Girl inside the doorframe so that the audience, when they had one, would be able to see the resolve coming into her face like a bank of stormclouds. David had said that about the stormclouds, weeks ago. He'd said he wanted the audience to know that the Girl had decided, even though the audience didn't know what the decision was. His comment had reminded Karen that David thought in metaphors. David had originally wanted to write his own plays and direct them, not direct plays that other people had written. Again Karen felt panic-pressure from the inside out, straining her ribs, and she didn't have any idea whether she'd conveyed the stormcloud-of-decision while standing in the doorframe. She didn't know whether she'd shut the door so that the window blind/screen was in place. She didn't know whether she was standing inside her taped box with her arm at the correct height and angle while she sighted at the X sightlessly and, from somewhere outside her body, pulled the trigger, jerking back from the force and the noise which was so much louder and more startling than the noise of an actual gun. Martin fell sideways out of the chair like a sack of potatoes, and the lights blacked out. The gun fell out of Karen's hand onto the floor.

"Jesus!" said Martin from down on the floor. "Is that the gun you just dropped?" Karen felt she'd crashed back in her body the same way the gun had crashed onto the floor.

"Yeah, sorry," she said, snatching the gun off the floor as the lights came back up.

"Let's do it again with the quick-change!" called David, which meant, That was perfect, let's keep the fuck going and finish.

"I need to reload it to do it again," Karen said. "I'm only loading one blank at a time. For safety."

Everyone stood around the props table watching as she opened the cylinder to confirm that the chamber was empty, loaded the new cartridge, pressed the cylinder back in the frame. Doing these things she'd done many times before and had total confidence doing Karen's hands felt shaky and unruly and she wished they wouldn't watch her so closely. She wasn't performing fucking brain surgery. To distract attention, theirs and her own, Karen talked through the steps the way Richie had done. "You always have to confirm the cylinder is clear after each time you use it. Basic safety. Your finger should be nowhere near the trigger and nowhere near the trigger guard until you're ready to shoot. Never point the gun at anyone, even if it's unloaded. Never squeeze the trigger, even if it's unloaded. The safest thing in our situation is if no one touches this blank gun but me. I'll bring it to and from the show, I'll move it to and from the props table, I'll load it and clean it. No one else should touch it at all, even if they're just trying to help. That's how accidents happen."

Then Martin and Karen and the gun all returned to their marks. Karen as the Girl again stood with Martin as Doc on the stage with the lights blazing on them. They spoke their lines again. They did their seizing embrace again. Through the door, stormclouds, door closed, find the marks, pick up the gun. Martin clapped his hands over his ears.

"What's that?" David called from the house. "Why are you doing that? We can *see* it, man. Doc's supposed to be waiting for death!"

"It's bloody loud, are you hoping that I should go deaf?"

"I think he's right," Karen heard herself saying. "We've done it once and I know how it feels, let's go back to 'bang' for the rest of rehearsal or we'll all end up deaf."

David was unhappy with this. He came up onstage, opened the set door, and stood scowling at them. "You're the safety expert. Seems to me like you should get used to shooting it for real in rehearsal. It's gotta go perfectly in performance."

"I am used to it. It will go perfectly. We've got the angle, I've felt the recoil. It's less safe to shoot the thing off every time we rehearse."

"You didn't think so before."

"I hadn't thought it all through."

"Well. You're the one holding a gun."

"Then let's take five so I can unload it again."

"For fuck's sake!" David said.

After that it mattered even more that the quick-change go smoothly. Karen remembered the quick changes she'd done years ago when they all were in school, the cold intimacy of pulling open Melanie's zipper, yanking down her dress to a pool at her feet, pulling the doughnut of the new dress swiftly over her head and her arms while she stepped out of the old dress, dropping onto all fours to grab her feet one at a time, push them into her shoes while she did up her buttons, all breathlessly fast in the dark. It was all business, it was not sexy, you were not meant to feel excited or strange as you roughly handled someone else's body and clothes as if they were a doll you didn't love. Yet it was sexy, exciting, and strange, or maybe only Karen felt that way, back when their feelings were so sternly policed that you got in trouble if you didn't feel one way on command and also in trouble if you felt another way that had not been commanded. And now it was Sarah grabbing hold of Karen's body in the dark, tugging her jeans down and holding them flat to the floor so that Karen could quickly step out, Sarah casing Karen's body in the tight dress, swiftly zipping it up with the flat of one palm running up Karen's back so the zipper does not bite her skin. Shoes, bag, a tiny light-up compact that Sarah snaps open so Karen can put on lipstick. The lipstick transforms the waif-Girl into something sharper and harder when she reappears onstage minutes later. Sixty seconds and Karen has sprung to her bit of glow tape. They've done it, first try. Karen even has time for her heart rate to settle back down.

During the quick-change something else has changed. It's happened just as quickly and just as wordlessly. Whether because they shared a task, or because they did it well, or just because they had to touch each other's bodies too efficiently to leave time to think, somehow the static between Karen and Sarah is gone. It's as if someone turned off a white-noise machine Karen hadn't remembered was on. While David gives notes, Sarah comes out from backstage and drops down in the chair next to Karen, and she isn't sitting opposite to Karen, haunting or besieging, she's just sitting there. She looks tired and slightly green beneath her permanent tan. Karen tries to recall her obsession with Sarah but can't retrieve the feeling-state. Losing that is like losing a limb. She feels light, not a lightness of heart but the lightness of being cut loose and set adrift in a void. At last, says Karen's inner therapist, so much more cost-effective than a real one. At last you're done crawling around inside Sarah, measuring all of the ways that she wasn't a good friend to you.

"Are you excited to be having a baby?" Karen asks Sarah when rehearsal is finally over and everyone is leaving while also talking, milling, smoking, and drinking.

"I don't know," Sarah says. "I felt like I had to have one."

"You *felt* that you had to have one? Or you *thought* that you had to have one? Thoughts are often false. A feeling's always real. Not true, just real."

"I thought I had to have one," Sarah says after considering briefly. "I really don't know what I feel."

"I had one," says Karen. They're back outside now, getting into Karen's car, on their way to The Bar, where Sarah will pretend to pay attention to Karen while only paying attention to David, and David will pretend to pay attention to everyone while only paying attention to Sarah. Is this why Karen lets slip her secret—because she wants to break into this circuit of David and Sarah, and seize attention, at last, for herself?

No. She lets it slip because she does. Don't ask her Why now? Ask her Why not every moment up to now?

They have the car between them. Sarah looks across its top at Karen, perhaps meaning to pretend to have misheard, as people sometimes do to buy time, when they think that what matters is how they respond, and not that the thing has been said. How to tell them their response doesn't matter, in fact isn't wanted? "Please don't say anything," says Karen. Her own voice sounds harsh in her ears, and clearly startles Sarah even more. Well, so be it. Karen watches Sarah struggle with her unwanted position—no way to prove her goodness and caring, no way to disprove her discomfort and guilt. They look at each other so long across the top of the car that the other actors and Martin and David and the tech people come babbling onto the sidewalk, and the moment is taken away, it doesn't end so much as stop. And that is satisfying to Karen, because nothing ends as in "completely to shut" from the Latin *conclaudere*. Nothing does that.

I ALWAYS LOVED opening nights. When I was little, before my parents split up, my mother and Kevin and I would go to opening nights at the outdoor theatre in the park and sit on a blanket eating peanut butter sandwiches and exclaiming in excitement every time something happened onstage that my father had done. If a flat glided in from the flyspace, or a set piece rolled in from the wings, or even if a pool of light appeared, if it was something he'd worked on we clapped as if the show's star had made an entrance. We hardly paid attention to the actors or the story. The whole production seemed to be a coded message to us from my father that confirmed our importance, our special place on the hill that formed most of the theatre's seating, its grass mashed flat from all the other blankets and all the other picnic baskets spread out under the pinkish night sky.

Ever since then I've been looking for that same secret message, that same confirmation that I matter most to whoever is sending the code. I'm sure all of us look for that message, although some people seem to receive it so early they don't recognize it's a message. They don't wonder who sent it. Their own importance is that well-established to them. But I've never been like that and doubt that

I'll ever be like that. Once you're old enough to recognize a hole in yourself it's too late for the hole to be filled.

The bar/performance space's women's dressing room was a janitor's closet with a bare lightbulb in it, but even though only I used it, because I was the only woman in the cast, when I opened the door and turned on the bare lightbulb and found a bouquet in a vase, I didn't think it was for me until I read the card. I had no friends in this town where I'd been born and raised. The only people I knew were involved in the show. I'd told my father I was David's props master, not that I'd be acting onstage, because I didn't want him to come see the show. Having someone in the audience who knows who you are is a certain reminder you're acting and I hadn't wanted to know I was acting.

The note on the bouquet said, "To lovely Karen from her lucky leading man. Break a leg, Martin." Reading the note, I knew that Martin had never forgotten. Over the past several weeks I'd convinced myself that he'd forgotten everything that had happened between us, but now I knew he hadn't, and that was harder somehow to digest than the thought that he had.

They were gorgeous flowers, actually. Karen put her face in them, and closed her eyes. It was a very self-conscious gesture she'd seen actresses do on TV and in movies but never had the chance to do herself. Then Karen put on her costume, the dingy jeans and hoodie of a runaway, and did her makeup, which was a lot of grayish powder to make her look starved and unhealthy. But she didn't feel starved, she felt full. She was already acting. She stayed in the closet as long as she could because she didn't want to see anyone else. She wished that she could do the play alone.

Somebody knocked on the door. It was Sarah. Sarah squeezed in and shut the door behind her. Sarah had made herself glamorous for the opening night of this show in which she served as a backstage dresser for the space of one minute. Just like when they were young, Sarah had glamorized herself painstakingly in the style of someone who has not made an effort. She was wearing stovepipe jeans with big rips at the knees, motorcycle boots, a slashed and draped top made of hoodie material that fell off one shoulder to expose her bra strap like the outfit in *Flashdance*, and gigantic bohemian earrings. Her hair was parted far to one side so that a lot of it fell in her face. Maybe her outfit was an homage to the eighties. She looked just like she'd looked in high school, except better, because the bones of her face had become more defined. Karen hoped David hadn't seen her or he'd be passed out drunk in the light booth before intermission.

"Mr. Kingsley is on the comp list!" Sarah said in outrage, as if even he should have ceased to exist once she'd pretended to write about him.

"He always comes to David's shows. They're good friends."

"How is that possible? How can David even speak to him? 'I won't rest until you cry'—remember that?"

"He said that to David, not you."

"That doesn't make me less angry about it."

"He was trying to help David get in touch with his emotions, and maybe it worked. David became a director, and he's really good at it and loves it. I've heard him call Mr. Kingsley a mentor."

"You're the last person I would have expected to drink the Kool-Aid."

"What Kool-Aid is that?" Karen said, because she can play dumb just as well as the next girl, particularly when discussing the person here called "Mr. Kingsley."

Sarah gave Karen a Look. "Mr. Kingsley is part of what happened to you," Sarah said, as if Karen deserved to be scolded for not holding the past to account.

"And here I thought he was part of what happened to *you*."

"I don't know what you're talking about," Sarah said after just a slight pause.

"Did you really expect me to go along with your revision? With

David it's one thing. He never knew in the first place and somehow still doesn't. But come on. 'Take five, sweetie'? That's rich, how you kept that and added a bow tie."

"I really don't know what you're talking about," repeated Sarah, who never could act her way out of a bag. By contrast, Karen knew she was going to be good. She could feel it. Tonight was her opening night.

"Five minutes!" someone called from outside, knocking sharply on the closet/dressing room door.

"Get to your place," Karen dismissed Sarah, turning away.

Nothing feels safer than watching a show from the wings. You might think it's a matter of upbringing, of Karen's childhood in the theatre that she mentions so much, but anyone can be made to feel safe hidden in the wings, watching the spectacle sideways, from outside the circuit the actors and audience make. The warmth of that circuit warms you but asks nothing of you. Karen loved her very late Act One entrance for how long it let her be a watcher in the wings, but she'd never felt so disembodied and free as she did tonight, ready to step out onstage and until then a being of pure curiosity shining her light on the darkened unknown. All these weeks of rehearsal she had willfully ignored the fact that Martin was the author of the play but now the play spoke to her in his voice and she understood something about him. Why, asked the actors onstage, had their friend killed himself? And why not? asked the others who argued with them. It was his Self to keep or destroy. Why should customs or, God forbid, laws interfere with the ways we dispose of our Selves?

Because we're none of us alone in this world. We injure each other.

Why should another be injured by choices I make for my Self?

You're choosing for another when you make choices. We overlap. We get tangled. You can't help but hurt.

That's a load of BS! Anyone tangled with me got that way by a choice of their own. If I shoot myself, they had fair warning.

What warned them?

The plain knowledge that *I* wasn't *them*.

The world is *me* and *not me*, Karen's therapist said. It's a difficult lesson to learn. Even over her therapist's voice speaking inside her mind Karen heard her cue spoken and walked onstage into the light. Her body was a wire bringing shock to the actors onstage just as much as to the audience out in the house. She did it. She felt the air crackle, and felt a curiosity to answer her own. That electrification took place that can happen in shows when the Selves in the room overlap and deliver their shocks across spaces of air. The act ended and backstage as if under a noiseless glass dome Karen loaded the blank gun and set it in place. Sarah came backstage glittering and gesticulating with her fingers and moving her mouth in ways associated with eagerness and excitement but whatever it was she was saying Karen chose not to hear. Karen had no need to speak to her dresser. The lights went down when intermission ended and came up again at the start of the act and the scenes that led up to her scene came and went and then Karen stood gazing at Martin through the eyes of the Girl who stood gazing at Doc, and Karen understood the injury that bound them together and knew that Martin understood it. Martin/Doc "seized her in a violent embrace."

Through the door, staring sightlessly out as the audience cringed from the stormclouds that formed on her face. Door shut, Martin in his chair, Karen on her marks, hot light throwing their shadows against the drawn blind. Shadow play. Karen raised the gun, sighted, and fired. With a strangled bellow and shriek Martin fell from the chair with his thighs and his hands tightly clamped at his crotch, and kept screaming and writhing once hitting the floor. Karen opened the chamber, looked in the cylinder, pressed the chamber back into the frame, took aim and fired again. Now Sarah was onstage with them in Doc's "room" behind the scene flat and screaming also, if not in the same way as Martin. "Oh my God!" Sarah screamed, and, "Doctor! We need a doctor—" Sarah's usual smoky murmurousness was now shrill and high-pitched while Martin's usual jagged singsong had gone moaning and low. From the house, scraping chairs and stamping feet and disputing voices and David, briefly flinging open the set door and looking at them before he went shouting away.

"What really pissed me off about what you wrote," Karen tried to tell Sarah as Sarah knelt screaming by Martin, as if Sarah had just one stage direction but was going to do it for all she was worth, "is how you wrote so much just like it happened, and then left out the actual truth. Why even do that? Who do you think you're protecting?"

"Oh . . . God . . ." Martin was keening, curled like a fetus on the floor, a fetus turning like a wheel. The way he was writhing in pain had him somehow rotating in place.

"What have you done to him?" Sarah screamed. As usual, not listening.

"You won't die," Karen reassured Martin. "You just won't be the same."

Trust
Exercise

I ENDED UP sorry I went.

I'm so sorry to hear that. Can you talk about why?

It was crowded. They had to simulcast it outside in the lobby. Even then, there were people who didn't get into the building at all. I got in. I'd arrived really early. I was so nervous, all I thought about was what I would say. Then I wound up in this mob. There must have been four or five thousand people.

That might feel overwhelming.

I didn't care about him. I was there for the audience. I just never guessed how large it would be. I felt like a fool afterward. Like I could have ever spotted someone in that crowd. Or like someone could have ever spotted me.

You were nervous about going and the fact that you went is what matters. Even if the outcome wasn't what you had hoped.

I don't know what I hoped. I know what I said I hoped, but did I really mean that? I was terrified it would come true. And then I got there and saw there was no way. And that made me wonder if I'd wanted it at all. If I'd set myself up for a disappointment that I'd actually hoped for.

Why do you think you would do that?

To tell myself I'm doing something.

You are doing something. You've done a lot of things, and they've all been very difficult things.

Thanks. I think that's all for today.

That's all the time you want for today?

Yeah. Thanks. I have to be someplace soon actually. Thanks for listening.

Of course. We can

CLAIRE CLOSED HER laptop. Then she foolishly felt she'd been rude. It wasn't as if she'd closed a door in someone's face. Whenever she opened the laptop again, there would be the reminder to tip and rate. Just thinking of it made her open the laptop again to complete the transaction in case, as she suspected, the amount of time she took to tip and rate was kept track of for whatever reason. As usual she clicked "30 percent" and "five stars," which represented the satisfaction level exactly opposite to hers. Like most economical options, this one didn't work.

Then she closed the laptop again. Then she reopened the laptop immediately so the screen wouldn't lock, closed the window inviting her to schedule her next session, and reopened the window to the school's Facebook page. She played the video of the tribute again. The same way she'd scanned the roiling, roaring crowd that afternoon, while feeling shorter and shorter and smaller and smaller and less and less able to hold her ground and not wind up trampled even wedged in a seat, she now scanned the depths of the video's frame, feeling as if she saw nothing. Even when she hit Pause to comb over each frozen granule, she couldn't seem to see a thing.

It hadn't been the same building she'd gone to almost three years ago. That building, squat and ugly with its bad old ideas about what might seem modern, had apparently already been declared obsolete the day she'd pulled open its doors. The ground had already been broken on its massive replacement. She hadn't known. There might have been an architect's model of Our Future Home! on display in the lobby, in fact it seems almost certain there was, but she hadn't noticed. She hadn't realized that the building might vanish, that its people might vanish, that she might lose her chance. When she'd left on that day almost three years ago, definitely not having seen an architect's model of Our Future Home! on display in the lobby as she plunged blindly back out the doors, Claire hadn't dreamed it might be her last chance. She'd thought okay, today wasn't her day, but she'd gotten somewhere. She'd stopped short, but she'd gotten somewhere. And another day she'd get farther. And she'd keep getting farther, a bit at a time, until she finally reached there, that place she was trying to go. It never crossed her mind that the building itself, where her answer was housed on some yellowed page or in some squeaky-drawered file cabinet or maybe just in some old person's wandering mind, could disappear, its ugly gray stones demolished and thrown into Dumpsters and carted off to the beach to become a fake reef for some project with oysters.

The new building where the tribute was held was huge, bright, beautiful, the opposite of the old building which looked like a bunker except for its goofy marquee. The new building stretched out over fake hills that had been built on the site and then planted with expensive-looking native blond grasses. Parts of the building, like the front, started at the normal ground level and were tall as a cathedral while other parts, around the sides, were low and halfway set into the ground with glass sections that opened directly onto little fake meadows of the native blond grasses that eventually rose into curved steps and formed an outdoor amphitheatre. The new building, in its resemblance to a LEED-certified eco-resort located in some northern European paradise like Finland, had actually taken Claire's breath away through a painful compression of her rib cage and lungs. It felt like a mockery of her perfectly adequate childhood that buildings like this now existed to serve as high schools. Claire had graduated high school only ten years ago but the building made her feel as though she'd graduated in a previous century that had thought a lot less of its children, or maybe had just thought a lot less of the way that it thought about children. This building emanated a smugness that if Claire hadn't already felt sick with self-doubt would have made her feel sick with disdain.

For all the time and money she'd spent anticipating this event, she'd less formed a plan than fostered a hope, that if she brought herself here, something would happen. Someone—not Claire—would say something, or do something, or be something, and then Claire would know what to say, do, and be. This hope of Claire's, if it could even be called that, was characteristically passive and uncertain. As usual, her Listener had undermined her efforts to not be this way by praising her as "courageous and determined" in "creating conditions for change." The few feeble ways she'd imagined creating conditions for change she gave up on arrival. The office, which she'd known was a long shot but at least gave her someplace to start, wasn't open. The crowd, which she had expected to resemble an audience at the movies—a couple hundred people sitting still, unsuspectingly allowing themselves to be closely examined—turned out to be a shape-shifting monster with no head or tail, a surging tide of thousands. Worst of all, her goal was still unclear. Even if she homed in somehow, using instinct or magic, what then would she do? Claire remembered the single time she'd broached the idea to her mother, years ago when she'd just started college. Her mother had neither scolded nor cried, as Claire had no reason to think that she would. But their closeness ensured that Claire would feel the vibration of sadness her mother failed to hide. "I always knew you'd want to know, and you should," her mother had said in a false, strident voice. "Dad and I can't be everything to you." "But you are," Claire had argued, as if the whole discredited idea had been her mother's to start with. Claire's hold on the idea had been so tenuous already that she'd been glad, at that moment, for the chance to abjure it. Her parents being everything to her at least was an idea that was robustly, reassuringly true. Claire's parents had prized her so much, tried so hard, organized their lives so completely around her, that the one thing they'd failed to give her was the reason she craved something more—something so potent, singular, and undefined that Claire was embarrassed to even share with a Listener she paid by the hour her private name for it. The Look: a grail that for all the time Claire spent imagining it, she could still neither see nor describe. Who delivered the Look, what exactly they saw Looking at her, were the urgent details Claire would learn only when the Look happened. She was, however, sure of how it would feel: the electric shock of being recognized, of being herself the object of a quest, the one thing someone else had been missing.

Instead Claire was plunged in this agoraphobe's nightmare where she lingered not courageously, as her Listener might claim, but because it was impossible to leave. The crowd groaned along like a glacier carrying with it all the squealing and hugging and crying people and her, until the force of it squeezed her into a seat. There the man next to her—he was maybe forty or thirty-five or fifty, she was terrible at guessing people's ages who were older or younger than her—talked to her with the assumption that she belonged there, saying Wasn't it so terrible, but Wasn't this incredible, and Had she heard who was going to be there, until at last he was interrupted by the lights going down and a screen gliding out of the ceiling and the audience roaring like the thing was a fucking rock concert. Projected on the screen, white on black, ROBERT LORD, 1938–2013.

A very highly produced tribute played, managing to take low-quality video and photos and make an asset of how low their quality was. The emotion in the room grew more audible the queasier the colors and the worse the resolution. By the time it was the early 1980s you could barely tell the gender or race or age of anyone in the murky black-and-white photos while the occasional image in color was almost unbearably elegiac, as if not only Robert Lord had expired but also whatever kind of special sunshine had once shone on his students, whatever better air they had once had to breathe. Everyone looked so young and beautiful and glad, although perhaps this was just Claire's anxiety racing to extract the possibility from each image before it dissolved to the next. At first certain images had elicited particular explosions of applause or cries of recognition but soon enough every single image elicited explosions of applause and cries of recognition until continuous full-throated yelling and continuous flesh-numbing slapping of palms seemed required. Claire must have looked as stricken and enraptured as everyone else. She hadn't anticipated this additional realm of possibility, photo after photo of Robert Lord midstride amid a changing crowd of raptly attentive kids in dance togs or ridiculous costumes or holding play scripts in front of their faces. But Robert

Lord thoughtfully stroking his beard, or retrieving his glasses from the top of his head, or sitting backward on a chair, or demonstrating a dance step, or forming his mouth in an elongated O as a youngish, then less young, then older, then oldish, then decidedly old man with hard creases cut from his nostrils to the ends of his mouth was not what Claire stared at devouringly. What Claire was staring at, her eyeballs burning with the effort, was the ever-changing constellation of kids clustered around Robert Lord. Claire meant to see to the heart of every long-ago young ancient face. She'd had the irrational conviction that she'd never see the video again, that this opportunity was passing so swiftly that if she so much as let herself blink she would miss it. Of course, she's rewatched the whole thing several times on her laptop, not seeing anything more than she did the first time. The lights came back up and the endless testimonials and live performances began. None of the speakers set off her alarms but even before she'd arrived she had already felt in her gut that it wouldn't be one of the speakers but a spectator, if one of these thousands at all. She toggled back and forth between absolute doubt and absolute certainty that it had to be one of these thousands. This event was a net that had dredged up possibilities from far and wide and deep into the past—if not here and now, where and when? Claire swiveled her gaze around, trying to scan every face in the crowd. But the crowd was so enormous it seemed not even made out of faces. It was a carpet of life that did not even have individual threads. Not even counting the excluded throng who'd had to settle for the simulcast, crammed in the lobby.

Finally, the current principal, a slim, sleek woman in a sleeveless black sheath, took the stage a second time. "As our cherished alumni community, most of you already know that this beautiful building expresses so much of Bob's vision. Working with our architects and designers, as well as with the Lewis Family Foundation, Bob was hands-on every step of the way, and it is difficult for all of us to lose him just on the brink of this amazing new phase of our school's history." Something in her comment had reversed the current and Claire realized that noises in the din she'd thought were hooting or cheering were actually booing. Seeming unsurprised the woman brought her face flush to the mic and her voice boomed out, drowning the others. "The conversation around the Lewis Family Foundation's bequest, and around naming rights, has engaged our community in a lastingly valuable way. Debate and dissent are the hallmarks of any inclusive community."

"Bob would have spared us the bullshit!" a male voice called out, and not just Claire's head but every other swiveled to take in the densely packed tiers of the grandiose space, trying to pick out the heckler.

"And though we can never say that Bob's death has a silver lining," the principal shouted determinedly in her mic, "I think I speak not merely for our school administration, and the Lewis Family Foundation, but for *all our community* when I say how delighted I am that our school's new name, at the suggestion of the Lewis family themselves, will not be the Lewis School for the Arts, as originally planned, but the *Robert Lord* School for the Arts." In the pandemonium of approbation that followed, Claire could barely hear what her seatmate bent close to tell her although his hot breath crawled over her ear.

"Bob would have fucking despised that. Being used as political cover. Y'know?" Claire nodded energetically, and kept nodding energetically as the crowd-glacier slowly reversed direction, first squeezing her away from her seatmate, who seemed to be working up to ask for her number although he had to be, she was now sure, at least twenty years older than she was; then squeezing her through the lobby past enormous images of Robert Lord hung from filaments high in the vault of the cathedral-like space that would bear his name; and finally squeezing her back through the doors, where she might have stopped and reflected but the crowd's force did not stop, it kept pushing her, down the sidewalk and across the parking lot until she was decisively at its far margins and then no part of it at all.

SHE'D VISITED THE old building almost three years before, on a day in June. She'd chosen the date carefully. She knew as well as anyone who's ever gone to school that June is the victory lap, with everybody killing time. She'd called ahead for an appointment. She'd said she had questions about the program and repeated herself when the admin in the office asked Was she a prospective student or parent? A member of the press? Acquainted with Mr. Lord? Mr. Lord was very busy.

"I have questions about the program," she'd repeated. She kept repeating the same six words not out of any courage but because she was so nervous she got stuck in the rut of the phrase. The admin put her on hold for so long that the line defaulted back to ringing again. The different voice that answered seemed completely unaware that Claire had not called that moment, but had been on hold for perhaps fifteen minutes. "Oh, of course, dear," the second voice said, and gave Claire an appointment, twelve twenty-five on a Friday, presumably lunch hour.

Before the appointment she hadn't known what kind of man he was. She hadn't known he was a local celebrity; she hadn't even known his name. She'd simply needed the head of the program for her own surely uncommon reasons. When the first admin had put up resistance, Claire had not been surprised because she always felt, when she called anyone, that she had to be bothering them. But arriving at the building she understood she'd accidentally been bold enough to ask for its king.

The women in the office traded skeptical looks when Claire said, "I'm here to see Mr. Lord. I have an appointment."

"You have an appointment?"

"At twelve twenty-five."

"Did you make it with one of us?"

"I'm not sure. I called—"

"What's the name of the person you spoke to?"

"I didn't ask—"

"Did she sound like an older woman?" Claire would have guessed both of these women were fifty or sixty or more. "It must have been Velva," one said to the other with a roll of her eyes. "I'll need to call Mr. Lord to make sure he's here in the building," she said reproachfully to Claire. "It's his lunch hour and he's *very* busy."

To hide her flushed face Claire turned to a mosaic of photos encrusting the wall. Young people played trumpet, declaimed, did the splits in midair. Most wore haircuts and clothes of the past. Behind her Claire heard the woman murmuring into the phone and then calling, "Julie!" A bare-midriffed girl appeared and received from the woman a molded plastic comedy-tragedy mask with the word "Visitor" plastered on it in sequins. "Julie will walk you to Mr. Lord's office," the woman said, turning back to her screen.

The girl's sneakers beneath her snug jeans landed flawlessly heel-to-toe as if on a tightrope. After many turns they stopped in front of a just-ajar door and the girl gave Claire the comedy-tragedy mask. "You're supposed to return this to the office when your visit is over. Do you want me to knock for you?" Now that she'd stopped, Claire could see the girl was very beautiful. Her natural makeup and lovely winged brows appeared professional, the look of an off-duty starlet.

"That's all right," Claire said. "I'll do the knocking."

"Have you met him before?"

"No."

"Are you interviewing him or something?"

"Yes," Claire decided to say.

"That's awesome," the girl said, craning her neck very slightly to peer through the crack of the door.

"Thanks for showing me the way," Claire said and waited until finally the girl went catwalking back down the hall.

"You're the Claire Campbell who wanted to see me? I'd started to think they had lost you," he said as he pulled the door open. He shoved it fully closed as soon as she stepped in, turning back toward his desk without shaking hands or otherwise introducing himself. There was a visitor's chair and she perched on its edge while he bent himself into his own chair, removed a frail pair of glasses from the top of his anvil-like head, folded the glasses, and laid them on his desk. He was not what she'd expected. She would never have admitted it aloud but she'd expected a fey man in a bow tie with a *Hello, Dolly!* poster framed on his wall. Not this granite-hewn, glowering man with dramatic black streaks in his white, lupine beard. Claire stared at his large, shapely knuckles. She was always surprised to encounter such actually masculine men, with their sword-tip eyes and their brooding brows and, when old, their somehow all the more menacing physical diminishments, as if their power hadn't been lost but just put in reserve.

"So." He picked up a pink While You Were Out slip from a pile on his desk, looked at it, and put it back down, without putting his glasses back on. A tic? A performance? "You had questions about our program." This was the moment Claire had mentally rehearsed so many times: not the stuttering phone call to make the appointment, nor the unintended rivalry at the threshold with bare-midriffed Julie, but this moment of belated disclosure, to this man she'd expected to be so unlike he was. Even more than information she'd expected sympathy. Kindly interest or as much as delight at the prospect of helping her. Why had she thought that would happen? Because she'd thought he'd be gay, and therefore sensitive?

"They're not exactly questions about your program. I have questions about someone I think was enrolled in it."

"And who might that have been?"

Claire had worked long and hard on a response to this antici-
pated question but now the words disappeared from her mind.
Instead she fumblingly took out the folder and held out the sheet.
He let her keep proffering it while he slowly unfolded the glasses
again, put them on, and unfolded a Look at her over their tops.
"You'd like me to read this?" he asked, still not taking it.

"That would be great, if you could. I think it'll be a lot more
clear than me."

"Are you saying your parents misnamed you?"

"I'm sorry?"

"Claire. They named you Claire," he repeated as she stared
dumbstruck at him. She couldn't fathom how he already knew. That
she'd had first one name, then another—but then she saw he didn't
know this. She'd misconstrued him, but it was too late to stop the
sensation of having been seen, which instead of being the recognition she always desired took the unpleasant form of a wave of heat
under her clothes.

"'Claire' means 'clear,'" he was suffering to explain to her.

"Right! No, I know that. I misunderstood you."

He let fall one last very protracted Look at her over the tops of
his glasses before he took the sheet and read the words she knew
by heart.

> Baby Evangeline, as she was known in this loving Christian
> environment where she spent her first months, was born
> January 1985 to a healthy Christian mother, Caucasian, age
> sixteen years. Birth mother's heritage on the maternal side
> Scotch-Irish, many generations in this region, on the pater-
> nal side German, also many generations in this region.
> Mother's mother attended secretarial school, mother's father
> vocational school, no college attendance in the family to
> date. Growing up, mother was a healthy active girl showing

normal development. Church attendance on and off due to divorce but Christian principles prevailing in both homes. Showed an early aptitude for acting and dancing and was accepted in the region's leading school for these arts; described herself, at the time of her residence with us, as an aspiring actress. Pregnancy normal, carried baby to full term and normal delivery. Nothing known of the father apart from Caucasian and Christian, good health.

He took much longer to look up from the sheet than it would take even a very slow reader to read it. At last he asked, "And what am I supposed to glean from this story?"

"'The region's leading school for the arts': that's this school."

"Is it? It's not even clear from this scant paragraph what the region is that it refers to."

"It's this region."

"Is it?" He made to pore over the sheet again, even running his finger down each of the lines.

"That's just an excerpt from my file." Claire caught herself twisting her hair. "What region it is—the rest of the file makes that perfectly clear."

"Makes it perfectly Claire."

"Yes." She tried to smile. Perhaps that was what he was after, less solemnity on her part, more banter. Already the appointment had become about what he was after. Remotely Claire remembered it was she who was after something. "The question isn't what region it is or even what school it is, because I know it's this school—there's no other school that it could be," she tried. "The question is, which student was it—of yours. Which student of yours was my birth mother."

"Is this you, then? 'Baby Evangeline'?"

"Yes." Had he not even understood that? There was something

shaming in his making her spell it all out. But he was old, she reminded herself, though he didn't seem old, if old meant befuddled or weak. He didn't seem that way at all.

He raised his still mostly black and very barbed eyebrows slightly when she said yes and kept them there, in a notched-up position. The longer he held the position the more meanings it seemed to imply. One of the meanings might have been, That's not what I expected. Another might have been, That's exactly what I expected. Another might have been, Now I understand why this person is here. Another might have been, I can't fathom why this person is here. "And what," he said, his eyebrows still in that notched-up position, "makes you think that your mother was ever my student?"

Claire's heart rate had been accelerating and now it was accelerated so much she thought it must be audible. Her cheeks had probably turned very pink. Sweat beads prickled her hairline. "Birth mother," she corrected him. "I know because the file—"

"The file says that she was accepted in the region's leading school for the arts. It doesn't say she attended."

"She did. I'm sure of it."

"Why? Is that also made perfectly clear, somewhere else in your file? I'm sorry," he said almost gently, when she didn't reply. "This must be difficult for you. It must be very difficult, to have so little information about something so important. But even if the young woman described on this page was a student here, and it seems very doubtful she was, I could never confirm it."

"Why?" Claire said, feeling him willing her out of the room.

"I could never violate a student's privacy in that way. As a woman, you must understand that."

Leaving the building, Claire had gotten lost. Or rather, she had never known where she was, and only went further astray. She'd found herself standing in a parking lot from which her car had disappeared, staring down at a hideous thing with two agonized faces and the word VISITOR spelled in hard little circles of metal. Eventually, she'd come to understand that she'd gone out an entrance on the opposite side of the building from where she'd come in. Both doors looked exactly the same.

THE DAY SHE showed her file to Robert Lord, Claire's mother had been gone just six months. Initially Claire had promised herself she would wait for a year before doing anything with the soft-edged manila folder with its surprisingly few sheets of paper that her father had given her after the funeral, sitting stoop shouldered on the "good" sofa it had always made her mother nervous to have people sit on, and making Claire's own shoulders stoop with the weight of his arm. "Mom wanted to encourage you," Claire's father said. "She even wanted to help. She just never figured out how." Claire had been crying too much to answer, but she'd known that what he said was the truth. Her mother had never planned to get sick. She'd only been sixty-six when she died. Her mother never having the chance to figure out how to help saddened Claire to the point of her making that promise, but she soon admitted to herself that not touching the file for a year was an empty gesture. The first time she read it, the strength of her grief frightened her. Her one articulate wish was that her mother was with her, that they were reading it together, that her mother agreed that the person described was a friend they both wanted to find.

Claire's father had grown up on a farm that his father lost when Claire's father was in his teens, resulting in a move to the city that had been the catastrophe of Claire's father's life. In her childhood, despite her steady lack of interest in nature, he'd often as bedtime stories described to her his favorite places on his childhood farm, the creek and the barn and the shade trees. After Claire's paternal grandfather's death, a "farm diary" had turned up in his basement, reams of curling faded yellow paper on which a spidery hand recorded births and deaths of animals, crop yields, and unusual weather events. The day after Claire showed Robert Lord her file, she rose extremely early and went to the print shop, although it was her day off, so that she could finish typing up, printing out, and binding the farm diary for her father. She'd been meaning to do this for literally years. Then she went to her childhood home, from which her father had been threatening to move, and ate a bowl of All-Bran while watching her father page through the all-new, highly legible farm diary, which she had even illustrated with some photos of West Texas pulled off the web. Her father's mouth formed a tight line as he read, by which Claire knew he was moved to the point of fighting tears. "Thank you, Boo-Boo," he said after he'd turned all the pages. Claire returned to her apartment and it was still only nine in the morning. She had not mentioned her visit to Robert Lord to her father. In fact, since receiving the file from her father, Claire had never mentioned it to him again. She'd understood that, in telling her about her mother's regret, her father had been saying far more on the subject than he would have if left to himself. This refusal of her father's to engage with the subject had never bothered Claire, while her mother's mere ambivalence about it had agonized her. Nor did her differing reactions to her parents bother Claire, although she recognized how unfair they were.

When an unknown number called, Claire only answered because she was just getting out of the shower and was blind from the steam. The rough voice that asked for Claire Campbell startled her with how familiar and unplaceable it was. She'd been wrapping herself in a towel, her hair a wet nest. No one ever called her at that hour of the morning now that her mother was gone. When she realized who it was her first reaction was to fear that she'd further offended him. How had he gotten her number? Of course she'd left it with the office when she made the appointment, but she didn't recall this daylight explanation until afterward.

"I regret the way our conversation ended," he said. He seemed to have to bend his voice into the phone the way a giant might bend his head through a doorframe. "Your surprising me at school as you did left me little maneuvering room. There are strict protocols. You must understand."

"I'm sorry," she said, shivering. "I didn't know where else to find you."

"I want to help you. But such matters can't be discussed on school grounds."

They made a plan to have lunch. A few hours in advance of it, when she was struggling with what she should wear, he called and told her lunch was a bad idea also, as he was a highly recognizable person. "Besides, Sofie and I can treat you to a much better meal here at home than we'd get at Butera's. And, it will be easier to talk." The mention of Sofie relieved an unease Claire had not been aware of until it dissolved, so similar was it to so many other species of unease, most predominantly her unease about whether she would get her answer. Preoccupation with the dread irresistible object marginalized every other concern. Now the meal would be dinner. He turned out to live in a rare high-rise with its own underground parking garage that she didn't see until she'd parked on the street. A somnolent lobby attendant pointed her toward the elevators without lifting his eyes from the horseshoe of tiny TV screens behind which he sat. Her destination was the top floor, eighteen—a novelty in this city of sprawl where Claire had never known anyone to live in a building with more than two floors. Leaving the elevator she gazed a moment out the corridor window at the orange-and-gray dusk before ringing his bell.

Claire imagined Sofie perhaps soft and flossy-haired and submissive; or sleekly haughty and European; or complacently Bohemian in tatty blouse and many strings of clacking beads. Wife of the great man, she could only exist in reaction to him. But what kind of reaction was she? He answered the door in a black turtleneck and black slacks, his still-copious hair like steel wool brushed straight back from the cast-iron face. Claire noticed in spite of herself that the beard had been trimmed. Its black-on-white stripes looked as if freshly painted. The beautiful apartment tempted her to gape with admiration in every direction, an impulse she tried hard to control while running her eyes over the laden bookshelves and dark tapestries, the little wooden tables inlaid with small tiles, the extremely large plants that touched her as she passed with the ends of their rubbery leaves. Classical music was playing. He led her through the labyrinth of European-looking things—Sofie had to be the European option, with a silver chignon and long, papery arms hung with thin tasteful bracelets—to a living room half in darkness from its view of what must be Memorial Park. An open bottle of wine and two glasses sat on a tray. Claire accepted a glass and sat sipping self-consciously. She rarely drank except at workplace holiday parties, and this was better-tasting wine than anything she was used to. She held the stem of the glass tightly pinched. He cupped his glass in an upturned palm, with the stem notched between his fingers. The way he held it bothered her in some indescribable way. He sat opposite to where she perched on the couch and saying almost nothing watched her while she talked as if she had to talk to breathe, about how beautiful the apartment was, and how beautiful the view was, and how unique it was he had one when everyone she knew lived in houses.

"You can take the New Yorker out of New York," he said at last, "but you can't take New York out of the New Yorker."

"You're from New York?"

"I'm from a sleepy little town called Bensonhurst, originally. But I ran away long, long ago, and my travels ended here—where yours began. I want to know about *you*, Claire. My story is not interesting."

For a long time she answered his questions. He was very good at asking questions, so much better than the online Listeners. This was what it must be like to have an actual therapist. Even the room, with its intellectual and faintly foreign furniture, seemed like a therapist's office. Perhaps not the wine. He refilled her glass while she was talking, for some reason, about her father's being forced into early retirement. She understood without having been told that some code to which he adhered required that he know her before he let her know herself, although he behaved as though his careful rummaging through her life would reveal what she sought after all her own rummaging hadn't. Each time she arrived at the end of an answer he slid a fresh question beneath the stream of her talk so that despite herself her own talk rippled on, uninterrupted though it was she herself who meant to interrupt, to finally stop answering and to ask what he had to tell her. Then he stood abruptly and said, "We should eat." Unsteadily she followed him down a corridor narrowed by bookshelves to a small dining room. The table was already set, with two more glasses, another bottle of wine, food already in large shallow bowls. "Ceviche," he said. "I hope you eat seafood? Sofie is a magnificent chef specializing in foods of her native Caribbean. If not for her I would have given up eating a long time ago."

"Is Sofie joining us?"

"Sofie? Sofie has gone home for the evening. Did you think Sofie was my wife?" He seemed very surprised that she might have thought this. "Sofie is my sainted housekeeper. I owe a great deal to Sofie, but even if she would have me, which I doubt very much, marriage isn't an experience I plan to repeat."

"You used to be married?"

"My most recent wife and I called it off as soon as our boys were grown. Now our boys are both married and seem to like it much better than we did. Perhaps the inclination skips generations."

This allusion to genetic heritage was Claire's best opening, yet somehow he kept her from taking it. First with stern attention to her trying the food, as if he expected her not to like it, and would scold her if this was the case. Then the food itself, sitting tentatively in her mouth. She'd never tasted ceviche and until he explained, between his own rapid mouthfuls, she could never have guessed it was raw fish somehow cooked with lime juice. Once enlightened her stomach and tongue seemed to turn cold and stiff as if being heatlessly cooked with juice, too. All her concentration was required to eat with a show of enjoyment. Undeterred by her silence he was now talking animatedly about Caribbean traditional festivals, at the same time as zealously eating. "Carni*vaaaal*," he kept saying, leaning hard on the last syllable. "You've turned pale," he said, dropping his fork with a clank in his now empty bowl. "Are you all right?"

"Maybe the wine," Claire admitted. She'd barely drunk from the new glass he'd poured when they'd sat at the table. She'd kept lifting it to her lips from politeness but when her tongue touched the tart liquid her mouth flooded with warning saliva.

"Some fresh air? I thought you might like the view from the roof. I have a private roof terrace."

This did seem like something she would have enjoyed at some previous time. "Okay," she said and swaying to her feet followed him again, up a short staircase of tight bends, out a door into the warm wet night air which was always so much more of a shock than the opposite plunge into clean sharp-edged climate control. That always felt like a falling away of exterior weight and returning, refreshed, to oneself, where stepping outside felt like being absorbed by some massive esophagus. The door closed at her back and he turned and in one step had plastered her full length against it, his unseasonal black knit turtleneck scraping the bare triangle of her neckline when he knocked her head back with his, stuffing his tongue in her mouth. He was strong, for a man she would have guessed was older than her father; as she gagged against the taste of masticated ceviche mixed in his saliva he seized her right hand

and pushed it inside the front of his pants, past the belt and the underwear waistband. "There," he rasped, "*there*." He scrubbed her hand roughly against the damp noodle of flesh which secreted warm goo but did not come to life. In her panic Claire wished that it would, was conscious of a failure and possible worse consequence if it didn't. She twisted and broke away, gulping mouthfuls of air as if stuffing her stomach with air would prevent it from hurling its contents. And it worked, she willed down her own vomit, the prospective shame of which was so great that it didn't cross her mind that her vomit might serve as a weapon. "Oh dear," he was tutting, with her wedged against the door again while swarming his hands like flesh spiders. "It's all right . . . sweet Claire . . . it's all right . . ." Finally getting her footing she kneed him. She missed but he lurched back and then stood glaring stormclouds of scorn.

"We seem to have had a misunderstanding," he said with admonitory coldness as she heaved, leaning on the door handle as if she'd just come up from swimming a race. "You've embarrassed me," he added as she yanked the door open.

"I'm sorry," she gasped. Shrugging through the door she rushed back down the stairs. She could barely find the front door again and almost left without her purse; riding the elevator she tried to fix her blouse and skirt and hair with her left hand while looking for something to wipe off her right. She'd only brought a little bag, not her usual tote, and didn't have any Kleenex. As the elevator counter came to G, she scrubbed her right hand against whatever the fibrous surface was that made the elevator's interior walls.

In the lobby the attendant did not look up, seemed in fact to make a point of looking down, as she rushed past. She had to pee, so much so she thought she might wet herself there on the street. That was all she thought about, driving back home. How much she needed to pee, how the need stuck like a spear through her brain and her crotch and drove out every other sensation. The next day, she spent close to four hours and two hundred dollars in "talking" it out with a Listener and forming a Plan—several Plans—but the Plans contradicted each other, as did the desires and emotions each meant to process and fulfill. How to talk to her father and how never to talk to her father. How to confront Robert Lord and how to forget Robert Lord. How to demand her answer and how to stop asking or wanting to ask. Obsessed, Claire spent far too much money and earned too many Loyalty Stars. Attempting to wean herself from that habit, she then formed the less costly but in certain ways equally costly habit of constantly checking the school's Facebook page. In Robert Lord's frequent appearances there, she sought clues as to what she should do. None of these were decisive and so she did nothing. Three years passed. Many school milestones were posted. One was the death of the school's longest-serving staff member, secretary Velva Wilson. One was the death of the school's longest-serving faculty member, Theatre Program founder Robert Lord. Claire went to his tribute and learned nothing new. When a subsequent Facebook announcement explained that the decision to rename the school the Robert Lord School for the Arts had been reversed due to "a credible allegation of sexual abuse from a former student," Claire finally unfollowed the school's social media pages.

BUT BEFORE THAT, the day she'd stood sightlessly grasping the comedy/tragedy mask in the hot parking lot—

—at last she understood she must retrace her steps, and going back in and down the main hall, she reentered the office, where it seemed everyone had gone out for their lunch but a dumpy and aged old woman who hadn't been there before. "Just returning this," Claire said, proffering the guest pass. The woman jerked back as if frightened.

"My God," said the woman, whose name tag read "Velva." "Sweet Jesus. Come closer to me."

As if in a dream Claire stepped close and the old woman hauled herself onto her feet. She reached a leathery hand to Claire's cheek. "Why, you must be more than twenty years old." Her breathy wonder repulsed Claire, frozen under her touch.

"Twenty-five."

"That's right," said Velva in triumph. She sank back in her chair, her gaze feasting on Claire. "What did they name you, sweetheart?"

It was such a strange question! "I'm Claire," Claire said brusquely and dropping the pass on the desktop went out, the right way this time, to the parking lot holding her car, the door and the key and the pedals of which she attacked with more force than required, leaving the gray stones of that building so far in her wake that it was only when the building was gone, the people she'd met in it dead, Robert Lord's name given then taken away from the fancy new building expressing his vision that she understood why that old woman had stared in that way all those years ago now.

Are we still recognized if seen by the wrong eyes?

But by then it was too late to go back and say, "Tell me her name."

ACKNOWLEDGMENTS

Writing fiction is like dreaming; the recognizable and the unthinkable, the mundane and the monstrous, coalesce in the least predictable ways, in the end turning into something entirely unlike real life, and yet hopefully relevant in some way to our shared human life. The writing of this book was no less a strange dreamlike process than writing ever is, but unlike most dreamers, I had lots of help. Thank you to Rebecca Lowe, Jason Nodler, and all my classmates and teachers at Houston's High School for the Performing and Visual Arts, emphatically the right-side-up to my fictional upside-down CAPA, and a place of dreams, not nightmares. Thank you to Seth King and Semi Chellas for their early enthusiasm for the manuscript and for some of the ideas which brought the dream-parts together. Thank you to Lynn Nesbit for early guidance, to Jin Auh for knowing when the story was done and for bringing the manuscript home, to Barbara Jones and everyone at Henry Holt for making that home so welcoming, and to the MacDowell Colony for precious space and time. Last but most, thank you Elliot, Dexter, and Pete.

ABOUT THE AUTHOR

SUSAN CHOI is the author of the novels *My Education*, *A Person of Interest*, *American Woman*, and *The Foreign Student*. She has been a finalist for the Pulitzer Prize and the PEN/Faulkner Award and winner of the PEN/W. G. Sebald Award and the Asian-American Literary Award for fiction. With David Remnick, she coedited *Wonderful Town: New York Stories from The New Yorker*. She's received NEA and Guggenheim Foundation fellowships. She lives in Brooklyn.